Jeremy lives with his wife, Jean, in Somerset where she, a talented musician, allows him to indulge in his favourite hobby, singing. It is probably for this reason that the children have long since flown the nest …

He was born (some time during the last century) with a naturally miserable looking face – probably an attempt at copying his mother's expression on first seeing him. This led to a senior officer, early in his army career, ordering him to stand in front of the bathroom mirror first thing every morning and grin at himself. It would, so the Colonel said, 'release his endorphins' and thereby make him a jollier person. And Jeremy's certainly been releasing them ever since! The maxim, 'One Good Laugh a Day,' seems to work to everyone's delight and, whilst narrowly evading arrest and the people in white coats, he can often be seen around the byways of Somerset grinning inanely at every person who doesn't see him first.

After ten years as a (grinning) officer in the Royal Artillery, he joined the BBC as a radio and television presenter and, in more recent times, enjoyed a successful transition into becoming a writer and playwright. Excerpts from his several books, plays and sketches can be viewed on his website www.cclpublications.co.uk.

Jeremy's dearest wish is to have this book seen by its readers as a substitute for their own bathroom mirrors …

RUNNING ON EMPTY

Jeremy Carrad

Running On Empty

Vanguard Press

A CIP catalogue record for this title is
available from the British Library

ISBN 1 84386 218 2

Vanguard Press is an imprint of
Pegasus Elliot MacKenzie Publishers Ltd.
www.pegasuspublishers.com

First Published in 2006

Vanguard Press
Sheraton House Castle Park
Cambridge England

Printed & Bound in Great Britain

To my dearest wife Jean and our great children, Lizzie and Chris, who have lived with a chap displaying at one time or another all the less attractive idiosyncrasies of each and every one of the Cavaliers in Oldthorpe House!

"She used to wear pink bloomers, you know. Elastic down to here."

His voice was hoarse with the enormity of it all. "She was putting up the decorations in the lounge. Up a ladder. D'you see? I was holding it for her." Basil's eyes gazed unseeing at the rooftops and trees bordering the garden. He didn't dare look at his friend. Again his voice became husky. "I glanced up."

There was a silence. Both were so aghast at the image invading their minds that they sat, immobile, seeing nothing, hearing nothing, hardly breathing.

Tubes broke the uneasy silence. "You would," he said, trying to comfort the tormented man. "You would. To see she was secure. Well anchored."

1

"You are Basil Charles Beresford Reardon?"

The quivering voice of the elderly Clerk to Flaxton-on-Sea Magistrates Court made the question sound more of a plea than the routine enquiry it was intended to be.

"I beg your pardon?"

Basil, who at this advanced stage in his life thought it strange to be told who he was when he was pretty sure he already knew, found himself familiarly confused. The clerk, with a voice now less sure than it had previously been, tried again.

"You are Basil Charles Beresford Reardon?"

There was now less of a question mark in the tone, the old man hoping that a statement might help the accused remember that indeed he was the chap named on the charge sheet.

"Who do you think he thinks he is? Diana Dors?"

The gruff, grumpy voice came from the depths of polished mahogany back in a gloomy corner of the courtroom. Four elderly men put restraining hands on the speaker.

"Quiet, Clarence."

"Shut up, you old fool."

"You'll have us ejected."

The whispers were clearly heard by the three magistrates occupying the Bench but much to the fury of one of the two junior ones the formidable lady in the centre, Madam Chairman, refused to utter a rebuke or even bang her gavel.

Basil felt that something was required of him. The old clerk looking up at him in the dock, pen poised, seemed to be about to burst into tears.

"I suppose I am, old chap. That's the way of it."

The clerk blinked. If the time it had taken to get the oath correctly recited by this old fellow was anything to go by it was going to be a hard day. Edwin Prosser had been called back to his former role as Magistrates' Clerk due to the sickness of his successor and already longed again for the peace of his armchair and the pile of ancient fly-fishing magazines. His fountain pen, as ancient as the fingers just about holding it, hovered over the little boxes which littered the new-fangled court documents nineteen-seventies Britain now required him to complete via ticks and crosses.

For a few moments the court was still, save for a distant drumming coming from just above the clerk's head. Had he turned and looked up – a combination of moves now way beyond him – he would have identified the sound as the fingers of the Chairman of the Bench drumming on her judicial blotter.

The eyes of the court, six set above the rest to denote their splendid authority, the clerk's two which had started to water with the intensity of it all and a number from within the body of the court, now settled on the slightly ramshackle figure standing as near to attention as he could muster in the dock. The said Basil Charles Beresford Reardon.

The military bearing was still there; something that once attained was never wholly lost. But it was fairly well hidden behind a thin head of hair that seemed to have recently lost a battle with a hurricane, a nicotine coloured moustache that would have looked better had it been clipped symmetrically, and a dark suit that had obviously served almost as long as its master. The only item to differentiate him from an undertaker was the regimental tie of the Royal Artillery with its vivid red zigzag pattern suggesting that the old man was on the point of detonation.

Having studied the document in front of him with a diligence almost equalling his study of dry flies and drifts, the clerk looked up and fixed Basil with a kind, if watery, eye. "I don't have a box for 'I suppose I am', I'm afraid."

Madam Chairman, sympathetic as she was with those within her own age bracket, wanted to get things over with.

"Would you please say yes or no."

It was a fair request and possibly it was the drama of the occasion that confused Basil.

"Right-ho. Yes or No." No one could argue that he didn't want to oblige.

Now totally confused, the clerk entered a tick in both boxes and, muttering, "Mister," ticked a third one.

"Major, actually, if it's all the same to you."

Seeing the hunted look in the clerk's eyes he was about to assure him that mister would be acceptable in the circumstances when the same thin, grim voice punched out from the back of the Court.

"MC. Military Cross. Shove that in your boxes."

The Bench, the clerk, and the accused heard the sound of scuffling from the far corner of the courtroom which ended with the voice, now urgently plaintive. "Where's the toilet? I need the toilet."

The clerk sat down with a bump. He really would refuse to stand-in again. It had been fine when you filled in the necessary particulars in neat handwriting…

"I fear I have no box for decorations but…" he looked up and smiled at Basil, "many congratulations."

The two elderly men who had been through a lot – and survived – acknowledged each other. The moment was interrupted by Madam Chairman who said in an equally kind voice to that of her clerk, "I think we'd better push on, Mr Prosser. Shall we hear the charge?"

With an upwards nod – not easy for anyone, let alone a septuagenarian now more used to looking down at his flies – that is those attached to his line floating in the water – Mr Prosser, the clerk, duly pushed on.

"And you are, I believe, an inmate at Oldthorpe House, Home for Retired Officers of Her Majesty's Forces at Thorpe Haven?"

His pen hovered over the 'Yes' box but descended no further because the proceedings were at this stage halted by what could only be described as an uprising in the dark recesses of the court. The Bench could just make out five shadowy figures, now on their feet, waving papers in the air and shouting in what Madam Chairman would describe as a deranged manner.

"Inmates?"

"I'll give you inmates."

"Do we look criminally insane?" were muddled together but one stood out above the rest.

"I must have the toilet."

A rather elderly arm of the law advanced on them, a policeman approaching retirement and put out to graze in the warm safety of the Magistrates Court. But before he could, from a safe distance, utter a word of admonishment, the gavel was wielded with some force and the protestors subsided.

Madam Chairman spoke.

"In any other circumstances I would clear the court, but in this case I do sympathise with those who objected to that word on the charge sheet. However, should there be one, just one, recurrence of this disgraceful behaviour I shall take appropriate action. Proceed, Mr Prosser."

The clerk now recited the damning words as required in the 'How to be a Magistrate's Clerk' handbook. He did, of course, know them by heart.

"Basil Charles Beresford Reardon. You are charged..."

"Major, Royal Artillery. Military Cross." The gruff voice had obviously not yet reached the lavatory.

Rap, rap went the gavel. "I really can't allow further interruptions and will have to exclude the public if they recur. Please continue, Mr Prosser." Madam Chairman had used as kind a voice as could be associated with such a reprimand.

The clerk tried the upward bow again but with even less success than the first time. He gave a good impression of a rather surprised stork.

"Major Basil Charles Beresford Reardon, Military Cross, Royal Artillery..."

Basil wasn't at all sure that he hadn't preferred the unadorned version. Blast old Clarence for having interfered. He so wished they'd all stayed away. They'd reckoned solidarity would do the trick but at this rate they'd get him six months.

"You are hereby charged that on the twenty-eighth of December in the year of our Lord..." Mr Prosser liked the old florid version now so sadly emasculated by the 'new thinkers'... "nineteen hundred and seventy-one, you did cause a disturbance of the peace by lying down in front of a Number Seventeen omnibus..." Well, that's what they were in his young day. "In, or perhaps to be more precise it should be on, Harbour Road in Thorpe Haven in the County of Suffolk..."

Madam Chairman's two colleague magistrates, flanking her, looked down on the glistening baldness of the Prosser head and rather wished that, prior to his recall to duty, a shark had, by chance, been on holiday in the river Alde and helped himself to Mr Prosser's fly, line, rod and the silly old butter himself. They would then have had a full lunch break. As it was, on he ploughed.

"...thereby impeding the said omnibus's progress towards Flaxton. How plead you? Guilty or not guilty?"

"That's a dashed tricky one, actually. In some respects, guilty. Indubitably. I mean, as you so eloquently put it, that's just what I did. But not for malice, do you see? For a very good reason. So I'm tempted to say, not guilty." Basil looked up towards the Bench at a pair of understanding eyes flanked by four which appeared to be somewhat hostile.

Mr Prosser had another bout of eye watering and wiped his gold-rimmed spectacles on a hanky that had seen better days.

"I have a little box for each and I fear it must be one or the other."

"Major Reardon," Madam Chairman felt it was time to lend a hand, "I note you have declined professional representation in this matter and must advise you that if you are not sure how to plead I must instruct that a plea of Not Guilty be entered. Is this all right with you?"

"Absolutely. Jolly good. Not Guilty it is, then."

With an audible sigh of relief, Mr Prosser's pen plonked a tick in the appropriate box.

"Of course he's not guilty. What's all the fuss?"

"I shall not warn the Public Gallery again." Madam Chairman was using her stern voice. "Rather than have you cleared from the court, I will offer you the alternative of coming forward to the front seating where I – we – can keep an eye on you."

After a slight pause, the culprits stood and, like five naughty schoolboys, heads down, made their way towards the Bench. Through habit they moved in order of long retired seniority: Brigadier Ainsley Bennington, Colonel Alastair Hunter, Commander 'Tubes' Potter, so nicknamed to honour his role as a submarine torpedo officer, Squadron Leader Freddy Foster and the troublemaker-in-chief – and to his shame, the eldest, Captain Clarence Cuthbert. There's no need at this early stage to know too much more about them, they'll appear in great detail later, but at this tense moment in the case of 'The Crown versus Basil Charles Beresford Reardon' they can best be described as elderly, slightly scuffed gentlemen who, through their military lives, had been through a lot in the service of others.

As one, they smiled weakly at Basil in the dock and he, in turn, smiled back – though for what reason he had no idea. Why, instead of gaining comfort from the closer proximity of his friends, was he experiencing a little tremor of foreboding?

Madam Chairman nodded at them and turned to the accused. "Perhaps you would care to sit down, Major Reardon."

"No, thank you. Most kind. On parade, do you see? Never sit on parade." Oh, but how he wished he could.

"Let's see if we can clear up this little matter quickly, shall we?"

Basil nodded eagerly. "Certainly, madam. The quicker the better."

It was at this moment as the due processes of the law were at last clicking into place that one of the supporting players, the junior magistrate on Madam's right, found it necessary to intervene. Percy Baldry, a plumber by trade known to most of Flaxton as 'Baldry the Bodger' because of the quality of his pipe-work, felt that there was far too much leniency in the air. He'd become a magistrate – Britain was at a stage in its evolution where it sought more Baldrys than Brigadiers on its Benches – to hand out rough, tough, justice to as many people as possible irrespective of guilt. He would have liked one day to settle a black cap on his head and send someone to the gallows but he'd probably have to move to another country to achieve his ambition. Many people in Flaxton, despite their reliance on his limited plumbing ability, hoped he would.

The plumber spoke, "Aren't we doing a bit of pre-judging here?" His whisper into Madam Chairman's ear was accompanied by a waft of Adnams Best Bitter laced with stale cigarette smoke. She winced more from the foul breath than the message it conveyed and dealt with the interruption as good Chairmen should by totally ignoring it.

"First, Major Reardon, we shall be hearing from the Bus Company that has brought this Action, then I will call upon you to give your…"

"Version of the events…" The plumber felt that doubt had to be noted and logged in the Court Record. It all seemed far too pally and far removed from black caps and gallows. Again Madam Chairman took no notice of the interruption – but words, hard sharp words, would be said later.

"And then I will call upon you to give your evidence. All right?"

"Absolutely fine by me, Madam. You do it as you wish. I'll tag along."

His comrades were mightily impressed. You could always trust old Basil to fit in and cause as little fuss as possible. None of them identified the whole sorry affair with the enormous fuss Basil had decided to make in the first place, thereby causing this most shaming episode in his long life.

Madam Chairman smiled at the accused but inwardly wondered if, for the first time since she had assumed her lofty role a decade or more ago, she wasn't very slightly losing control of the proceedings.

"Mr Usher, please call…" She glanced at her papers and was as confused now by the name written on them as she had been when first reading it. "Mr Seymour Seymour."

Giggling from the body of the court – particularly amongst the naughty boys – was mixed with a squeaking of door hinges and the scraping of feet as a gangling youth was shepherded to the witness stand. Madam Chairman eyed him sternly. She wasn't well up on Mr Elvis Presley and therefore failed to understand or appreciate why this untidy young man was so ludicrously dressed and had his hair glued into such a weird shape. She gathered herself and nodded at the Usher.

For the second time that day the oath took a long while to get right, Seymour Seymour evidently having trouble with even the simplest recitation – a fact already well known to his various unfortunate school teachers.

"You are Seymour Seymour?"

"That's not your real monicker surely?" The plumber needed fuller and better particulars. "You look more like Elvis."

"Thank you, ta, for that. The greatest ever." Seymour Seymour felt he could get on with that geezer up there. He hoped the old biddy would leave the questioning to him. For the moment he wasn't to be disappointed.

"Why have it twice? Your mum and dad must have been bonkers when they named you."

Seymour Seymour suddenly went off the man. If they were going to go on like this he'd miss his lunch break. Better clear it up and get on.

"They call me Seymour 'cos I can read a number plate at a hundred yards. Better than anyone else. And one of my mates…"

He got no further. With a sigh Madam Chairman intervened.

"Your real name, if you will, please, Mr Seymour?"

"Desmond Elvis Seymour. It was my mother's idea, the Elvis. She's in love with him"

It has to be said that throughout all this the public in the Courtroom had been sitting open-mouthed – most metaphorically but, in the case of Captain Cuthbert who was now fast asleep, actually.

"Mr Prosser, I'm afraid you will have to change the name on your documents."

The Clerk stared down at his box-covered pages which he had been ticking and crossing as best he could as the proceedings progressed. Now he felt that nasty feeling overtaking him again. His heart beat faster, his hands shook even more than usual and his glasses began to steam up as the eye-watering got underway again. It was like that moment when the fishing line goes taut – but not half so much fun. For a start he had no ink eraser to delete the written-in Christian name but, far worse, even if he could clean the box it wasn't long enough to put in the two names. The form designers had boobed, there was no doubt about it. He turned and tried to look up at the Bench but his neck muscles only allowed him to stare at the mahogany a few inches above his head. It would have to do.

"Madam Chairman…"

After all that effort he was wasting his time. Madam Chairman moved briskly on.

"You were, I believe, driving the number seventeen bus along Harbour Road in Thorpe Haven at the time of the alleged incident?"

"Yeah. Not fast though." He didn't want this lot squeezing in yet another speeding fine to blight his day. "Meandering sort of. I was good and early…"

"For once." Tubes Potter couldn't resist it. Being a naval chap he was a stickler for punctuality and the Flaxton buses, he had noted, were far from that. He was surprised to receive a little smile from Madam rather than the expected reprimand.

"And just approaching the stop when that madman over there…" He pointed at Basil in the dock, "flung himself in front of my bus."

"Flung himself?" The plumber couldn't believe it.

They all looked at Basil. Less of a flinger it would be hard to find.

"Well, maybe not flung." Seymour adopted a pose as if he was about to strum his Elvis guitar. It tended to give him confidence. "He was sort of eased down by the other old buffer. I think it's him there." He interrupted a silent rendering of 'You aint nothin' but a hound dog' to point at Tubes Potter.

As the picture of the events emerged, the Bench, in their own individual ways, found it hard to maintain the serious composure expected and required of them.

"Do you recognise the person in the dock as the man to whom you are referring?"

"Yeah. I just said so didn't I?"

"Then what happened, Mr Seymour?"

"I jammed on me brakes and we came to a stop just by the geezer's nose. If I'd been driving any of our other buses I'd probably have squashed him but this one had just been done."

From somewhere in the dim recesses of the Courtroom there came a loud hiss. A senior representative of the Flaxton Omnibus Company was less than pleased with his employee's assessment of its vehicle servicing record. Neither was the aspersion lost on Madam Chairman who made a note for future reference. She smiled a sweet, but on this occasion false, smile.

"And what happened then, Mr Seymour?"

"Nothin."

"Nothing? Were not the police and an ambulance called?"

"Oh yeah. Some passer-by. The police didn't want to do

nothin but the old geyser on the mattress…"

"The mattress?"

"Didn' I say?"

"No, you most certainly didn't, Mr Seymour. Where did the mattress come from?"

"I never saw. It must have been put there before I come along. It wasn't there on me previous run."

"The chaps put it there for me, do you see? The road's very hard at that spot. Jolly decent of them." Basil nodded a thank you at his friends below him and they duly nodded back. That's what friendship was all about.

"You'll have your turn in a moment, Major Reardon. Not just yet."

The plumber grimaced. If he'd been in charge he'd have yelled 'Silence in Court' and had the prisoner taken down.

"So you are sitting at the wheel of your bus and just in front of you Major Reardon is lying on a mattress in the road."

"Spot on."

"Does that mean yes?"

"Yeah."

"For how long were you there?"

"About ten minutes. I had a fag or two and then the coppers arrived and ordered the bloke to move and he wouldn't…"

"Yes, thank you. They will tell us this in due course. What happened after that?"

"The ambulance men helped him up, brushed him down and took him into the house. That Oldthorpe place for old soldiers and the like. I was so early that I had time for another fag and then pushed on."

The Bench appeared to be deciding in a democratic manner, as British Benches would, if there was any more required of Desmond Elvis Seymour. But appearances can be misleading. In fact Madam Chairman was telling her colleagues that she'd had more than enough of the weirdly dressed fellow and she didn't want any more questions. Her method regarding the due processes of the law was much quicker than that laid down in the Court Procedure manuals.

"You may stand down, Mr Seymour and wait in the lobby. Off you go."

In such a way was Flaxton's answer to the 'greatest of them all' dismissed. With a final silent strum and extravagant wave to the missing multitude he was escorted from the Courtroom by the policeman who, judging by the tight grip he administered to the Seymour arm, was no great Presley fan.

It was a rather sombre lunch in The Anchor pub in Flaxton's High Street. The six of them sat at their favourite table, brimming pints of Adnams Best Bitter in front of them, but they couldn't muster the accustomed bonhomie nor the cut and thrust of their usual banter. In truth they were all cowed and somewhat overawed by the atmosphere in the Courtroom. It was all far removed from the pleasure they had experienced when Basil had outlined his method of protest to them. Then it had all seemed good, clean fun but now the due majesty of the law was turning it into a frightening drama.

They had all experienced Courts in their time but only as officers providing mitigating statements for their erring troops who had committed wicked crimes, usually on the younger female population of garrison towns. But this was different.

"I wonder how long you'll get. I bet Matron Maud will ban you from Oldthorpe. We'll miss you." Squadron Leader Freddy Foster, the master of tactlessness, was running true to form.

"Shut up, Freddy for God's sake. Basil's got enough to put up with without your inane comments." Ainsley was feeling very strongly about all this partly because, as the senior officer in Oldthorpe, he shouldn't have allowed it to happen – although, with no authority, he couldn't have prevented Basil from doing it anyway – but also because Seymour's evidence had shown how dangerous the stupid prank was. Basil could have been killed.

The others, for once, sat quietly and demolished their pints in unusually small gulps.

Freddy, never down for long after an admonishment, flew his hand onto Basil's shoulder and gave it a squeeze. "Dashed rotten of Matron not to let any of the staff come along. You need all the support you can get."

It was meant kindly but earned another stern rebuke from Ainsley. Just time for a stale cheese roll each and then it was back, battling against the North Sea's icy winds and the cheerless January streets into the dreary gloom of Flaxton-on-Sea Magistrates Court.

Back inside the overheated Courtroom, try as they might, they couldn't prevent falling into a communal light doze as the police, in formal and, to the layman, almost unintelligible language stated its case from the witness stand. The sergeant assigned this important duty seemed unfazed by the sight of the accused apparently asleep on his feet. He'd seen many like him in his time and put it down to a mixture of drugs, drink and senility which, though partly true, was a trifle unfair.

Basil was jerked awake by the sound of his name.

"Major Reardon, you have heard the evidence against you, such as it is, would you like to move to the witness stand and explain your behaviour to the court?"

"Ah well, Madam, thank you." Basil pulled himself together and, escorted quite unnecessarily by the policeman, moved across to the other side of the Court. He smiled upon them all and noted his dozing comrades with some disgust. Hoping that Clarence wouldn't let out one of his little noises – they tended to pop out when he was asleep – he launched into his carefully planned defence.

"You see it's the bus stop – or rather the imminent lack of it."

That, thought Basil, clears up that little matter. Clear, concise, one round of gunfire, problem solved. Time for another quiet pint or two with the chaps in The Anchor.

It might be thought by the silence this simple explanation caused, that his assessment of his little speech was correct; that there was, indeed, nothing more to be said. But he was wrong. Madam Chairman, lost for a moment in admiration of this delightful man, was rudely brought down to earth by another foul smelling plumber's whisper.

"What the hell's he going on about?"

She passed it on to Basil via a judicial translation.

"Could you, maybe, enlarge on that a little, Major Reardon?"

Basil was flummoxed. Why did it need enlargement? Hadn't he said it all? Explained it? Cleared it up? It was at moments like this that you called upon your friends, which, after all, was what friends were there for. So he did. But his glance at the five elderly faces in various disgusting facial contortions of sleep only confused him.

"We will need rather more explanation than that, I am afraid, if we are to judge this case fairly."

Madam Chairman speared her gaze each side of her as she stressed the last word. The timid soul on her left nodded somewhat over-enthusiastically and her gulp echoed and bounced around the mahogany. The plumber let out a loud 'huh' which collided with the gulp creating a rather unpleasant noise. Captain Clarence Cuthbert jerked awake, shouted, "Pardon," and then relapsed back into a deep sleep.

"Ah well, what more is there to say?" Basil would like to oblige if he could.

"A fair bit, I hope, Major Reardon." Madam Chairman looked benignly on the accused.

"There'd better be." The plumber was unbenign.

"Well, if you're sure you've all got the time I'll run through the whole caper for you. Perhaps sitting would be in order?"

The court policeman, pleased to be of some useful purpose and eager to rekindle the excitement of his early years in the Force, picked up a chair and placed it in the witness box. The noise of scraping, puffing and blowing awoke the sleeping comrades who, as one, looked at each other, the Courtroom and the Bench, shuffled, and pretended that they'd never been asleep at all.

Basil, now thoroughly comfortable, crossed one leg over the other, folded his arms over his chest and set off on a gentle ramble.

"We had this letter delivered to Oldthorpe, do you see, from the bus chappies…"

Ainsley, knowing Basil and his innate ability to meander through the highways and byways of the English language, and feeling the need for more sustenance at The Anchor sooner rather than later, decided to move things on. He clambered to his feet.

"Decided to take away our bus-stop. The one close by Oldthorpe House. Just remove it…"

"Not just shift it." Tubes Potter, as ex-submarine Commanders will do, bellowed out his contribution, "Do away with it. How can we get anywhere?"

"Gentlemen." Madam Chairman could bellow as well as anyone when required. The clerk waved his arms – he felt it might help – and appeared to be conducting the steady beating of the gavel that Percy-the-plumber had, quite improperly, taken upon himself to wield.

As the cacophony, and its resulting mahogany echo, began to die away, Colonel Alastair Hunter, now standing on what only his colleagues around him knew to be his one real leg, was left almost shouting "… get to The Anchor for our medicine without a bus?"

Again there was one of those pauses, pregnant with a mixture of confusion and misapprehension. An anchor? Medicine? It was all lost on the Bench but to Madam Chairman this was not the issue. Other matters took precedence.

"I will not have this, gentlemen. This is not a debating chamber. It is not a meeting place. It is Her Majesty's Court of Law where rules, strict rules, apply. I advise you, if you do not wish to join your colleague in the dock, to remember where you are."

That did it. The reference to Her Majesty, to whom all those under rightful castigation had sworn an oath of allegiance on her ascendance to the throne, shut them up with a wallop. To their consternation they saw Basil nodding in agreement with Madam Chairman. He really didn't want them sharing his little dock. He was quite comfy there on his own.

Madam Chairman was about to get things moving again when the little colleague on her left tugged at her arm and whispered, "How do they get medicine from an anchor?"

How pleasant it was to experience toothpastey breath for a change thought Madam Chairman, however stupid the words borne upon it. She decided to ignore the interruption.

"Please tell us more, Major Reardon."

The smile was sweet and Basil felt a funny little feeling not felt for many a long year. In some confusion he felt for his pipe and tobacco pouch. This was the longest waking time he'd been without a smoke and it would, he knew, put such strange feelings to rest. He wondered if he might ask permission to light up but, knowing the answer, made do with taking the pipe from his pocket and sucking on the comforting cool stem.

"You can't do that!" The plumber was speaking with indignation.

"I fear you can't, Major Reardon." Madam Chairman would have loved to light up one of her own small cigars.

Basil cheerily waved the offending object at them. "Not lit. Certainly not. Most improper." And then with a rare flash of inspiration, "It'll help me move the story along, you see. Save time."

"We give you permission in its unlit state."

Judging by the plumber's expression, 'we' was somewhat of an exaggeration.

"As the chaps have said, the bus company told us in its letter that the stop was being removed and we – well, those of us brave enough to defy Matron Maud Montague – it is she who refers to us as inmates, and doubtless told the police so when they called regarding my protest – and inmates we most certainly are not, but voluntary residents who made the mistaken assumption that Oldthorpe House would be a welcome refuge for us at this latter stage of our lives and …"

He paused. There was silence. Total silence. No movement. The moment was broken by Basil himself.

"Where was I?"

"I fear we are still at the start, Major Reardon. Shall we move on?"

Ainsley leapt to his feet. "Might it not be better if I…"

"NO."

It seemed that even Madam Chairman had an explosion point and Brigadier Ainsley had neatly found it.

"Thanks old chap but I'm really coping splendidly. Why don't you all cut along to The Anchor? I'll be with you in a jiffy – unless, of course…" Basil looked enquiringly at the Bench as if to ask them how many months he'd get so that he could make suitable arrangements.

"You must only address the Bench, Major Reardon."

Even Madam Chairman was beginning to despair. She had put this case down as a quickie ending with a warning as to future conduct; a rather pleasant interlude between the welter of petty thieves and rascals who regularly filled the lists. It wasn't turning out like that at all.

Basil brought out an old envelope on which were jotted a number of little phrases thought up by them all at an illicit late-night meeting in his room at Oldthorpe.

"We rely on the bus do you see? It's our only means of escape from the clutches of Matron Maud. Our link with the outside world. We're about the only people who use it in Thorpe Haven, everyone else has a car. And then we got this letter telling us that the bus would no longer stop in the village but speed through to Flaxton. Matron thought it would be a good idea but that's typical of her. Do you know, she even checks up on our…"

"Major Reardon. We're slipping from the point again. And you were doing so well. On we go. You'd received this letter…"

"Um. Dash. Memory gone. Sorry. Happens sometimes when there's an interruption."

He scanned the envelope but it seemed to offer up no support. It was obviously time for some help from the chaps. He glanced across at them and was disturbed by what he saw. Ainsley and Tubes, were mouthing what he imagined to be helpful advice. They looked, he thought, like fishes thrown onto the bank gasping for air, or water, or whatever fishes out of water gasped for. Alastair was laughing, thoroughly enjoying his friend's predicament, Freddy was, as usual, using his hand as a late-lamented Spitfire and doing stall turns in the air around him, and Clarence was still fast asleep. Basil felt he might handle the moment better by ignoring them.

Madam Chairman sighed again. It seemed to be turning into one of those cases that evoked a lot of sighing. "So having received the letter what did you decide to do?"

"Ah well. You all know that don't you. That's why I'm here." That seemed to wrap it up nicely.

"In your words please, Major Reardon?"

Basil consulted his envelope again.

"Right ho. We'd phoned them – that's the Bus Company – and called in, but nobody would see us. They just sent a message saying that a few passengers a day couldn't justify maintaining a bus stop."

Tubes jumped to his feet again.

"Falling to bits. Hasn't been maintained for years. They're talking poppycock." He caught Madam Chairman's eye. "Sorry."

"One more word..." Madam Chairman made a sweeping gesture with her arm towards the door. All those in court were sorry that it didn't inadvertently clip the ear of Percy-the-Plumber.

"We decided that a protest would bring it to everyone's attention." Basil sat back and sucked deeply on his empty pipe. "We did that in India once. Rawalpindi. Or was I in Kamptee? Dashed if I can remember. Brain's gone. I was a young pup at the time. Second Lieutenant. Bit of a rascal. We young chaps didn't like the way the Mess was being run. Put a big sign on the roof. 'FREE TEAS'. The natives flocked in. Families, the lot." He chuckled, rubbing his hands together with the memory of it. "They sat amongst the old Colonels and Majors. They were apoplectic. Speechless. Children and babies yapping about. Fearful racket. Great fun." Eyes closed, he started laughing at the memory and, in a gesture of solidarity, his friends joined in.

The sound of heavy hammering clicked Basil's eyes open again and revealed what the reporter for the Flaxton Chronicle described in his article as a 'Disturbed Bench'. Madam Chairman appeared dismayed, as if her favourite nephew had let himself down in front of her friends, the little lady Magistrate on her left seemed about to burst into tears as a child would when a grown-up joke goes over its head, and Percy-the-Plumber was standing up pointing an accusing hand on the end of a similarly accusing arm at Basil. It was he who got his oar in first.

"You can't call Indians in India natives. You should be rearrested for inciting racial – something."

Percy was obviously an early disciple of political correctness, even if his knowledge of the law was as sketchy as that of the circlips and O-rings he inexpertly fitted to Flaxton's taps.

"Major Reardon I really do despair." Madam Chairman looked as if she really did.

"I'm sorry to hear that, Madam. Is there anything I can do?"

From anyone other than Basil Reardon this remark would be seen as the height of sarcasm but he was made of finer stuff. He sat forward earnestly wishing to help a maiden – well, more a matron – in distress.

Her voice was very gentle, almost pleading. "Tell me about the protest, Major Reardon."

"Ah, right. I'm so sorry. I rather felt I had."

The Bench, in unison, shook their heads.

"Ainsley controlled it all, gave orders and suchlike, Alastair phoned the paper to send along a chappie, Freddy took Clarence and his zimmer to the corner of the road to signal when the bus was approaching and Tubes and I were on mattress duty. Then, on Ainsley's signal, they lowered me onto it – because, do you see, it was my idea in the first place."

Basil, pleased with the clarity of his description of the protest, smiled with satisfaction at his colleagues but was disturbed to see that they all appeared not only agitated but as if they would dearly love to strangle him. It was hardly surprising. The Court policeman, they noted, had slowly sidled in their direction throughout Basil's evidence and they feared that arrests could be expected at any moment.

Madam Chairman, only too aware that today's fiasco could be multiplied five times if the law took its due course, quickly decided to use the powers vested in her and ignore the implications of the exposé. She moved swiftly on.

"You saw the bus and dropped onto the mattress."

With a couple of swift well-practised movements of her hand she snuffed-out not only a complaint from the plumber regarding leading the witness, but also Basil's apparent willingness to enlarge on her statement which would probably have lead them all back to India or some other far-flung military station.

"Thank you, Major Reardon. We have no more questions, have we? – good – then please return to the dock where a chair will be provided." It was said all in one breath and further hand movements ensured that she was not interrupted.

"I – that is, we – would like to hear from Mr Seymour again. Usher, will you please find him and bring him here."

Madam Chairman's unilateral decision to recall Flaxton's

answer to Elvis Presley was as much a mystery to her colleagues on the Bench as it was to those in the body of the Court. They were united in their opinion that they had already seen more than enough of the nasty little man and judging by the way the policeman marched him to the witness stand, so had the Law.

"You are still under oath, Mr Seymour. Two questions I – we – should like verified. First you spoke of arriving in Harbour Road ahead of your schedule. This is so?"

Seymour Seymour – or, more accurately, See-more Seymour – paused. Was this a catch to book him for speeding? He decided to move warily.

"I wasn't speeding if that's what you mean."

So much for wariness.

"Maybe not. But you were very early."

"No passengers, you see. A quick drive through and more time in the canteen. Obvious."

There was another hiss from the depths of the Courtroom. Elvis was in for a bus-load of trouble when he reported back for duty. Madam Chairman scanned her notes.

"After Major Reardon had been taken back into Oldthorpe House you say you sat and had a cigarette before continuing into Flaxton. I quote, 'I had time for another fag and then pushed on'. When did you, as you say, push on?"

Even someone so totally insensitive as Seymour Seymour felt it. A sudden change of mood as if a window had blown open, filling the Courtroom with a blast of cold January air. This was serious stuff; the jousting was over. With remarkable ease the witness fell hook, line and sinker into the hole carefully dug for him by Madam Chairman.

"I checked the timetable and left the stop on the dot, so don't you go accusing me of being late. We pulled in dead on time at the bus station."

With that, Flaxton's Elvis flamboyantly strummed a series of chords on his imaginary guitar and, grinning at his audience, presented them with a mouthful of yellowing, nicotine teeth. It was enough to freeze all movement and for a moment or two it did.

The pause was, however, deliberate. Madam Chairman knew a bit about the theatre. Hadn't she been a rather over-commanding presence at Flaxton's AmDram Society for the past decade or two? She allowed the pause to register and then said unusually quietly, "So your enforced stop in Harbour Road put you back on the correct schedule?"

After what seemed like an age, the simple fact put forward by Madam Chairman sank home and Seymour nodded. "Probably."

"Thank you, Mr Seymour. You may step down."

Another strum on the guitar, this time accompanied by the real sound of inaccurate humming of the first line of 'Hound Dog', and the artist left the stage. But instead of frenzied applause and unmentionable garments being hurled at him by young ladies, as was the way with his god, he just earned a stiff rebuke from the bench.

"No humming in my Court."

"Hold very tight please, ting, ting." Tubes couldn't resist it.

The stern gaze of Madam Chairman swivelled from the departing Seymour to the group of naughty boys. It was enough to earn Tubes a swift dig in the ribs from Ainsley.

"We have one last duty to perform before retiring to consider our verdict. If available, we will call a witness as to the character of the accused." She swung round to Basil. "I'm sorry about this, Major Reardon, but it is customary."

As one, Basil's colleagues clambered to their feet. Captain Clarence, who had been asleep again, rose rather later than the others and was helped up by Squadron Leader Freddy.

"Is it over? How long did he get?"

The flat of Freddy's hand flew a quick sortie and landed gently across Clarence's mouth. It wasn't a particularly pleasant experience for either party.

Madam Chairman, fearing that any one of the quintet would provide a near identical fiasco to Basil's performance, was willing to clutch at any alternative straw.

"Have you, perhaps, a relative in court, Major Reardon?"

Basil blinked. Relatives didn't feature much in his life. The only one he could think of was his sister in Bexley but they'd only known each other for the years up to his seventh birthday when he was packed off to boarding school. He doubted whether such early memories of him would be of much help. He was about to suggest that his old friend, Tubes, might fit the bill when a young female voice piped up from the back of the court.

"I'll do it, if it's all right. I work at Oldthorpe House."

"Thank you, madam. Please come down to the Bench where we can see you."

A splendidly buxom girl, resplendent in nurse's uniform, appeared from the shadows gently escorted by the usher. She was obviously nervous and was wringing a small hanky in her hands.

Basil was on his feet now. "Lisa, you shouldn't be here. Matron will be furious."

"That will do, Major Reardon, thank you. I'm sure this young lady is aware of what she is up to."

Madam Chairman smiled at the girl and directed her to the witness stand. It was a great relief to hear the oath rattled off in great chunks rather than word by word.

"Please state you name and occupation."

"Miss Lisa Mary Roberts. I'm a nurse, well, in fact the only nurse at Oldthorpe House."

Mr Prosser, the clerk, was in seventh heaven. Everything was fitting neatly into his little boxes.

"She's an angel." Captain Clarence wanted it to be known and Madam Chairman was surprised to find her admonishing glare returned by an even fiercer one.

"Please tell us how long you have known Major Reardon…"

"The accused." The plumber was still thinking of black caps and gallows but the look he received from his superior was rather more frightening than being sentenced to death.

"As I was saying, how long have you known Major Reardon and what is your assessment of him?"

Lisa took a deep breath as she had been taught to do at times of panic and launched into her carefully prepared piece.

"He was at Oldthorpe when I came there three years ago. He, and Brigadier Bennington, and Colonel Hunter, and Commander Potter and Squadron-Leader Foster and, of course, dear Captain Clarence, are the dearest people I've ever met. Major Reardon is so kind and gentle. I would have loved him to be my father because he's so sensible and wise…"

Basil was annoyed to find that at this totally unfamiliar moment when things were being said of him that he'd never heard before and were, he was sure, an enormous exaggeration, he was getting a tickling feeling in his eyes. They appeared to be watering without any help from the usual clouds of tobacco smoke he wafted at them.

"It doesn't matter that he sometimes sets fire to things with his pipe or that he's rather untidy, he's lovely to have around the place."

With a plonk, Lisa dropped down onto the chair. She felt dizzy and out of breath and wasn't at all sure that she might not burst into tears.

"Thank you, Miss Roberts. You have been of great assistance in this case. You may stand down."

The magistrates each side of the Chairman took the tight clamping of their wrists to mean that if they uttered a word she would break them.

"We shall now retire for a short while to consider our verdict."

The atmosphere in the small lobby outside the Courtroom was fraught, not so much due to the high drama of 'The Crown versus Basil Charles Beresford Reardon', but rather the thickness of the smoke from the defendant's pipe. With no opening window and the doors closed in due accordance with the law, the cloud ceiling was rapidly lowering.

The six protestors were huddled on the hard wooden benches in one corner and over by the door Seymour Seymour, all his Elvis cockiness gone, was receiving a wigging in what sounded like single syllable Anglo-Saxon words from a man dressed in the tea-stained uniform of a Flaxton-on-Sea Omnibus Inspector. It was he who had provided the hissing during the proceedings.

Ainsley Bennington felt that some corporate support for Basil was required at what could well be a watershed in his life.

"If circumstances called for it we'd do it again. Never fear."

Basil couldn't quite fathom that one out. Would we? It hadn't seemed much of a team effort there in court. Not that he minded. It had been his idea and for some strange reason he was happy to be facing the consequences on his own.

Freddy wanted to lend support. His hand made a perfect landing on Basil's knee.

"We'll all stand by you, old chum. Visit you often."

It was Clarence's turn to rally round and he clasped Basil's arm with a shaking, bony, hand.

"I'd share a cell with you. Keep you company."

Basil just managed to hide a shudder. The thought of Clarence, with his internal problems, little noises and a need to spend most of his waking hours in the lavatory, living cheek by jowl with him in a prison cell made a death sentence seem almost attractive. He didn't know, of course, how much one of the magistrates would like to have obliged him!

Alastair Hunter, to whom this stage of life had to be as cheerful as possible, the previous stages having been hell, roared with laughter.

"What are you all on about? Basil lay on a mattress in front of a bus. He'll probably be fined a bob or two. We'll all chip in and that will be that."

They sat in silence, each wondering how many bobs it would be. Financial resources were meagre to say the least.

Tubes, for once, had no contribution to make. He felt way out of his depth – worrying for all submariners. He couldn't see how Basil could get over this one. Any fine, however small, would make him ineligible to stay in Oldthorpe House. Where on earth would the poor chap go? And Tubes knew that he would have to go with him. He'd never leave Basil to face the outside world on his own. Heaven knows what he'd inadvertently get up to.

They all jumped when the Courtroom door opened. The usher, appearing far sooner than expected, did some ushering and, with slaps on the back to denote solidarity but, in fact, inflicting a degree of grievous bodily harm on him, the defendant marched towards the dock.

Taking the cue from him, his colleagues, in single file, did the same. Even Clarence kept roughly in step.

"This has been an usual case in many respects, not least for the various interruptions I – we – have been subjected to during the course of the day. Whilst abhorring this behaviour it has caused us to be aware of the support the defendant has from his colleagues at Oldthorpe House. But, I must warn you all, enough is enough."

Madam Chairman swept her eye over them all and then, with an occasional glance at her notes, launched into what appeared to be very much her own judgement. Her audience was not to know that it would be entered in the Court records as a two-to-one decision – but that didn't worry her in the least.

"There are many strange twists to this case. The one that is germane to our judgement is the behaviour of the bus in question – or, to be more precise, its driver Desmond Elvis Seymour." She made 'Elvis' sound like an unfortunate disease. "By his own admission he left Loxton early so as to reach his destination here in Flaxton in time for a lengthened break in the bus station canteen. This, of course, meant that he reached Harbour Road, the scene of the incident, early. Now let us consider the legal implications of this."

Basil wondered if he'd wandered in to the wrong case. There was no mention as yet of his mattress or the flinging of himself upon it. Surely, that's what all this malarkey was about?

Madam Chairman was warming to her task.

"Under the statute granting the Flaxton Bus Company the license to operate a Stage Carriage service in this area is a requirement to keep to the published timetables. It therefore follows that if they are deliberately not adhered to the license is being flouted and it further follows that the vehicle is therefore not operating a lawful service."

Yes, thought Basil. They're dealing with another case first. Might as well sit down until my turn comes. A glance at Madam Chairman indicated that this was not a popular decision and he quickly stood up again.

"I hope you're all following this?"

It wasn't put as a question but everyone, even Percy-the-plumber, realized that this was not the moment to suggest otherwise. They nodded enthusiastically.

"So the unlawful bus arrived and found its way impeded by a mattress and, upon it, the defendant Basil Charles Beresford Reardon. Now we must stress that despite all this, Major Reardon's act in impeding a vehicle on the highway is an illegal act but what if it had been a stolen car? Or a get-away car? Or a runaway car? In other words, a vehicle going unlawfully about its business?"

Admiration for Madam Chairman was growing by the minute. Whilst the plumber would always be a dissenter and Elvis was barred from having an opinion because nobody liked him, everyone else would vote her to be Lord Chancellor or any other eminent legal position she would care to choose. They gazed at her adoringly which almost put her off her stride. Slightly flustered she spent a moment considering her notes then, her composure regained, she marched on.

"What particularly struck me – us – was that the driver admitted in evidence and re-evidence that, after the mattress was removed, along with the defendant, he continued sitting there, smoking another disgusting cigarette, before proceeding– on time – into Flaxton. It was, therefore, the mattress and, per se, the defendant upon it, that changed the bus from an unlicensed service to a licensed one."

Madam Chairman sat back triumphantly. So much more fun than most other cases. She glanced around and saw precisely the same uncomprehending expressions still on her adoring public's faces. She wondered whether anyone had understood a word that she'd said. Better get it done with.

"All that being so my – our – judgement is that the defendant, Basil Charles Beresford Reardon…"

"Military Cross, Major, Royal Artillery."

Basil did so wish that Clarence would shut up – or go to the lavatory again.

"Yes, indeed, all that as well." She was thoroughly enjoying herself.

It was more than could be said for Mr Prosser, the Court Clerk, who could find no spaces on his new-fangled forms to set down any of these words of wisdom. The squares provided called for 'guilty' or 'not guilty' ticks.

"As I was saying, you, Major Reardon, have no case to answer and you are therefore free to leave the Court without a stain on your character."

It was at this moment that fate took a splendid hand. Instead of polite applause and mumbled congratulations, and before the

Bench could rise, exchange the customary bows and retire, Basil Charles Beresford Reardon, Military Cross, Major, Royal Artillery – burst into flames.

The over-zealous Flaxton Chronicle reporter was the only person present to actually speak of flames – indeed he referred to an inferno once he really got going in his article – and it was a pity both for him and his drama-seeking readership that, as we shall see later, none of it was subsequently printed in the paper.

First, though, was the small matter of the blazing Basil. It would come as no surprise to those knowing him that the seat of the fire was his breast pocket wherein was his beloved pipe. It suddenly erupted into clouds of smoke letting off the revolting smell of burning material. It would take a connoisseur of fine cloths to identify it as conflagrating worsted of a superior quality but, indeed, that's what it was.

His suit jacket started to burn merrily, ably assisted by the usher, the policeman and his somewhat stunned comrades who barged into each other trying to beat him out thereby causing a healthy draught for the fire to latch on to. The flames were well and truly fanned.

The British are undoubtedly at their best when a drama suddenly strikes them and now they duly demonstrated it. The judiciary were hastily bundled by the ushers into the inner sanctums of the Courthouse behind the Bench. They were swiftly followed by Mr Prosser who gathered up his precious sheaf of little boxed forms and rushed to his office to prepare another set in the name of 'The Crown versus Basil Charles Beresford Reardon'. He was sure that arson regarding one of Her Majesty's Magistrates' Courts was high on the list of indictable offences.

Calmest of all were Basil and his fellow protestors. They hadn't fought in goodness knows how many wars to be fazed by the sight of a chap on fire – even a close comrade.

In no time the jacket was off and they were stamping out the flames, giving, Captain Clarence would report later, a fair imitation of a Nijad African tribal fertility dance which he had often witnessed.

The fire was out long before the Fire Brigade arrived –

Flaxton's own Appliance and two from Ipswich; when it came to burning Courthouses the authorities took no risks. All the firemen found was a small heap of charred cloth and six greatly embarrassed elderly men. Their only task was to move into the well-drilled 'make safe' procedure which involved the usher's dustpan and brush and a rubbish bag. In no time, except for a foul smell of burnt cloth, a slight thickness of the atmosphere and a small patch of less-polished floorboards, there was no sign of Basil's little conflagration.

It was a week before Basil was officially told that he would not be 'proceeded with' regarding the fire. He wasn't to know that Madam Chairman had wielded her not-inconsiderable authority in this decision. She weighed the obvious enormity of setting fire to a Courtroom, however unintentionally, with the thought of another Basil Reardon trial and came down heavily against prosecution. In this she was empowered to make a unilateral decision – which was just as well because Percy-the-Plumber would certainly have seen it as a hanging-drawing-and-quartering offence.

The week was not without other incident. Flaxton-on-Sea Omnibus Company agreed to withdraw its plans for the removal of the bus stops in Thorpe Haven.

To everyone at Oldthorpe House – other than Brigadier Ainsley – this about turn was directly attributed to Basil's selfless action and they all praised him mightily. That is, everyone except Matron Maud Montague and her immediate subordinate, Sister Amelia Newbiggin who castigated him for making an exhibition of himself. For their opinions he and his fellow conspirators cared not a jot.

So why was Brigadier Ainsley the odd one out? What did he know that the others didn't?

Years before, near the end of the Second World War he had serving under his command a Liaison Officer called Vernon Rogers who had been Editor of the Flaxton Chronicle and, on demobilisation, had returned as such to the paper. It was he who, years later, had introduced Ainsley to Oldthorpe House. Now they rarely met, but old comradeships die hard and it was to Vernon Rogers that Ainsley turned for help in two directions.

First, he suggested to Vernon that an exposé of the Bus Company in his newspaper would, if the driver's evidence was anything to go by, reveal sloppy management of staff, poor time-keeping and mechanical maintenance. Vernon might suggest to the management that printing such a story would be catastrophic for all of them. However, if the bus stop plans were withdrawn they would be showing to their customers that they cared for them and then it would be inappropriate to print the exposé...

Secondly he stressed to the Editor that it would serve the residents at Oldthorpe well if the report on the trial could be kept to a minimum and Nurse Lisa's contribution left unreported.

It showed the degree of respect that Vernon had for Ainsley that the editor defied all his journalistic principles and placed the story, reduced to a couple of column inches, deep in the depths of the middle pages.

So Ainsley had done well – or nearly. Later in the week the six of them were sitting around the fireplace in Oldthorpe's lounge, staring at the puffs of smoke drifting upwards from the five or six small lumps of coal.

Clarence, referring back to the stamping out of Basil's burning jacket, had just described, in breathless and querulous tones, the lurid details of a Nijad fertility dance, dwelling at length on the nakedness and bouncing-up-and-down of the young maidens, but it had all got a bit too much for him and Nurse Lisa had taken him to his room for a lie down.

For a while they let their fertile imaginations run away with them and then Alastair Hunter broke the silence.

"After the Lord Mayor's Show."

Freddy looked up from reading Punch.

"What is, old fruit?"

"The excitement's gone. Back to dull monotony."

"I'm glad you found my humiliation exciting," said Basil a touch tartly.

"You did damn well." Tubes needed to get something off his chest that had been worrying him ever since that revolting Elvis character had let slip a worrying piece of evidence.

"Damned brave – but was the possibility of death worth the removal of a bus stop? I happen to think not."

Basil smiled indulgently. "We considered that at the planning stage didn't we, Tubes. We knew there was no risk otherwise, I assure you, I wouldn't have done it. Not for a bus stop."

Tubes wasn't satisfied. "But the thing only stopped an inch from you. And that was only because that useless driver jammed on his brakes."

"We allowed for that in the plan, didn't we? As soon as Freddy and Clarence signalled the bus was approaching you helped me onto the mattress then hid behind the hedge. I closed my eyes and then Ainsley stood by the mattress and signalled the bus to stop."

It took a moment to sink in and then Ainsley had one of those nasty icicle feelings at his various extremities. He'd completely forgotten to carry out that bit of the plan. He did, however, remember finding the cover behind the hedge rather cramped for him and Tubes...

They looked at each other. Two white-faced conspirators. Freddy's hand took off into a steep climb.

"But you weren't..."

Tubes was quickly in.

"Shut up, Freddy. Go and see if tea's ready."

2

Lucy Banbury, every inch the retired headmistress, neat, petite and precise in all details of dress and behaviour, lowered her book and shifted uncomfortably on the slatted seat in what Flaxton-on-Sea dared to describe as a 'shelter'. It was a poor description in that it faced the North Sea and was open to anything Russia, Scandinavia – in fact all the northern archipelago – could hurl at it, making it more a receptacle for foul weather than a shield from it.

It wasn't, however, the icy January wind blowing onto East Anglia's exposed coast that afternoon that was causing the shelter's sole occupant discomfort, she was well wrapped up against that. It was the male posteriors: six of them at varying heights from the ground, packed tightly together only a few feet in front of her. With mackintosh and coat tails flapping they presented a thoroughly disturbing sight and the best that could be said about them was that they acted as a windbreak.

But Miss Banbury, created in the image of her genteel, God-fearing and now long-gone parents, would have much preferred a howling North Sea gale in her face rather than this posterior shield. Never in her life had she considered this particular part of the anatomy, never given it a moment of her time although, as she saw amongst the graffiti that covered much of the available wooden walls around her, many others in Flaxton obviously did!

She quickly pulled her eyes away from the scratched vulgarities of Flaxton's bored teenagers and returned to her book. Anthony Trollope's Barchester Towers was a great comfort to her at these especially sad times and, strange though the behaviour of Bishop Proudie and his infuriating wife was, life a century-and-more before seemed preferable to today.

As Lucy absorbed herself once more in Trollope, the human windbreak stirred into something approaching life. Had someone from nearby Oldthorpe House been walking on the seaward side of it they would have immediately recognised the owners of the posteriors as Brigadier Ainsley Bennington, Colonel Alastair Hunter, Commander 'Tubes' Potter, Major Basil Reardon, Squadron Leader Freddy Forbes and Captain Clarence Cuthbert and doubtless given them a cheery wave, but to Lucy this collection of retired officers of Her Majesty's Forces was, at this early stage in their acquaintance, merely an assembly of flapping coat tails.

She heard, during the brief lulls in the howling wind, the murmur of their voices and at this particular moment in her life it gave her comfort. But for someone brought up to use words sparingly and wisely she would have been dismayed at the inconsequential nonsense that came so naturally to these elderly men. Words, any words, rather than silences, kept them sane and aware of at least some purpose to their extended lives.

Freddy yawned into the gale.

"I'm on jumper duty with Clarence. Sister says so. Urgent. She won't have his old one in the house another minute. She says it's a hazard to our health."

He gave the old man next to him a gentle nudge but Captain Clarence, with the excuse of age, was quietly dozing, held up by the closeness of his colleagues.

Ainsley nodded, for once agreeing with Sister Newbiggin.

"She's right you know. He's got more food on that pullover than they had in the last days of the siege of Mafeking. We shall all be relieved." He allowed himself a small chortle at his witticism but it was lost in the gale.

"She said I must get a colour to camouflage the food." Freddy, his left hand acting as a substitute for his late-lamented Spitfire, performed a tight vertical roll followed by a stall turn.

Tubes also felt that Sister had a point. His voice boomed from within a forest of white beard. "There always seems to be a profusion of gravy on it. Get him a brown one."

Basil, drawing heavily on his ever-burning pipe and thereby dispatching an unwelcome smokescreen back towards Lucy, was unhappy with this suggestion. He'd studied the offending pullover from far too close quarters through many a ghastly meal.

"Custard. That's Clarence's main problem regarding spillage. A goldish colour would be best."

It was now the turn of Alastair to add fuel to this ludicrous discussion.

"I've noted the man can't eat tomatoes – well, not without squirting the innards over a wide area." His Midlothian lilt gave no hint of the depths of his disapproval of clumsy tomato eaters. "Predominantly red. That's what the jumper needs to be. Definitely."

Ainsley noted how emphatic his friend could be when important decisions had to be made. He uncharitably found this unusual in an infantry officer but then, being a 'tank' man himself, he probably would.

Freddy was losing interest in jumper duty.

"Any advance on brown, gold or red? I very much doubt if our friendly outfitter, Mr Baker, will stock such a racy item."

"I've noticed smatterings of blue." Basil closed his eyes the better to visualise the offending article. He had always found colour difficult to define.

Blue? They were all silent as they searched their food cupboards for squirty blue food but were saved too much of this unwelcome effort by the quivering voice of the squirter himself.

"Quink." Clarence spat the one word tetchily into the gale with surprising force. He didn't see why his little failings regarding the transfer of food into his mouth and the safe keeping of it there should be bandied about with such abandon by his colleagues. There was another long pause and finding their silence at this explanation unnerving he ploughed on. "Can't get the blasted ink to the pen-nib without giving it a good shake. Anyway, I don't want a new jumper. There's lots of life left in my old one."

"There certainly is, old chap," Tubes nodded. "Mostly crawling from one morsel of food to the next."

Clarence thought the general chortling extremely childish.

Freddy, seeing the white spume on the rollers breaking noisily on the shingle, had a moment of inspiration.

"We're all wrong as far as the main colour is concerned. It's white isn't it? More of that than any other colour."

There was further silent pondering as they searched their minds for white food that Clarence would have dribbled.

"Not ice cream," said Basil mournfully. "We never have ice

cream."

"Semolina, tapioca, that'll be it." Alastair had had enough of this ludicrous conversation and hoped that his pronouncement would be seen as the final solution to this totally unimportant matter. He wanted to get down to the real reason for bringing them to this desolate spot and making them endure the full force of the January north wind. But his hopes were dashed by Tubes who, a stickler for accuracy – as a Torpedo Officer would need to be – was still not satisfied.

"More cream than white. Although it's usually been in the tin so long it's more grey."

They were about to embark on a discussion regarding their perception of the colour of Oldthorpe House semolina and tapioca puddings when Clarence tried again to put an end to this whole embarrassing business.

"Gibbs."

It was another of his one-word conversation stoppers – and it worked. He paused as they floundered around him and then put them out of their misery.

"Dentifrice. When I clean my teeth." He couldn't understand why they didn't just say 'Right, old chap' and take him to the warmth of the pub for a pint or two but they obviously needed more help before they'd budge.

"The nail brush."

"The nail brush?"

"In the washing bowl. Before I put them in."

Each of them experienced his own image of this terrible ritual and, shuddering, silently stared out to sea.

"Do them every Sunday. Regular as clockwork."

Maintaining their collective silence they considered this terrible revelation for a while, knowing each others' company well enough to be aware that such moments often led up to a shell suddenly exploding amongst them and, sure enough, it did.

"Corporal Tremlett was a messy eater."

As one, they groaned. Ainsley Bennington's tank driver, whilst obviously experiencing a full and eventful war – he would have won many a Victoria Cross and served innumerable months in detention if he'd experienced only a fraction of the stories attributed to him – filled many a boring hour with increased boredom at Oldthorpe House.

"We were laagered up…"

"In tank parlance rather than a football fan's I imagine?" Alastair could not resist a bit of Ainsley baiting even if it lengthened the blasted story.

Ainsley was wise to this sporadic gunfire during his interesting dissertations; he saw it as the lot of the experienced raconteur.

"Tremlett and my signaller, Corrigan, had bagged a couple of chickens that strayed into our path…"

"I'm surprised they weren't squashed flat by the tank tracks." Freddy took off at speed with his left hand and had it smacked away by Tubes who saw any interruption as a delay in getting the unlikely tale finished with.

"They'd knocked the birds up…"

Clarence stirred from his doze. "We had a lot of that in France in the first lot."

They were saved further unpleasant, if illuminating, detail of Clarence's French philandering that doubtless delayed the 1918 armistice, by Tubes who, using his Torpedo Officer voice which had sent many a rating scuttling into hidden corners of his torpedo room, boomed, "Will you all shut up and let Ainsley finish. Then we can get down to some serious drinking in The Anchor."

As was usually the case at these times Ainsley hardly heard the interruptions being so absorbed in the tale he was unfolding.

"They'd knocked the birds up into a stew. Delicious. Particularly with a rather fine Sauvignon I'd found in a nearby cellar…"

"It must have been hell."

"Not really – although I've always found Sauvignon a little too dry with chicken."

His enforced listeners continued to feign interest and wondered why they really bothered.

"Corporal Tremlett had just lifted his mess-tin to grab at another piece…"

"Didn't the chap know how to use a knife and fork?"

"ALASTAIR PLEASE."

None of them heard the slight clucking of disapproval

behind them. Even Trollope couldn't hold Lucy's attention when the windbreak started shouting.

"And this bullet hit it." Ainsley slapped his hand on the balustrade causing them all to jump. He turned an accusing eye on Alastair. "If he'd used a knife and fork he'd have been a gonner." Alastair returned the stare and winked, ruining everything.

Basil sighed. "What a blessing." He was a kindly soul.

Tubes nodded. "It certainly would have been."

"It was a glancing blow and caused poor Corrigan, my signaller, double anguish. The mess-tin was torn from Tremlett's hand and deposited its contents all over the poor chap's pullover and the bullet took off his ear."

This took even more digesting than most of the Tremlett stories but at last Alastair, as baiter-in-chief and self-appointed adjudicator, gave his verdict.

"Hogwash."

Basil continued in his kind vein. "Poor old Corrigan. What was the outcome?"

"Tremlett had to make do with a spam sandwich."

"Ah." There wasn't much more one could say.

Tubes stirred. He was freezing cold, a state rarely experienced in the snug, fetid air of a torpedo room.

"Why are we here, Alastair? Why pull us off the bus at this stop and submit us to this arctic purgatory – and blasted Corporal Tremlett – when two stops on there's the warmth and comfort of The Anchor?"

"Because, my friend, what we have to discuss is for our ears only."

"Lucky old Corrigan isn't here." Freddy would never learn. "He'd only half hear."

Their stares said it all but the venom was lost on Freddy who dived on into thick cloud. "Only having one…"

"SHUT UP"

"Right-ho."

Alastair seized the moment. He had decided that very morning, after an even more vituperative than usual episode with Matron, that now was the time to discuss well away from eavesdroppers the discontent that had plagued them all since their descent into the misery of Oldthorpe House. There had to be a solution.

"She's got to go."

Alastair made the four words an emphatic, no nonsense statement.

"So must I."

Clarence shakily transferred his gloved hands from the balustrade to his two walking sticks. He added nervously, "Quickly!"

"Come on, old fella. I'll give you a hand."

Freddy looped-the-loop with his left hand, executed a stall turn and laid it to rest on the old man's arm. He hoped the misunderstanding of last week's visit to the seafront 'Gents', when another reliever had found his zip manipulation on his old friend unusual, would not be repeated.

With the human windbreak reduced to four bodies Lucy, whilst still having her view of the shingle and beached fishing boats partially restricted, could now feel the strong breeze and taste its salty tang. She was finding the snatches of conversation blown across to her so intriguing that it made it difficult to concentrate on the affairs of Trollope's Barchester so she decided to give her reading a rest for a few moments.

Back at the balustrade Ainsley felt that sufficient time had passed since Alastair's four word statement, but even though he had no need to expend the energy on his question, already knowing the answer, he felt it had best be asked.

"Who must go?"

"Matron Maud Montague of course." The others noted that Alastair always snapped out the wretched woman's name; she had that effect on him. "Damned woman. Runs the place like an asylum. I came for rest, peace and tranquillity in my old age. Only this morning…"

"Not before time after the life you've led," said Ainsley dryly.

Basil blew out a cloud of tobacco smoke into the gale. He had this ability to talk with a pipe clenched tightly between his teeth and still more-or-less make sense.

"D'you know what my nephew said the other day? You know, that chappie who looked in last week? Can't remember his name. Something odd." He wasn't good on names.

There was another long pause and as no one seemed to want to know, Basil told them. "Running on empty." He slapped his thigh with glee and let out a sound halfway between a guffaw and a snort causing Miss Banbury to blink. "Running on empty. I like that. Us, old codgers. Gadding about to no purpose, d'you see? Clever, that lad. Clever. That's university for you."

"Often did – nearly," boomed Tubes. "Run on empty. Near the end of a patrol. Couldn't surface. Enemy all around. Batteries nearly flat. Desperate to be relieved."

"Absolutely." Clarence with Freddy, his fighter escort, had rejoined the group. He added, unnecessarily as far as the others were concerned, "Much relieved, thank you."

Basil stared for a long moment at the horizon. Much as he loved dear old Clarence and would defend him with his life he felt yet again how easily his friend dragged down any conversation into something approaching lunacy. That young nephew of his was right. They were running on empty. Their active lives now over they were serving no useful purpose to anyone. Relations nearly all gone and those remaining duty bound to make an occasional visit or, more likely, make do with a Christmas card. He searched for a word to sum up his feelings adequately and found it.

"A bugger." Generally he would only swear to himself but he felt the need to share it this time.

A further clucking from behind made them jump and, as one, they turned. Miss Banbury, sitting bolt upright, fixed them with a reproving but not wholly malevolent eye. In perfect unison they raised their hats.

"A thousand apologies, madam." Basil, the perfect gentleman, was distraught to have been overheard by any stranger, let alone a lady, saying such a word. "I had no idea you were there."

Now aware that they were blocking her view, they split to each side of the shelter, leaving a gap at the balustrade. They all felt awkward, as if they had invaded another's privacy.

Lucy smiled. "I, too, am running on empty." She waved a woolly-gloved hand at them. "Forgive me. I could not help overhearing. You were, dare I say it, a little loud." She patted the seat each side of her. "Come and sit with me for a moment. It is nice to speak other than to oneself now and again."

Sheepishly, like little prep-school boys, they did as they were bid, squeezing into the shelter. One, she noticed, had a gammy leg.

"May we know your name?" The others had never heard Ainsley speak so gently.

"Lucy Banbury." She jumped as each man, in turn, leapt up, removed his hat, bent down and warmly shook her hand.

"Ainsley Bennington."

"Alastair Hunter."

"Tubes Potter."

"Basil Reardon."

"Freddy Foster."

"Clarence Cuthbert." Without Freddy's restraining hand the old man would probably have collapsed onto her lap.

Lucy, delighted to discover that old-fashioned manners were still to be found in Flaxton, wasn't to know that they had automatically introduced themselves in descending order of military rank. They may be 'running on empty' but entrenched disciplines still prevailed – even if they were all now under the command of a particularly officious Matron Maud Montague.

"Retired Officers' place. Out at Thorpe Haven." As he said it Ainsley felt that it was superfluous information for this elderly lady but his embarrassment in telling her came through more as gruffness.

Basil felt the need to ameliorate the tone and added, gently, "Oldthorpe House."

Speaking socially to a woman was a rarity for them these days and now they lapsed into uncomfortable silence, gazing out to the shingle beach.

"Piers."

They jumped, wishing Basil wouldn't do things like that.

"Piers. That was the lad's name. Dashed funny one if you ask me." He was agreeably surprised that his memory hadn't totally deserted him.

"I've got a granddaughter called Tiffany," Ainsley added mournfully. "Sounds like a restaurant."

"Didn't someone have breakfast there once?" Freddy's

higher pitched cheerful voice, was, felt Lucy, like a splash of fresh water amongst the dark soup-like quality of the others' but it made no difference to them; they ignored their younger friend's interruption as they usually did – and the perfect three-point landing he made with his left hand on the balustrade.

"There used to be a pier here."

Lucy's voice was quiet, almost lost in the wind sweeping around the shelter, but there was now something uncannily still about her, as if she was in a trance beckoning them into her private world. Such was the effect that no one moved, even the wind seemed to drop for a moment.

"Just out from here. Where we're sitting now. With an enormous theatre sitting on the end of it."

Their eyes swung in unison from her to the shingle and sea in front of them then back to her. A pier? It seemed hard to believe.

She was smiling again now. "I used to go to it when I visited my aunt. It was so lively, so funny. Music Hall, you see. All the soldiers and airmen waiting to go and fight," her voice dropped to a whisper, "and die."

Her gloved hands, fingers tightly entwined, started to beat gently on her knees. Ainsley, sitting next to her wanted to stay them but felt that he shouldn't. They waited quietly, respecting her silence.

"Nineteen-forty." The memories were becoming painful now and she needed space to accommodate them. She went to the balustrade, staring out to the horizon, her voice just reaching back to them. "What's that? Thirty-two years ago. The pier went. Burnt down. The North Sea did the rest. I know. I watched it slowly disappear over the years." Her voice trailed away. "Every last trace of it."

"You moved here – to Flaxton?" Ainsley stood to join her but Alastair, feeling that it would somehow be inappropriate, pulled him down again.

Lucy turned to them. "After my aunt died. Killed by a bomb. Here in Flaxton." She found it strangely cathartic to say the simple sentences out loud.

"Good God." Tubes was amazed. "Bombs here? I never knew that. I thought Hitler kept them for the big cities."

"One morning a lone German bomber came and dropped its bombs on the High Street. My aunt ran the Post Office. It was a direct hit." She turned back to the sea. "She never knew. I needed to be where she died," Lucy's voice rose now as if to justify her actions, "so I moved here."

Why was she, such a private person, telling these complete strangers all this? She knew, of course that this meeting had to be coincidence but it was uncanny that she found herself willing to share with them her most intimate thoughts, so long bottled up within her. It had been such a long silence and she identified it as having started on the day she retired as Flaxton's Primary School Headmistress. Then, somehow – why she couldn't fathom – she'd closed into herself, refused all invitations to attend events, join worthy organisations, meet and chat. Her only outings, other than to the shops, were to this shelter on the promenade and weekly to the Church where she was known as the little lady in a back pew, sitting bolt upright, kneeling to pray with hands clasped and eyes shut. She came and she went. No one felt it right to invade her private, many assumed troubled, world.

And now, today, she was here to observe, in all sadness, a birthday. Thirty-one years to the day – January the fifteenth, 1941 – since the first major catastrophe in her life. Rupert, the baby of the family; the 'afterthought', and loved all the more for that. His nineteenth birthday. He and his Hurricane fighter at rest just two miles out to sea from this very spot. Deep below the waves.

Today he would have been fifty years old. And his two older brothers? Both amongst the war dead; they would have been in their sixties. Three catastrophes. Her parents killed in the blitz. Four. Five. Her aunt killed here in Flaxton. Six. Each gentleman here represented one of them and she suddenly realised how grateful she was that they were here and that Rupert now had guests at his fiftieth birthday party. It had been a solitary annual ritual for far too long.

It was extraordinary. Why was it that she found herself telling them of Rupert and her family? It poured from her, oblivious to the wind rising to almost gale force and the rain that now fell, clattering on the roof of the shelter. After years of containment the dam was well and truly broken as she told these men in such detail that, as she calmed and came near the end, they felt that they had known the three slain brothers, her parents, and her Aunt Alice killed in the Flaxton Post Office. It was as if they were all here now, and this was a moment to celebrate rather than mourn.

When it was done there was really nothing they could say; nothing that should or could be said that wouldn't sound trite or banal. Even Freddy Foster who usually managed to put his big foot firmly into any situation at the most inopportune moment remained still. But then he too had flown – and lived.

The unfamiliar cathartic experience had drained her and she felt exhausted. "You must go now. I hope we shall meet again. You will never know what kindness you have done me." With an effort Lucy rearranged herself neatly on the wooden seat and opened her book.

"We must see you to your home. Please allow us." They all nodded in agreement with Ainsley.

She shook her head. "I shall be very comfortable here for a while with my thoughts. However, there is one thing I would ask of you before you go. I would like a note of your names. I used to take home form lists on the first evening of a new school year and I pride myself that I never forgot a single child's name and could, in no time, put a face to it."

"Of course. Freddy will write them down now." Ainsley was at his most commanding.

"Jawohl, mein Capitaine." How could he – and at a moment like this? The five freezing stares he received from the others said it all.

"Sorry, Silly. Right, here goes." He scribbled on the back of an old envelope and handed the result to Lucy who examined it as she would a scruffy piece of homework.

"And ranks, please."

"Right-ho." More scribbling.

"And decorations. I'm sure there are many."

Tubes felt he should put his naval oar in after a long period of unusual silence. "You won't need all that malarkey, I'm sure."

Lucy studied the poorly presented homework and her voice

was at its sternest, "Similar malarkey, as you rather unfortunately call it, Commander, hangs in three separate picture frames on the wall of my sitting-room. Bravely won, proudly displayed." She handed the envelope back to Freddy, "If you would, please."

She was pleased to see him adding the required detail to the list of names as he whispered to each of his colleagues and they, with much embarrassment, provided the necessary information.

"We call ourselves 'The Cavaliers'." Freddy, who never allowed his crassness to trouble him for long was back to his chirpy best.

Oh Lord, thought the others almost simultaneously, I wish he'd shut up. Such childish nonsense was the last thing they wanted to share with an outsider, particularly one as intelligent as Lucy Banbury.

"Now why should you call yourselves that?" As they feared, the question was asked as if to a ten year old.

Ainsley and Tubes were about to vie for the unwelcome task of leaping in to neutralise the silly subject and at the same time silence Freddy but Alastair was ahead of them. Having invented it he was rather proud of the sobriquet; anything to get back at Matron.

"Matron Maud has segregated the goodies from the baddies, do you see. Put those who unquestionably conform to her monstrous demands in the grand front bedrooms and we..."

"Who don't."

"Yes, thank you, Freddy. We, who do question and don't toady, are housed in the side wing. No view do you see? Of the sea. So we feel we're the Cavaliers."

"And the cringing majority are the Roundheads." Freddy just had to finish it off.

Lucy's response to all this was, as they had guessed it would be, a slight pursing of the lips and a look, long practiced over the years, of resigned tolerance. She was tempted to suggest that their assessment of the Civil War protagonists was far too general but, instead, took the envelope and placed it carefully in her handbag. "Now, off you go to your tea and buns. I shall sit here for a while until the storm passes. I need a little more time."

Ainsley had a brain-wave. Perhaps the meeting could end in

a lighter mood. "We've got a bit of trouble with Captain Clarence's pullover."

"No we haven't." Clarence could feel more washing of his dirty pullover in public. "My pullover is no trouble at all. It and I are very close."

"That's half the trouble," murmured Basil.

Ignoring the interruptions Ainsley ploughed on. "Sister has decreed that we are to buy him a new one and our bright idea is to match his most common food stains, which suggests it needs to be– er…"

"Brown," from Tubes.

"Red." Alastair was emphatic. He had no doubts.

Basil saw Lucy's knitted brow and mistook amazement for concentration. He provided extra detail. "Gold, for the custard and so on."

"Blue – unless we restrict him to pencils only." Ainsley, as commander, was happy to impose restrictions.

"I think the old chap should have a white one." Freddy chipped in. "Care of his teeth must come first."

To Lucy, who had not been privileged to hear the earlier discussion other than brief extracts blown on the wind, all this was utterly incomprehensible but she'd experienced many equally inarticulate explanations in her classroom over the years – admittedly from children – and, quickly stripping it down to the essentials, came up with the perfect solution.

"Fair Isle."

"Pardon?"

"A Fair Isle jumper. A multi-coloured pattern. From the Shetland Isles. Your friend will look very smart in it and can get pleasure from adding to its many colours. I'm sure Mr Baker in the High Street will have one."

They were all amazed. This was undoubtedly a woman to be reckoned with. If they didn't have her as an honorary Cavalier in next to no time they'd eat their various hats – which they now raised and, clasping the small, gloved hand, moved away.

As they went out of her sight Lucy studied the carefully scribbled envelope.

Brigadier Ainsley Bennington CBE, DSO, late of the Royal Tank Regiment.

Colonel Alastair Hunter DSO, late of The Queen's Scottish Regiment.

Commander 'Tubes' Potter DSC, Royal Navy.

Major Basil Reardon MC, Royal Regiment of Artillery.

Squadron Leader Freddy Foster DFC and Bar, Royal Air Force.

Captain Clarence Cuthbert MC, Royal Signals.

She stroked it gently with her glove. She was sure she'd read something about them recently. Now would come the fun of putting faces to the names, assessing them in her mind as she would her new pupils.

First, Ainsley Bennington. Tall, gaunt, every inch the senior officer. Shoulders still well back, small expertly clipped moustache and, when his hat was removed, a head of perfectly combed though thinly spread silver hair. He'd been, Lucy felt, a bit of a patrician in his time; no nonsense tolerated, no excuses accepted. She felt confident to place him in the back row of desks amongst the well-behaved.

Colonel Alastair Hunter, the one with the gammy leg, hadn't said much but Lucy could detect an impatience with the female authority now imposed on him at Oldthorpe House. He was of medium height, ruddy complexioned, and stocky with a definite paunch suggesting a predilection for good food and drink. He seemed to favour tweeds and corduroys and had a moustache which Lucy felt sure that he would twirl at the girls. Had he, perhaps, too much of an eye for the ladies but too little training in how to behave in their presence? She'd sit him near the front, well surrounded by other boys.

This was fun, the best fun in years. Lucy looked up. The wind had dropped now and the rain had moved on inland. A weak sun not far above the horizon glinted on the wet shingle and the beached fishing boats in front of her. She'd stay a while longer and work down the list.

Commander Tubes Potter. Strange, 'Tubes'? He'd mentioned submarines. Probably something to do with torpedoes. She was sorry she'd reprimanded him because, thinking back, he'd meant no offence, only a modesty which all, less that Alastair, seemed to possess. Short and stocky, a head of white hair and full beard and, where skin managed to show through, a bright red complexion which, Lucy felt, there being no sun in submarines, was probably mainly fuelled by gin, whisky, rum and every other spirit known to man. He'd be all right near the back of the class.

Basil Reardon worried her. He was delightfully unkempt with unruly hair, a lop-sided, badly trimmed moustache and ill-fitting clothes but as Lucy had so often found amongst her new charges, appearances could deceive. Major Reardon was, without doubt, the epitome of the perfectly mannered gentleman even if he would smoke that beastly pipe – and knock out the still smouldering tobacco with no thought for its ultimate destination, which in this case was any of them upwind of him. Yet something was wrong. She saw sadness and some grief in his eyes; he was, she felt, a bit of a tortured soul. She'd keep him near the front where she could keep a motherly eye on him.

And in the very front row, just below her desk would be Freddy Foster. A rascal if ever she saw one. But a rascal with a silvery voice. She would soon have had him in the school choir. Younger and smaller than the rest, he'd been able to hold on to his youthful high spirits despite the terrors he had obviously been through. But the terrors were, of course, still there: his 'flying hand' exposed the torment still near the surface of his brain. She looked at the envelope. Two Distinguished Flying Crosses. She understood the affection she had for him: she saw in him her brother Rupert as he would have been now. Small, dapper, as if made for a Spitfire's cockpit, and with the obligatory fighter pilot's moustache. He had obviously been a devil with the ladies and, as she'd already discovered, was a master of tactlessness. Yes, front desk for him – and a word with the girls in the class to refuse any trips behind the bicycle sheds.

Lastly, there was dear old Captain Clarence Cuthbert. She checked the list. Most junior in rank and senior in age. He must be well into his eighties. Deaf as a post and thin as a stick, his

57

skin had taken on the transparent parchment texture of the very elderly and crippled. Probably arthritis. She guessed that he will have done most of his soldiering in the first conflict.

Then she remembered another plus mark for Freddy Foster: great kindness. He obviously saw a duty to his old friend and for this she would forgive him all his many undoubted transgressions.

So there they were. The class of seventy-two! She sat for a while, oblivious to the present and totally immersed in her past life with its high ration of sadness. Yes, it was sad but, conversely, strangely comforting to remember what happiness there had been in the early years.

It was the bitingly cold wind that brought her back to the present. The sun had gone again behind heavy cloud and she realized how cold and stiff she was. She looked up at the grey sky and her voice was clear as a bell in the now-still air. "Thank you, God, for bringing them to me this day."

Lucy stood and slowly, carefully stretched. Once sure of her balance and that her limbs would do more or less what was expected of them she started off towards the High Street and home. How she would have loved to join them for tea and cakes in the Cosy Cot Café but it wouldn't be right. A cup at home and then a little rest in front of the electric fire to get over the unusually active afternoon.

It was just as well that Lucy decided not to seek out the six of them in the café. On leaving her they more-or-less marched along the High Street and, having steered Clarence and Freddy into the outfitters, without breaking step or giving it a sideways glance, swept past the Cosy Cot and on into the saloon of The Anchor at the southern end of town. They came to an abrupt halt on finding the bar unusually full at what was, for most people, tea time. Their usual table was occupied and so, with help from the landlord, stools were found and they perched uncomfortably in a line up at the bar. It was a relief to find that the beer – Adnams Best Bitter – tasted as good as ever.

Later Lucy, at a considerably slower pace, followed the same route to her home which lay near the end of the road leading south from the town. She would like to have glanced into the café if only to see the six of them again but training and discipline kept her eyes fixed on the pavement ahead.

It was the sound of loud chatter coming from the bar that made her automatically glance into the brightly lit interior of The Anchor. She stopped, turned and stared through the window. It was uncanny, unbelievable. There they were again; the same six rear ends, tightly packed in a line and one, she noticed, had over his upper half a very smart Fair Isle pullover. No coat-tail flapping this time, but instead she could just make out the arms being raised as the pints slipped down.

"So much for running on empty," she murmured happily as, with a smile, she let herself into her cottage. It had been quite an afternoon.

She sighed, more in contentment than sorrow, her voice hardly audible above the quiet murmur of the passing traffic in the High Street. "Happy birthday, Rupert."

3

Chef Jean-Paul, better known to his mother by his baptismal name, Clint, gave the gong in the hall a mighty biff. The gesture, and its resulting boom, was considerably out of proportion to the luncheon it heralded which consisted of a rather tired shepherd's pie, watery greens and semolina pudding. This would be the mid-day fare for the residents of Oldthorpe House on this bitterly cold February day and doubtless add to the many hues of Clarence Cuthbert's Fair Isle pullover. The creation of this unspectacular menu had taken the chef most of the morning to produce and stretched his culinary skills near to their limit.

He stayed for a moment half expecting a rush of eager, hungry elderly gentlemen to swarm past him from the lounge to the dining room at the rear of the house but he should have known better by now. To the fifteen residents the gong merely announced a necessary revictualling exercise rather than the prospect of a table laden with haute cuisine.

Sister Amelia Newbiggin, thin, ramrod straight and as starched as her uniform, watched from the landing as the chef sloped untidily back into the kitchen and then, in reluctant dribs and drabs, her charges, chattering quietly, made their way, as if for execution, into the dining room. One remark she did hear.

"One good thing about the food here…"

"What's that?"

"It doesn't stay long enough inside you to do much harm."

Sister had one of her frequent headaches and really didn't want to bark at anybody just at the moment – and in the mood she was in, bark she undoubtedly would at such an unfair dig at the fine wholesome fare provided for her charges – so she hung back to avoid being seen.

Once the men were clear she descended the stairs and, going into the lounge, let out one of her more unpleasant 'tsks', a sound unique to her which usually preceded an angry explosion. The room looked as if the blizzard raging outside had penetrated the walls hurling the contents in all directions. Newspapers were strewn untidily on the armchairs, tables and floor, over-filled ashtrays balanced precariously where ashtrays shouldn't be and the chairs themselves were pulled out of the straight-lined precision she required them to be in. Why, oh why couldn't men conform and do as they were told? Wasn't that what military people were supposed to do? And then there was the tobacco smoke that hung over the room in a thick cloud. Had none of them any idea of the dangers to their health all this smoking was causing? All these damning rhetorical thoughts were accompanied by more 'tsks' as she cushion-pummelled her way around the room.

But there was still worse to come. As a final mark of extreme untidiness, two of the troublesome Cavaliers were still in the room: Commander Tubes Potter and Major Basil Reardon.

"Commander, Major, why are you still here? Did you not hear the gong?"

She tsked again and dived frantically into the mess scrunching the newspapers into heaps, lining up the chairs and, one of her favourite and, to the residents, most aggravating habits, pummelling – she preferred plumping up – the cushions as if they had personally offended her.

Tubes, rocking on the balls of his feet in front of the fireplace – 'feeling the ship' as he called it – found Sister Newbiggin a pain in the backside at the best of times but today it was all just too much.

"Belay there, Sister."

"Don't you belay me, Commander."

"Fear not, Sister, you will never be belayed."

Basil was silent for a moment exploring Tubes's witty sally which had been accompanied by a covert wink at him. Could there be a hidden meaning? Surely not. But these 'ranging rounds' of gunfire didn't auger well. He feared that battle was about to commence.

And so it appeared. Sister advanced on Tubes and for one exciting moment he thought that she might engage him in a bit of wrestling but the move was only to push him to one side so that she could empty the ashtrays into the fire.

Basil, the cause of much of the ash and most of the smoke

cloud hovering over them, looked up from the mess that was his armchair.

"I hear you're off for a week, Sister." He risked a wink back at Tubes but it was hidden by smoke.

"That is right, Major." She tried unsuccessfully to take his ashtray.

Tubes noted that her lips were in advanced purse position which usually suggested that all was far from well. It seemed right to press on to see if they could ignite her volatile fuse – which would be fun.

"Somewhere nice, I hope?"

They knew – and she knew they knew and probably everyone knew – where she was off to and that this seemingly innocent enquiry was an attempt to bait her but still she fell for it and ploughed on.

"I am attending a course in London. Our new owner, Mr Cartiledge, has discovered that a grant can be obtained if one of the staff has a particular qualification and he has elected me to go."

Tubes and Basil, having been charged by their fellow Cavaliers to find out if this unexpected turn of events would interfere in any way with their established way of life at Oldthorpe, dug deeper.

Basil drew heavily on his pipe thereby undoing much of Sister's tidying up. "I remember courses in the army. Good excuse for wining and dining and generally lying about."

"There'll be nothing like that, Major, I assure you. I shall be there to learn." She nearly added 'though how that pip-squeak Cartiledge, can dare to suggest there is anything I need to learn regarding controlling elderly persons I can't imagine'.

"And what will you be learning, Sister?" Tubes's voice positively purred.

She turned from their penetrating gaze and adjusted the window curtains mumbling, "Caring for the elderly."

"Oh good," more purring. "We'll look forward to having you back full of some bright ideas to ease us through this painful stage in our lives."

Basil banged his pipe out in the newly clean ashtray and much of the surrounding carpet. "Tubes and I could come along and offer some ideas if you like. We could all pop up to London together."

Tubes nodded. Not half they couldn't!

"These will be experts, Major. Far younger than you two. They've studied these matters."

Bingo. Time for the kill.

"I would have thought that we, rather than those you call 'younger experts' are more aware of what the elderly need with regard to care, wouldn't you?"

It was the very point that all the residents, Cavaliers and Roundheads alike, had been debating since the news of the course reached them on the grape-vine – that is to say, Nurse Lisa Rogers. Basil nodded his agreement to Tubes.

Sister felt that a change of tack was needed. "You may well nod, Major, but look at you. You talk blithely of 'care' but do you care with that pipe of yours? Poor Nurse Lisa. Got the shock of her life when she sat on that burning ash last week. In the dining room. It singed her, er, frock."

Tubes chuckled, "Certainly made her eyes water."

"And look at you, Commander. A man in the prime of his life…"

"Now steady, Sister." Tubes had once before heard a woman saying dangerous things like that to him.

"Soft and flabby. Unkempt, the lot of you. Some of you only bath once a week and when you do…"

Sister advanced on Tubes who abandoned the balls-of-feet exercise and retreated as far as he could into the fireplace. She stood with her face only inches from his.

"When you do, you just lie there and play submarines with the loofah."

Loofah sounds silly at the best of times but takes on an element of surrealism when screeched in a loud high-pitched voice. Basil blinked and couldn't avoid a giggle but Tubes, to whom bathrooms and all that went on within them were sacrosanct, was seriously un-nerved and knew when to abandon ship. His voice became rather pathetic.

"How do you know that, Sister?"

She marched to the door. "Well, if you aren't doing that, heaven knows what you're up to. The shouting, splashing, gurgling. You can hear it from the kitchen."

The few bits of Tubes's face that showed through his white whiskers were even redder than usual. "You've no right to listen. You might just as well climb in the bath with me." He knew when he said it that it was a mistake.

Basil staggered up from his chair and laid a hand on his friend's arm. "Steady, old man, steady. The mere thought..."

Sister stared out of the window. Her eyes saw nothing but her mind saw another bath and a handsome, strong man from, oh, so long ago. With shaking hands and an unaccustomed colour to her cheeks she unarranged a vase of snowdrops.

"I find the mere suggestion offensive – and silly. Anyway, the baths here are far too small."

Tubes and Basil glanced at each other. What was happening? Sister seemed to have become very strange, almost as if she were somewhere else.

She for her part was confused. Why on earth had she said that? Yet again these old men had got the better of her, riled her into speaking without thinking. It had the usual effect of making her crosser than ever. Their movement to the door made her head jerk round to them.

"Yes, well. Come on. Shepherds pudding and semolina pie. Before it gets cold. I've got work to do."

The departure of Sister Newbiggin for her week in London was not the cause for celebration that some might think it would have been. Everyone, including the staff – notably Nurse Lisa Roberts – knew that they had all jumped out of the frying-pan into the fire. Now, on duty all rather than only half the time would be Matron Maud Montague. And it took only a day for the full impact of this dire situation to surface...

"Idling in the toilets is forbidden. Come out at once, Captain Cuthbert."

The Glaswegian twang of Matron Maud Montague's voice bounced off the landing walls producing at least as many decibels as any army bugler sounding reveille – and it had the same effect. Every bedroom in Oldthorpe House on that Friday morning experienced a sudden transformation from snorting snores to groans and grunts as their inhabitants discovered, to varying degrees of relief and surprise that they had yet another day ahead of them,

Nurse Lisa Roberts, late twenties and 'comfortably' built, who was at the receiving end of Matron Maud's lavatorial dictum, blinked away a tear as the matron punched her way downstairs and towards the front door. Over her shoulder she added her usual venomous rider.

"You were the night nurse. Get him out of there and sort him out. I won't have mucky officers soiling the toilets."

With that she stormed out of the door adding as an after-thought, "I'm going to the surgery to deal with Doctor Hamoud. He dares to question my drug – that is – medicine administration."

She hurled herself into her Cortina and, with a gravel-squirting of rear wheels, injected herself into Harbour Road en-route to take on the General Practitioners of Flaxton-on-Sea.

"Night nurse, indeed. Oh yes, I'm sure." Lisa brushed away another unwelcome tear. "Oh yes. Night nurse, day nurse, wet nurse, dusting and polishing nurse, 'help me 'cos matron's being horrid' nurse," now she was yelling at the long departed car, "I'm every type of bloody nurse and I'm fed-up." Her voice rose to nearly the same level of Matron Maud decibels, "BLOODY FED-UP." And then, rather losing steam, she added chokingly, "so there."

From somewhere deep within Oldthorpe House came the growing sound of applause harmoniously mixed with the flushing of a lavatory cistern.

As night-duty nurse – a ridiculous title seeing that she was the only one of such lowly rank alongside Matron Montague and Sister Newbiggin – Lisa was very well aware that her basic duty was to at least ensure that the same number of residents were in the house each morning as had been there the previous evening. And now, so it appeared, there weren't.

Having, with understandable reluctance, checked every upstairs lavatory, she came to the inescapable conclusion that one resident was missing and no one, whether resident, nursing or domestic staff, would need a second guess to name the culprit: Captain Clarence Cuthbert, an eternal nocturnal wanderer.

She wasn't unduly worried as she toured the house searching for her lost charge. She was a born optimist and her cheerfulness matched her large frame, well-endowed as it was in all the parts where her adoring elderly gentlemen expected and appreciated endowment. She'd acquired the efficient bustling movements of a nurse in the eight years since she'd simultaneously come-of-age and qualified, and was more – far more – of a match for the fifteen residents who all but filled the available bedrooms in the house.

Her aim was to have Clarence accounted for and re-assimilated into the daily routine before Matron Maud returned from her verbal assault on poor Doctor Hamoud, and that gave her about three-quarters of an hour to find him and sort him out. Washing, shaving, dressing and loo could just about be accomplished in the time available provided the old rascal could be run to earth soon.

Briskly Lisa first visited one of the most obvious places. She banged on the hall cloakroom door thereby surprising Brigadier Ainsley who was checking the runners in the three-thirty at Lingfield whilst performing other necessary functions – senior officers had to be multi-skilled – and asked if Captain Cuthbert was in there. Through a haze of Capstan full-strength smoke she was tartly informed that officers of Field rank never consorted with their junior colleagues in the latrines.

The rest of the ground floor gave up no trace of Clarence and with mounting exasperation Nurse Lisa ran up the stairs at a startling speed for one so well built. Many of her less stable bits trembled alarmingly, not so much through the brisk movement but more at the thought of what she now had to do and what she would be up against – not literally, she fervently hoped.

The trouble was that all these elderly men had seen so much of life – the staff felt far too much – on their travels in the service of the various Kings and Queens of England who happened to be reigning during their military careers. This heady mixture of experiences containing every shade from danger to wild uninhibited abandon (they talked mostly about the latter) had given them unbounded confidence, particularly when operating as a group, and a worldly knowledge of matters which equally shocked and amazed the female staff. Conversely, they displayed a vulnerability when alone which they overcame by relying on the nurses to both nanny and mother them. As the

Matron often remarked in her frequent loud, exasperated moments, "You never know where you are with this lot from one moment to the next."

The next dozen-or-so minutes were going to be, thought an out-of-breath Lisa, an exception to her superior's oft-repeated observation. She felt she knew darned well where she would be for quite a few moments to come. In a word, embarrassed.

The first rooms she visited were those of the Roundheads at the front of the house. As she expected, all she received from her polite enquiry through their doors was a gruff denial of any knowledge of the whereabouts of Captain Cuthbert. That was the easy part done but at the end of the landing was the wing of rooms which, to her, represented nothing less than a minefield. This was Cavalier territory.

In some trepidation she knocked on Freddy Foster's door – and made her first mistake. Had she merely said, "Have you seen Captain Cuthbert this morning?" she would probably have received a shouted, "No" – or "Yes." As it was, she said rather too sweetly, "Squadron-Leader?"

There was only a moment's pause before the door was flung open and there the small man stood, fingering his moustache and clad only in a large white bath towel that looked dangerously loosely knotted around his slim waist. Lisa couldn't help noticing that even so dressed – or undressed – he looked very neat.

Freddy, having been told of the old man's disappearance, performed a steep climb followed by a stall turn with his hand and then rested it on her arm. "I'll be with you in a jiffy, Lisa. Just give me a moment."

With that the hand went to the towel knot and, with a quick, "No rush, well there is, actually," she sped to the next door which was Captain Clarence's room.

Just in case he'd returned from wherever he'd been she decided to look in and, after a discreet knock, poked her head around the door. Inside the two remaining loves in Clarence's life were performing to an empty unmade bed: Vera Lynn, 'The Forces Sweetheart', was revolving at a steady speed on Clarence's pride and joy, his tape recorder. The machine had been given to him by his relatives on his eightieth birthday. He was far too straight a man to realize that it was a sop intended to excuse any visits by them in the future and, in turn, they were too vain to know that he much preferred the recorder as his companion to any visits they might deign to make. Lisa always felt a great sadness in this room. Despite his cantankerous ways she loved the old man dearly and felt him somewhere near her at this moment. She realised that it was probably the room's familiar smell; a mixture of old body and strained cabbage – the latter wafting up from the kitchen below his room. Gently she closed the door and resumed her search.

Basil Reardon opened his door furtively to her hesitant knock. He seemed to be in every sort of mess and Lisa would dearly have loved to wipe the shaving soap from his ears, comb his hair, tuck his shirt-tails in, unravel his braces and plonk a kiss on his cheek; he was that sort of rather pathetic, elderly man. Through the pipe smoke that now poured onto the landing he gazed at her with watery, bloodshot eyes rather like a kindly spaniel. "Poor old devil. It's the lav, you see, Lisa. He goes there in the night and then gets lost."

A voice behind her made her jump. "We all keep our doors locked otherwise he'd be in bed with us in no time." Tubes Potter stood with legs slightly apart, immaculately turned out in corduroy trousers and a giant polo-necked white sweater which confusingly merged neatly into his white bearded face. "He forgets which is his room," he boomed. "Nothing sinister, do you see? Ghastly thought, though, having the old devil bunking up with you, don't you think?"

Lisa, feeling that this applied to them all rather than just Captain Clarence, smiled weakly and, to make the point, nodded vigorously. Now came her greatest trial: Colonel Alastair. She knew that one squeak of a female voice would cause the door to be flung open before another breath could be taken and heaven alone knew what state of dress, or more likely undress, the wretched man would be in; he made the Squadron Leader appear like a Trappist monk.

Salvation came in the form of Tubes who, having padded along the corridor behind her, yelled out, "Is old Clarence with you, Alastair?"

The answer saved any need for closer contact. "Certainly

68

not. Bugger off, there's a good chap," was all they got in response and with that Lisa made her way back to the stairs.

Hearing Tubes still marching along behind her she now panicked and changed direction towards her room in the staff wing. Why was she so edgy and nervous this morning, it wasn't like her at all? She decided an aspirin might help to calm her nerves before reporting to Matron who, to put it mildly, would be somewhat hysterical at the news of Captain Cuthbert's disappearance.

The first thing to hit her as she entered the still curtained dimness of her room was a zimmer frame. She grabbed at it to restore her balance and, at the same moment, glanced at her bed. There, comfortably tucked in, deep in what was apparently a period of blissful sleep lay the gaunt figure of Captain Clarence Cuthbert.

The shock to Lisa's already frayed nerves was exacerbated a thousand times more by the voice of Tubes close by her ear. "Any port in a storm," he boomed, and rudely shook the old man out of his deep sleep.

With a wild curse which only those living in the area of Inverness would fully understand and appreciate, Alastair Hunter struggled upwards from his pillow and assumed a moderately successful sitting-up position. It wasn't just being rudely awakened from an interesting dream by Tubes that angered him, it was, of course, the usual pain. He reached under the bedclothes and rubbed the leg that wasn't there and, as always, the aching eased even though his hand touched nothing.

He lay back on the pillow to calm himself. All those years ago and still he wondered who had laid the landmine. Was the chap still alive? A loving grandfather maybe? Wouldn't hurt a fly. A pillar of his community. Perhaps he had a faith? 'Deliver us from evil…' Imagine that moment of laying that small round metal object under the sand, so carefully. And then more of them. And more again. And into it they had walked, crouched, pitch black, then a searing heat and flash, deafening noise, unbearable pain, – and no leg. Montgomery of Alamein? Why not 'Hunter of Alamein'? And all the others…

This wouldn't do. That's what he said out loud every

morning but today there was something in his drowsy sub-conscious that suggested a lighter spirit was hovering around him. It took him a moment to place it and then, with a grin and a shout of 'Jocks w-hay' – the cry of the Queen's Scottish as they swirled into battle – he eased himself out of bed. It always struck him at this moment in the day that one compensation for being one-legged was that only one foot froze on the linoleum covered floor.

Mechanically he glanced across the courtyard to the staff wing to check if Nurse Lisa had opened her curtains or, at least, left a chink in them so that he might view her slipping into her nurses' uniform. He had done this every morning since he first came here five years ago and, due to the unfortunate route his first interview with Matron had taken, been allocated a 'baddies' room in the rear wing. Basil Reardon had whispered to the rest of them over soggy cornflakes at breakfast one morning that he had once looked out and seen the nurse in her bra. Being the delightful chap he was he had been deeply embarrassed and would doubtless be surprised that all the other Cavaliers now followed this ritual every morning – just in case. But today the curtains were tight shut.

With practiced skill Alastair hopped to the washstand and, eyes still partly glued with sleep, examined himself in the small mirror. It pleased him that only his head and torso were visible and what he saw lifted his spirits and brought a smile – more like a schoolboy's grin – to his face. He was handsome, no doubt about it. Seventy-one years young, and the latter fifty or so of them flirting, fraternising, lusting, laughing and loving again and again with more women than he could ever remember – or would care to. Many a heart had been broken along the way and for that he was as much surprised as sorry; he lived for the ecstatic moment, never for the ties that true love might bring and, to his initial amazement, he found that one leg attracted far more women to him than most of his colleagues with two. Perhaps the girls were sorry for him. He chuckled. They soon learned there was nothing to be sorry about.

Perfectly balanced through long experience he went through the familiar routine of washing and shaving and then, sitting on his bed, slowly dressing.

The army base hospital to which he had been rushed as soon as he could be evacuated from the front line in '44 had done all that could be done, but then it was back to England with a medal – the Distinguished Service Order – and, as only the army could, having acknowledged his valour, a rocket for 'leading from the front'. Commanding Officers in this war were expected to send their troops into battle, not lead them, he was reminded. And so, after a desk job which he hated and an artificial leg which he hated even more, he was let loose on the civilian world. Several unsatisfactory jobs and a host of women later, he had sought the pleasure and comfort of his own kind and moved south of the border into East Anglia and Oldthorpe House – and the unyielding regime of Matron Maud Montague.

From the first moment Matron and Colonel Alastair Hunter met it was clear that their individual chemistries made for a volatile mix. He saw her role as one of servant and, when necessary, nurse. Matron Maud, for her part, treated her elderly charges as children: silly children: silly, fractious children. She saw them returning to messy, uncoordinated, ill-behaved childhood as a deliberate, wilful act of rebellion on their part and so she tamed them with a combination of scolding, reproach, threat and malice relieved very occasionally with a small pinch of love and gentleness – but only when she deemed that it would serve her nefarious purposes. This rare apparent sweetener to the bitter gruel of her behaviour was provided only to those who had totally surrendered to her will – and the inhabitants of the rear wing bedrooms did not, under any stretch of the imagination, enter that category.

There had been no gentleness in her Glasgow upbringing and she had learnt none since. As if especially constructed by God to suit her personality she was tall, thin and gaunt – similar to a fair number of her charges – and, dressed in her severe Matron's uniform with an obligatory bun of tightly pinned grey hair supporting her cap, she presented a forbidding sight to those who had the misfortune to meet her on her daily rounds.

But like all tyrants she had her weaknesses which, if exploited, could well spell her downfall. In her case it was gin, the ruin of many an otherwise puritan soul, and to minimise the risk of the discovery of her guilty secret, she consumed it in a tumbler, mixed with clear Italian Vermouth, passing it off, should she be seen doing so, as a glass of water required to wash down her nightly aspirin. The maxim that the simplest subterfuges are the best had so far worked in her favour – or so she thought...

And then, only yesterday – Thursday – providence, in the form of a Premium Bond, swooped down like the proverbial dove upon one of her charges. None other than Colonel Alastair Hunter came into a totally unexpected large sum of money (the only free gift the Government would ever hand him) and, immediately leaping desperately at a route every man-jack of them would have followed given his luck, decided to leave forthwith and buy a comfy bit of sheltered accommodation where he could pursue his amorous dalliances unhindered by petty rules and regulations.

He only shared this amazing news with his fellow Cavaliers and was at first hurt and them moved that they received it with dismay. Whilst they were delighted with his good fortune they would sorely miss their ally who had, over the years, been very much the ringleader in their constant battle with Matron Maud. Aware of this, the intrepid Colonel decided to deliciously sugar the bitter pill of parting. He asked them to join him after supper in his small room – an act which was in itself an adventure because it was against Matron's strict orders that forbade the residents to congregate in each others' bedrooms.

In they trooped, delighted to be breaking the rules. The Colonel silently called the roll and, having not as yet seen beyond his good fortune at winning so much money, was only now aware that he would soon be leaving them all and would miss them greatly. He looked around him with affection at this group of friends who were seeing each other through the last chapter of their lives.

Now that they were settled as much as their stiff joints would allow and had filled their tooth-mugs with illicit tots of the winner's whisky, Alastair whispered his parting gift to them: they would conspire together to rid Oldthorpe House of Malicious Matron Maud. No more, no less.

Clarence gulped and gasped at the same time causing some

delay whilst he was brought back to consciousness, and then they were all chattering excitedly, expressing their appreciation of their friend's selfless thought for their well-being once he had gone. It soon emerged, however, that his plan wasn't going to be all 'give' on his part: there would be a fair dollop of delicious 'take' as well.

It was well known to them that the gallant Colonel's dangerously active amorous streak had, on more than one occasion, descended with considerable gusto on none other than Matron Maud herself! These best undescribed moments amazed the others being, in their view, not only way beyond the call of duty but also grotesque. Alastair, however, took the opposite view seeing them as both the ultimate challenge – particularly on one real leg – and rather sexually satisfying.

The tactical skills that had steered the six intrepid warriors through the Battle of Britain and on into Europe to the very gates of Berlin – Captain Clarence, due to his age, actually only got as far as Epping Forest but that wasn't his fault – were now deployed and came up with a simple ruse. They would substitute the contents of the Vermouth bottle with neat gin. As simple as that. Both were clear liquids and, unless closely examined, could not be told apart and, they were sure, fairly strong gin tasted pretty similar to neat gin – until it was too late!

So, relying on the heavily doctored bottle of Martini and Matron's known predilection for a fair quantity of nightly 'gin and It' which occasionally led to the aforementioned touch of slap and tickle with the Colonel, the trap was set. They were, however, less confident about the outcome on hearing from Alastair that dear old Clarence's strange and constantly malfunctioning lower intestine was also to play a valuable part.

It was also helpful to the plot that the ever-changing GPs persuaded by the new owner of Oldthorpe House, Gregory Cartiledge, to minister to his elderly charges all had a dislike for Matron – hence the reason why they were ever-changing. They strongly objected to her arbitrary use of every type of known drug to keep her charges quiet and compliant and could be relied upon to report any misdemeanour they came upon in the course of their reluctant visits.

After some slightly slurred discussion the scene of the

action was set for the next evening, a Friday night when careful surveillance had elicited that Matron tended to launch more heavily into the gin bottle than on other evenings, probably as a form of celebration and thanksgiving that another week was all but over. It also coincided with the residents' weekly toe-nail-clipping session which always stretched her nursing vocation to the limit.

It was known to them that Matron indulged her wicked ways regarding the gin and Italian Martini bottles in the kitchen once the staff had cleaned up and gone home. She had a fear of drinking in her room upstairs rightly seeing it as a quick route to a gin-soaked end.

Thus it was that the plans were laid to end Matron Maud's unjust rule over them all and, at the same time, send Colonel Alastair Hunter to well-deserved retirement in his very own retirement home.

As the Cavaliers trouped off to their beds that Thursday night filled with the intoxication of two spirits – whisky fortified with the tingling excitement of a battle to be won – Basil Reardon had a niggling doubt concerning its outcome. The gallant Artillery Major tossed and turned in the narrow tightly-sheeted confines of his bed until both the doubt and a solution had been identified. He then took a short trip along the landing to another bedroom and, after a few whispered words, retired back to sleep the sleep of a contented fellow conspirator.

4

The first salvo of the Matron Maud Offensive occurred at suppertime that Friday evening. Precisely according to plan Clarence collapsed in a heap on the dining room floor groaning and clutching his lower stomach. The others were both impressed at his acting skills and delighted that their painstaking tutoring of him throughout the day involving demonstrations on his bedroom floor accompanied by shouted instructions and energetic sign language had worked. As it turned out later their satisfaction at a job well done was somewhat misplaced because the old man had understood none of their antics and, by coincidence, had genuinely suffered one of his internal intestinal dilemmas.

Innocent of any of these carefully devised plans Lisa, concerned at the severity of the attack, summoned the latest doctor with insufficient reason not to attend Oldthorpe House. As planned, Freddy and Tubes hovered near the hallway ready to delay him if he arrived before what Alastair rather indelicately referred to as 'the frontal assault' was being executed in the kitchen.

Sure enough, at eight o'clock that evening, as predicted in the masterly tactical plan, Matron Maud, as a lamb to the proverbial slaughter, slipped into the kitchen carefully shutting the door behind her.

It was an anxious ten minutes for the plotters as they waited in the hall imagining the matron getting out her stash of gin and 'doctored' Italian vermouth, popping what she thought was a mix of the two into a glass and taking a few gigantic swigs.

At last the moment was right and, more nervous than he had been at the start of many a charge across open ground, Colonel Alastair Hunter launched himself into the kitchen and, literally, into the arms of the enemy.

An old saying by some chap or another came to mind and was suitably mangled by him. It was, he felt, a far greater thing that he was now doing for his comrades than he had ever done before – and they had ever done for him!

What happened from that moment onwards was best described by Alastair himself the next day at a celebratory session in The Anchor saloon bar. What added even more spice to the occasion was that the Matron was under the impression that the Cavaliers, rather than being in the pub, were at a Saturday morning children's performance of the film Bambi at the Flaxton cinema. She had sent them there to restrict their contact with the other residents until the Owner arrived to deliver justice to her assailant.

"I really caught her with her trousers down." Alastair liked dramatic metaphors which painted disturbing pictures.

"It is indeed, Alastair old friend." Clarence struggled upright to the relative security of his zimmer. "Sorry it was so obvious, I'll be back soon. If I'm not you'll know where I am." With that he staggered away towards the Gents. None of them showed any surprise. Clarence was forever moving either towards or from the lavatory and it was a strange fact that the only words he heard – or misheard clearly were those associated with this, to him, regular irregular activity.

Now the five of them huddled forward together at the small round table in the Bar. The Landlord, unused to having their custom at this early time of the day, cast his eye over them as he wiped the smears into his partly washed glasses. These old chaps always seemed harmless enough and with the professional skills needed for summing up his customers he'd decided long ago that they were obviously 'gentlemen', but gentlemen who had fallen on rather hard times.

"I had just got my fingers and thumbs on her rear suspender knobs…" Alastair's whisper was hoarse more with excitement than consideration for anyone overhearing him.

"Shouldn't we get Clarence? He's long overdue." Freddy, strangely embarrassed at such detail, weaved his hand into a perfect landing on the table.

"He'll emerge when he's ready or…" Ainsley shuddered, "thinks that he's ready. Go on, Alastair. You weren't under the uniform were you? Those fingers? Suspender knobs?"

"Certainly not." He was horrified. "Not the behaviour of a

Scottish Cavalry Officer as you well know, Ainsley." His eyes twinkled. "Of course, you Tank chaps..." He left the monstrous innuendo unsaid but none of them wanted to pursue regimental rivalries, not when suspenders were about to be undone. "I was working through her frock, of course. And then the doctor came in."

Alastair sat back a bit, indicating that the supreme moment of excitement, as far as this event was concerned, was done. Ainsley couldn't believe his ill luck, and turned accusing eyes on Tubes and Freddy. They had been charged with delaying the doctor until the right moment, and hands probing suspender knobs was unnecessarily premature.

Freddy felt a need for more detailed information. "When you burst in on her you immediately grabbed her suspenders?"

Alastair often despaired of Freddy. "Of course not, you idiot. I apologised to her for barging in, suggested a drop of harmless Martini in her, ahem, water, would help calm her after her long day– and filled her quarter-gin-filled tumbler to the top with, of course, neat gin!"

Basil, who had become increasingly unhappy about all the deceit, drew heavily on his fiercely burning pipe, exhaling a vast cloud of smoke. "Didn't she guess we'd – oh Lord – I'd substituted gin for the Martini?"

"It needed a diversion right enough." Alastair was forward again. "I asked her if she'd like to be a Colonel's Lady. Cast nursing aside and embark on a life of unencumbered bliss."

There was an appalled silence as they considered the terrible thought. It was broken by the wavering voice of Clarence who had appeared leaning gauntly on his zimmer frame.

"It was, thank you. But nothing more, I'm afraid."

"Bliss, Clarence old chap." Freddy leant forward and gently fastened the old man's fly buttons, then they moved up and eased him into the circle.

"So, she was drinking neat gin." Ainsley needed to know if his tactical appreciation of the battle had gone according to plan. As the senior officer present he felt the familiar tingle of high command.

"In a series of large, noisy gulps. The thought of hitching

to me obviously was affecting her deeply." Alastair, surprised at his shaking hand, took his latest double whisky at one attempt.

"So I should imagine," Ainsley murmured.

"It was then ..." the voice was hoarse again, "that I grabbed her and fondled the knobs."

Clarence fell forward, his balance not being so certain as the others. "You what, old fruit? Her knobs? The jobs at the front?"

They re-established Clarence behind his zimmer and he stared wild-eyed through it thinking of the many bosoms he had known.

"Down, Clarence." Ainsley's voice was soothing. "Suspender knobs. You remember?" He regretted it as he asked it.

"Ah," the old man collapsed back into his seat and seemed to fold into almost nothing. "This girl, Phoebe– or something. Up in the hills. India. Turn of the century. We…"

"Shush, Clarence." Basil patted his arm. The others felt that his sense of propriety could sometimes be infuriating. Clarence's memories of Phoebe could even out-fantasise their image of Alastair and Matron locked in an amorous embrace in the kitchen.

"Did you get them undone?" Freddy saw no need for subtlety and was ready to move on through scenes of increasing lust until they were writhing naked on the kitchen table. No such luck.

"She was just getting really going – you should have heard her – when the damned doctor burst in. Propelled…" he laboured the word whilst looking accusingly at Tubes and Freddy, "propelled by you two idiots speaking dialogue only ever seen on that damned Independent television channel." He mimicked, "'Matron, look who's here. The doctor. Goodness gracious, is this lust? Are you performing with a resident?' And you, Tubes, really. 'Unhand the poor man, Matron. He suffered enough in the last war.' I ask you. Pathetic."

They fell about laughing, relieved that the fearful business was over and the dreadful deceit done with but, as one, satisfied that Matron had got all she deserved. She was vicious, cruel and, above all, endangering the lives of those in her care.

"Right. De-briefing." Ainsley resumed his position of high command.

"Never got that far. Mind you…" Alastair sat forward, a sheen of lustful perspiration on his brow.

Ainsley cleared his throat loudly. "A de-briefing session you idiot. "What happened after the reinforcements arrived?"

"I unhandled her knobs of course?" Alastair waved his empty glass in the air and Clarence absentmindedly waved back. It created no other reaction and he feared he might have to buy the next one himself.

"None of that language in the Saloon Bar, please, gentlemen." The Landlord who, in their time, would have been on saluting terms with their seniority, now held command. With dignity, and stomachs well filled with a variety of alcoholic liquor, they rose more or less as one and moved to the door.

"The doctor was appalled. He informed Matron that she would be reported to the appropriate authorities." Alastair laughed. "He's found me a vacancy on his overfull panel. 'In recognition of services rendered' he said. The rest you know. Bye-bye, Matron!"

Ainsley sighed, "And hello, Acting-Matron Newbiggin. There's still work to be done."

Freddy studied his watch. "When does Bambi end?" Tubes, now took command. "In one more pub's time. Your round, I think, Clarence. You spend too much time emitting rather than buying."

With arms around each other's shoulders they marched cheerfully down the High Street for another lengthy pause, this time at The Pier Head Tavern.

As happens so easily in war a victory can quickly turn into defeat. On their return to Oldthorpe House two setbacks hit them as soon as they entered the hallway.

First, on being sweetly asked by Nurse Lisa, in the hearing of Matron, if they had enjoyed the film about Bambi, Clarence, on his way to the downstairs cloakroom, blurted out that he felt films about Indian martyrs were boring. The difference between 'Bambi' and 'Ghandi' was far too subtle for eighty-four year old ears.

The second setback, far more serious, was the obvious fact that Matron was still in residence and, judging by her tirade regarding the intended film trip, very much in charge.

Sister Newbiggin, almost as severe as her superior but blessed with more than a few sparks of humanity, was charged with telling Colonel Alastair Hunter that his fate regarding the heinous assault upon the Matron's person, would be decided by no less a personage than the new Owner of Oldthorpe House himself, Gregory Cartiledge the very next morning. Until then he was to keep a low profile.

And so it was a muted band of conspirators who filed into Alastair's room that evening. Spirits were low, so low that poor old Clarence, still shaking from the wigging he had received from Matron and his colleagues over the 'Bambi' fiasco, went to his room early, was tucked into bed by Nurse Lisa and given an extra-long embrocation rub which was the only bright spot in his otherwise rotten day. She whispered night-night to him, pecked him on the forehead and asked him to try to only use his own bed through the coming night.

Sunday morning, and the atmosphere in the house could have been proverbially cut with the proverbial knife. Saturday had been just about endured by both residents and staff as they all awaited the arrival of Gregory Cartiledge to, as Matron delicately put it, "rid the place of its evil influence," by which, of course, she meant Colonel Alastair Hunter.

"We misjudged the enemy, do you see." Tubes was at his favourite spot in the lounge standing at the fireplace, feet apart, hands behind his back, gently rocking on his toes and heels. In stressful times he felt better with a bit of movement around him even if he had to create it himself.

Ainsley threw The Times to the floor in disgust, not so much at his inability to do today's crossword but rather with their misjudgement of Matron Maud. "You'd think we'd know the unspeakable depths to which she'd sink by now, wouldn't you?"

"Tubes should," Freddy executed a tight roll with his hands, "being a submariner. Heaven knows what unspeakable depths he's sunk to in his time."

Ainsley turned, crossly stabbing a finger at him. "If that's meant to be a joke, Freddy, it's most inopportune. Poor Alastair is holed up in his bedroom awaiting Court Martial and all you can offer are inane remarks. And for God's sake stop flying your confounded hand around the room and SIT DOWN."

With a sad sigh Basil lowered his Daily Telegraph. "It won't help, you know, for us to fall out with each other. It's a united front we need just now. I think we can save Alastair from prosecution but until I can find Clarence who seems to have disappeared yet again I can't be sure. Come and help me search for him, Tubes old chap. If we know our Clarence we shouldn't have far to look."

They went off into the hall leaving Ainsley fretting at the window expecting to see the Owner arriving at any minute. Freddy, becoming more and more confused at the turn of events riffled untidily through Basil's Telegraph. "She might push for sexual harassment you know. That could mean a spell in the chokey."

Ainsley clamped his jaws together causing the few remaining teeth still physically attached to him to ache abominably. Why couldn't the damned chap shut up? Freddy's amazing lack of tact was always infuriating but at a time like this…

Freddy was saved from further mental admonishment by the startling sight of a very large gleaming silver Rolls Royce purring into the driveway. What was even more startling was the fact that it seemed to be empty! Ainsley pressed his nose against the net curtains and could just make out the tops of two heads in the front seats, the driver's as bald as an egg and the passenger's carrying on its wavy blonde top what appeared to be a bird's nest.

Rumours had been spreading all week about the mysterious new owner of Oldthorpe House who, it was said, was very wealthy having made his fortune buying and selling army surplus equipment to dubious regimes around the world. Whilst the residents deplored such behaviour they were willing to turn a blind eye on his activities provided that, as he had rashly promised, some of the proceeds would be ploughed into refurbishing, redecorating, re-plumbing and re-chef-ing the establishment.

The first setback to their beautiful dream had been a letter pinned to the notice-board from Mr Cartiledge stating, in very bad English and even worse grammar, his unqualified support for Matron Maud and her splendid colleague, Sister Amelia Newbiggin. And now here he was, hastily summoned by Matron this Sunday morning to oversee the removal and probable prosecution of Colonel Alastair Hunter DSO, late of the Queen's Scottish Regiment.

Ainsley, now joined at the window by Freddy, watched in amazement as, in perfect unison, the two front doors of the Rolls swung noiselessly open and the two diminutive occupants almost jumped down onto the gravel. That is where unison stopped and discord, rather than harmony, took over. At great speed and with giant strides for such a small man Gregory Cartiledge made for the front door. Half a dozen paces behind him the little bird-nested lady pattered with tiny steps in his wake.

On any other occasion the watchers at the window would have found this amusing but given the reason for this visit, Ainsley and Freddy merely stared through the lace in disbelief. Before they could make any comment to each other, the door was flung open and the strange little man burst into the room followed by Matron Maud and, a few tiny steps behind, the little lady with the bird-nest hat.

Matron was already in full verbal flow. "I've confined the residents to their quarters as a safety precaution, Mr Cartiledge." She stopped dead in her tracks causing a collision with the following small body. Brushing the little lady away from her she fixed Ainsley and Freddy with her gimlet eyes. "What are you doing down here, Brigadier and Squadron Leader? Were you not confined…"

"I am not here to be confined, madam, but to be cared for, cosseted and…" Ainsley thought 'caressed' would sound good with the other two words but felt in the circumstances it might be going a bit far.

He was saved from finding a suitably sounding verb by Freddy who chipped in, "I don't think any of us are in the confined game do you, Matron? We certainly won't be – and you never would be. If you get my point."

The sheer indelicacy, audacity and unsubtlety of the remark actually made Matron speechless just long enough for Gregory Cartiledge, who had understood none of the exchange and was becoming increasingly restless, to take over. Well aware that the care of these elderly men could secure him a long-coveted knighthood – the only reason he'd bought the blasted place – he put on a sickly smile and advanced on Freddy. At great speed and with the sharp twang of London's East End he barked, "Stand at ease. AC plonk Gregory Cartiledge, lowest of the low in the Raf, now a millionaire. And you are?" He thrust out a podgy hand which was not taken.

"Squadron Leader Frederick Foster, DFC and Bar, Royal Air Force, and it is you who may stand at ease."

It was a brave and, for its pomposity, totally uncharacteristic speech by Freddy which left him breathless and Gregory Cartiledge totally unabashed. Putting the proffered hand up to his forehead in mock salute he was interrupted in his move towards Ainsley by a quiet titter from apparently somewhere within Matron. Closer examination found that it came from immediately behind her, uttered by the little bird-nested lady.

"That's telling you, Gregory Cartiledge," she said, clutching her handbag to her bosom as if for protection.

"Quiet, Gloria," hissed Gregory. "This is my lady wife, Gloria Cartiledge. Come around from behind Matron, Gloria, and say how-do to the gents." He swung round to Ainsley. "And you are?"

Ainsley pulled his gaunt frame up to its full height and balefully gazed downwards into the little man's eyes. "Brigadier Ainsley Bennington – and good-day to you, Mrs Cartiledge. Welcome to our very humble, seen-better-days, needs-a-lot-spending-on-it abode. I trust you had a good journey here?" Then he added as an afterthought, "Although I doubt if either of you saw much of it, down there in the depths of your grand motor."

Matron, who had watched all this verbal exchange in unaccustomed silence felt it had all gone on quite long enough. She pulled back her shoulders causing various starched bits of material to squeak, and took over.

"I suggest you go to your rooms as I had previously ord – er – requested, gentlemen. Mr Cartiledge, perhaps you would like to inspect the premises before you carry out your duty as owner and deal with Colonel Hunter." With that she swung out of the room.

"Carry on." The Owner waved his hand in the air, dismissing himself from their presence, and marched into the hall. Gloria pit-patting behind him, turned at the door and smiled warmly.

"So nice to have met you all."

"Come along, Gloria." Gregory had to have the last word.

The dual guffaws that were about to roar out in the lounge from Ainsley and Freddy were silenced by the unexpected and breathless arrival of Alastair through the French windows.

"Been out for a walk. Thinking things over. Got back in time to hear all that. Damn poor show. The devil of it is that it doesn't affect me, I'm off anyway. It's all of you who'll suffer. Poor bit of planning. Never under-estimate the enemy." With that he hurled his walking stick into a corner and sank into an armchair.

Ainsley wasn't having this. "Nonsense, old boy. And enough of this defeatist talk. A battle isn't lost until…" he searched for the word.

Freddy helped out. "It's lost?"

Ainsley turned on him – it seemed to be a morning for turning on Freddy. "Rubbish. Do something useful for heaven's sake, man. Go to the door and keep a look-out. We don't want the staff to find Alastair down here."

Freddy reluctantly drifted across the room tipping over an ashtray as he flew his hand at zero feet above the coffee table and, leaning on the door jamb, resumed his reading of the Daily Telegraph.

Tubes came in and stood by the window. "We've found Clarence. In the staff one. He says the paper's softer there. I checked and, do you know, it is! Monstrous. The old chap's with Basil now."

The ensuing silence, as they each considered different textures of lavatory paper they had known, was almost louder than the chatter. It was broken by Ainsley.

"I'm sure the doctor will confirm that it was a, er, mutual encounter."

Alastair shook his head. "As soon as the doctor came into the kitchen the damned woman started screaming like a stuck pig. It sounded as if she was being ravished on the spot. She pulled away from me and rushed around the table and out through the door with her hands over her face yelping like an injured stag." Alastair's metaphors usually relied on his past penchant for game hunting, shooting and pig sticking.

"Sounds like more than fingers on suspender knobs to me, you randy old devil." Freddy chortled and resumed his study of the cricket scores.

"You damned fool." Alastair was angry now. Freddy had that ability to light the touch-paper. "She was embarrassed and aware that her career was in jeopardy. It provoked the same reaction as an assault would have."

"That's women for you." Tubes had no idea why he'd said it but it seemed right at the time.

The next silence was broken by an explosion of angry voices from the hall. Freddy, surprised that Len Hutton had been clean bowled for a paltry seven runs, completely failed in his look-out role and was brushed to one side as a white-faced Matron stormed into the room followed by the Cartiledges.

Matron was near her hysterical best. "Gone? Gone? He can't be gone. I gave strict instructions…"

Gregory interrupted her, "Well he has, hasn't he. Not in his room. He's scarpered." For such a small man the new owner had a very loud voice.

"Who precisely are you so loudly looking for?" The calm voice of Alastair stopped them short so that once again Gloria cannoned into, not Matron this time, but the more familiar buttocks of her husband. They stood as a tableau, pressed together, with Gregory at the front, Matron towering behind him looking over his head, and pressed like a slice of ham somewhere in between, the tiny figure of Gloria.

"Are you Hunter?" The question was shouted upwards into the handsome face of Alastair.

"If you are asking me if I am Colonel Alastair Hunter, late

of the Queen's Scottish Regiment, yes I am."

Freddy added even more weight to the statement by saying firmly, "Distinguished Service Order – DSO to you."

Gregory was totally unimpressed. "Then you're out, now. Do you hear me?" No one in the house could fail to. "OUT! NOW! PRONTO!"

"Unless, of course, there's an explanation." The little tinkly voice of Gloria calmed the charged atmosphere.

"Quiet, Gloria. Of course there isn't. There'll be charges brought and no mistake. We'll see to that won't we Matron? Serious charges."

"Grabbed and molested. Defiled. Sexually assaulted." Matron was warming to her work.

She would have found quite a few more vivid expressions to describe the Colonel's vile acts if Tubes, who had been rendered speechless for a while by the extraordinary behaviour going on around him, hadn't stunned her. "Hard to believe. One thing I'm sure my friend the Colonel is not, is blind." Having dug the hole he decided to jump into it. "And he has impeccable taste!"

Heaven knows where all this would have led before Alastair – and probably Tubes – were unceremoniously ejected from the building had not events taken a very different turn with the arrival on the scene of Basil leading in on a tight rein Clarence and his zimmer. The old man was even more bent than usual due to the lead from a pair of headphones around his neck being pulled urgently by Basil who was carrying a large black leather-covered box to which the lead was attached.

"Major Reardon, will you please take Captain Clarence back to his room and then go to yours until further notice." Matron had resumed her composure and was making a mighty effort to retake control of the situation. "And whilst we're about it I wish you, Brigadier, and the Commander, and the Squadron Leader to do the same."

No one moved.

Gregory Cartiledge now resumed his undisputed authority over them all. "I don't care who goes or who stays except you, Colonel Hunter, and YOU GO NOW!" For a lowly ex-aircraftsman he was very good at giving orders.

"Unless there's an explanation." Again the tinkly voice of Gloria was pouring some soothing balm on the proceedings but before she could say more her husband was back in again.

"Quiet, Gloria. There is no explanation to sexual misdeeds. Never is in my experience."

"And how great is your experience in that direction?" Freddy's tactlessness could be very useful sometimes.

Gregory was saved a further search in his limited vocabulary for the right phrase by Basil who, having left Clarence to huff, wheeze and puff at his black box, was lighting his pipe in front of the fireplace. This was a time when he, rather than Tubes, needed to be on the bridge of the ship.

"Matron, are you quite sure that matters between you and the Colonel were exactly as you have described them?"

They all turned and looked at the elderly man who had suddenly assumed, with evident ease, the role and posture of a fictional detective about to solve a crime. Their authors always seemed to have them standing at the fireplace with the cast of characters spread before them, one of whom was the villain. Now here was Basil, his comfortable woolly clothes hanging loosely around him and his lethal pipe pouring smoke in every direction.

"Major Reardon, I won't tell you again…" Had Matron's voice taken on even a touch more shrillness than usual? "To your room please. And that applies to you all – NOW!"

Again no one moved. Aware of the raised voices, Nurse Lisa and Sister Newbiggin were now at the door and behind them the hall was quickly filling with the other residents and staff.

Basil poked his pipe dangerously at the Matron. "You say that Colonel Hunter was forcing his attentions on you. Your phrase, I believe."

Before the Matron could answer, Gregory Cartiledge decided to resume command of the situation.

"I don't know who you are but…"

He got no further, interrupted by a high-pitched hiss escaping from Gloria Cartiledge's lips followed by a voice as sharp as a scalpel, "Quiet, Gregory."

In any other situation the old men would have collapsed in

peals of laughter, but not now. Everyone in the room felt the tension and both Matron and the Owner knew that something was beginning to go very wrong.

Basil seemed in no way put out by any of the blustering being aimed at him. Another mighty suck on his pipe and again he literally disappeared in a thick fog of smoke through which came his calm voice.

"Forcing his attentions on you, you say. Grabbed and molested. Worse still, defiled. Even worse, sexually assaulted. Your description of the events if my memory serves me correctly. Grave charges indeed." Basil was warming to his task.

"Absolutely right, old man." Tubes felt his old friend needed support as he inexplicably dug this hole into which he would undoubtedly shortly disappear and came to stand alongside him on the bridge. He'd miss him and he did so wish that the old fellow would shut up and not get further involved.

Basil didn't even hear his friend's remark. "I wonder, do you feel that this is an indication of attentions being forced on you, Matron?" With a grasp of theatre of which Sherlock Holmes himself would have been proud and which surprised them all, he dramatically pointed a finger at Clarence who was now humming quietly as he tinkered with his black box.

They all stared at the old man. Clarence became aware of the silence interfering with his humming and looked around at them. "Ready, Basil?"

With a gritting of teeth to hide the frustration of a moment of high tension wasted, Basil nodded furiously.

Clarence opened the lid of his box to reveal the deck of his tape recorder and, with his old, gnarled and shaking forefinger, pressed a button. The reels began to turn.

Vera Lynn's rendering of 'There'll be blue birds over the white cliffs of Dover' was always captivating and still brought a tear to many an eye, but it was a trifle mystifying to everyone assembled in and outside the residents lounge as to why it was so important to Basil at this time.

The pure, silken tones of Vera were now somewhat masked by a tinny sound accompanying each note.

Captain Clarence jammed his headphones on and off again. Was his beloved tape recorder– or his as beloved Vera – going on the blink? He treasured the tapes of his heroine and couldn't bear the thought that they were damaged in any way. Then he spied out of the corner of his eye the cause of the trouble.

"Shush," he commanded in a most ungentlemanly way – and Gloria immediately stopped humming along to the tune.

"Sorry," she whispered.

Freddy couldn't resist it. "Quiet, Gloria," he whispered back, and they both giggled.

"Now look here…" Gregory was more impatient than ever.

"The shepherd will tend his shee…..kiss me you great big hunk of a man.' Vera had suddenly given way to the slurred Glaswegian twang of – surely it couldn't be? *"Stop being so coy you old scallywag. Let yourself go, Ally my old pet. I'm all yours. Let's get…"*

Almost Maud Montague's last positive act as Matron of Oldthorpe House was to stride across the room and, raising her fist high, bring it down towards the turning reels of the recorder. In an instant, with a strength that amazed everyone, not least himself, Clarence held the fist still aloft in a steel-like bony grip and directed it away from the machine. Then he gently pushed the 'off' button and, by so doing, cut off Matron in what appeared to be very much her prime.

"There is more, much more." Basil relit his pipe and was infuriated to note that his hand was shaking. Maigret – or Poirot – certainly not The Saint – they'd never have shaking hands.

"The recording goes on until the doctor bursts in. Do you want to hear Matron's screaming – of discovery, NOT assault?" He paused for full effect and, as if to join in the drama, his pipe deposited a lump of burning tobacco on the carpet. Tubes, used to following on behind Basil dealing with the minor conflagrations he caused, leapt across him and ground his foot onto the burning fabric leaving yet another brown blob to add to the fading pattern.

Matron Maud stared for a moment at the burn, her automatic reaction to such desecration rising in her throat and then, realizing that all was lost, turned on her heel and marched from the room. In total silence the crowd at the door parted and let her through.

Basil fixed Gregory with a steely eye. "We thought that

Matron might try to lure one of us into her..." He couldn't think of the right word.

"Sexual forays?" volunteered Tubes.

"Excellent, old chap. Sexual forays it is. You see, Cartiledge, we've been so dashed frightened by her, er, demands towards us whenever she's raided the gin bottle that we decided to catch her at it."

Ainsley, Tubes and Freddy had spent some time just staring in disbelief at the authority oozing from Basil and, even more amazingly, the technical prowess of dear old Clarence. Now they nodded vigorously in support of whatever it was that had been done to ensnare the wicked woman and send her packing.

Gregory Cartiledge had never experienced anything like this before. As a lowly airman the ultimate test of command – handling a swift advance that, in a flash, becomes an even swifter withdrawal – had never been part of his service training. But he was not a millionaire by chance. When in doubt, do a bit of bullying, create fear. It never failed.

"Right. That's different then. She'll go. Dirty business. But watch it, all of you. I've got your measure. Any more nonsense and you're out. The lot of you. Savvy?"

He'd said all this as he marched up and down the room and now he stopped in front of Basil by the fireplace and stared up into the Major's bloodshot rheumy eyes. "No smoke without fire," he barked.

Basil took a long draw on his pipe and exhaled prodigiously. "No, indeed, Cartiledge. The finest Holborn Extra Mixed. You should try it. It might calm you down."

A tiny voice came from somewhere near the sideboard. "Pigs might fly."

Coughing and spluttering and with eyes watering from the cloud of smoke that had just engulfed him, Gregory turned on his heel and strode from the room.

Gloria turned at the door. "So nice to have met you all." Then she was gone.

"Come along, Gloria," boomed from the hall, mimed in perfect unison by the Cavaliers in the residents lounge.

They all crowded to the window and watched as the two diminutive figures clambered up into their giant car. With much crunching and spraying of gravel it turned itself around and purred out of view. Their last sight was of a tiny hand waving above the birds-nest hat.

The Cavaliers arranged themselves around the lounge and for a moment there was silence as they tried to digest the extraordinary events that had taken place in the midst of their dull repetitive lives.

"How did you do it then? Get it? The recording?" Alastair fiddled with the tape recorder only to have his hand smacked away by a possessive Clarence but in doing so he inadvertently pressed the 'start' button again. *"Run your hands through my hair, you naughty man. I've got a big surprise for you…"* Alastair had no intention of allowing them to know what the big surprise was.

"Turn the wretched thing off, Cuthbert, or I'll Court Martial you on the spot."

Again there was a silence as the others created wild fantasies as to what the big surprise might have been but Clarence was busy fiddling with the machine.

"Microphone hung down from my bedroom window, you see. Outside the kitchen window which Basil had opened. He did most of the work because I suddenly had to go to the lav. I felt this peculiar…"

He was hurriedly stopped by Ainsley. "Yes, Clarence, thank you. But what gave you the idea, Basil?"

"Vera Lynn, old boy. Hearing her ceaselessly on that blasted tape. I swear it's the only one he's got. I was lying in bed and it struck me that our battle plan was flawed. What if Matron blamed Alastair for the assault? I've had more stick from her than you lot due, it seems, to my habit of dressing rather casually. I was sure that she'd try some way of turning the tables and who better to scotch her than 'The Forces Sweetheart' herself – aided and abetted by old Clarence here. Thank God that Gruesome Gregory man has gone."

Further discussion was interrupted by another crunch of gravel outside. They all leapt up and got to the window just in time to see Matron Maud's Cortina, laden with boxes and cases, appear from the back of the house and speed out into the road.

As if to signal her departure the lunch gong banged out

from the hall. Freddy flew his hand towards the door. "Grub's up."

They left the room, moving in close formation as if to protect each other as they entered an unknown non-Matron Maud future. From the lounge Vera Lynn, having been switched on by Clarence who hadn't heard the gong or seen them leave, sang silkily, 'there'll be love and laughter, and peace ever after…'

Not if Sister-now-Acting-Matron Amelia Newbiggin had anything to do with it…

5

"This..." the newly promoted Acting Matron Newbiggin proclaimed to the specially assembled residents and staff, "is a new beginning."

She paused for the rapturous effect the play on her surname would have but all it elicited after a telling silence was one of Captain Cuthbert's little noises, louder than usual as if to especially mark the occasion.

Tubes Potter, who likened these oft-heard noises to the siren of one of Her Majesty's ships entering port, complimented the sound as he always did with a cry of "Land, Ho!" This caused a nervous titter to riffle through the lounge which the newly Acting Matron took to be a warm response to her joke, rude noises being so much a part of her everyday job.

The Acting Matron was using for this important occasion her high, tinny voice of authority which, whilst in complete contrast in tone and pitch to the booming baritone of the recently departed Maud Montague, still made listeners drop things, break into trots and catch their breath in anticipation of what was to come.

On being given the welcome news by Gregory Cartiledge that she was to become Acting Matron she had been nearly delighted and her face had lit up with one of its rare smiles. Nearly delighted because she had expected immediate promotion and considered a period of probation as both demeaning and unnecessary.

Now she had assembled the fourteen remaining residents in the lounge, the Cavaliers and Roundheads packed together in a rare and rather unwelcome alliance, and had taken up her position at the traditional place of command: the fireplace. This did not please Tubes Potter; the bridge was no place for women.

"There will be no more mention of Mrs Montague, no mention whatsoever." In one neat stroke she felt that she had removed the risk of any comparison with her predecessor but it was a forlorn hope, the subject being, for her charges, far too satisfying a pastime. She went on, "There will be changes."

This was red-rag-to-bull stuff and Ainsley Bennington, as the senior retired officer in the Home, felt that something needed to be said.

"Sister…" He got no further.

"Acting Matron now, Brigadier, if you would be so kind."

No, he was damned if he would. "Sister – for that is, I believe, still your substantive rank and is so much more, how shall I say, companionable, than Acting Matron…"

There was a murmur of approval from around the room, strengthened by another little noise from Clarence.

Sister Newbiggin adjusted her starched cuffs angrily and pulled in another notch on her belt. Her anger was the stronger for having noticed Nurse Lisa Roberts at the door joining in the murmurs. That would need to be dealt with soon, unequivocally. She needed the woman on her side – and by that she meant totally compliant – if her planned changes were to be implemented and enforced. She was about to speak but Ainsley hadn't finished.

"As I was saying, Sister, you would receive more attention from us were you to adopt phrases such as 'may I suggest' or 'do you agree that' or even 'it might be nice if', rather than 'there will be' and other such commands." He was enjoying himself and, as often happens in such a state, became a trifle careless. "We got rid of Matron for …"

Tubes was quickly in, "Getting your syntax a bit muddled there, old chap. Matron got rid of herself, if you remember."

Clarence Cuthbert unwittingly saved the awkward moment. "They tried that in Bombay. But it didn't work. Nearly caused a mutiny."

There was now silence as they all stared at the old man sitting crouched over his faithful zimmer. "You can't enforce a sin tax. How do you decide what sin is in the first place? I remember a little filly…"

"Please, Captain Cuthbert. Squadron Leader, perhaps you would be so kind and take him for a little walk – to cool down. It does him no good having such, er, dangerous memories, not in his condition."

Freddy Foster, pleased to have an excuse to leave, gently

guided Clarence to the French windows. "Come on, old sport. Let's take a turn round the flower-beds."

Clarence stopped dead. "Why's she going to turn round our beds? I like my view through the windows. You can see all sorts of things. If Nurse Lisa forgets to…" Mercifully Freddy managed to manoeuvre Clarence and his zimmer over the sill and they disappeared out of view.

The interlude had shifted attention from Ainsley's gaff but the point he had been making had sunk home with Sister Newbiggin. She was well aware that Oldthorpe House and, more personally, her job, depended on the residents who, with assistance from various military charities, their pensions and whatever savings they had scraped together during their active lives, provided its only means of income.

"I assure you, Brigadier, that I only have all your interests at heart."

This tended to make matters worse rather than better. Memories of schoolmasters wielding canes and saying in strained, disturbed voices to bared posteriors, "This will hurt me more than it hurts you," flitted across several of the residents' minds causing them to shift uneasily in their chairs. Basil Reardon, with dreadful memories of many a flogging through owning up and often taking the blame for others, needed reassurance.

"I believe our interests, Sister, to be a quiet life, good food and a relaxed atmosphere. Something we have sorely missed in the past. Are you to provide that for us now?"

The Cavaliers amongst the residents saluted this bravery with gentle applause and appreciative murmurs. The Roundheads would like to have joined in but, wishing to have their bread buttered on both sides, remained silent.

"Major Reardon," Sister, with great effort, prevented her indignation from showing and displayed a dangerously warm smile. "All these things shall come to pass, I assure you. We have, as you know, been rushed off our feet which has caused a little friction."

Tubes, glad that Clarence was out of earshot and therefore not handy with a further far-eastern memory associated with friction, muttered behind his hand to Ainsley, "The understatement of the year."

"What was that, Commander?" Sister sensed mutiny.

"Your statement brings good cheer, Sister. Do please go on with your assuring."

Sister Newbiggin fixed the submariner with a baleful stare that would have caused many a man to look down at his boots, but retired Torpedo Officers were made of sterner stuff. Through the blanket of white whiskers covering his face, two steely blue eyes stared back.

"We need at least one new maid – two ideally. Unfortunately so far no one has applied but despite being short-staffed we must all do the best we can. As for the food …"

"Splendid. Like school dinners. Love it." Clarence came clattering into the room from the garden and moved at remarkable speed towards the hall door, scattering his colleagues feet, many stubbed by his zimmer frame, as he went.

"Off to the loo and then a dose of Vera Lynn." And with another little noise he was gone.

Freddy dropped into an armchair. "Semolina pudding."

"And a choice of plain or chocolate," broke in Sister wrongly believing the memory would comfort them.

Freddy nodded. "Indeed, plain or chocolate semolina pudding. Each as disgusting as the other. Watery greens, tasteless meat, soggy suet…"

"Squadron Leader, please." Her pep-talk wasn't going at all as she had intended. She tried again. "The food is carefully selected and prepared to help your digestion to work efficiently. To have," she unnecessarily added, "a safe route through the body."

Tubes nodded, "Pity in Clarence's case that it so often finds a cul-de-sac."

Again there was a smattering of laughter. That's better, thought Sister, oblivious to the joke, they're settling down now. She ploughed on displaying her uncanny ability to misjudge those around her. "It's not the diet that is at fault. It's what you do to your bodies between meals."

There was some uncomfortable shuffling at this remark as they all interpreted it according to their consciences but they were saved delving too deeply as she continued, "Too much lying around lost in your own thoughts. We must think of ways to provide more activity for you all. Physical exercise, walking, gardening – now there's a good idea, we have a splendid garden but, sadly, no gardener. Let's make it your project to keep it in perfect trim."

Sister Newbiggin really didn't know her men – well, not the Cavaliers anyway. They stared at her in every type of aghast that they could muster. What was she talking about? PT? Walking? GARDENING? When, for heaven's sake? There was reading to be done – the racing results, cricket scores, football scores and, when they were fully digested, the world news to dissect and reshape. Then there was talking. So many reminiscences to share over and over and over again. And there was a prodigious amount of drinking to be fitted in. How could the many and varied Flaxton-on-Sea pubs survive if they diverted their time to Sister's mad ideas? And then after all that hard work there was, of course, a need for rest. Their heavy schedules demanded that time be put on one side at frequent intervals for a little nap or two during the afternoon – and morning if breakfast had proved too strenuous. In a nutshell their schedules were already severely over-stretched.

"I'm glad you're giving my plans such deep thought. We'll devise a roster so that you don't get under each other's feet."

I'd like to get you under my feet, thought Ainsley most ungallantly but before he could express his feelings regarding all this nonsense Sister Newbiggin bustled out leaving her residents more agitated than they had been for many a long day.

How well the meeting had gone, she congratulated herself as she went up to her room. She had calmed and reassured them all and they had made no objections – as she had feared they might – to her ideas for more activity in their dull, listless lives. This augured well for her future she was sure. Matron Amelia Newbiggin. How well it sounded; a splendid rhythm to it. It was only a matter of time – a short time, she hoped.

"I sometimes wonder if it was all worth it, you know."

Ainsley took a bite of his toasted teacake transferring a fair portion of dripping butter to his moustache which could be savoured at a later date. Basil was puffing contentedly at his pipe, watching his fellow officer and Lucy Banbury consume the

Cosy Cot Café's most popular comestible in their very differing ways, Ainsley's in large untidy chunks and Lucy's in carefully cut tiny portions.

As so often happened these days the two of them had run into their new friend in the shelter on Flaxton's promenade and had, with very little persuasion needed, moved her into the warmth of the café where they could bring her up-to-date with events at Oldthorpe House.

Lucy was, to her own astonishment, a changed woman since the first cathartic meeting with the Cavaliers. She had popped out of the shell into which she had locked herself on retiring from teaching and was now busily joining a host of committees around the town.

She couldn't fathom how these elderly men had done it. Maybe God had decided that they should be the vessel into which she should pour all the bottled up anguish caused by the deaths of so many loved ones? It was, she felt, a purging of the darkness that had enveloped her soul and with it had come an emergence into a new, brighter world.

She would see at least some of them most days and their chats together, although to an outsider appearing somewhat banal, were to both sides extremely therapeutic. They were, in a way, a form of confession as each related the events of the day to the other and then discussed them, often simplifying what had seemed insurmountable problems and thereby solving them.

"What do you sometimes wonder, old boy?"

Basil disappeared behind a blanket of smoke to which Ainsley was required to reply.

"The Matron caper. All that plotting. A successful offensive. Enemy routed. And then, blow me if another well-armoured one doesn't pop up to take her place. It's Normandy all over again."

The two of them sat in silence for a while but it was an uneasy interlude. Lucy, whose school-teaching antenna could spot a mood a mile off knew that something was wrong with Basil, the body language said so. Eyes didn't meet, his hands played nervously with the crumbs on his plate and, although he would never believe that he did so, he brought out his fairly clean hanky to wipe away the tea splashes on the table.

"You're not happy about it, are you?" Lucy neatly dabbed at her mouth with her table napkin.

Ainsley couldn't understand it. Basil had seemed out of sorts since Matron Maud's ignominious departure. He had been keeping to himself, creating more smoke clouds than ever and, despite the paucity of it, picking at the Oldthorpe cuisine.

"Come on, old chap. Spit it out." Ainsley realized subtlety was needed. "You're like a wet weekend in Whitby. What's up?"

Basil absent-mindedly put his tea-stained hanky into the breast pocket of his blazer, knocked his pipe out very noisily in the tin ashtray, prepared to refill it, and then sat bolt upright and stared at them.

"Subterfuge. Conniving. Deceit, do y'see? Wrong. All wrong. Not the way we were brought up. Poor show."

"Ah." That was better. Ainsley had feared some dreadful disease, or bankruptcy or, perish the thought, love: a bit of passion getting in the way. But it was only conscience. That could soon be sorted out.

Lucy gently touched Basil's arm. "I fully understand, Major Reardon, but you see, as I sometimes had to explain to my young charges, there are moments when we have to fight our conscience and, to put right what is obviously wrong, embark on a plan of action that is totally abhorrent to our nature." And then, looking down at her plate, she added very quietly, "my three brothers died doing that."

"Absolutely, Miss Banbury, bang on the nail." Ainsley thought he probably knew what she was talking about. He sucked some butter out of his moustache and gave Basil a playful biff. "War, old fruit. D'you see? And what lay at the basis of battle planning? Subterfuge, deceit, a bit of conniving, a bit of cunning. And for why? To defeat an enemy that was trying to impose a harsh regime on its subjects. And what does that remind you of?" He didn't wait for a reply. "Matron Maud and us, of course."

Lucy felt that Ainsley's manner was far from the right one when his friend was so obviously in anguish but she couldn't find fault with his sentiments.

Basil digested all this but was only slightly heartened

because he had never found the justification for war easy to accept. Tyrants should certainly fall if their subjects objected to their ways, but all those innocent lives? Ainsley's analogy was too simple, too 'pat'.

"Matron Maud was hardly Hitler." He looked at Lucy for support but only received a fleeting smile in return.

"Ah, Hitler." Ainsley signalled for the bill and looked back to find Basil mopping the table again. He lent forward and drew the others to him. They wondered what amazing revelation regarding the late unlamented Adolf he was about to share with them. His voice dropped to little more than a whisper.

"Hitler. Corporal Tremlett..."

Basil exploded, "O dear Lord, Ainsley. Not another Tremlett story." The residents of Oldthorpe House generally moved as a man to their various bedrooms at the mere mention of the blasted fellow's name.

Ainsley was totally unabashed. "Corporal Tremlett, yes. I wouldn't be here, you see, if it hadn't been for a few large slices of cunning and deception."

He finished the dregs of his tea. Basil looked at him trying to figure out if there was a way to prevent yet another Tremlett saga.

There wasn't.

"We'd at last cleared Caen. You remember, Basil? Monty assured everyone that the battle for Normandy was going according to plan – but then he always said that, didn't he? Well, as we know only too well, it wasn't. I was leading my squadron of tanks. Mine brewed up. Blasted German Tigers and 88s. We found refuge in a farmhouse. Only an old chap in it – but a fighter if ever I saw one. He told us the Boche were at the bottom of his orchard. Tremlett, my driver, was either shell-shocked or so used to popping his head out of the hatch to see where he was going that he did just that. He popped his head above the windowsill and said far too loudly – he'd been a Sunderland supporter, d'you see …"

Lucy was losing the gist of all this but she had to give Ainsley the benefit of the doubt and hope that something of consequence would come out of the story. "I don't quite see…"

"They're always loud, Sunderland Supporters." He looked

for agreement from the two listeners but got none.

"Anyway, Tremlett shouted, 'Where are the Boche? I can't see them.' Of course his voice easily carried to the end of the orchard – and all hell broke loose. Small arms, mortars, you name it, we got it. The old farmer got us into his barn across the yard and, to our amazement, a terrific battle started with as much gunfire being returned from the house to the orchard as it was receiving!"

This was all getting a bit much for Basil. "How could one old man do it? Doesn't make sense, Ainsley. Doesn't make sense at all."

"Cunning and deception, you see, old boy. That's how he did it, cunning and deception. When he got back to the house having hidden us, he was confronted by a platoon of German infantry who'd arrived through the front gate. He told them about the platoon in the orchard."

Ainsley sat back and slapped his knees with glee. "Clever, eh?"

Basil just looked at him. Artillery chaps weren't supposed to understand infantry tactics. It was all a bit much. Ainsley saw that the point hadn't gone home and remembered that he'd missed a vital detail.

"Told them there was a British platoon in the orchard, d'you see? Brilliant. We watched from the barn as the two German platoons pasted each other until the orchard lot advanced with a white flag and the ruse was up."

"And the old man?" Lucy, concerned for his safety, needed to know.

"He'd disappeared – very wisely. Probably became the local Mayor after the war."

"And you and your tank crew?" She needed the story tidied up a bit.

"Ah. A problem there. Corporal Tremlett. He popped his head up again to take a gander at what was going on and shouted back to us, 'They've surrendered' which, of course, jerry heard. There was nothing we could do but walk out with our hands up."

Basil knocked on the ashtray with his pipe, scattering burning tobacco.

"So, cunning and deception let you down in the end."

Ainsley dabbed at the hot ash. "Not at all. A few moments later a shell – probably one of yours, Basil, blew the barn to smithereens. Tremlett saved our lives."

"But you became prisoners of war." Lucy felt that the story still wasn't tidy enough.

"Only for a couple of days. Our captors were overrun before we could be shipped back." He turned to Basil. "But you do see, old man, don't you? We couldn't do without cunning and deception – then or now. And Matron Maud was a pig. The worst sort. Took advantage of us. Some chaps in despair. Rotten egg."

Lucy gathered up her handbag and coat and they went out into the chill early evening air. Forming up each side the two men escorted her down the High Street towards her cottage.

Feeling rather hemmed in she said, "I shall be quite safe if you want to go over to the bus stop. I'm sure the next one to Thorpe Haven won't be long."

"Just time for a snifter in The Anchor before home to supper."

She declined the invitation to join them – such behaviour would never do and after a cheery farewell walked on to her cottage.

Once the two foaming tankards of Adnams were on the table in front of them and Basil had disappeared behind his familiar smokescreen of Holborn Extra Mixed he was ready for a bit more information.

"What about this Tremlett chap? Court Martialled?"

Ainsley chuckled. "I'd have given him a medal. By sticking his head above the parapet he saved our lives – twice. In the house and in the barn. Brilliant."

Basil was doubtful about this but, as he knew, in war it was often the idiots who became the heroes. He was now reasonably convinced that if Matron decided to wage a form of war between the staff and the residents at Oldthorpe House then drastic steps did need to be taken and, yes, a bit of cunning and deception to clear the air was probably in order. Well done, Ainsley – and Lucy.

They stayed contentedly in the Saloon Bar, comfortable in each other's presence, until it was time to cross the road to the bus stop. Ainsley himself was well pleased with the outcome of his chat with Basil. The man's whole body language had changed for the better, his step was jauntier, he was swinging his arms and his head was high – and, dear Lord, he was humming! Tunelessly maybe, but a hum's a hum however ghastly the noise might be.

He was also well pleased with his storytelling ability. Had the event actually happened? He sometimes shared his colleagues' view that maybe the gallant corporal's escapades were a figment of his imagination but he really couldn't be sure after all this time. Still, it had won over dear old Basil. Just another bit of cunning and deception…

The next morning was cold but bright, a clear blue sky allowing the weak February sun to spread a tiny element of warmth over East Anglia. Tubes and Basil had drifted down to the summerhouse at the end of the garden after breakfast already aware, from the noise Sister was making as she surged around the house, that indoors would be no place to be once they'd all been chivvied out of the dining room.

Excusing themselves from their fellow residents and willingly foregoing a second slice of burnt toast in return for the only two available spaces in the rickety structure at the bottom of the garden, they were now well wrapped up and comfortably settled in equally rickety deckchairs.

For some time there was silence only broken now and again by the rustle of their newspapers as they turned the pages. And then, slowly, dreamily, Basil lowered his Daily Telegraph and, with his eyes focused on nothing at all, let out a deep sigh.

"She used to wear pink bloomers, you know. Elastic down to here." His voice was hoarse with the enormity of it all.

Tubes, who had been reading an interesting account of the strange doings of a female 'starlet', a male masseur – he hadn't come upon one of them in any of Her Majesty's submarines – and a giant loofah, slowly lowered his newspaper. There was his old friend Basil indicating with both hands just below his right kneecap the point to which the bloomer leg had reached and been held by the said elastic.

As if to make the matter even clearer and the image more

ghastly than ever Basil shifted his hands, now holding his pipe, to his other leg and repeated the demonstration in case Tubes might not be sure that ladies' bloomers had two legs – to match their occupants. As he did so he deposited a fair portion of burning tobacco onto his corduroys which he absent-mindedly brushed away.

Although he was impatient to return to the mysteries of the giant loofah, Tubes, realizing that Basil had gone to some considerable trouble to illustrate his point, showed mild interest.

"Who?"

He started to lift his newspaper back to a comfortable reading position but loofahs were quickly replaced in his somewhat over-fertile imagination by Basil's answer.

"Matron. The last one, that is." Then he added huskily, "I don't know about the Newbiggin jobs."

"You old rogue. I thought the late lamented Alastair Hunter was the only dark horse amongst us when it came to shenanigans with the un-late, unlamented Matron Maud Montague. Well, my dear chap…"

Basil was very confused. "Are you all right, Tubes? Not suffering from the bends or anything? Surfaced too quickly? Stop drivelling, there's a good fellow."

They went back to their newspapers, Tubes to the starlet, masseur and giant loofah and Basil to a page of unseen type as his memory clicked in even more vividly on the events surrounding Matron Maud's pink bloomers.

"Last Christmas," his voice came from behind the middle pages of his Telegraph.

Tubes, rather wishing he'd stayed on for the second round of toast, betrayed no interest even though, to his annoyance, these large items of women's unmentionables were beginning to take the place of giant loofahs in his daydreaming.

The paper was lowered again but now Basil, needing to expiate his guilt by sharing it, leant across and tapped his friend's knee with his pipe. He hardly waited for Tubes to brush the smouldering ash from the sharp crease in his flannels before he was blurting out his terrible secret.

"She was putting up the decorations in the lounge. Up a ladder. D'you see? I was holding it for her." Basil's eyes gazed unseeing at the rooftops and trees bordering the garden. He didn't dare look at his friend. Again his voice became husky, "I glanced up."

There was a silence. Both were so aghast at the image invading their minds that they sat, immobile, seeing nothing, hearing nothing, hardly breathing.

Tubes broke the uneasy silence. "You would," he said, trying to comfort the tormented man. "You would. To see she was secure. Well anchored."

Basil's eyes were still staring into the distance. "Probably. There they were. On each leg."

This had all gone on for long enough. Tubes felt it would be safer for him to return all his attention to the giant loofah.

"They would be," he said firmly with all the authority of one who, in his youth, had fleetingly glimpsed a maiden aunt similarly under-attired. "That's the way bloomers are."

With that he firmly put the entire contents of Monday's Times between him and Basil – and the bloomers. He intended to force Basil to do the same with his Telegraph and, by so doing, wrench the chap away from his unsavoury meandering but he'd underestimated the degree of memory-stirring going on in the dark, one might say murky, recesses of his friend's mind.

The next utterance paled all the others into insignificance.

"It reminded me of my father."

Tubes gulped, snorted and, as a result, choked. A glimpse up a lady's frock at a pair of pink bloomers, however accidental or brief – the glimpse, not the bloomers – was one thing, but being reminded of one's father in association with the wretched garment was quite another. He felt it his duty to comment but feared that all this was becoming too deep, even for a submariner.

"Your father? Women's undies, eh? Dashed awkward. I'd never have known looking at you. Fear not, Basil, your secret's safe with me."

Basil seemed to be totally oblivious of Tubes or, for that matter, anything else around him. He pulled out a slightly grubby hanky, still tea-stained from the table cleaning in the Cosy Cot yesterday, and wiped a watering eye.

"He used to put up the decorations, every Christmas. In

India. Up a ladder. Me holding it."

With a telling flick of the pages and a somewhat aggressive sigh Tubes resumed his Times reading and was just reacquainting himself with the starlet/masseur/loofah trio when another salvo, even more deadly than the previous ones, landed on target.

"It finally killed him."

Basil's voice was now so mournful that Tubes feared that all this reminiscing might prove too much for his old friend.

"I'm so very sorry, old chap. A stroke?"

"Two hundred and thirty volts – or was it a hundred and ten in India? The fairy lights, d'you see? There he was, putting one up the angel's skirt and down he went. Straight past me."

They sat in companionable silence for a moment and then Basil relit his pipe and picked up his newspaper. His voice, now stronger and more relaxed, brought the matter to a close.

"I carried on holding the ladder," he said proudly.

It was these little intimacies that were so important to the residents in Oldthorpe House. All of them had experienced so much during their careers in the Armed Services and now, for much of their waking hours, they were locked in their own little worlds, seeing each other moving, at differing speeds, back to the helplessness of childhood. And then, out of the blue, triggered by something they had seen, heard or read, would come some reminiscence, vivid in its detail and so often poignant in memory which they would find themselves sharing with whosoever was in earshot.

Tubes, having found the giant loofah saga tawdry alongside Basil's early memories of fairy lights, put his paper down and surveyed the scene of apparent bliss outside the summerhouse. The air was unusually calm for February on the East Coast and the sun shone brightly on the bushes and shrubs bordering the lawn. He knew the names of none of them – horticulture and submarines didn't really go together – but he could see that some of his fellow residents, their breakfasts more or less digested, were very much at home with them, snipping and tying. One, at a small easel, was painting a bush full of what he expected were roses, those being the only flowers he'd ever heard of.

These industrious souls were, of course, Roundheads who, for a quiet life, had accepted Sister's idea of gardening to brighten their days and, as so often happened – much to the fury of the Cavaliers – appeared to be thoroughly enjoying themselves.

Tubes saw Nurse Lisa come bustling out of the house, her large comfy body uneasily encased in the confines of her light blue starched uniform. She chatted to the gardeners and admired their handiwork, gave two of them their pills with glasses of water and then, waving to him and Basil, went back indoors to the disciplined regime of Sister Newbiggin who, from time to time, could be heard, voice raised in agitation, berating some miscreant who had incurred her wrath.

Something was nagging Tubes and he couldn't for the life of him work out what it was. He trawled back into his recent memory. Starlets, masseurs, loofahs, Matron's bloomers, fairy lights? No, it was none of those.

They sat quietly for a while, he nagged by the missing link and Basil, eyes closed, thinking of childhood, India, and his father. They were both jolted by another shouted command from Sister Newbiggin somewhere in the area of the kitchens. "What bright spark put Captain Cuthbert's underpants in with my washing?"

That was it! Well done, Sister. Bright spark. Electrocution. Basil's poor old father. It reminded him of an incident on – which submarine was it? There had been so many. 'Sea lion', that was it. Pacific. '41.

"I remember one of our electricians …"

Oh Lord, thought Basil. Tubes is off again. Another reminiscence. Where did the chap dredge them from? He was glad he wasn't one to delve into the past.

"Fused all the submarine lights – or he would have done if he hadn't stayed hanging on to each end of the broken cable."

Basil now lowered his newspaper. Was Tubes having him on? An old sea-dog's tale? Being an artilleryman he wasn't up on electricity but it all seemed a bit far-fetched to him. Tubes ploughed on unaware of the scepticism being wafted towards him.

"We had to release him eventually when we sighted land.

Buried him at sea."

With that, he picked up his newspaper and the telling final shot was fired from behind it.

"Fired him through a torpedo tube."

He peered around it at Basil who had found the imagery of it all rather too much so soon after his greasy breakfast.

"My job, you see, old man. Being torpedo officer."

Feeling that some acknowledgement, however brief, was in order, Basil summed it all up in one word.

"Terrible." And then he was back in the safety of the Telegraph.

"It was," agreed Tubes. "We were on emergency lighting for seven days. Cold food. You're right, it was terrible."

Now they both subsided again into silence as they scanned the obituary columns in their respective papers. The residents found it a chilling but strangely necessary exercise to check up on those who had 'handed in their dinner plate', particularly fellow Officers. The relative ages when they performed this selfless act brought differing reactions from the readers. Some who had gone were younger – 'dear Lord, can't be long now', others a similar age – 'any moment now. Anything I don't want found after I've gone?' and a few were older – 'still plenty of time, I'll cut down on the drink and smoking – soon'.

With some difficulty Tubes levered himself out of the deckchair. "Off to the heads, old boy. Nature calls." He ambled across the lawn, pausing at the amateur artist to glance at his watercolour, now slightly resembling a bush covered with a mass of flowers. "Roses. Dashed good," he said encouragingly, and ambled on.

A sharp, clipped voice followed him. "Camellias."

Basil found his eyes closing. This wouldn't do. Wouldn't do at all. He glanced at his watch. Ten-thirty. This age thing. Eat, read, sleep, eat, read, sleep, and so on. And then the reading drops away. And then the eating. And then just sleep is left. Eternal sleep…

This wouldn't do at all, not at all. He relit his pipe for the umpteenth time and concentrated on the Court Circular. How busy they all were. Dashing here, dashing there. Bowed and scraped at, gawped at, curtsies and bouquets. And here he was, here he was, retired major, Royal Artillery. Seventy years old and a sister in Reigate. That's all, that's the lot…

The newspaper fell to the floor, his hands flopped loosely into his lap. Basil Reardon was comfortably and contentedly fast asleep.

6

The subsequent Inquiry, carried out with due diligence by Sister on behalf of the owner, put the time of the conflagration at a few minutes past eleven o'clock on that sunny, February morning. The statements from witnesses to the event covered every aspect of it and painted a clear picture from which a conclusion should have emerged. Sadly for Sister, blame could be placed nowhere – but suspicion was a very different matter; it rested firmly on the shoulders of Basil Reardon.

Basil's evidence was very hazy and, try as she might, Sister could pin him down to no germane facts whatsoever. He had, he said, been experiencing a very confusing dream set in India which, itself, was evidently set in a submarine which, itself, became a sailing boat with a large pink sail which, itself, became a certain large article on a washing line which, itself, became a string of fairy lights held in each hand by a person or persons unknown who walked into a long tube, a door was slammed shut, someone shouted "FIRE" and it became very hot and smoke choked him. The next minute, clothes smouldering, hair singed and face blackened he found himself being ejected, partly by the explosion and partly by rescuing hands, from the blazing summerhouse.

That, in a nutshell, was all he could tell Sister Newbiggin who could make nothing of it that was of any value to her Inquiry. Basil, always willing to help those struggling around him, added an embellishment: he wasn't sure if the Queen hadn't popped into the dream at some moment or another. Then he withdrew for more soothing ointment to be administered by the cool, soft hands of Nurse Lisa to various singed extremities of his body.

Other eyewitnesses – the gardening residents, and Clarence Cuthbert from an upstairs lavatory window – described a sudden, mighty explosion as the old wooden summerhouse burst into flames. They saw Basil stagger to the door and rushed to help him away, their willing hands tearing at his burning clothes with a frenzy that subsequently reminded him of a night in a Delhi nightclub – the last time anyone had tried to rip off his clothes.

In no time at all the building was a smouldering ruin. No one thought to try to extinguish the flames; there was no real point and, anyway, they saw a nice new replacement soon standing in its place.

Clarence's evidence to Sister contained nothing to do with summerhouses catching on fire but rather centred on his visit to the upstairs lavatory and all matters pertaining thereto, and however hard she tried to bring him back to the issue in question she found herself writing down an account that provided a graphic insight into Captain Cuthbert's faulty drainage system leading to the moment when the explosion caused him to fear that his end, as it were, was nigh.

So immersed was he regarding his innards that he failed to mention the strange sight he had viewed from the window of his old friend Tubes Potter, behind the summerhouse and therefore unseen to everyone else, literally crawling on his stomach towards the flames holding a garden rake which he swished around in the heart of the fire. Clarence saw him retrieve a tiny blackened object which he pulled back with the rake and hid in the flower bed.

The Court of Inquiry, made up entirely of Sister Newbiggin, visited the site of the catastrophe and rummaged around in the remaining debris of ash, nails and broken glass, but found no evidence of anything suspicious that might have caused the blaze. On being recalled for further questioning regarding his pipe, Basil professed a hazy memory of the events before he had dozed off and was saved further interrogation by Nurse Lisa who said that she would swear on oath, if need be, that he had no pipe on him when she took him indoors for treatment to his injuries, and – she almost stamped her foot because she was so cross – if it's remains weren't in the debris, he obviously hadn't had it with him.

Tubes said nothing – and kept well out of the way. The 'tiny object' had already been retrieved from the flowerbed and thrown away and those who needed to know briefed on his expedition with the rake.

An uneasy week followed 'The Great Fire of Oldthorpe', as the Cavaliers amongst the residents had dubbed it. A frosty air of suspicion and rumour existed between Sister Newbiggin and her charges not helped by her anger that anything untoward should happen during her probationary period as Acting Matron.

The residents could feel in their elderly bones that, whatever the outcome of the Inquiry, they would end up the losers. There would be reprisals and, almost as bad as not knowing what they would be, they had no idea when they would manifest themselves. Coupled to this was the loss of their only means of refuge when they were thrown out into the garden as part of Sister's new regime to, they were assured, 'improve their health' – which they knew really meant getting them from under the understaffed staffs' feet.

"Who spilt custard on the floor?"

The residents who were having their after supper sit in the lounge groaned – as much from the knife-on-glass voice of Sister as the heavy indigestible weight in their stomachs. She was obviously somewhere in the kitchen area and the answer to her question was sullenly inaudible.

"Why didn't you get him to mop it up?"

More murmuring.

"Then you should have held his zimmer while he did it. Custard on the floor is not permitted."

"Oh Lord." Clarence struggled to his feet. "I think I'll go to the loo."

Freddy made a gentle landing with his hand on the old man's shoulder. "Just stay here, Clarence, old mate. We'll handle this."

The next moment Sister rushed into the room. "Captain Cuthbert…" She got no further.

Tubes held up his hand. "Sister, why was poor old Clarence here being made to carry custard in the first place when it's quite obvious that…"

Sister Newbiggin marched to the fireplace and banged a wooden spoon that she happened to be carrying on the mantelpiece. There were more important matters to discuss than careless Captain Cuthbert's custard – and now was an ideal moment.

"Your attention gentlemen please. I have news for you from our owner, Mr Gregory Cartiledge, who has now weighed up the evidence contained in my report to him of the Inquiry I conducted into the summerhouse fire."

Dear Lord, thought Freddy who was, as usual, draped in an armchair, she's got as much wind as poor old Clarence, even if it does come from another vector.

"First, I should tell you that he congratulated me on my thoroughness and diligence in its preparation…"

"But you didn't find out how it happened, Sister." Tubes spoke whilst quietly indicating to Basil that it might be prudent to put his pipe away for a moment or two. "Wasn't he a tad bit unimpressed regarding this somewhat fundamental omission?"

"Not at all." Sister tried a steely look again forgetting that, with the Cavaliers, and Tubes in particular, it didn't work. "He understood the complexity of the matter and has been willing on this occasion to see the cause as an Act of God."

"I must protest, Sister." Ainsley was having none of this. "Since when have any of us – and here I refer only to the residents – and Nurse Lisa – I can't speak for the rest of the staff – incurred the wrath of God to the extent of him sending a thunderbolt to land on a tinder dry, dilapidated, ramshackle nonsense of a building enshrining our very own beloved Basil? It is sacrilege to even hint at such a thing. And at Church Parade on Sunday we shall, as one, make just such a representation to the Padre."

Sister was completely taken aback by this verbal assault which had, so it seemed, the full backing of everyone present – and probably God.

"Yes, well," she took a deep breath to calm herself and was surprised to feel tears prickling in her eyes. "Those were Mr Cartiledge's words. You'll have to take it up with him."

"Who? God?" Freddy was being either naive or very mischievous; it's doubtful whether even he knew which.

"Mr Cartiledge, of course, Squadron Leader. Now, enough of this. I am merely the spokesman – person – in this matter. It is decided that from this moment onwards there will be no smoking either in the house or the garden. Mr Cartiledge has decreed…"

113

"Caesar Augustus," murmured Basil.

"What was that, Major?" As she said it she knew she shouldn't have asked.

"The chap who decreed. In the bible. Friend of Herod who slaughtered the children if you remember. Gruesome Gregory might as well do that to me if I can't smoke my pipe any more. It's the only thing that keeps me going. Stupid, vicious man."

They were all staring at him. It wasn't like Basil to vent his feelings so forcefully and it did strike Tubes, close friend that he was, that it was a trifle rich considering it was he who had destroyed the blasted summerhouse in the first place and caused all this fuss. But, of course, it was at times like this that friends must stick closely together.

"Suppose we refuse to obey this grossly unreasonable command?"

"Then, I presume, Mr Cartiledge will have to consider the future of Oldthorpe House."

That silenced them, but Sister knew that it was probably only a lull before an even greater storm erupted. "And there will be no replacement summerhouse."

Sensing the mood, she decided to get all the bad news over whilst they were still in shock and ploughed on with the last and most cruel bit of all.

"Mr Cartiledge has ordered me to inform you that there will be doubling up."

At first most took this to mean that, whatever their age, they would be required to run from here to there or, if more appropriate, from there to here. How on earth could they? Why should they? The man was patently as mad as a hatter.

As the dam of indignation was about to burst all around her Sister hurried on, making the breech wider than ever.

"Certain of you will be required to share your rooms thereby making it possible for the Owner to take in more residents and, in so doing..." she paused in disbelief at what she was required to say, "make the Home more viable." She knew better than anyone present that the owner must already be making a very handsome profit out of his investment.

Now there were mutterings of deep discontent coupled with agitated fidgeting as these men, who had commanded so many troops in battle and fought the hun on land, sea and in the sky tried to come to terms with their impotence at the hands of this petty dictator who, unlike their previous adversary, Hitler, had not even risen to the rank of lance corporal.

The dam burst scattering anger and fury around the room. Everything from the fairly mild 'how dare he' to 'I'd like to stick one of his blasted rifles'…

The rest was mercifully lost to Sister's ears by a sudden bellow from Ainsley who caught out of the corner of his eye the flickering television screen transmitting in silence the regional evening television news programme.

"Good God, there's the blighter himself." He sat forward and grimaced at the screen and decided that he disliked the look of the dreadful owner of Oldthorpe House as much via electronics as he did in the flesh. He fiddled with the remote control to increase the volume, and the familiar bulbous features turned from their usual scarlet to beetroot. Finding the right button he flooded the lounge with the man's distinctive East London twang.

Everyone had by now pulled forward, staring at the television set, experiencing a rare viewing of the early evening regional news.

GREGORY CARTILEDGE
Chairman – Cartiledge World Armaments

The caption flashed beneath the jutted-out chin of Gruesome Gregory as, with a voice spluttering with indignation he berated the police, British justice, the entire UK road haulage system in general, a local haulage firm in particular, the road network and, of course, the Government.

Try as she would, the hapless interviewer couldn't lead him to a coherent account of the story surrounding the theft of two lorry loads of crates filled with rifles for a far-clung African nation that were needed urgently to quell an uprising by its oppressed citizens.

Gregory Cartiledge's face grew darker and darker, the veins standing out even where veins shouldn't be. His spell-bound viewers in Oldthorpe House gripped the arms of their chairs.

Would they have the stupendous good fortune to see their Landlord actually expire before their very eyes – maybe blow up like his summerhouse?

Sadly, no. The interviewer brought the entertainment to an untimely close. "Mr Carbonage, thank you. And now, some more of the day's news." Behind this sentence could be heard a strangulated distant snarl, "Cartiledge."

Ainsley watched this exchange with less than his usual degree of detachment for all matters relating to television news programmes, partly because it had featured their beloved owner making even more of an ass of himself than usual but also because the embryo of a plan – a wicked plan – was taking shape in his mind.

Gregory Cartiledge sat at his vast desk, smoking a vast cigar, in his vast office at CARTILEDGE WORLD ARMAMENTS and fumed, his small frame physically shaking with anger as he contemplated the monstrous assault on his company, his bank balance and, worst of all, his ego. This triple whammy he found mind-blowing.

For a band of villains to steal, in broad daylight, a consignment of arms destined for a group of terrorists was, to him, a criminal act of such proportions as to warrant the death penalty. That many innocent people would undoubtedly have died as a result of the use of the arms he was providing to the terrorists didn't enter his head. The fact was, he'd been cheated, and that didn't suit Gregory Cartiledge, it didn't suit him at all.

The vast door opened to admit his Personal Assistant who had to advance some distance into the room before she could see the tiny man behind his vast desk. She cleared her throat nervously.

Gregory looked up and saw this stranger peering at him. He had no idea who she was but, by her deference and obvious nervousness, assumed rightly that she was the woman whose desk he'd passed as he strode into his office that morning. He wasn't in any way surprised that he didn't know her; his Personal Assistants never stayed long enough for him to know their names – why, he couldn't imagine. They all left for a number of extraordinary reasons: sudden deaths, instant marriages, terrible sicknesses, allergies, contagious diseases, every excuse under the sun.

"Yeah?" snarled Gregory looking up at the unfortunate woman shaking before him.

"There's a Mr Robin Bennington on the telephone…" she got no further.

"Get rid of him. I've told you before that I don't want – won't – be disturbed by any…"

With supreme bravery she broke in. "From East Anglian Television."

This was different. An apology, probably, for the appalling way he'd been handled by that stupid interviewer. Right. He always had time for an apology and the more cringing, crawling and abject it was, the better. He rubbed his chubby little hands together.

"Don't just stand there, woman. Put him on."

With a mixture of fury and relief she scuttled out determined to look in the 'Jobs Vacant' section of the local newspaper before this, her first day at CWA, was over.

"Mr Cartiledge, good morning to you." The voice was purring and well educated – the antithesis of its addressee. "Robin Bennington here. I'm a Documentary Producer at East Anglian TV. I saw your, er, splendid interview regarding the, er, monstrous theft you have experienced, and my colleagues in the newsroom feel that you would make an excellent subject for our 'East Coast Profile' programme I produce each month. Maybe we could meet to discuss the idea?"

Gregory sat spellbound – a sensation of tranquillity that had rarely ever enveloped him. At last here was the recognition that he coveted and from no less an influential organisation than a television company. But old habits die hard.

"How much?"

"We pay no fee, Mr Cartiledge. The exposure it provides for you and your business is, we feel, reward enough."

How soft and gentle was the voice. Almost sinister, felt Gregory.

"Right. Let's get on with it. Meeting here, tomorrow. Nine a.m."

"Shall we say Friday?" the voice continued smoothly.

"Here. Eleven-thirty. My secretary will contact yours regarding the address and so on. Goodbye 'til then." There was a click and then the dialling tone.

Gregory wasn't used to such treatment but, in an unusual show of diplomacy, decided to ignore the insolence of this young pup; there was too much at stake. The proposed programme would lead to riches and fame – probably the first steps towards the knighthood he so richly deserved and for which he had bought that blasted old codgers' home in the first place.

A further reason for doing something so totally uncharacteristic as spending a smidgeon of his ill-gotten fortune on Oldthorpe House had been to mollify his once timid wife who was becoming dangerously bold and critical of his 'manners and methods', as she called them. He had considered ditching her as he had the other two, but Gloria had once been his secretary and knew far too much of his 'manners and methods' with regard to his business activities to be safe unattached to him. It was better to humour her from time to time. The Rolls, furs, jewellery, the estate and servants were easily bought and seemed to be effectively binding as far as she was concerned. There was also the little matter of the Nuptial Agreement that, to his fury, had been foisted on him just before the wedding. Put a foot wrong and much of his fortune would slide effortlessly into her bank account. And that would never do.

It was with such thoughts that he stood at his vast office window overlooking his vast empire of warehouses containing every make, type, size and calibre of deadly weapon that man had yet devised. He was successful – and clever, very clever.

But his cleverness hadn't, over the years, restricted itself to achieving a thriving, highly profitable business, it had also been mightily employed in the methods used to gain the success. He had dealt equally ruthlessly with his competitors as he had with his customers who were made up of a raw mixture of 'soft' regimes in far off places ripe for overthrow, weak Heads of State and strong gangland bosses. All were either coerced, set against each other, blackmailed and bullied or, where necessary, pampered, flattered, paid-off and 'provided for' by the CWA Empire.

And then, of course, there was the manipulation of the Inland Revenue. Oh, Gregory Cartiledge was clever, cleverer than most. He knew it, and all those who had the misfortune to touch him knew it.

But then, as he watched from his window another consignment of arms being driven out in now heavily protected lorries, his smile of satisfaction – more a grimace – faded as a terrible thought struck him; what if the television people, through some research in their preparation for the programme, alighted on even a very small insight into the way he did business? The more he thought about it the more he saw that, even if they were all as apparently inept as that stupid young pup, Bennington, it would be difficult for them not to find someone or something he would rather not have relayed into people's homes via their television sets.

With mounting concern another horror struck him: the Inland Revenue. What if, due to his magnetic personality, the programme was repeated countrywide, even worldwide?

He lit another cigar, sat at his desk, stabbed the intercom and yelled for his Personal Assistant to attend him – this instant.

The subsequent phone call, when his Assistant had at last tracked down Robin Bennington, was not a success and this, on top of every other disaster since the theft of his lorries, was almost more than the pressure of blood in the various Cartiledge arteries and veins could stand. Almost, but sadly for all those unfortunate enough to have met the man, not quite enough.

His 'Personal Office', a team of four brave souls, on hearing his even more than usual maniacal yell through the intercom, put their well-rehearsed survival plan into operation and vacated the floor on various spurious pretexts whilst he roamed around kicking, smashing and shouting at anything in his path. Gregory Cartiledge threw his toys well and truly out of the pram.

The phone call had started well enough.

"How can I be of assistance, Gregory?" The soft, reassuring, almost doctorish tones of Robin Bennington were completely in contrast to his stern expression as he purred at the ghastly man. As he spoke he glanced at the revolving spools on the tape recorder with its microphone attached to the telephone earpiece.

119

Cartiledge, at once thrown by the media's use of Christian names with almost complete strangers, took a moment to adjust and then adopted his comfortable bull and china shop technique.

"Forget it. The programme. Changed my mind. Not interested. Private person. Good day." But before he could replace the handset three quietly spoken words set it back to his ear.

"I think not."

"What was that you said?" He couldn't believe his ears and so added, "Eh?" to make the point more strongly.

"I think not, Gregory. You see we have already started on the research and what we're finding is – how shall I say – fascinating. I predict, with my knowledge of these things, that the programme will be, I assure you, a great success. I would almost say sensational."

Unseen by his tormentor, but faithfully picked up on the recording tape, Gregory Cartiledge gulped.

"You haven't listened, man." His voice was getting dangerously loud and Robin Bennington adjusted his volume control accordingly.

"I said forget it. I haven't time. Too busy. A private person, you see. Don't like publicity." He found that he'd poured every argument he'd jotted down in preparation in to one short staccato outburst.

"Ah. What a pity. I so much prefer it when we have the full co-operation of our subjects. We do, however, have a sister programme here called 'East Coast Exposé'. It explores the lives and activities of those who, perhaps, need to be a bit more open in the way they relate with the world around them. A colleague of mine produces it and I will, if you're sure you don't wish to take part in the Profile, pass the file to him. I think he will see great merit in using you as a subject for one of his programmes."

It is said that old habits die hard and whoever thought up such a profound statement could not have asked for a more appropriate subject to pin it to than dear old Gregory Cartiledge.

"Now you see here, Beckington," the voice bubbled and spluttered, "if you so much as whisper anything – ANYTHING – about me or my Company to another living soul I shall be delighted to send my men to sort out you and, if you have one, your family – kids, the lot. And believe me, their ways are nasty. Very nasty indeed. If you value your fingers, toes and any other extremities …" He got no further.

"Steady, Gregory, steady. The needle's going right off the dial. Whilst you're providing marvellous material for my colleague's programme you're making the recording of this conversation terribly distorted, and we at East Anglian Television pride ourselves on the technical quality of our work. Now let's see, you were threatening me, weren't you? Do please continue, but try to enunciate more clearly, speak more slowly, and lower the volume. Right? Cue."

There was silence. For once in his life Gregory Cartiledge could think of nothing to say. He was smart enough to know when he'd been sewn up, packaged, sorted and turned into a ball waiting to be kicked into touch whenever his tormentor wished. He took the only route that he had ever known to work in such situations – and he only knew what that route was through hearing others say it pitiably to him.

"How much do you want?"

"My dear sir. You are surely not attempting to bribe an employee of a British television company? I fear that if that is the case my masters will see it as an important news story to pass on to ITN in London who will, in turn, probably sell it worldwide. It will then have the advantage of reaching all your customers."

He – and the tape – heard the groan and a sound almost like a whimper. It was time, thought Robin Bennington, to put the revolting man out of his misery.

"There is, actually, a way out of this mess you find yourself in…"

The news that greeted the residents at Oldthorpe House, relayed by an incredulous Sister Newbiggin, revitalised every one of them and lifted the atmosphere of gloom that had descended since the 'Great Fire of Oldthorpe' Inquiry and its subsequent resulting edicts from the owner.

The ban on smoking was lifted giving over half the residents the will to live again, the threat of doubling-up was removed and all bedrooms would be redecorated in the coming months followed by the downstairs public rooms. No less than two new maids and a gardener would be persuaded to join them and their recruitment would be helped by an increase in pay for both nursing and domestic staff. Finally, wonders of wonders, a new, larger and far smarter summerhouse would be delivered and assembled within the week!

All this had been conveyed to Sister in the grating voice – even more grating than usual – of Gregory Cartiledge himself and confirmed in a personally written, excruciatingly grammared letter to be pinned to the notice board.

Ainsley Bennington chose to use a public telephone in The Anchor hostelry to pass on his grateful thanks to his nephew Robin at the East Anglian Television studios. The young man had been delighted to be of assistance and had found the whole experience exhilarating. There had even been a rewarding spin-off. He had taken the idea of an 'East Coast Exposé' series of programmes to his Executive Producer who had seen great merit in it and instructed Robin to search out some likely characters to feature. Robin set to work with a will but, sadly, one person who would not be on the list was the Chairman of Cartiledge World Armaments – unless, of course, he misbehaved himself again.

Ainsley rejoined his friends in the bar and gently reminded Basil that it was his round. But Basil had to get just one thing off his chest before he could really relax. From a fog of pipe smoke he fixed Ainsley with a reproving and, as usual, watery eye.

"You see, old friend. We don't need to get angry and upset with the establishment all the time. This has proved that there's good in everyone at heart – and, as we've seen, that includes Mr Cartiledge. A little bit gentler in the future, eh?"

Ainsley Bennington choked on his beer but decided to say nothing. On this occasion not even Corporal Tremlett came to his rescue.

7

Brigadier Bristowe looked out of the train window at the passing April landscape, but saw very little of it. The brain did strange things at a time like this: detached itself from the present by shutting down the senses serving it. Sight, sound, smell, touch contributed nothing to the immediate state of mind, which was in considerable turmoil.

Funny thing, the brain. Six months ago it had inhabited a fit, strong body full of enthusiasm for life, fuelled with knowledge that all was very well with the world. Ahead there was a well-earned retirement at the end of a long, distinguished Service career, strong financial investments to provide a well-heeled standard of living and a senior army rank attracting respect from the community. All these beckoned after the last salute had been taken and the retirement dinners with their accompanying eulogies and subsequent indigestion were over with.

Just six months ago…

The Brigadier sighed a long, deep, slightly gurgling sigh. Other passengers in the crowded Second Class compartment noted it and glanced across and then at each other. Children paused in their loud games and messy orange eating and their parents nodded, knowing only too well what brings on a sigh like that; everyone has a cross or two to bear in their lifetime. They were perplexed, though. This distinguished looking fellow traveller somehow seemed very out of place in this noisy, smelly, untidy, second-class carriage.

Six months ago…

It had started with a brief, rather abstract letter from someone overseeing the Lloyds Underwriting Syndicate into which the financially unworldly Brigadier had deposited, on excellent advice, the vast majority of every pound, shilling and penny earned in over thirty years of military service. Safe, secure, set to multiply astronomically, a pot of gold to secure the very best of everything a person could need in the long years of retirement ahead.

And then had come the Stock Market crash. Every invested penny was gone together with nearly every other possession. What was left? A suitcase of clothes, a few personal mementos deemed of little or no value by the assessors and a basic pension: those constituted the Estate of Brigadier Bristowe CBE; the residue of a lifetime of service to the Monarch. Had there been a partner the blow might not have been so severe, but frequent moves around the world had never provided the opportunity for marriage and, until now, this had never been regretted.

The Royal British Legion and similar charities were quick in providing all the help they could and, with much relief, came the offer of a place at Oldthorpe House which, from the brochure provided, was described as a Home for Retired Officers of Her Majesty's Forces. It didn't help that it was apparently a long way from anywhere at a place called Thorpe Haven on the East Anglian coast.

The Brigadier's shudder and sigh at the prospect of what lay ahead caused further concern from the other passengers and a brief, blessed moment of silence amidst the orange sucking. The sigh was followed by a glance through the window at the beauty of the passing countryside but it failed to register. However, what did break through the cart wheeling turmoil of doubts was the reflection of a prematurely old, lined face reflected in the glass.

This would never do. Certainly not. Made of sterner stuff than this. A bit of shaping-up was what was needed. Adversity had often been got through before and would be again now. Brigadier Bristowe sat bolt upright, let out a 'humph' that again silenced the railway carriage, and set about completing The Times crossword.

The Brigadier changed at Ipswich onto the branch line to Flaxton-on-Sea, being the nearest station to Thorpe Haven, and it was coincidence that as the train entered the outskirts of the town it should pass so close to another new recruit to the ranks of Oldthorpe House.

Phyllis Coombe was pottering around, humming cheerfully, in her tiny kitchen at 8, Gas Lane from which she could see, through the polished glass of the window and across the small neat garden, the railway line running some thirty yards from her back door.

She could see the line – but on this occasion she didn't. Having been born and brought up at number 8, the sensation of a diesel railcar apparently passing at regular intervals through the centre of the house, whilst it might draw the attention of others, had no effect on her whatsoever. On this bright Spring afternoon, as Brigadier Bristowe flashed by, her humming never wavered and she continued making breakfast for the rest of the Coombe household. It was good to have her hubby Albert home again and, as she always did after he'd been away for a spell, she marvelled at how cheerful he could be when his life seemed to be dogged with a never-ending stream of bad luck. And now their boy, George, seemed to have inherited his father's misfortune.

Phyllis frowned – a rare expression for her. Her loved ones: two upright, healthy men conscientiously going about their business on the night shift at some factory on the estate – she could never remember its name which, in fact wasn't surprising because they had never mentioned a name to her. What she certainly did know was that they were constantly hounded by the local constabulary who, using obviously trumped up evidence – the Coombe family preferred the word 'dodgy' – managed to have them both detained for varying periods of time at 'Her Majesty's Pleasure' in Ipswich gaol. That's how Albert, who had always been good with words, described it; the pimply detective, who spent almost as much time at number 8 as did its two male occupants, preferred a less melodious phrase: 'banged to rights'.

Whichever, Albert and George, much to Phyllis's pride, maintained a phlegmatic, almost serene, cheery disposition through all their trials and tribulations. They went off each evening in their smart, freshly laundered black boiler suits carrying their tool bags and Phyllis's freshly prepared sandwiches, and returned exhausted from a night of labour to her welcoming pot of tea, and then bed. That was, of course, provided the fuzz – as Albert and George called the hard-pressed constabulary – didn't lay a hand on their shoulders.

Now, with her diamond encrusted wristwatch (dear Albert)

125

showing three p.m. Phyllis climbed the steep stairs holding in front of her at shoulder height a tray containing a plate of eggs, bacon, sausages, tomatoes, black pudding and, floating in a sea of fat, two slices of fried bread. Alongside the plate was a full toast-rack, a pot of tea, a cup and saucer, the necessary cutlery, and a table napkin encased in a solid silver ring engraved with an elaborate 'A' which Albert had evidently found lying in the gutter. Under her arm was tucked today's Daily Mirror. Time the boys were moving.

Two minutes later she was downstairs again, and another two minutes after that she was trotting along Gas Lane to catch the bus to Thorpe Haven and her first shift as housemaid at Oldthorpe House. Waiting at the bus stop it struck her, as it so often did, that coincidences popped into the Coombe family lives almost as often as the strong arm of the law. Amongst them had been the finding of the napkin ring with, amazingly, its engraved 'A', just outside their house. And then there had been that sack of stolen ornaments and jewellery that a burglar, obviously in a panic, had hidden in their coal hole. She had found it and Albert, grabbing it from her, had rushed off saying he was going to the police station to hand it in. Good old Albert, so public spirited and yet so often misunderstood.

Then there was that fuss at the local football club, Flaxton Athletic. 'The only thing athletic about that lot is the speed of their beer arms', Albert had jocularly quipped on one merry occasion, but they evidently still entrusted him with their silver trophies from a bygone age which he had brought home in the boot of his old banger. He told her that the club officials had met him in a pub and asked if his wife would clean them and, being of a kindly disposition, he'd said yes. She'd spent a whole afternoon at it and they looked really grand when she'd finished. And then, horror of horrors, someone stole them as he was taking them back! That had been just before his lucky win on the 'dogs' and their dream holiday in Benidorm.

Such thoughts flitted smilingly through Phyllis's mind as the bus carrying her across Flaxton paused at the railway station. She watched an elderly person with two heavy suitcases win a strongly worded argument with the unhelpful driver and then clamber on and sink, exhausted, into a front seat. Of course neither she nor Brigadier Bristowe was as yet aware that they were both bound for Olthorpe House. Yet another coincidence.

The bus jolted to a halt in Thorpe Haven much to the aggravation of the driver who, despite having a job which entailed taking on and setting down passengers, found it irksome, inconvenient, and a damn nuisance to do so. Now he was forced to go through this tiresome procedure by this little woman who had come forward to the door – a sure sign that she wished to alight. Then he remembered the toff who had dared to invade his bus at the railway station with two large suitcases. Bloody cheek bringing cases onto a bus. And this high-falutin' voice had demanded to be told when they reached Thorpe Haven.

"Thorpe Haven," the driver growled.

The two of them stood on the pavement in Harbour Road enveloped in the blue exhaust smoke of the departing bus. Phyllis, full of her own thoughts, set off towards Oldthorpe House where, a week previously, she had attended an interview with what she described to Albert and George as 'a starched cross-patch'. She had only taken a couple of paces when a voice behind her said, very pleasantly, "I wonder if you could direct me to Oldthorpe House?"

So, together, each carrying a large, heavy suitcase, Brigadier Bristowe, new resident, and Phyllis Coombe, new domestic, set off to discover the delights awaiting them at the hands of the 'starched cross-patch' herself, Sister (Acting Matron) Amelia Newbiggin.

Sister had woken that morning in a confused state of mind. Before full consciousness took over, she could feel that there was a mixture of two extremes ahead, good and bad. As she sat up the cogs fell into place and she saw before her the satisfaction of at least one new maid arriving and possibly, although she hadn't yet interviewed the other applicant, two. That was good – although what on earth Mr Cartiledge was up to suddenly pouring money into the place having been so stingy up until now, she couldn't imagine.

The feeling she had experienced on first waking turned out to be more unsettling then bad. It was the arrival of a new resident. This would mean extra work and patience, the latter being a commodity it would be hard for her to adopt as she directed him along the path she wished him to take.

She really couldn't understand why, when she had very clearly defined the said path and its clear boundaries, about half her charges seemed to delight in treading over them thus creating disordered mayhem – and disordered mayhem was something that Sister Newbiggin would NOT tolerate in any circumstances. This new arrival would have to be made very clear about that fact right at the start. Educate him early and all would be well and he would find himself amongst the compliant group who were rewarded with the bigger front bedrooms with their newer, uncracked wash basins. Catch him late and as sure as eggs are eggs that unruly element calling themselves the Cavaliers would devour him.

Sister dabbed a touch of rouge to her cheeks and a smidgeon of lipstick to her pursed lips. She pulled them in and pressed them together staring in the mirror at her taut, stern face. And then, extraordinarily, two big tears rolled down her cheeks followed by an increasing deluge. Mascara and rouge were washed away as she sank onto the bed and, like a small child, sobbed her heart out.

It didn't last long. Why had it happened? During the cosmetic repair to her face she reasoned out the answer. All this was really a charade. The aggression, sharpness, anger, petulance and so many more emotions had been learnt at the knee of those who had trained her. The real her, the real Amelia Newbiggin had a heart full of love, compassion and caring for those in her charge, particularly, she was surprised to discover, the rascals around her. It was the teachers who had been at fault, those senior to her in her career in institutions around the country who had, to their eternal shame, pumped the 'command through fear' philosophy into her. Not for the first time she wished she'd followed her parents' advice and taken the gentler hospital path in her nursing career.

But this would never do. However much she regretted it, she knew that if there was to be any change in her style of command it would have to be very slowly implemented. Any sign of weakness would be pounced upon and as she worked out her period of probation as Acting Matron any more disasters, like the recent summerhouse fire, would mean the end of her dreams.

She straightened her uniform and checked in the mirror to ensure that everything was where it should be – seams straight, pleats sharply pleated, cuffs and collar to a starched perfection and cap well secured. Sister (Acting Matron) Newbiggin was set for another day in loud, authoritative command.

It was obviously going to be a 'Grade One Alert' day at Oldthorpe House – a designation coined by Tubes Potter who had witnessed many such days deep beneath the oceans in his submarine, not that he and the crew had ever had to cope with anything as lethal as Amelia Newbiggin. The residents always had early warning of the impending storms to come by the early arrival of Sister who, when the mood took her, would appear at breakfast and start fussing around their greasy portions of dried egg, fatty bacon and sausages.

Her unnecessary interference confused everyone including Nurse Lisa whose carefully prepared distribution of pills and potions was thrown into total disarray by the distraction. This inevitably resulted in her having to take them all back again – those that hadn't already been consumed – and redistribute them. Then, quite often, there would be a hysterical repeat of the procedure with a few aspirins thrown down her own gullet for good measure. This generally calmed her and reduced the threat of her driving the chef's long, razor-sharp knife between her senior's shoulder-blades.

With breakfast out of the way and Sister's appearance amongst the cornflakes registering the coming waking hours as a 'Grade One Alert' day, the residents split to their various morning activities. Many chose the garden, there being, according to one enthusiast, plenty of propagating to do in the greenhouse. Propagating? The Cavaliers had doubted certain aspects of this particular retired officer's character for some time and this seemed to confirm their worst fears.

With the compliant Roundheads out of the way and soaking up a dangerous cocktail of sun and fresh air whilst they propagated, the Cavaliers settled themselves in the lounge, quickly concealing themselves in Basil Reardon's smokescreen. There was serious mental work to be done – crosswords, obituaries, the Stock Market, Court Circulars and, hopefully, a number of column inches of salaciousness.

Tubes had often pondered the paradox that such stories of naughty goings-on tended to be more graphically reported in the broadsheets than the tabloids. Many hours of such pondering, and even longer spent in earnest discussion with his fellow Cavaliers, had led him to conclude that The Times, Telegraph and others of that ilk went into such detail because they respected the depth of intelligence and social concern of their readers who felt that they could handle the rude bits more maturely than those who dribbled over the tabloid accounts. Such mature people were also less likely to give it a go to see if it worked.

This didn't stop the Cavaliers from also dribbling over the tabloids themselves but only, of course, as a means of comparison which they felt was a necessary element of their research.

Tubes, as instigator and leader of this vital insight into the nation's social behaviour, was of a mind to offer himself to Women's Institutes and other such socially conscious bodies as an authority on 'salacious reporting' using his colleagues to read out extracts to illustrate his doctrine. Whilst noting his enthusiasm and wishing him well the others felt that this was probably the worst idea Tubes had come up with since he opted to choose Oldthorpe as his final port of call.

So the lounge was now an area of calm tranquillity, studious thought and deep concentration. Tubes, enthusiastically assisted by Freddy, was busily passing practiced eyes over today's papers – purely for research purposes – and finding a disappointing lack of reported dubious activity, Ainsley was noting a downward trend in his meagre Share portfolio and Basil an upward trend in Royal Family activity. Clarence Cuthbert, displaying solidarity with his fellow Cavaliers, was fast asleep in a deep armchair, only visible by his zimmer frame.

Through the open French windows could be heard the song of the birds and happy chatter of the Roundhead gardeners potting, planting and propagating to their hearts' content. These sounds, counterpointed by a few of Clarence's little noises now and again, suggested to Ainsley that, just for this moment at least, all was right with the world.

Then, of course, the peace was shattered, and who better to shatter it than the practised peace shattering voice of Sister Newbiggin which, as usual, preceded her into the room.

"We're expecting a new resident in a day or two to replace Colonel Hunter. Let us hope that he will fit in rather more easily with us than did the Colonel."

Ainsley was about to protest at this slur on their friend but Sister hadn't finished. She turned on him. "Same rank as you, I believe, Brigadier." She held up her hand as they all started talking at once. "I know no more than that. It is all that Mr Cartiledge has told me."

Ainsley now became very agitated. If this chap was senior to him on the Army List it would mean that he would assume unofficial command at Oldthorpe in his place and that would be bad news indeed.

"You must know his name, Sister, surely. I'll need to look him up – so that we can welcome him properly."

Sister Newbiggin was now at the hall door. "Oh, Bairstowe or something. The line was very bad and Mr Cartiledge tends to speak…" she wanted to say 'appallingly' but checked herself in time, "rather quickly."

"Now, all of you outside, please. We have this room to clean and polish before he arrives. We want to make a good impression, don't we?"

She was already bustling around, chivvying them out of their chairs and doing grievous bodily harm to the cushions. They stood awkwardly clutching their newspapers. One thing was certain – absolutely, categorically certain – they would not be bullied and would leave in their own good time.

Sister, now busily rearranging the furniture into neat lines, continued addressing them with hardly a pause for breath. "No new maid yet so we need help from those – that's you – who have nothing useful to do. There's dusting, hoovering, polishing…"

She looked up from retrieving a sticky sweet wrapping from the depths of Clarence Cuthbert's chair – and found she was talking to herself. The room was empty.

"Here we are. Oldthorpe House. Grand, eh?"

Phyllis Coombe put down the Brigadier's suitcase for a moment and flexed her numb hand. What on earth was in it? A phrase drifted through her mind from all those years ago when her Albert decided they'd get married. 'All my worldly goods…' She suddenly felt so sorry for all those poor souls finishing their lives in places like this one. And there she was, so happy in her little home with Albert and their George – when the two of them weren't, through no fault of their own, 'banged to rights'. And their boy had been so proud of her and Albert when they had got married. She smiled at the memory. He'd taken the day off school and had actually washed and worn a tie.

The Brigadier surveyed Oldthorpe House and, with great relief, recognised the imposing, double-fronted Victorian façade as something very similar to a number of Officers' Messes that had been a temporary home in all those different postings around the world. This would do. A half smile. This would have to do.

Without a word the two of them picked up the suitcases and trudged over the gravel to the front door.

Nurse Lisa Roberts had just about had enough. Since getting up at a stupidly early hour she'd helped the most elderly residents to dress, tended various minor ills with ointments, pills and spoonfuls, supervised breakfast, dispensed and redispensed medicines, checked the drug cupboard, ordered replacements, chatted and cheered up the down-hearted and generally lifted everyone's spirits with her warm, caring personality. And that was fine. Exactly what she was at Oldthorpe to do, and thoroughly enjoyed doing. BUT, and it was a very big BUT, once that morning routine was over and she should have been putting her aching feet up in the kitchen for a few moments' peace and a mug of coffee, she wasn't. Sister had decided on a spring clean and delegated to her a thorough going through of the hall, landing, lavatories and downstairs cloakroom.

This was not why she'd become a nurse and it certainly hadn't been in the job spec. for 'Supervising Nurse' at Oldthorpe House. It was, she decided having trawled the length and breadth of her vocabulary, a liberty, a right liberty.

She knew the problem of course: lack of domestic staff. But if that fat, greasy little owner, Gregory Cartiledge, had dipped into his pocket for a minute portion of his loose change, which he wouldn't even miss, they wouldn't be in this pickle.

For a moment, a week ago, it had seemed that something might happen. For some unaccountable reason the dreadful man had phoned Sister and, reversing all his previous meanness, ordered all manner of expensive changes to take place including appointing a new maid – maybe two – and increasing their measly pay to a semi-measly level.

Pigs might fly!

Sister had actually interviewed a would-be maid a few days since. Lisa had caught a glimpse of her and she'd seemed really nice; sort of motherly and maybe a little 'simple' but, Lisa reasoned, anyone coming here and working for Sister Newbiggin would need to be. Anyway, it probably wouldn't happen. Greasy Cartiledge would have changed his mind by now.

For the umpteenth time she resolved to look around for another post. Huh! How often had she said that? Every time she'd made the decision she'd thought of all these dear lovable old men. What would happen to them if the one 'bright spark' – that's what they called her – moved away to be replaced by a Matron Maud/Sister Newbiggin clone? It just couldn't be done.

So here she was. And here she'd have to stay.

With one more swirl of the lavatory brush around the inside of the pan she surveyed her handiwork. A spick-and-span downstairs cloakroom. But for how long? Poor old Captain Clarence. The others said that it was lucky he hadn't been in the Royal Artillery because his aim was so terrible. With a sigh she returned all the cleaning paraphernalia to the kitchen.

The afternoon was spent in uneasy calm by both the residents and staff. Sister Newbiggin, having raised the last vestiges of dust as she rushed around on her final inspection, had retired to her room with a self-imposed headache. If there was one thing that would totally scupper her chances of substantive Matron rank it would be a new resident's dissatisfaction leading to an early withdrawal and this, the Sister was determined, WOULD NOT HAPPEN.

Ainsley spent the siesta time making a fruitless search of the Army List, a mighty tome showing in order of seniority every serving and retired Officer in Her Majesty's Service, but couldn't find the name Bairstowe or anything like it under Brigadiers, Colonels or – perish the thought – Major Generals. He gained some comfort from finding his own name sandwiched amongst the Brigadiers.

Having been the senior Officer in the Home for so long, to be outranked would be devastating and it had never struck him that it might – or could – happen. It wasn't, he reassured himself, that he had ever 'pulled' rank. Of course not. The residents were one big happy family. He saw himself as just one of the crowd but, when the chips were down, as they so often were at Oldthorpe, someone had to be in charge and that someone must be him – because he was the senior rank – even though he saw himself as equal – which he wasn't – being senior.

Becoming seriously confused he calmed himself with a splendid phrase dredged from the deep recesses of his mind: 'First Among Equals'. Splendid. Even though, of course, he wasn't – being senior.

Brigadier Ainsley Bennington closed his eyes and willed himself into a troubled snooze.

Nurse Lisa was putting right the grandfather clock on the landing which, since one of the residents had attempted to mend it, now kept totally arbitrary time, when she heard through the open front door the sound of feet on crunching gravel. She quickly set the hands to eight minutes to four and scampered down the stairs. This was the big moment; a moment she had been waiting for ever since the last maid had stormed out hurling invective – words Lisa hadn't heard since school – to any and everyone in range of her.

Lisa's heart leapt up another notch when she saw that the crunching was caused, not by one person but two, each unaccountably lugging an obviously heavy suitcase. Two new maids. It was too good to be true.

"Front door open. No one on duty. Careless."

Luckily Brigadier Bristowe was so out of breath that these curt comments were lost in the gravel crunching, but with no more ado the two newcomers marched into the hall and, in perfect unison, dropped the cases onto the carpet.

"Oh wonderful, wonderful. Hello. I'm Nurse Lisa Roberts. General dogsbody, who's been 'Jack of all trades' round here for far too long. I'm..."

"That'll do, Nurse, thank you very much." The high, tinny voice of Sister cut through Lisa's excited gabble like a knife and, with a frosty smile, she brushed past her and advanced on the two women standing inside the front door.

It being unusual to have any activity at this quiet time of the day before tea brought the place to life again, it was a small audience that assembled at the various doorways leading off the hall. Ainsley and Tubes roused themselves from their siestas in the lounge and were ideally placed to see the lot, the chef eased open the kitchen door, and Clarence, ensconced once again in the downstairs cloakroom, peered out through the thinnest of cracks.

Sister surveyed the new arrivals and immediately recognised the small dumpy one. "Right, Lisa, this is Mrs Coombes..."

"Coombe, dear. But you can all call me Crumb. Everyone does. Well, those I know, you know. Not those I don't know."

Phyllis beamed her most beautiful smile to all of them in their various vantage points. It was what had first won the heart of her dear Albert who had been so overwhelmed that he had ravished her there and then – well, very nearly there and very nearly then. It still took him that way so she made a point of rationing the particular expression for moments when it suited her. And this was one of them.

Whilst all the others smiled back, Sister, being one of the few people to be totally unmoved, did not – and ravishing never entered her mind.

"Very well, Mrs Coombe," she emphasised the end of the name which annoyed them all, players and audience alike. "And please refer to me as 'Sister' from now on – what in heaven's name have you got there?" She had noticed the suitcase, and then the other one. "You're not thinking of boarding here, are

135

you? Quite out of the question."

Brigadier Bristowe, severely frowning, witnessed this extraordinary dialogue with a mixture of disbelief and frustration. It seemed that there would need to be a great amount of sorting out to be done.

Lisa now took over. "Come along now, dears. I'll show you where everything is. Sister wants you to meet everyone and see how we work before you start for real tomorrow."

She was bustling around them and her chivvying seemed to be having some effect because both of them found themselves moving towards the kitchen door where, to their consternation, the way was blocked by a large, unprepossessing man, holding a long, obviously very sharp knife.

"Mind out, Clint." Lisa brushed the chef to one side still chattering. "You can split the duties. Polishing, dusting, hoovering, washing, lavvies – look, that's Captain Cuthbert..." She wasn't sure why she did it, but she pointed to Clarence peeking through the cloakroom door. "You'll see a lot of him as you flit from one to the other. It's undies day tomorrow. That'll introduce you to our residents well enough."

Clarence mercifully stopped Lisa's flow just as it seemed to be getting out of control by pushing through them all, his zimmer, as usual, unerringly finding toes, before reaching the safe haven of the lounge and his fellow residents.

"Brigadier Lesley Bristowe." It was more of a command than an introduction.

"Dear Lord, no surely not. Not now. Where?" Sister pushed through to the front door and scanned the drive. "He could have waited until I got you two sorted."

"She, madam, SHE!"

"Stop making silly noises, pet. Off we go." Lisa tugged at the Brigadier's arm, but to no avail. Neither the arm, nor that to which it was attached, was going anywhere.

No one had noticed the brief absence of Sister, but now she returned at speed through the front door.

"He's nowhere to be seen. What were you talking about, Mrs...? I don't know your name. The Agency didn't tell me you were coming."

"BRISTOWE." This was ludicrous. "In all my years of

Service I've never …" The Brigadier got no further.

"Bristowe. Sounds familiar." Sister absentmindedly adjusted Phyllis's coat collar and brushed off some stray hairs. "Ah, yes. Oh Lord, this is going to be confusing. We have a new resident arriving with a similar name. Bairstowe or something like it. Now, you'd better come to my office and tell me about your years of service and all your other particulars."

"STOP."

They all stopped.

With such a command delivered with a power that belied the gaunt stature of the deliverer, there was no other course open to any of them. Pins would certainly have been heard dropping.

"I want no one to move or even whisper until you have listened very carefully to what I have to say. My name is Lesley Bristowe. I retired recently as a Brigadier in the Women's Royal Army Corps, I am honoured to be a Commander of the British Empire and am, the Lord help me, a new resident in your Home. And now if one of you will take me to your Matron Montague, you may all return to whatever it was you were doing before I and this kind lady arrived."

Still no one moved – except Ainsley who whispered to Tubes, "No wonder I couldn't find him in the Army list. He's a woman!"

"Is he now?" Tubes said a touch laconically.

Ainsley whispered on, "I didn't look under women."

"I did – once." Clarence shook a little more than usual causing his zimmer to rattle. "Nearly arrested. In the Far East. I was just looking at – oh, what was it called?"

Both Ainsley and Tubes moved Clarence back into the lounge and sat him firmly in a chair.

"Quiet, old boy." Tubes put his zimmer strategically out of reach. "You don't need to remember what it's called. Bits like that aren't for we chaps to know about."

Phyllis, having been brought up to respect the deep divide that exists each side of the green baize door, felt that none of this hoo-ha should be witnessed by the domestic staff and glided into the kitchen deftly taking the cook and his carving knife with her. This left Sister, Nurse Lisa, Brigadier Lesley and two large suitcases to act out the unfortunate scene on their own.

"Er, Brigadier?"

"Yes."

"It's you being a woman, you see."

"What is, Sister?"

"Pardon?"

"What is me being a woman, you see?"

"We thought you were a man."

"Really. What part of me deceived you into thinking that, Sister? My body? My clothes? My voice?"

"No, no. Please don't get me wrong. It's Matron Montague, you see."

"What is Matron Montague?"

Lisa felt that all this was getting none of them anywhere. Sister seemed to have gone all to pieces, and if she fiddled with her cuffs and collar one more time she'd strangle her.

Sister adjusted her belt and smoothed her pleats. "Matron Maud has left, Brigadier, and gave no hint that the new resident – yourself – would be a woman so we have all been rather – er, how should I say – startled." She swung round to Lisa and used her curtest voice. "I suggest you go about your duties, nurse. It is my place to sort out this – er – confusion."

Lisa was about to add Sister strangulation to her many other duties when her would-be victim, as if reading her mind, flew her hand to her neck.

"Oh Lord. I've put you in Colonel Hunter's old room between Brigadier Bennington and Major Reardon. That'll never do."

"I see no reason why they should be offended by my presence."

"Maybe not. But I see every reason why you should be offended by theirs. I'll put you in Matron's old room for the time being. Nurse, find Coombes…"

Brigadier Lesley was quickly in, "Coombe."

"Crumb." Lisa was not far behind. She drifted to the kitchen door to set in motion the transfer of bedding and other essentials from one rear wing to the other.

"You must excuse Nurse Roberts, Brigadier."

"On the contrary, Sister. I felt she kept a level head throughout this misunderstanding. Now, I should like to wash and brush up and then I'll be ready to meet my fellow residents. Perhaps you would arrange a pot of tea and some biscuits in my room. I am a trifle fatigued from the journey." With that Brigadier Lesley Bristowe ascended to the landing, leaving Sister standing in total confusion in the hall.

Ainsley and Tubes winced and waited for the explosion but to their amazement there was none. "Carry yer bags, lady?" Tubes whispered and winked as he and Ainsley took a suitcase each and lugged them upstairs.

As if on cue the grandfather clock struck midday.

If only it was, thought Sister. I could go out and miss the entire afternoon's fiasco. She looked at her fob watch. She'd have to wait a while before ringing Mr Cartiledge. He'd not be back from work before seven so it would give her a couple of hours or so to work out how she was going to break the news to the dreadful man. He'd undoubtedly explode and become confused so she would have to explain the mix-up simply and very clearly. She must emphasise that it was caused by her predecessor, Maud Montague, and that no blame could be placed on her own shoulders thereby affecting his decision regarding her elevation to the rank of Matron.

Perhaps a couple of aspirins and a little lie down for a few minutes might be a good idea…

8

Ten minutes after going upstairs Lesley Bristowe came out of the bedroom allotted to her by Sister onto the landing. Why was she so breathless? She'd only ever fainted once in her life and that was many years ago as a teenager but those first dizzy feelings had come back to her in a flash now. She leant against the doorframe and closed her eyes. In something approaching a panic she found the blackness to be infinitely worse and jerked them open again. She must focus on something – anything – to steady herself. The grandfather clock was the only furniture in sight and her pleasure at forcing herself to get a sharp image of it was rather spoilt by noting that it was about four hours slow.

Being a stickler for preciseness her automatic reaction was to put the clock hands right but she checked herself realizing that it was, at this moment in her life, about the least important thing she might do. What had she done? Surely there had been an alternative to this? Anything?

Nothing. She'd been through it all so many, many times.

Perhaps the room would look slightly more habitable once her bits and pieces were around it. What bits and pieces? A few photos of the family and others of major events in what had been an illustrious career. Amongst them was a picture taken after the investiture of the CBE at Buckingham Palace with her mother and sister. Her mother so proud – thank the Lord she wasn't alive to witness this – and her sister, then so jealous, now so smug – and she had a right to be; a successful husband, loving family...

Enough. She was spending far too much time these days in the unfamiliar state of feeling sorry for herself. It would have to stop and from now onwards she would put the past behind her and launch positively into the future. She would make a go of it come what may.

She was disturbed that despite never having set foot in Oldthorpe House before there seemed to be something familiar about it. She stood at the top of the stairs looking around but it was her nostrils that solved the mystery: the smell; a hot, elderly body smell, so uncannily similar to the nursing home where her mother had been incarcerated for the last part of her life. Near the end she had spent so much time with her and never, in her worst nightmares, had imagined that within such a short space of time she would be in a similar place. Hot, elderly body smells. She'd soon change that...

With a spirit of determination she hadn't shown for many a long month Brigadier Lesley Bristowe marched downstairs ready to take on all-comers – to be met by the old man with the zimmer, Captain Cathcart or something, coming out of what was obviously the cloakroom.

His face broke into a kindly, crinkly smile. "I've put the seat down as Sister commanded," he said as he crossed the hall towards the lounge.

"Jolly good." It was all Lesley could think to say.

"Pop it up again when you've finished there's a dear."

And with that he zimmered through the door.

In the lounge, with Clarence installed deeply in his armchair and, in no time gently snoring, Ainsley and Tubes considered the ramifications of the arrival of a female in their midst. Having spent their lifetimes steering well clear of women other than nurses, nannies, mummies and the odd – sometimes very odd – flirtation, the thought of, as Tubes rather ungallantly put it, "being shacked up with one until the dinner plate's handed in," frightened them out of their wits.

There were so many things to consider and these they whispered to each other as they looked out on the still-toiling gardeners. They'd have to watch their manners – Clarence would certainly have to suppress his little noises. Then there was their language which tended at times to be rather too expressive, their dress – zips zipped, braces braced, ties tied, matching socks and so on, and their stories – did they have any reminiscences suitable for female ears? The list of restrictions seemed endless.

Tubes grinned mischievously. "Don't let's tell the others. We'll get a bit of fun to compensate for the gloom ahead."

Ainsley wasn't at all sure that this would be acceptable or proper and feared, not for the first time, that the correct degree of etiquette was seriously diluted in certain branches of the Royal Navy, particularly submariners, immersed as they were in water for so much of their lives. He did, however, feel the need for a bit of fun after the severe shock to his system so, providing the good lady was not embarrassed – well, not unduly embarrassed – he reckoned he could go along with the idea. After all, it only meant not saying anything.

The two of them turned from the French windows – and received the fright of their lives. There, examining the bric-à-brac that posed as ornaments on the mantelpiece, was the Brigadier lady herself. How long had she been there? Had their whispers been whispered enough?

Before they could decide one way or the other who should come sauntering through the door but dear old Basil. Seeing the back of a tall thin woman at the fireplace he made a number of immediate assumptions and, in true army officer style, quickly 'appreciated the situation'. Here, he deduced with a degree of inaccuracy surpassing even that usually found in Artillerymen, was an unknown woman dusting, and that suggested a new maid already at her work. Courtesy decreed a friendly introduction.

"Ah, hello there. Reardon, Basil, Major, Royal Artillery, retired."

The lady turned slowly towards him. He began to feel a little unnerved as he often did when the opposite sex stared at him. He took a step backwards, always a difficult manoeuvre for him even on the parade ground.

"Yes, well, right. Jolly good. Glad you're here. Hope you'll get the laundry right. Last girl kept on giving me Freddy's underpants. Gunners wearing RAF-type knickers. Probably a Court Martial offence. Bad show. Don't mind me. Keep dusting."

Now thoroughly exhausted and wishing to escape what had become a penetrating gaze from a pair of gimlet eyes, Basil, his own eyes hollow from the ghastly experience, rushed towards the French windows where stood his two closest chums each, it appeared, in the early stages of hysteria.

"Extraordinary."

The imperious voice swung Basil around in mid rush causing him to lose balance and clatter into the Cuthbert zimmer.

At that moment he knew that something had gone terribly wrong. He was saved by Clarence who, awakened by the attack on his metal strength and stay, suddenly jerked upright.

"Kuala Lumpur. That was it." The old man subsided and the dust both metaphorically and literally settled again.

Brigadier Lesley bent over the old man rather, as Ainsley would recount later, like a heron about to take a fish.

"I beg your pardon?" This was clearly a query rather than an apology.

Clarence opened his eyes and, seeing this female face rather too close for comfort, sank even further into his armchair.

"Kuala Lumpur. Where I looked up the girl. That was it. Sorry."

This, thought Ainsley, is just it. The problem. Rude stories. Recipe for disaster. Time to assume command. "Clarence, old friend, I rather think…"

"I was twenty or so. Exploring the world. My mother told me to look up my cousin in Kuala Lumpur. Ugly little monster she was. Spots and all that. Why am I telling you all this?"

Being aware that Clarence's contribution was, as so often happened, leading events in totally the wrong direction, his question was ignored by everyone.

"Brigadier Lesley Bristowe." Her hand extended, she advanced on Basil who, believing she was announcing the arrival of the new resident, saw salvation and escaped past her towards the hall.

"Ah, good. We were expecting him. Come on chaps, let's welcome him to Oldthorpe House, poor old devil." He turned at the door and waved airily to Lesley. "Carry on dusting."

No one moved.

"What d'yer mean, she's a woman?"

Such a question from a very obviously world-wise man such as Gregory Cartiledge might have caused a moment's brow-knitting to a lesser person than Sister Amelia Newbiggin but she was made of sterner stuff and weighed straight in with the perfect answer.

"She is a female, Mr Cartiledge, of the female gender. Brigadier Lesley Bristowe, CBE, is, and I have no reason to doubt, always has been, a woman."

She had wisely chosen her bedroom phone for this awkward conversation with the owner and now, putting her hand over the telephone mouthpiece, let out a deep sigh which was quickly replaced by a large slug of that which she knew had ruined the career of her predecessor and, frankly, caring not a jot, would probably ruin hers. She remembered a splendid phrase she'd heard on some trashy television soap she had caught a few moments of: she'd 'had it in spades'. The gin anaesthetised her very pleasantly which she found comforting.

Gregory Cartiledge was in no way fazed at Sister's detailed explanation regarding the gender of the new resident nor its heavy sarcasm. Nor was he enlightened. He dug deeper.

"How can Leslie be a woman? Is he a – you know, one of them? Women's clothes an' all that? Hand on hip? Cascara?"

Sister's boiling point was usually fairly low but with the owner, in whose grubby hands lay the path to her future as substantive Matron, she forced herself to make an exception.

"Mascara, Mr Cartiledge and, no, he doesn't – I mean she doesn't wear women's – I mean she does – because, as I hope I have explained to your simple – er – I mean as simply as you – er – would wish me to, SHE IS A WOMAN."

The last four words were shouted but, she hoped, pleasantly, into the mouthpiece which was then covered again as a fresh supply of gin was poured into her glass.

"Leslie? Sounds daft."

"LesL-E-Y," she spelt the last three letters for him and knew as she did so that the hole into which she frequently popped herself whenever she attempted to converse with this stupid man was, as usual, getting deeper and deeper. After all, judging by the travesties that went for letters and his atrociously hand-written notes for the Home's notice board, he hadn't the first inklings of how to spell the simplest words.

Sister's voice was now at such a volume that everyone on the first floor could hear her. Luckily the cause of this dilemma, Brigadier Lesley, was in the garden admiring the Roundhead gardeners' handiwork, but Ainsley, Tubes, Basil and Freddy, pretending to be doing useful things on the landing, had been drawn towards Sister's bedroom door enthralled by her virtuoso performance.

Her realisation that correct spelling would be of little help was dead right.

"I don't care how he spells his name. He's money to me, and money – INCOME – is what the Home needs. Whatever you may think of him, we need him. Right?"

"HER. HER. Mr Cartiledge. Will you please come here ..." was she really saying this? "and see for yourself. SHE IS AS MUCH A WOMAN AS I AM."

"More, by the look of her." Tubes chuckled.

Basil approached the statement from the other end, as it were. "I wish she was a chap. I'd know how to deal with her if she was a chap."

"K.V." Squadron Leader Freddy, in his accustomed role of look-out, smiled somewhat inanely at Nurse Lisa as she came round the corner, his hand making a perfect landing on Ainsley's shoulder.

Lisa, a girl amongst four brothers, knew a gang of naughty boys when she saw them. "Gentlemen, please. The Staff Wing is strictly out of bounds as well you know. If you don't mind."

"I CAN'T HANDLE A WOMAN, Mr Cartiledge."

The voice through the door was higher, louder and tinnier than ever.

"Too true," murmured Lisa as she went on her way to her room.

The men, now back on their own territory on the landing strained to hear more, but to no avail. Sister's voice dropped to normal as did the temperature of the conversation and then, with no warning, her door was flung open and she marched out.

As one, the four of them sprang at the grandfather clock, each trying to get at the hands to adjust them and then, with their years of training to co-ordinate procedures in any emergency, they fell into an ordered routine. Ainsley held the glass door open, Tubes adjusted the hands, Basil studied his pocket watch and Freddy, still smiling inanely, flew a quick sortie over the banisters. The tableau was quite graceful and delicately formed in its own way but its finer points were totally lost on a very disturbed Sister Newbiggin.

"What are you all up to? Does it take four men to put a

145

clock right?"

"Only when it's very wrong, Sister." Basil had no idea why he said it but it just came out, its banality totally lost on Sister who had hardly been aware of her question, let alone the answer. She stormed down the stairs.

"Is the owner coming, then?" As usual Freddy set a whole squadron of cats amongst the pigeons.

Sister stopped dead on the bottom step and looked up at eight troubled eyes. "I see," was all she said as she marched into the kitchen.

Tubes sighed. "Well done, Freddy, old boy. Another landing with your undercarriage up."

"Like Laurel and 'Ardy, we was."

Phyllis Coombe paused in ironing her eighth sheet and chuckled. She was enjoying her first afternoon's work at Oldthorpe House and already felt very much at home in the kitchen. The chef, Jean-Paul, had allowed her to do some tidying up and drawer sorting, and then Nurse Lisa had bustled in and suggested a spot at the ironing board before helping to lay the tables for supper. That suited her well, and when it was done she would go back to Number 8 and tell Albert and George all about it before they set off on their night shift.

Jean-Paul, cursing the fact that however much he sharpened his big knife it wouldn't cut through the brisket's gristle, tapped Phyllis on the shoulder with it. "Who are they, then, Lorry and whatsit when they're at 'ome?" He set to sharpening the knife.

Phyllis looked up at him. Even though she had the kindest, gentlest of natures and wouldn't want to hurt a fly she couldn't help noticing how incredibly ugly the cook, for all his flashy ways, was.

She wiped bits of gristle from her shoulder. "Y'know? Them comedians. Americans. Laurel and 'Ardy. On the filums. And there we was in the 'all there. Me, short and fat – well, plumpish – and the Brigand tall and, well she needs a few square meals I reck'n. And there was Sister all 'et-up and you – ooh, you should've seen yourself. Laugh?"

Jean-Paul paused in his knife sharpening and wondered, doubtless accurately, whether Phyllis would be an easier dissection than the brisket. Phyllis, totally unaware of causing any offence, resumed her ironing.

"There you was with that knife in the doorway an' you reminded me of my George the other day at 'ome. 'E's about your age. Such a lad. Wouldn' 'urt a fly. This copper 'ad come to question 'im and my Albert about some coincidence regarding finger-prints and George, who 'ad a kitchen knife like yours only smaller in his 'and – I can't remember why – suddenly tripped over the edge of the carpet and sort of lunged forward, poor lad. If the copper 'adn't shifted smartish 'e'd 'ave been a gonner and no mistake. An' do you know what?"

"Don't tell me."

"I will. They 'ad 'im on attempted GBH." She put down the iron. "It was my evidence what got 'im orf. I said 'e'd always 'ad dizzy spells, and so 'e 'ad. Since a nipper. The doctor confirmed it. 'E said that if they still 'ad the right sort of places 'e'd recommend they took George in for a rest." She sounded very proud about this and added, "But they 'aven't no more. So they can't."

For some reason he couldn't fathom Jean-Paul was beginning to feel somewhat uneasy alone with Mrs Coombe and was rather glad to have his big knife handy, but before he could think of a way of stemming the flow, Nurse Lisa rushed in.

"Hello. Jolly good. Settling in. Lovely ironing. Oh, Jean-Paul, can't you cut that up a bit?"

All this was said at great speed as, whilst hurtling around the room, she saw the chef pick up the uncuttable gristle and drop it into a saucepan in one big lump.

Jean-Paul shrugged. "It'll boil nicely for 'em. Something to suck on."

This deserved a stinging admonition but Nurse Lisa was now way beyond the brisket. She seemed to be carrying out a fairly intimate examination of herself, kneading, feeling, prodding and squeezing parts that her charges around the house would love to have kneaded, felt, prodded and squeezed for her.

"The key. Dear Lord. The key. The drugs cupboard. Padlock. Damn Sister. Sorry. It's gone."

Phyllis had no idea what she was talking about but Jean-Paul knew only too well. He'd witnessed the ructions the day

Sister took over from Matron, when she'd insisted that a padlock and hasp be fixed to the drugs cupboard to augment the door lock as extra protection. Nurse Lisa saw this as totally unnecessary and had, subconsciously probably, got some satisfaction from never putting the extra key on her bulging key ring. And now she couldn't find it.

"They'll need them at supper. Their medicines. Sister will be furious. Livid. She's in a bad enough mood as it is. Oh Lord..." She collapsed at the table and put her face in her hands.

"There you are, luvvie. It was inside all the time. You must 'ave shut it in last time you used it."

Lisa couldn't believe her eyes. There was the drugs cupboard wide open and Phyllis handing her the padlock and the missing key.

"I find these so useful." She held up a ring on which were a number of short metal probes all shaped differently. "Albert gave 'em to me one birthday. He said 'e'd bought them in Woolworths or somewhere. I'm such a scatterbrain. Always losing keys." Then she went back to the ironing.

"It's really nice to make your acquaintance." Gloria Cartiledge took Brigadier Lesley's hand, giving it a little squeeze. Such were their differences in height that, whilst Gloria had her arm above her shoulder level, Lesley's was hardly above her own waist. "I can't imagine why my husband thought you were a man."

"Sit down, Gloria."

The command was hissed at her by her equally minute husband but after years of reminding herself that she was not now his secretary but, God help her, his wife, she no longer scampered when so commanded; instead she made gracefully towards an armchair and delicately sat herself down in it.

The arrival of the Cartiledges had produced the usual hilarious charade for the watchers at the lounge window; the enormous Rolls rolling up, the occupants' heads just poking above the window sills, then the two of them jumping down to the ground and Sister's awkward curtsey-like welcoming followed by the procession into the house with Gregory storming ahead, Sister talking fit to bust and trying to catch up with him, and little Gloria, the same bird's nest balanced precariously on her head, making her own way, at her own speed, very much her own person.

In no time they were in the lounge, and those residents who had decided to attend the confrontation between the owner and the new resident moved from the window to various vantage points around the room. They had decided on this simple tactic to help throw confusion on the proceedings by making their target, the Gruesome Gregory, shift from one to the other as the shots were fired.

Whether Lesley would have approved of this is doubtful. Not wishing to be the centre of attention she wanted a clear, concise exchange and an acceptance of her position at Oldthorpe. Then they could all get on with their own lives.

"Of course you know you can't stay." Gregory did not believe in preamble and knew neither the meaning nor the spelling of subtlety.

"Oh really, Gregory…"

"Quiet, Gloria."

Lesley sat herself slowly in an armchair and Freddy, for no reason whatsoever other than inborn etiquette, adjusted a cushion behind her head. With infinite calmness she fixed Gregory with an icy stare.

"I know of no such thing, Mr Cartiledge. Your Matron was, of course, well aware that I was – am – a woman and she was happy to accept me with that knowledge. The contract was signed accordingly."

"Matron's gone."

"I am now aware of that but, I would hazard a guess, as your delegated representative at the time, the contract is still binding."

This generated loud murmurs of, "Hear, hear," "Well done," "Thirty-love," and similar support from the others in the room.

A flutter, similar to a small bird flapping its wings, came from the depths of Gloria's armchair as she more or less silently clapped her hands in agreement.

"Right, Sister, I want everyone else out – now. This is a private matter." Gregory struck a pose at the fireplace that reminded Basil of Mussolini. A remarkable resemblance, he thought.

"I think not, Cartiledge." Ainsley stepped forward. "If our splendid new resident is happy for us to be here, we stay. After all, I assume that it is we rather than you who should be making the decision in that we shall be living with her – and she with us."

More supporting murmurs greeted this but inevitably it merely added fuel to the fire. Sister decided to chuck a can of petrol into the blaze.

"Mr Cartiledge is the owner, Brigadier, and it is he who decides who lives here and who doesn't and ..." her voice became tinnier than ever, "that applies to existing as well as new residents."

Before the inevitable explosion at this sycophantic rubbish could erupt, Gregory, who had been trying to speak when Sister interrupted, swung attention back to himself in the simplest possible way – and one which had served him throughout his doubtful career as Chairman of Cartiledge World Armaments: he shouted.

"SHUT UP."

This elicited three distinct reactions. Sister sat down very suddenly and feared that, for the second time in one day she might burst into tears, Ainsley, tall and gaunt, advanced on Gregory making the little man retreat further into the fireplace and Clarence woke up with a start and made a little noise.

"Land Ho." Tubes signalled his usual response to the ship's siren-like sound from Clarence and there was a moment's respectful silence.

"Pardon?" Gregory was confused by Tubes.

"Not at all, old boy. I thought it was good old Clarence here. It can happen to the best of us. Beans for breakfast?" Tubes knew how to confuse confusion. Life in a submarine was full of noises.

"What? Oh, to hell with it. If I says she goes..."

"SHE? SHE? Have you no manners, sir?" Ainsley was enjoying this.

Again bird's wings fluttered in Gloria's armchair.

Lesley's stare hadn't wavered from Gregory's puffy eyes. "Let us get back to the point. Obviously my fellow residents will have their say and I would be willing to consider abiding by their decision. As for me, I have no qualms, no qualms at all about being amongst them. After all, I've messed with men most of my service life."

Whilst the audience fully understood what Lesley meant by the last sentence, Gregory, with no knowledge of Officers' Messes, took the obvious interpretation and was about to make a scathing remark when Clarence interrupted not, this time, with one of his noises but, instead, a loud laugh.

"Manuella was like that. We were warned to steer clear of her. Spain it was. I was passing through. Very few escaped Manuella. I remember one night…"

"Squadron Leader." Sister was tugging Clarence from his chair. "As usual it would help us all if you would take Captain Cuthbert out for a walk in the garden." She steered Clarence towards Freddy who, fearful that if he didn't leave quickly he himself might perform a pre-emptive strike on Gruesome Gregory, was only too pleased to lead the old man and his zimmer out into the garden.

"I assume she was finding it very hot because she took all her clothes off…" Clarence's voice died away leaving all those in the lounge in different states of silence and contemplation.

Tubes was the first to recover. "So, what do we think? Come on, we're all here. You lot in the hall, come on in." The Roundhead element sidled reluctantly into the room. "Five, seven, eight, right, eleven, fourteen of us. How do we say? Brigadier Lesley stays?"

There was no doubting the emphasis in his voice as he raised his own hand quickly followed by Ainsley and Basil. Clarence at the French windows, having taken one look at the garden and seen enough, raised a quivering hand and Freddy behind him flew a sortie into the clouds as his sign of agreement. Five so far. Not good enough.

Ainsley, feeling a push was needed, turned to Tubes. "You know that idea of yours for football in the garden. Grand idea. Goal posts at each end – those bamboo canes in the vegetable patch will do…"

Tubes was straight in. "Nets from the fruit cages. Flower beds as ball stoppers. We'll need to hack up the lawn a bit…"

Ainsley passed the ball back. "Splendid. Two teams. Cavaliers versus Roundheads. Didn't you play rugger, old man?

Dirty player I believe."

"And you were a boxer. No rules. Just pitch in."

"Unless…" Ainsley held his hand up. "Unless Brigadier Lesley were to bring a rather calmer influence to bear on us."

After all their hard work in the garden neither was surprised to see six Roundhead hands raised around the hall door.

"Unanimous, I think. So there we are, Cartiledge old bean." Tubes settled himself into an armchair and his fellow footballer did the same.

"Now look here you…" Gregory was Mussolini-ing again.

"Potter. Commander Tubes Potter, Royal Navy."

"All right, Potter. What I …"

"Commander Potter. Ranks are important to us here, Cartiledge."

"Mr Cartiledge…." Hands on hips. He had to be Mussolini.

Freddy piped up. "Aircraftsman Cartiledge. As we said, ranks are …"

"QUIET." Gregory actually stamped his foot, just like El Duce. Then he ruined it all. "I'm a millionaire!"

There was silence for a moment and then, uncontrollably, they started to giggle and the bird's wings flapped fit to bust. Gregory suddenly felt very silly. "Well I am. So there. And what I says goes."

Basil winced. "Say goes."

"Hate the stuff." Clarence tottered into the room. "And semolina. But Sister won't listen. We have to eat it all up."

Lesley marvelled at the old man. How did he always manage to stop everything in its tracks? There was total silence as he made his way through to his hall cloakroom hide-away, zimmer legs making painful contact with toecaps as usual.

Gregory had had more than enough. "So, that's it. Decided." He marched up to Brigadier Lesley. "I'll give you a couple of days and then you're out. Right? It won't work. And anyway, it'll show you all that I'm the owner. I decide. And what I says – say – goes. So there." In a stunned silence he marched through the door, scattering Roundheads as he barged through.

"GREGORY." They'd never heard such volume from Gloria. She was out of her chair in a flash and storming after him. "You can't. You can't possibly. It's not fair."

Through the net curtains they all watched the end of the dreadful episode as Gregory heaved himself up into the Rolls, his voice so loud that it seeped through the glass.

"Fair? Fair? Why should I be fair? I own them. Own them all. Get in. We're off."

Sister helped Gloria up into the car and with a mighty churning of gravel, it swung out into the road.

And that was, undoubtedly, that.

The atmosphere in the Rolls was decidedly chilly. Gregory and Gloria, lost in the sumptuousness of the big leather seats, were each deep in their own thoughts – which was hard on other road users because Gregory, unable to keep a chauffeur for more than a few days at a time, was at the wheel.

His thoughts ranged over every aspect of the recent Oldthorpe meeting: Sister's lack of control; the previous Matron's idiocy in accepting a woman resident; the woman herself – hoity-toity and too clever and stuck-up by half; those blasted men who, he was sure, were mocking him but he couldn't work out when and how. On top of all that there was his own Gloria who seemed to be getting too big for her tiny little boots. She'd taken to reminding him of their Nuptial Agreement. Thinking it was something to do with sex he'd happily signed it at the wedding ceremony without reading it and then, when Gloria had insisted that he did, he saw that far from the pleasures of the flesh, the content concerned itself with the distribution of the Cartiledge fortune should, perish the thought, the marriage founder – and the distribution appeared to be heavily weighted in his little wife's favour.

Fuming, Gregory stamped on the accelerator causing the Rolls to surge forward alarmingly. He could see the inscription on his tombstone now: 'He failed to read the small print'.

Gloria's thoughts were fewer and less sweeping than her husband's. She just thought that her Gregory was a chump!

The big car glided on. Those Rolls Royce advertisers were right, thought Gloria, you could hear the dashboard clock ticking but only in between her husband's grunts and curses. And then the cork popped out of the bottle and the fizz that was Gregory's pent up anger squirted everywhere. True to form he poured his fury on the person nearest to him who, at this time, was of course his wife.

"I saw you flapping your arms. What happened to loyalty?"

Gloria smiled. "Credit where it's due, love. I didn't think you'd want any support – certainly not from a woman." She stressed the last word so that maybe even her silly husband could get the point, but irony was not something that Gregory Cartiledge would ever understand.

"I sorted them though. Sorted them proper. How dare they try to pull one on me. How DARE THEY?" The end shout was accompanied by a loud blast from the two-tone horn as a small mini-car was sent scuttling into the gutter. "Pulling rank they were," he snarled. "I outrank them all now. Ex-AC-plonk sorting out all them officers." His chuckle sounded like a sink emptying and made his wife feel rather sick.

Gloria dared to smile again. She was enjoying this. "But they all wanted the lady to stay. They put their hands up. They're the ones who've got to live with her, not you, pet." She was tempted to add, "She wouldn't half sort you out," but decided that as her life was literally in her husband's podgy little hands at this moment it would be rather unwise.

"Women should know their place. You know your place."

Anywhere but here, thought Gloria, as a cyclist was sent off down a side road that was not his intended route. Gregory fumed on.

"Women officers. Rubbish. Take orders from a woman? Rubbish."

Not for the first time Gloria was struck by the paucity of her husband's vocabulary.

"I'll give 'em orders."

You do, indeed you do, but thank heavens, no one at Oldthorpe seems to obey them. Gloria was disappointed that she hadn't said that out loud but the sight of a pram-pushing woman about to set off across a fast-approaching zebra suggested it would be unwise.

"When I says run, people run. Else they're out."

Yes, but which way do they run? Judging by the regular resignations of most of his office and domestic staff it seemed to

Gloria to be a one-way race. Again, she said nothing but as she sat gripping the seat as her husband literally swept everything before him a simple plan was forming in her mind. How vulnerable they are, these men, she thought. How very vulnerable.

With a jerk the Rolls turned into the long driveway leading to Cartiledge Towers. Gloria sighed. The end of another long, noisy, bad-tempered week. Tomorrow was Sunday. And she hated Sundays.

Phyllis Crumb was back at 8, Gas Lane by eight o'clock exhausted but happy. It had been a grand introduction to Oldthorpe House and she'd loved every moment of it. They'd all been so kind, and Nurse Lisa had plonked a big kiss on her forehead, which was as far as she could bend down at that time in the evening, and said, "Oh, Crumb, you're a breath of fresh air. How we need you." Lovely. Tomorrow she'd teach Jean-Paul how to handle gristly brisket. Not a problem. Albert had given her a lovely set of kitchen knives only the other day that looked nearly new.

The house was unusually quiet. Eight o'clock? They didn't usually leave for work before ten or eleven. Strange. The note on the kitchen table in Albert's big capital-letter writing explained it all.

FUZZ HAS TAKEN US IN.
MISUNDERSTANDING AS USUAL.
SUPPER IN MICROWAVE. PRESS HIGH AND
FIVE MINUTES.

Poor Albert and George. Had the police nothing better to do?

The corned beef hash was delicious. She washed the plate and, slipping into her cerise frilly nightie, popped into bed where all her hard work soon had its effect; in a matter of minutes she was fast asleep.

A moment later she sat bolt upright.

What microwave? Where had that come from?

"Is Little Red Riding Hood ready for a visit from the Big Bad Wolf?"

Gregory Cartiledge loved Sunday mornings. They'd played this game ever since Gloria, astutely gauging the possibility of a radically changed lifestyle from the misery in which she was then living, had succumbed to Gregory's amorous advances and become 'Mrs Cartiledge the Fourth'.

The Big Bad Wolf slipped out of his vast bed in the vast bedroom in his vast mansion and drew his thick cotton nightshirt over his head. Then, as naked as the day he'd been unfortunately born, he padded across the vast carpet making revolting wolf-grunting noises towards Gloria's vast bed on the far side of the room. It was as far away from him as she could get and still, technically and legally, 'sleep with him' as the carefully drawn-up Nuptial Agreement had stipulated.

The Sunday morning ritual was, as far as Gregory was concerned, going according to plan and now would come the moment when his ardour – and other bits – would be roused by the sight of little Gloria apparently shaking with fear in her bed, the sheets drawn tightly up to her chin.

For her, in this macabre game, the shaking had never been a problem: it was automatically caused by giggling hysterics at the ludicrous apparition both bearing and baring down on her.

But this Sunday morning the ritual suddenly went seriously wrong. There was no Gloria shaking in the bed: there was no Gloria at all. Instead, on the pillow, lay a card on which was written:

"The Scheduled Service has been WITHDRAWN until further notice"

Gloria was proud of her wording even though she knew that it wasn't original having copied it down from a sign she'd often seen at the bus station.

Her husband stood there, nakedly quivering. Ardour gone, rousing gone, grunting gone. He looked just like a little boy who'd lost his toffee-apple and was about to burst into tears. But no tears were forthcoming; Gregory Cartiledge's tear ducts had dried up and fallen off many years ago. Instead, his system clicked into a much more familiar programme: he flew into a rage.

"GLORIA?" He bellowed onto the landing.

"Yes, dear?" The little, calm voice of his beloved came from just alongside his left ear and, despite being little and calm, made him jump out of his goose-pimpled, naked skin.

"Why not pop something on, pet? It might stop our most recent housekeeper from leaving even before she's unpacked her bags."

Gregory pulled his fully-dressed wife into the bedroom and slammed the door. With a little shudder she draped a dressing-gown around his shoulders and other bits. Men looked so silly naked and Gregory, she didn't wonder, sillier than most.

"What's the meaning of this?" He held up the notice.

"It means, dear husband, exactly what it says. To take a phrase you yelled at me in the car yesterday evening just as you were trying to send an innocent cyclist to his Maker, women do know their place. It is to see that their husbands do the right thing. That they're fair. Considerate." She realized that she was ladling it on a bit thickly as far as Gregory's health was concerned, but with him speechless for once it was too good an opportunity to miss.

"So, until you carry out the wishes of all those dear old men at Oldthorpe and agree that the Lady stays …" She opened the bedroom door and stood on the threshold, "Normal Service will NOT be resumed."

With that she smiled, inclined her head, and left, gently closing the door behind her.

On Tuesday morning the news reached Oldthorpe House via a curt telephone message to Sister from the owner that, after due consideration, Brigadier Lesley Bristowe CBE would be installed as a resident of the community.

No one, of course, knew of the tense, noisy and damaging two days of negotiations that had just taken place in Cartiledge Towers.

The Big Bad Wolf and Little Red Riding Hood would tussle together again in their Sunday romps – but who, now, would have the sharper claws?

9

Lucy Banbury was the first person to spot that all was not well at Oldthorpe House or, to be more precise, amongst its resident Cavaliers. They were now roaming into Flaxton and joining her in the promenade shelter pretty well every day; not just one or two at a time as was usual but all five of them together. And that wasn't all; they appeared listless, like little boys who couldn't think of a game to play, which, in effect, was exactly their problem.

Their conversation, once lively and interesting, was now dull and punctuated by long silences. If there had been pebbles to kick around they would probably have kicked them but, as a substitute, they took to hurling shingle from the beach as far as they could throw it, which, as it swiftly became a macho competition, she felt was better than nothing. Eventually, after scoring a direct hit on a couple of young lovers hidden below the distant shingle ledge, causing them to jump up in alarm and very little else, Lucy, summoning all her school teaching experience, ordered the Cavaliers to stop being silly – which, of course, they immediately did.

After two weeks of this childish behaviour she gathered them into the shelter and sat them down on the hard wooden seat. It was, she felt, time for a bit of straight talking.

"I expect you to tell me if I am interfering but you won't be surprised I am sure if I mention that you all have seemed a trifle quiet and, well, not yourselves these past two weeks. Have you a problem you would like to share with me?"

The silence that followed this gently put inquiry was as much to do with their surprise that they appeared to others in any way different from their usual selves as the fact that none of them could think what to say. As usual on such occasions they turned to their senior officer and he reluctantly accepted the challenge.

"It's this new woman, d'you see, Lucy?" Ainsley found this hard to do. It was like being hauled up in front of the class to confess a misdemeanour. "We feel constricted. Not able to get on with our ordinary lives. We've been used to being…" He was lost for the word.

"Men?" Lucy came to his rescue.

"Precisely that."

"Have you thought about what it is that has so changed your lives since this woman joined you all?" Like all good schoolteachers her tactic was to get her charges solving the problem themselves by dint of some gentle questioning.

Tubes always felt uncomfortable in these situations and said gruffly, "No idea. The blasted Roundheads don't seem fazed in the slightest."

"Perhaps they're more used to women," Basil added mournfully.

Lucy cleared her throat but decided to let the indelicacy of the remark pass. Basil obviously didn't mean any offence being, she felt, the most gentlemanly of them all.

"Is that really why you think your friends the Roundheads are, to use your word, unfazed? It's hardly likely, is it?"

"Can't think of another explanation." Ainsley wondered if they should ever have started this.

"And what is it you cannot now do that you were doing before she came?" Again the quiet but firm voice. They felt that any moment now they were going to be given detention.

"Er, well…" Ainsley decided to delegate. "Tubes?"

"Now we have to watch the language. Be careful with jokes. That sort of thing."

"The 'sort of thing' you employ when you're with me?" Lucy smiled sweetly at them.

"Absolutely. Because you're a woman, do you see." Ainsley thought the reason was pretty obvious but felt obliged to offer it to Lucy.

"And your new resident – isn't?"

Now they were stumped, clean bowled and caught at the wicket. No appeal was necessary, the innings was very definitely closed.

In the ensuing silence Clarence, assisted by Freddy, reappeared from his usual trip to the gents which provided them with an opportunity to try to retrieve the situation by changing the subject.

Ainsley felt that he again should take the lead. "Jolly good. Welcome back."

"Everything all right?" Basil's offering opened the way to a dangerous downward spiral involving Clarence's little problem.

"I think so although I may have to go again in a moment. You see…"

He got no further. Tubes, feeling that they had shared intimacies for long enough, sprang up and advanced to the balustrade. He turned to them and with legs apart and hands clasped behind his back took his favourite 'command of the bridge' stance, gently rising up and down on the balls of his feet as he was wont to do on such occasions. He addressed them from somewhere deep within his white, woolly beard.

"It's simple. Our trouble, chaps, is that we are now being required to act like the gentlemen we once were. For too long we've been behaving like smutty boys. It's time we mended our ways."

Not bad for a torpedo officer who had spent much of his life in the smut of the wardroom.

Freddy nodded vigorously. "Absolutely, Tubes. Keep the smut for The Anchor, eh?" He could always be relied upon to douse any crowning moment with a bucket of water.

Lucy stood – they all stood. She pulled on her gloves and hung her handbag over her arm.

"Well done, Commander. I think you've solved your little problem. Of course you must be allowed to let your hair down occasionally, we all must, but your new resident has given you the opportunity to behave as the real gentlemen I know you to be."

It was usual for the Cavaliers to stroll along the High Street with Lucy and then duck into the pub but today they stayed back at the shelter after she had set off home. The truth of the matter was that, like Tubes, they felt rather chastened and embarrassed at the exposure of their shortcomings in front of a stranger. No one said anything for a while and then Ainsley broke the unusual silence.

"Well done, Lucy, getting to the nub of the problem. I trust you weren't including me in your allusion to smut, Tubes? I well remember putting Corporal Tremlett on a charge for insubordination…" He got no further.

"Your round, I think, Ainsley." Tubes set off at a brisk pace towards the pub. "Then we must get on back and mend our ways."

The Cavaliers were not the only residents to feel the strain of the arrival of Brigadier Lesley; so did she! As her newly acquired colleagues manoeuvred around each other in an attempt to avoid treading on her toes or causing any sort of confrontation, she became more and more frustrated to the point when she would have happily boxed all their ears.

As they summoned up every vestige of etiquette and courtesy which in their long careers had been displayed automatically, but in monastic retirement had now sadly lapsed, they would have been surprised and somewhat miffed to know that all their efforts were causing her deep discomfort and not a little dismay. Try as she might she couldn't find a way of relaxing everyone short of hanging naked from a chandelier and singing bawdy songs. With no handy chandelier and a reluctance during her Service life to hear, let alone learn, any of the bawdy songs sung on various occasions in Officers' Messes, she was saved having to make a 'will or won't' decision.

Sister Newbiggin was also treating her very warily. A bit of elderly man bullying – she called it cajoling – was one thing, but trying the same tactics on an older, far more world-wise and sophisticated woman was quite something else. Nurse Lisa, on the other hand, had no problem whatsoever; she just mixed easily with everyone provided they were pleasant to her, and once Brigadier Lesley had accepted that she was a nurse and not a servant they got along swimmingly.

The positive result of all this wariness was a newfound peacefulness around the place. No one shouted, no one scoffed, no one schemed, everyone felt fitter and more at peace with the world and, miracle of all miracles, Captain Clarence's innards settled down and whilst not functioning totally normally at least stopped having a rather noisy life of their own.

There was, however, one fly in the ointment. The five Cavaliers, having no excuse for a joust, cut, thrust or parry, were bored. It was no good talking about 'mending ways' when all it did was stop you doing the things you enjoyed most, leaving a chap with no alternative but to aimlessly mooch about the place. Desperate times called for desperate measures and so, with much foreboding, they each sought their own solution.

Freddy, under cover of dusk, went on a sortie out into the garden dragging Clarence as his wheelbarrow behind him. Whilst his fellow Cavaliers lolled in front of the television jumping up and down every time Lesley entered the room he took instruction from a Roundhead gardener and was allowed to do a bit of tidying up.

He entered into this new activity with an abandon previously reserved for his wartime Spitfire sorties ordering Clarence to move in V formation just behind and to his left pushing his zimmer to which was attached an open sack. Freddy could then more or less hurl rubbish over his shoulder whilst devoting all his concentration on deciding what was, was not or might be, suitable for chucking. Unfortunately Clarence, having been in the Royal Signals rather than the RAF, had never flown in formation and would have brought certain death to anyone around him if he had, so the result was a scattering of weeds and bits of precious plants all over the lawn and himself. It was not long before the Roundhead gardeners forcibly ended their sortie and landed them in armchairs alongside their TV viewing colleagues.

As part of his boredom-relief Brigadier Ainsley chose a moment one morning to pop into Miss Gribble's topiary class. All sorts of plants were provided for snipping, and the regulars – needless to say, Roundheads – merrily snipped away producing from Yew and Box shapes which, with considerable degrees of imagination, might be birds, mammals, gnomes and occasionally anti-aircraft guns and battleships.

How much nicer they looked in their natural state, thought Ainsley, but, nothing ventured, nothing snipped. Miss Gribble completed the shaping of a stunning peacock, leaving a few stray twigs for the Brigadier to practice on. Snip, snip went the scissors, "eek," or something similar went Miss Gribble, and onto the floor went the complete tail still sporting its exquisitely fashioned fan!

He did, of course, apologise gracefully and very fully. He even offered to find some sticky tape and perform a tail graft but Miss Gribble, in a shaking voice, declined the offer and suggested that, for the next week or two – she hoped forever – he might care to watch rather than wield. Ainsley, with a slightly stiff little bow, withdrew.

Basil had only a little more success with his foray into interesting activities. He found in a cupboard full of board games – the Cavaliers had long since changed the spelling to 'bored' – something that was labelled 'Painting By Numbers' which suggested that it was 'fun for young and old alike with mixed abilities'. He showed it to Tubes who observed that the description well suited his friend who could behave both childishly and decrepitly almost simultaneously and, as an Artilleryman, certainly had mixed abilities. Then, whilst Basil was elsewhere, he displayed his own brand of infantile mischief by changing over the numbers on the top of the paint pots.

Basil set to with a certain degree of will and, to Tubes's surprise, failed to notice the wicked deception as he applied as neatly as he was able with a shaking hand and through a fog of tobacco smoke the numbered paints to the same numbered squares. The picture, which was intended to be a reproduction of one of Renoir's jolly scenes in a French café, began to resemble the surface of a very untidy artist's palette but Basil who, like all boys, failed to refer to the plans – in this case the original picture on the cover of the box – painted on.

Tubes, having at first found the wheeze hilarious, began to have serious doubts regarding the deception as his friend toiled on day after day. He was eventually forced to raid the artist's studio and put the lids back on the right pots. He knew this would be too late to completely retrieve the situation but it might help from now on. To his surprise the painting continued on its downward path due, it later transpired, to Basil's misunderstanding regarding number matching from pot to paper and the fact that he was partially colour-blind.

Tubes wasn't to know that near the start of his career in the Royal Artillery Basil had been quickly removed from the gun site due to his inability to differentiate between red coded high explosive shells and green coded smoke shells. The result was that an enemy destined for slaughter found himself merely kippered.

Tubes himself, noting with dismay the decline into reckless activity that boredom had brought upon his fellow Cavaliers, took to standing for long periods of time in front of the lounge fireplace perfecting his habit of rising and falling rhythmically on the balls of his feet. He felt that 'feeling the ship' was the best contribution he could make at this time and it also saved him having to get up every time Lesley came into the room.

Near the end of this fortnight's lull which was, thought Sister, rather like a muggy spell before a thunderstorm, she came bustling into the lounge and found Tubes 'balling' up and down, his blue eyes lost in the mass of white whiskers covering his face.

"Really, Commander. Here you are again. Everyone else at it and…"

"And I am not at it, Sister." The blue eyes twinkled and, to her dismay, Sister experienced a tiny frisson of a 'turn'.

"You Cav…" no, she wouldn't admit to knowing their silly nickname, though she did rather like it. "You five, you're all the same. So unlike my front-room residents."

Basil, now very cheery with his discovery of the latent artist in him – his Renoir, declined for exhibiting in the lounge by his colleagues, hung proudly in his bedroom – drifted into the room. "How dare you liken me to Tubes here, Sister. Or Ainsley. Or Freddy. Or even dear old Clarence. Whilst I am pure of mind, these bounders are riven with grievous faults. I have none." And with that he plonked into an armchair.

"Except setting fire to things." Sister lined up the chairs.

"Except setting… Now then, Sister, what an accusation. As you know, your Court Martial exonerated me. No deadly weapon was found in the ashes."

"I wonder why that was?" Sister did a bit of GBH to the cushions.

Tubes, as the remover of the said weapon from the scene, resumed his up-and-downers rather more urgently. In that he had absolutely no answer to the question it seemed the best thing to do.

Basil could stand no more of this deceit. It just wasn't his style.

"Sister, I think I should..."

As Tubes was contemplating smothering his friend under one of the newly plumped-up cushions, a saviour appeared in the shape of a familiar large motor car purring into the drive.

"Oh no, surely not. The Owner." Sister rushed from the room.

Gregory Cartiledge's Rolls Royce whispered to a halt at the front door. Tubes and Basil crowded to the window to watch the splendid tableau that was identically re-enacted whenever the beastly little man and his charming little wife graced Oldthorpe with their presence, and sure enough it started with the usual obeisance from Sister. They were trying to decide whether to giggle or be sick when, to their amazement, the routine was thrown into disarray because, instead of Gruesome Gregory, a smartly uniformed chauffeur stepped down from the driving seat and, with a military bearing of which the audience approved, marched round to the passenger door and helped Gloria Cartiledge to dismount. The next moment the three of them were on their way to the front door.

"Do please come in here, Mrs Cartiledge. Gentlemen, perhaps you would retire to your rooms – or somewhere." Sister was bustling again. Sister's bustle was always a dangerous sign and usually, as now, brought out the worst in Tubes.

"We've already retired once, Sister – and look where it got us."

Basil, embarrassed by such behaviour in front of non-inmates of Oldthorpe, butted in quickly.

"Of course we will, Sister. Good afternoon, Mrs Cartiledge and...?" He raised an eyebrow at the chauffeur.

"Simmonds, sir." Obviously one of us, thought Basil. The chap nearly saluted.

Gloria sat daintily on the settee. "Pop into the kitchen, Simmonds, and ask cook for a cuppa. And don't move, please. I want a bit of family around me just now and you're the nearest I've got to one. Tea all round, Sister?"

It's rather difficult to speak coherently through clenched

teeth but Sister just managed it. "Of course, I'll tell cook, er, chef." She marched out.

Everyone seems to be marching this afternoon, thought Basil, jolly good.

"Come and sit down, boys. Everything all right?"

Boys? Good Lord. They hadn't been called that for a good while. Feeling not a little bemused the two boys, one a highly decorated Commander, Royal Navy and the other an equally decorated Major, Royal Artillery, with a combined age of one hundred and thirty-six, sat primly on the edge of two armchairs.

Sister quick-marched in. "Are you sure it wouldn't be better...?"

"Sit down, Amelia. Take the weight of your poor tired feet. Slip your shoes off if you like, dear. We're all family here."

This was getting all too much to handle, thought Sister. Amelia? Shoes off? Family? Whatever next?

As if reading her thoughts, Gloria slipped her shoes off which, as her feet were several inches above the floor, dropped with a satisfying clunk to the carpet and then, with the utmost decorum, she slipped her legs under her and sat back on the settee.

"Ooh, lovely." In came the tea on a tray many sizes too large for Mrs Coombe who plonked it on the low table.

Gloria smiled sweetly at her. "Well done, dear. Crumb, isn't it? How are you, love? Settling in all right?"

"You remember Mrs Coombe?" Sister felt that she was falling helplessly through space.

"Of course I do. But she likes to be called 'Crumb', Amelia, don't you dear? Much more jolly."

"I'm loving it, ma'am. Sister – Amelia" – she made it sound like 'Ameliar' – "is so very kind." With that she did a little bob, winked unseen at Tubes and popped out, closing the door behind her.

"Now then, loves. I'm not here just for fun, although fun it certainly is. I want to break some news to you before you hear it from anywhere else. Gregory's banged-up."

This news, delivered as it was with no frills, had two differing effects on the three of them: Tubes and Basil thought GOOD, Sister wondered what 'banged-up' meant.

Gloria saw that, judging by the total non-reaction of her audience, clarification was needed.

"Amnoria. Or Ameronia was it? Arminervia – or something."

Still no reaction.

"Where he is. A big deal it was – or should have been. The anti-Government lot. Much nastier than our politicians. They needed arms, rifles and that, you see. And Gregory has them. But the Government got wind and took him in."

"My dear Mrs Cartiledge…" Basil was at his charming best.

She corrected him. "Gloria, dear."

"My dear Gloria, we're so dreadfully sorry." He eyed Tubes to say something.

"Anything we can do, dear lady, of course" – like throw away the cell key. But Tubes didn't actually say the last bit, which was probably for the best.

"What will happen to Oldthorpe House?" Sister saw redundancy ahead. "Er – I mean, Mrs Cartiledge, we are all most dreadfully sorry and wish him a speedy er… "

"Recovery?" Tubes found Sister quite infuriating at times like this.

"Return," the feeling was mutual. "I'm sure our Embassy…"

"Oh they will, but if I know them – and my Gregory – they'll leave him to stew for as long as possible."

"As they used to do only a decade or two ago." Basil unwittingly undid all his good work and now, in panic, sank deeper and deeper into the mire. "Stewed them. You know. Big pot, um …"

"Major Reardon," Sister bristled.

"Steady, old boy," Tubes chuckled.

Their unison admonishments were drowned by Gloria who, rocking backwards and forwards on the settee, was giggling, then laughing and finally, in hysterics, pounding the cushions.

"Wonderful, wonderful. Tough though. They'd need good teeth. Ooh wait 'til I can tell him. What a joke. What a lark."

The three of them sat in varying degrees of awkwardness with Sister well out in front and Tubes, who started a chortle of his own, lagging behind.

"Must be off." Gloria studied her diamond studded watch whilst draining her cup, which the two men thought very dexterous. "Fetch Simmonds will you, Amelia? There's a pet."

The teeth-gritted pet marched out.

"You'll be off to set the diplomatic wheels in motion eh, Gloria?" Tubes stroked his white whiskers.

Basil nodded. "No stone unturned. Relentless pressure. Get those Foreign Office blighters earning their keep. Not a moment to lose."

"Humphrey Bogart." Gloria jumped down from the settee and smoothed her skirt.

The other two thinking it might be an East London swear-word they hadn't heard of, stood awkwardly, towering over the little woman.

"Mustn't be late. Gregory hates the flicks. Won't let me go. Says I'll be molested in the back row. Fat chance."

She herded Simmonds through the front door. "Let's get shifted. If I miss the start I don't understand a word of it."

Tubes and Basil watched the Rolls, for once being gently manoeuvred, swing out into the road.

"I want this kept to yourselves." Sister was back in, punishing the cushions yet again.

"On the contrary, Sister." Tubes resumed the balled feet routine. "Gloria intimated that she wanted everyone to know now. That's why she came. To be with her family. I think we should respect her wishes, don't you?"

Not for the first time Basil was impressed with his friend's command abilities. But then, he reasoned, you'd need them, being a Torpedo Officer. Press the button at the wrong time and you could blow up Portsmouth.

"If you must, Commander." The teeth were clenching again. "Just the facts. No more."

"Fear not, Sister." Tubes performed a little bow. "We shall, as usual, be the souls of discretion."

Sister, for once aware of the sarcasm, turned in desperation to Basil. "Major Reardon, I appeal to you." And she was gone.

"Not all that much, Sister, actually," Basil muttered.

Tubes stared at his friend. That was dear old Basil's

greatest strength. You never knew if he was serious or joking. Deadpan. That was the word for him. Deadpan.

Deadpan would be a good way to describe Lesley Bristowe's features at about that moment. She was having her photograph taken. This was something the Brigadier had loathed since she was a tiny child, but today, at 6.04 p.m. as recorded in the Desk Sergeant's book, it was more loathsome than ever because the act was being performed in a back room at Ipswich Police Station.

She had already gone through the indignity of having her finger-prints recorded and now here she was, holding a board on which was a long number meaning absolutely nothing to her, being told not to smile, indeed, not to affect any expression whatsoever until permitted to do so. That, she felt, was no problem.

A few moments later she was being placed in a cell and the door firmly bolted.

20954163 Bristowe, Lesley, was well and truly 'banged-up'.

It seemed to be becoming a habit with those associated with Oldthorpe House.

She'd had a really pleasant afternoon. Lesley was settling in well, but the mountain she had to climb was formidable and life in the confines of Oldthorpe House was proving harder to bear than she had imagined.

It had seemed an easy option at first. An ordered existence in a disciplined environment, living cheek-by-jowl with a group of men, all this seemed fine; it was Officers' Mess life. She knew it well and had enjoyed it during her long Service career. But it quickly proved to have other ingredients that she had totally overlooked.

First, for some reason, the residents were governed by the staff and had no say in the day-to-day running of the place. That would have to change. The Home was there for their benefit and the staff should be there to help, not rule them.

Her second bone of contention was the nursing. Few of the residents, she felt, actually needed much medical care. Mind you, having seen the bizarre behaviour of some of her fellow residents, a bit of nursing might be appropriate – but more of the psychiatric kind. The serious point was that the more medicines you pushed into a person, the more they needed them and that, coupled with endless chatter about health problems could do nothing but harm to them all. Of that she was convinced.

And then there were the residents themselves, moving around as if they were walking on eggshells. And their stupid factions. Cavaliers and Roundheads! How ludicrous, how banal. She'd always fought the idea of factions in the Messes of which she had been a member, and now in retirement here she was having to choose. Ridiculous. All she wanted was a quiet life.

So, should she be a Roundhead?

Why, in heaven's name, was she drawn to the Cavaliers? Perhaps it was a reaction. She'd heard the perfect phrase on the telly only last evening. A detective story and the suspect being questioned had said, "I was being stuffed so I said, stuff 'em." She'd thought then, "You're right, that's me. So a Cavalier I'll be…"

And now here she was, neither one nor the other. At this moment, in the eyes of the police, she was a 'suspect'. Being questioned.

In the confines of the sanitized police cell she shivered. Why? Why? It can't be. It's not me. I didn't – did I?"

She'd enjoyed herself in Ipswich, shopping for bits and pieces. Tight budget. Only essentials. Then she'd seen it. Through the jeweller's window in a cabinet. It was a simple piece, a gold cross encrusted with amethysts hanging on a delicately thin gold chain. It appeared to be identical to her Confirmation present from her parents. Gone now. Lloyds decreed…

She'd walked into the shop just to see it and had stood for a few moments, staring, her mind bombarded with such memories that she became totally unaware of the present. Her whole life flashed in tumbled, jagged scenes from such early promise and achievement through great success and then a downward spiral of lost loves, rejections, financial disaster – and now this; her remaining years in an Institution.

As ever, she pulled herself together. Self pity? Not the way to behave. Not how I was brought up. Not how I was trained. With one last look at the pendant she marched out of the shop.

"Excuse me, madam. If you would be so kind as to step back into the shop. We have a little problem."

It had taken a moment or two to register. This young man. Blue suit. Clean shirt. Smart tie. Tidy. He had his hand on her arm. Of course she protested, vehemently. People glanced at them. Mother and son? A tiff?

To avoid embarrassment she allowed herself to be steered back inside. The shop now was empty of customers and had obviously been emptied.

"The alarm, you see, madam. I'm so sorry. These electronic marvels can so easily go wrong. Do forgive us. I wonder if you would be so good as to allow us to check your coat – in your presence, of course. And maybe Sylvia here could just look through your shopping bag and your handbag?"

At first, in the tiny office at the back, the search revealed nothing. She sat there, dazed, as this stranger poked through her handbag and the manager emptied the pitiful contents of her shopping bag onto the desk. Boiled sweets, a birthday card, biro, paper hankies – and two wrist watches.

The manager picked up the watches, each still with a little white price tag attached by thin cotton. He held them close to her. Out of habit she looked at the tag rather than the watch. £240.

"Of course you have no receipt for these, do you?" The voice had changed. It was now hard and unfriendly. "You see that screen up there?"

Lesley looked up at a television screen showing the shop, busy again now.

"It's a new idea. Just installed. Records everything. You'll be on the tape of course." It was said in an almost bored voice. "Miss Roberts will call the police. I suggest you sit there and say nothing."

Then the walk through the crowded shop escorted by a policewoman and across the busy pavement into the police car. It seemed to Lesley that all of Ipswich was there. Stopping. Staring.

And now this cell.

"It can't be. It's not me. I didn't – did I?"

The telephone call reached Oldthorpe House at seven that evening. Sister, for once sharing news with the residents because she felt deeply out of her depth, watched Brigadier Ainsley and Major Basil set off for the police station and then, doubting the wisdom of entrusting Lesley Bristowe's dilemma in their hands, telephoned Gloria Cartiledge. Matters moved quickly after that.

Ainsley and Basil were refused any contact with the prisoner and were sitting disconsolately on the wooden bench in the waiting area when Gloria and a smartly dressed young man marched in. The man was admitted into the innards of the station and Gloria joined the two of them.

"Sit down, boys. That's Philpott, Terence. From our solicitors. He'll have it all sorted in no time. Mistaken identity. Bound to be. Soon have her back. Daft ha'p'ths. They must know she's innocent."

Gloria was right about the time but not the outcome. After a few moments she was taken into another room and then, as Ainsley and Basil continued their silent, awkward vigil, she reappeared with Lesley and the Philpott and led them outside to where the Rolls was parked on a double yellow line with Simmonds at the wheel.

"Silly lot. Don't you worry, love. Soon have it sorted. We'll all go back to my place and have a cuppa – or something much stronger. You go and sort it out, Terry. Off you go."

The smartly dressed Philpott disappeared at a trot.

The drive to Cartiledge Towers was conducted in total silence. Lesley appeared to be in a daze and said nothing and no one else felt they could start a conversation, certainly not in front of the chauffeur. Even the novelty of a ride in this amazing car failed to register with the two men. To break the embarrassment Basil started to hum until dug in the ribs by Ainsley.

Whiskies and soda in the vast drawing room helped to thaw out the rescuers and, as the power of speech returned, the details of the terrible event started to emerge and plans were made.

Gloria had provided surety and Lesley had been released on police bail. The Philpott was in charge to find out all he could, and Ainsley and Basil were to return to Oldthorpe and say little.

Lesley was easily persuaded to stay overnight with Gloria, and the men were despatched in the Rolls with a list of requirements for Sister to gather from Lesley's room and send back in the car.

Basil sighed, "So far, so not very good."

"Do you think she did it?" Ainsley's whisper had to be very low to be not heard in the silence of the Rolls.

"Of course she didn't. Good grief, Ainsley, are you mad? She's an Officer and a Gentle – er – person. Would you do a thing like that?"

"Not and get caught. No."

"Seriously."

"Of course I wouldn't. How dare you even ask."

"Well, there you are then. It will be sorted out. I'm sure of that."

Simmonds noted the doubt in the old man's voice. These officers. Hopeless without their NCOs.

He steered the car into the Oldthorpe driveway and its two passengers received the only delight of the entire episode so far. Sister rushed out, half curtseying, and opened their door. The speed her smile faded was exceptional even by her standards. With a 'humph' she led them into the house.

10

Nurse Lisa and Phyllis Coombe were at the kitchen table the following afternoon surrounded by an impressive array of silverware, mostly sporting trophies won by the residents of Oldthorpe during their long Service careers. It was the weekly silver cleaning session. Around them, looking as if he was there to guard the valuables, hovered the Chef, Jean-Paul wielding the long, sharp kitchen knife which had become something of an adjunct of him; whatever damage he was doing to food he never seemed to be without it.

"Pig Sticking? What's that when it's at 'ome?" Phyllis blew heavily on the inscription on the silver trophy and gave it another hard rub.

"Sounds horrible." Lisa took the cup from her. "'Lieutenant B. Reardon. 1932.' Can't see old Basil doing something horrid. Pig Sticking. Why do men enjoy such strange pastimes?" She spoke as one who had experienced quite an array of them in her time.

"Like sex." Phyllis breathed heavily again, but more to gain extra shine than through lustful thoughts. Jean-Paul, thinking it was a question, was about to answer firmly in the affirmative when Phyllis ploughed on. "My Albert seems to enjoy it. It just gives me a few quiet moments to plan the shopping list."

Lisa roared with laughter. "Oh, Crumb. You're so good for us all here. Under Matron Montague we quite forgot how to laugh."

"What's with you women and sex?" Jean-Paul and his knife towered over them.

"That's quite enough of that sort of talk thank you, Jean-Paul. Don't be smutty." Lisa rubbed unnecessarily hard on a silver golfer in mid swing.

Muttering, the Chef resumed his slaughter of an innocent cauliflower.

"1937 Shove Ha'penny Champion. HM Submarine Firefly. Sub-Lieutenant Archibald Potter R.N.' My young George is good at that. Practices at the pub 'til all hours." Phyllis smiled the smile of a doting mother. "Bless 'im."

Tubes an Archibald, thought Lisa. Well I never. Something to store for a special occasion. She now changed from golf to cricket and was buffing up some little shields on a bat when Sister came rushing in. She always seemed to be rushing these days, as indeed she always seemed to be 'tsking'. Now she uttered a long stream of tsks to signify that all was not well, or worse, nothing at all was well.

"Lisa, why are you cleaning silver? The whole purpose of Mrs Coombes here…"

"Coombe, luvvie – but I wish you'd call me Crumb. Everyone does. Even posh people. So you certainly can."

The unintentional innuendo was mercifully lost on a non-innuendo-aware Sister.

"I've told you before. Don't call me Luvvie, Mrs Coombe."

Lisa paused in her buffing. "It's my break time, Sister, and I'm bored doing nothing so I thought I'd help Crumb, here. And silver polishing is very relaxing." The buffing had an angry edge to it.

Sister sank exhausted at the table and subconsciously polished those pieces already done to perfection.

"You've said nothing, I hope, Nurse. Oldthorpe – er – business is not to be discussed as I'm sure you appreciate."

"I find it hurtful, Sister, that you should think for one moment that I would do such a thing."

The silver being buffed was near meltdown. There was a silence broken only by heavy breathing from the buffers and chip-chopping of vegetables. Phyllis saw her reflection in a polished cup and took the opportunity to check her perm.

"Shame about that nice lady, Lesley Thingy. And poor Mr Cartiledge."

It was said in such a chatty way as another hard-won trophy joined the gleaming pile that for a moment or two the comment didn't register. When it did it became another of Sister's many final straws. She leapt up.

"Mrs Coombes…"

"Coombe," shouted Jean-Paul in considerable glee.

"Crumb," Lisa joined in the fun.

"Shush," Sister's hand went up as if in the Fascist salute. They shushed. "I clearly said…"

"It's all over Flaxton, Luvvie. It's the fuzz, you see. As leaky as a colander. It'll be in the Press tonight. I don't believe a word of it. The Brigand, that is. I know a villain when I sees one. My Albert taught me that. Whenever he's been inside he's studied them, you see. An expert is my Albert. There, all done." Phyllis collected the cleaning things and started to stand but Sister pulled her down again.

"Inside? What do you mean, inside?" Her voice was even more strident than usual.

"Clink, dear. But Albert and George are back home now. Resting. They were taken in but no evidence, you see. And I should think not. George had found these car radios in someone's dustbin and fearing they'd been thrown away by mistake, he rescued them." She blew a few crumbs off the table that inadvertently landed on Sister's lap. "Like his father. So public spirited. He'd kept them safely in his bedroom that night and then there was the fuzz at the door with a search warrant. I ask you. Coincidence. That's the Coombe cross we bear, luvvie."

Sister hauled herself upright. "I think I'm going to go and lie down for a little while. Perhaps, Lisa, you might bring me a cup of tea at, shall we say, four?"

"As a nurse I could bring you medicine, Sister, but I'm not sure if my duties…"

"DON'T say any more, Nurse, please."

The door closed quietly.

"Poor soul. Getting towards the difficult time in her life I shouldn't wonder. She'll be better when it's all over."

"I think, Crumb, it might be wise not to say too much about your Albert's – er – busy life. If Sister reports it…"

"Mrs Cartiledge thought it sounded great fun. She hooted with laughter when I told her. She's evidently got a relation who suffers from the same problem we have. She looked at me and said 'Coincidence? My Aunt Nellie!'"

Lisa was about to say something but thought better of it. Dear Crumb may be simple but she had a heart of gold – and that was good enough for her. She opened the door and they went into the hall with armfuls of silver.

At that same time another meeting was taking place but with a far more sombre agenda than buffing up silver. A Council of War was in full swing in the vast drawing room at Cartiledge Towers.

Gloria was in the Chair, tucked up on one of the vast settees, and around her were dotted her chosen team. The Philpott, surrounded by briefcases of documents, was appearing to be both very learned and very busy, thereby apparently earning the massive fee his law firm would charge the Cartiledges. Lesley Bristowe, in contrast, sat motionless, still in deep shock, all the stuffing knocked out of her.

Ranged around them were Ainsley, Basil and Tubes, all co-opted at Lesley's request.

"As a first offence, I am of the opinion that the Magistrates will prove lenient and impose a fine rather than a custodial sentence."

The mournful legal-speak of The Philpott, emulating his television hero, Perry Mason, did little to get the meeting off to a bright start. That was left to Gloria.

"Poppycock, Philpott. Come on, Terry, you can do better than that, dear. We want an innocent verdict. Unanimous. Not guilty."

"But are you, Mrs Bristowe? That's the question." The Philpott had adopted a censorious Prosecuting Council style.

Gloria seemed to have taken up permanent possession of the witness box. "Of course she's innocent. And she's a Brigadier so don't you forget it, you young rascal."

Deflated, The Philpott returned to his files unaware of and totally disinterested in the mysteries of military rank.

"I just don't know any more." Lesley sat forward in her chair. "I really don't know. Did I? I can't believe it. I was so unaware of anything – everything around me. Just thinking back to my childhood actually. Miles away. But why would I pick up two wrist watches? And put them in my shopping bag?" She let out a deep sigh. "And yet it seems I did."

"That's what I was saying." The Philpott was Perrying again. "Plead guilty and ask…"

"For heaven's sake, man, shut up." Ainsley was getting impatient with the young pup. "You heard what Mrs Cartiledge said. We're here to get Brigadier Bristowe off the hook whether she did it or didn't."

"If she did…" Basil always preferred to fear the worst.

"She didn't," Tubes inclined towards the positive.

"This isn't getting us anywhere, dears. Come on, Terry, in return for your extortionate fee, what do we do now?"

The Philpott rose and Perry-ed around the group, causing them all to crick their necks to keep him in view.

"I would have advocated a guilty plea…"

Gloria was becoming quickly disillusioned with her Philpott. "Yes, we know."

"But, Mrs Cartiledge, there is one fact that causes me to pause."

They sat still, their necks seriously cricked. One thing you could say for young Terry; he'd learnt from Perry what suspense was all about.

"Why have the police returned the videotape to the jewellers? That puzzled us – er – me on reviewing the evidence to date. Had they copied it? Evidently not. They told the plaintiff that…" he pretended to study a file in true Perry-style, "Ah, yes, here it is. 'The tape will not be required in evidence'." Slowly he closed the file as if the very act saw the prosecution's case in tatters. He almost heard the theme music.

"Well?" Ainsley's impatience with the man was simmering again.

Tubes stood up and tried a little balled-feet routine at the vast fireplace which caused more neck-cricking. "I see what the chap's on about. There's no evidence on the video whatsit of Lesley pinching the watches, so…"

"Of course there isn't, Tubes, because SHE DIDN'T." Ainsley's patience was being exhausted.

Basil was the only one present to care little for his friend's wrath. "We don't know that, old chap," he said quietly, "even Lesley herself says she isn't sure."

"Come on, dears. None of this is getting us anywhere. I want some bright ideas – now." Gloria swung her legs from under her, jumped up and advanced towards Tubes at the fireplace, a finger thrust out in front of her. For his part, Tubes, fearing a digital assault on his person, took avoiding action and swung to port. The finger, like an avenging torpedo, missed him by inches and found its target: a large bell-push.

"There are two avenues to pursue." Perry Mason was back. "The accused ..."

"I won't have you calling our Lesley that." Ainsley was up now.

'Our Lesley', thought Lesley. That's nice.

Basil did his calming act. "Let him finish, old chap. Let him say his piece."

"A guilty plea..." he held up his hand to quell the rising murmurs, "A guilty plea will mean that every possible mitigating circumstance must be chronicled to help reduce the sentence. May I suggest that you, Mrs Cartiledge, handle that. Mrs Brigadier Bristowe will find it easiest to share such information with another woman."

Where did they find these pups, fumed Ainsley. Mrs Brigadier indeed.

"A not guilty plea – and you know I have trouble with this route – means that evidence must be found to support it. Something, or someone will need to be produced in evidence to prove innocence."

The bell-push assault had resulted in a trolley bearing every known type of alcoholic beverage being wheeled into the room by Merryweather, the butler, and its contents dispensed in large quantities according to each person's wishes. They all gulped gratefully and began to feel a little better.

"The videotape! Of course. I bet they were all locals. View the tape and chase them up."

The Philpott sipped his sweet sherry. "A very long shot but better than nothing, I suppose. I will contact the jewellers back at the office."

"No time like the present, Terry. Phone's in the hall. Off you go, dear." The Philpott blinked. His client obviously hadn't been a devotee of Perry Mason. He would never do the menial bit. He'd leave the phoning to the reliable Della Street. He slunk out.

"How does any of this help?" Basil was sorry but the point

had to be made. "Even if we trace the people, what are they going to say? At best it will be 'we didn't see the lady take anything' but that won't be enough. The facts are that Lesley didn't steal the watches, but they were in her bag when she left."

There was silence now. They all realized one other fact: they just weren't up to this. It was way beyond them. Perhaps The Philpott was right after all. Plead guilty and they'd all band together to pay the fine. It was probably the only way out.

Lesley now stirred. "Perhaps they dropped in. Or someone thought my bag was theirs. Or – or the tape will show that I did do it. Yes, the videotape's the answer. Just to resolve it." She'd spoken quietly, very un-Lesley-ish. Near defeat.

Any more debate was abruptly ended by the return of The Philpott. "They won't release it to us. I suggested they let us have a copy but, no, on no account. It is evidently safely in their safe. They were completely unhelpful. Hardly surprising, I suppose. After all, they are bringing the prosecution."

"Damn. The tape was our only hope." Tubes could see surrender ahead but he supposed that, rather than be depth-charged, a guilty verdict was probably the only way.

Ainsley drained his glass and stood up. "It's been most kind of you, Mrs Cartiledge – Gloria – to include us in this meeting. I fear we must rush back before Sister, who thinks we're in the Cosy Cot Café, sends out a search party. If something comes up we will, of course, contact you."

Almost urgently he herded Basil and Tubes to the door. "How long do we have?" The question was shot at The Philpott.

"The case will be heard the day after tomorrow and probably adjourned for, er, medical reports." Even he felt the embarrassment of such a procedure.

"Tight. Work to be done." The three Cavaliers left and in the Rolls Ainsley outlined his plan. A long – very long – shot but it was all the ammunition they had available to them in this darkest of dark hour.

Simmonds dropped them off in Flaxton's High Street and after a pause at a phone box they more or less automatically sauntered into the Saloon Bar of The Anchor. Then they got down to work.

The Landlord acknowledged their arrival with a cheery

wave. These old men might not spend much but they were regular customers and for that he was grateful. They usually arrived about this time – five-ish – and then rushed out to catch the bus back to their Home and, he guessed, a pretty awful supper. But today, he noted, it wasn't long before they were joined by two men who, it seemed to him, were not the sort with whom they should be associating. He'd been an NCO – a Sergeant – in 'the last lot' and respect for those who were or had been his senior was ingrained in him. But these other two were strangers and, quite obviously, not of officer class. Rough diamonds, he thought. More for the Public Bar than the Saloon.

The gentlemen, however, seemed happy enough with their company and, judging by the rolled wad of notes produced by the older stranger to pay for the first round, he'd swell the bar takings better than the three gents put together!

"It won't be easy, Gov. No question. Right out of my league. Winders to get through, combination locks, alarms – lots of 'em – the safe itself – modern – tough as nails. That's where it is, y'see. The fuzz told 'em to lock it in there." His younger companion touched his nose with his finger. "Insider knowledge. Done me 'omework."

They didn't think it fair to tell him that The Philpott had already found that out.

"But can it be done?" Tubes was beginning to share Basil's gloomy prediction about the outcome of Ainsley's plan. He saw the three of them joining Lesley in clink which would undoubtedly be a record for one Old Folks' Home at any one time.

"Wiv the right 'fingers', yer, of course. My lad 'ere knows better'n what I do."

The younger one slipped the remaining half pint of mild down his gullet in a couple of noisy gulps and handed the empty glass to Basil, then he performed the accepted and expected drill of running the back of his hand over his mouth with a precision that impressed the old soldiers. His voice was softer than his father's. Ainsley was reminded of Corporal Tremlett but, for once, forbore to say so.

"I got the man but he's expensive, see. He'll do it. No problem."

Basil, as he bought the next round, was impressed that secondary education had advanced to the use of 'h' in everyday speech in the course of just one generation.

The negotiations proved harder than most battles the three of them had fought in their long careers but in the course of the next hour, and four more pints each consumed by their guests, the die was cast and plans set in motion for that night. As they left, one final condition had to be met.

"The old lady mustn't know about this. Right? My Phyl is very – what's yer mum, George?"

"Sensitive, Dad. Better she don't know nuffing. She'd only fret."

"Totally understood, old chap. Fear not. The secret's safe with us."

Gravely, Ainsley, Basil and Tubes shook their collaborators' hands and Albert and George Coombe sloped off to make their plans.

Whilst daring deeds were being debated in The Anchor, Oldthorpe House was receiving an unwelcome visitor. With Nurse Lisa detained in a bedroom rubbing in a bit of embrocation and Phyllis hoovering the sitting room, Sister answered the doorbell.

"Dan Pinkerton, Flaxton Chronicle."

Not a good start.

"No thank you, Mr Pinkerton. I have no comment to make."

But Reporter Dan would not be that easily put off. "No comment about what, Matron?"

Sister warmed slightly to the man. 'Matron' sounded good. "About Brigadier Bristowe. A terrible mistake. She is, of course, innocent. Completely innocent."

Whoops!

"Ah. So the story exists? A good start. The story we have and shall be printing suggests rather the opposite of innocent. An open and shut case. Impossible for it to be otherwise. Obviously our readers would probably get a rather more sympathetic feel for the lady if we could paint a warmer picture of her home life and her – er – standing amongst her peers."

The ways of journalists were a mystery to Sister and,

already defeated, she stood aside. "You'd better come in," she sighed resignedly. "Mrs Crumb – Coombe – will you hoover somewhere else please, and CAPTAIN CUTHBERT, WAKE UP." She saw in the garden Freddy, flying a sortie with his hand. "Squadron Leader, please come and wake Captain Cuthbert and take him somewhere."

Freddy zoomed in landing his hand in the Reporter's and energetically shaking it.

A quavering voice came from deep in the armchair, "Is this your young man, Sister?"

"Don't be silly, Captain Cuthbert. Look, here's Squadron Leader Foster. He'll take you."

"But I don't need to go at the moment. Hello. Are you Sister's young man?" A quivering hand snaked out of the armchair. "Clarence Cuthbert. Nice to meet you. Do sit down. We don't get many visitors."

This, felt Sister, had all gone totally wrong even before anything had started. She looked down on the three of them, now settled in the chairs, and felt there was nothing she could do but follow their example. The final straw was delivered by Phyllis Coombe.

"I'll make us all a nice pot of tea." And off she went.

Reporter Dan studied his pristine notebook. This was his first real story since being let out of the newsroom.

"Tell me about Brigadier Lesley Bristowe."

Clarence struggled forward in the chair. "Banged up. That's what Ainsley calls it. Pinched a couple of wrist watches. I remember, about 1910 in Cairo. This young filly…"

"I think we'd better go into the garden." Sister was up again. "I'm afraid lunch is being prepared in the kitchen so…"

A hand performed a vertical climb within inches of the reporter's face. "Brigadier Lesley Bristowe, Commander of the British Empire – that's CBE to you young fellow – is as fine an example of a British Army Officer as you will find in this Sceptred Isle." When he tried, Squadron Leader Freddy could lay it on with the best of them.

Reporter Dan was writing as fast as he could. Lesson One of his shorthand course couldn't help him here, but he was saved from having to ask them to speak more slowly and thereby risk ignominy by the considerable upheaval of Clarence rising from his armchair and making for the downstairs cloakroom.

"We've got three lavvies. Four if you count Sister's," was his parting shot.

Dan stood up and was slightly unnerved by Freddy over-energetically doing the same.

"Would it be possible to see her room? Perhaps I could phone for a photogr …"

"Certainly NOT." Sister was appalled. "It would be a grave infringement of her privacy."

"You wouldn't like anyone rummaging in your nooks and crannies now would you, young fellow?" Freddy slapped the Reporter slightly too forcefully on the back.

"Well then, can I please speak to her? I know she's out on bail."

"In shock, old chap. Speechless." Freddy advanced on him until he was only a few inches from his face, and then enunciated slowly, "In-comm-uni-ca-do."

The diagnosis of this strange behaviour was shared by both Sister and the Reporter: Squadron Leader Frederick Foster DFC and Bar was undoubtedly mad. As if to prove the point he performed a delicate aerial manoeuvre with his hand and brought it in to a perfect landing on the back of the armchair.

Reporter Dan wiped his brow with his handkerchief.

"Why do you wave your hand about like that?" As he asked he knew it was a mistake but, being in an inquisitive profession, he couldn't help himself.

"Like what?" The question was fired at him and Reporter Dan recoiled from the impact.

"Sorry. It doesn't matter." Desperation was taking over. One last try.

"Do you, perhaps, have a photograph of the lady?"

Sister had been watching this exchange in a mixture of exasperation and disbelief. What was Squadron Leader Foster up to? His behaviour was so unlike him. Manic movements, barked questions and the occasional leer which for all the world suggested that he was a raving lunatic. She must stop it.

"Squadron Leader Foster, perhaps you'd like to go – somewhere. Have a little rest in your room, maybe?"

Freddy appeared to be unaware of Sister's presence. He watched as Phyllis brought in the tea.

"Why do you want a photo? Do you collect them? Of ladies? A bad habit to get into, young man. Dangerous. Leads to all sorts of, how shall I say, unsavoury…" – more over-enunciation – "un-sa-vou-ry thoughts."

Phyllis handed a cup to the Reporter. "Our George had them. My Albert and me spent ages thinking of a way of curing 'im. Albert had the answer, bless him. He knocked the bleedin' daylights out of 'im." With a smile and a wink at Freddy she bustled out.

There was a deathly silence, broken eventually by Reporter Dan.

"A photograph for our article." It came out as a squeak. "It's common practice."

"Is it, indeed?" Freddy's hand did a stall turn.

Reporter Dan was now severely unnerved. On this, his first big story, to return to the newsroom with his pristine notebook still pristine was a thought too appalling to contemplate. He must try one more time.

"May I sit down?" A simple, humble request.

Sister was about to say, "Yes, of course," but again Freddy manoeuvred ahead of her. "Better not." He waved his non-flying hand around the empty room. "They're all taken, I'm afraid. Cause a riot if you invade their spaces."

"Squadron Leader. I insist …"

"It's all right, Sister. Leave this young blade to me." He swung round violently on the Reporter who jumped back in alarm.

"Any more questions, just fire away. Rat-tat-tat." The three rounds of cannon fire were each accompanied by hard finger jabs to the young man's chest.

Reporter Dan had suffered enough. He broke off the engagement and made for the door.

"We'll have to do what we can with what we've got. Thank you, Sister, for your trouble, I'll find my own way out."

Scuttling across the hall he was confronted by a tall, sallow man dressed as a cook, holding a long, sharp knife. With a yelp, he legged it across the drive to the relative safety of the road.

Sister, who had rushed into the hall on hearing the yelp, hustled Jean-Paul back into his kitchen and then returned to the sitting room to find Freddy comfortably installed in an armchair, reading the Daily Express.

"Squadron Leader, I despair."

"No need to, Sister. I handled it for you. It was a pleasure."

"But ..."

"Has your young man gone?" Clarence zimmered into the room and plonked himself down.

"For the last time, Captain Cuthbert..." They both knew the signs: the tinny voice tinnier, volume rising, quivering delivery. All was not well with Sister. With considerable effort she controlled herself.

"Have you any idea what you have done, Squadron Leader? Have you any idea what will now be printed in that wretched newspaper? 'Oldthorpe House – Home for the Insane'; 'Fighter Pilots driven to madness by their wartime air battles'; 'Rooms full of imaginary people'; 'Madmen wielding sharp knives'." Sister was warming to the subject. Perhaps she'd missed her vocation and should have become a scribbler herself.

"Do you feel, then, that I may have gone a wee bit over the top?"

"Nice fella." Clarence really didn't know when best to keep quiet. "Reminded me of a young subaltern we had in Mesopotamia. 'Non-stop Davenport' we called him because the girls said he never knew when to ..."

"I really don't know if I can stand much more of this. What is the phrase Brigadier Bennington uses when you go too far, Squadron Leader?"

Clarence chuckled, "Landed with his undercarriage up."

"Precisely." Sister retired to her room for at least two aspirins and a few minutes lie-down.

Whilst Sister, Freddy, Clarence and Phyllis were 'handling' the media, the War Council was assembling for a sandwich lunch at Cartiledge Towers. This time they met in the vast dining room, Gloria almost lost in an enormous carving chair at the head of the long table, Lesley, Ainsley, Basil and Tubes down one side and opposite them The Philpot sitting uncomfortably close to

Albert and George Coombe. Despite their number they only filled about a quarter of the table's vast length.

"Cor, what a night!" Albert rubbed his palms together in satisfaction. "Knackered. We was on watch. Took bleedin' – beggin' your pardon, ladies – ages. Our 'Fingers' did bleedin' – begging your pardon – marvellous."

Then, as if rehearsed, he and his son embarked on a quick-patter double act.

"Alarms orf," said George.

"Safe open," said Albert.

"Tape out."

"Off to the video shop."

"Broke in."

"Copied the tape on their machines."

"Back to the jewellers."

"Tape back in the safe."

"Sealed up."

"Alarms reactivated."

"Scarpered."

They were somewhat surprised to receive a round of enthusiastic applause led by Gloria.

"Bravo. Bravo."

Both looked down, sheepishly.

"So no one knows we have the copy?" Ainsley needed reassurance.

"Not a foot or finger print. Clean as a whistle."

Gloria clapped again. "You've done really well, boys. And our regards to, er, 'Fingers'."

The Philpot fiddled in agitation with his countless files.

"I'm really not sure I should stay. I find myself already severely compromised."

"That'll do, Terry. You and your firm have been compromised since the first day you worked for Gregory. Now, let's take a look."

The under-table buzzer was buzzed and as if by magic the double doors opened and Merryweather and another servant wheeled in the trolley. But this time, instead of being laden with drinks, it held a small television set and video machine.

Basil expected an intoned, "You rang, madam?" but instead

187

there was a fair degree of muttering as the men connected the machinery to the mains electricity and, with a perfunctory bow, left the room.

They all looked at each other, the four 'Oldthorpes' and The Philpot embarrassed that they had no idea how to work the wretched machines. Gloria was contemplating a return of the butler when George dragged his chair back and slouched up to the trolley. In no time the busy interior of the shop appeared on the screen.

Lesley wasn't ready for the shock it gave her. To see herself almost at the moment of her greatest shame was too much and she hid her head in her hands. Gloria stroked her arm gently.

"Better look, dearie. Just in case."

There really wasn't much to see. The small shop was busy and Lesley was almost at the centre of the picture viewing what must be the gold cross pendant in a showcase. On one arm was her handbag and in her other hand the shopping bag. People bustled around her in the confined space.

"Did you see where the watches were displayed?"

Well done Tubes, thought Basil. None of us have asked Lesley that and it's an important point.

"I think I saw them in a counter display case at, let me see …" Lesley twisted her head at various angles, "Yes. Down at the bottom left-hand corner of the screen."

They sat intrigued at the activity recorded on the tape and then they saw Lesley walking out.

As the manager left after her, Ainsley called, "Stop it now, if you would be so kind." He didn't want Lesley's humiliation seen by any of them. He looked at The Philpot. "So, that's it. No sign of Lesley pinching the watches. Will it help?"

"I fear very little. I can see why the police returned the tape. It wouldn't help the prosecution, but that is immaterial to them. They will major on the stolen goods in the shopping bag. They don't have to show how and when they got in there. They will argue that it's obvious."

The Philpot felt that Perry could hardly have put it better; it would have earned an adoring smile from Della Street. He looked around. All it got here were stares containing varying degrees of dislike for having made this unpalatable statement.

They now lapsed into an embarrassed silence, no one knowing what to do or say until, at the very moment when Ainsley opened his mouth to say something – anything – to try to cover their disappointment, they became aware of some deep rumblings coming from the Albert and George direction. With a screech of chair leg on polished wood George slouched his way back to the machine and reversed the tape. Then he started it again.

"There. Put it slow there." Albert, almost hunched double, scampered round the table and peered closely at the screen. Those whose view was not obscured by two Coombe posteriors saw the action jerk through in slow motion.

"Stop. Back. Again. Do it again. Stop. THERE. The bugger." He swung round, "Beggin' your pardon, ladies. But I done it. I cracked it. Janglin' Joe Crutchley. The bugger – beggin' your pardon again."

All this was shouted in considerable glee as Albert, with more palm rubbing, almost danced back to his place and, as a finale, crashed his fists onto the solid mahogany table.

They looked at him. They looked at each other. And then they looked at the frozen picture on the television screen.

They saw Lesley, her bag in her left hand, and alongside her a little man in a raincoat and trilby hat. He looked rather like a jockey, dapper and obviously well-heeled.

"Give it another run, George."

Now they followed the action with Albert's commentary.

"See 'im? Look at that. I'll say this for 'im, Janglin' Joe's good. There it is. See? Dropped in. You'd never know."

They didn't! The tape had to be run again and again before the viewing innocents saw the deft movement of the man's hand dropping the watches into the bag but, in evidence, there would be no doubt whatsoever. Then the man was gone, shortly to be followed by Lesley.

"Then what?" Ainsley was seriously out of his depth as, indeed, were the others.

"'E waits, don't 'e? His 'carrier' comes out – that's you, lady." Albert pointed at Lesley, "and 'e snatches you." He sat back and saw the blank faces in front of him. "Snatches your bag. Oldest trick in the game. You take the risk. If you're caught – as you was – 'e slinks off and does it again somewhere else. No sweat. 'E's probably doin' it again now at this moment."

The Philpot cleared his throat and they all swung their eyes to him.

"It certainly puts a new complexion on the case, but I foresee a problem."

"What's that, gov? No big court fee?"

They all laughed nervously – except The Philpot.

"How do we explain the tape? We would have to admit burglary."

They swivelled back to Albert.

"It won't come to that, will it." It was a statement, not a question. "I've got a score to settle with Janglin' Joe. An' we professionals has no time for someone who'd do an old lady like what you are – beggin' your pardon I'm sure, ma'am. Yers. Another copy of that bit of tape delivered anonymous and then, wiv a bit of 'elp from the lads 'e's goin' to pop into the local nick. That'll put 'im away for a nice while. 'E's spent longer inside than my George an' me put together."

"Why Janglin' Joe?" Tubes had to ask. They needed to be prepared for such questions back at Oldthorpe.

"Jangles with jewellery. Always. Covered in it." Albert collected the tape and chivvied George to the door. "You can see why, can't yer. I'll be in touch. Ta-ra all."

They all just sat there. The Philpot began to noisily assemble his files but Gloria stayed him with her hand. They needed silence for a few moments.

Lesley was first to stir. "Does that mean…?"

Ainsley touched her hand. "It means, Lesley, that – to coin an Albertism – you're orf the 'ook. No charge to answer."

Lunch in the Orangery, which had been planned as sandwiches and light wine to suit the sombre occasion, turned into a feast of everything the Cartiledge Towers' kitchens could provide washed down with large quantities of Gregory's finest champagne.

Early on in the celebrations Basil saw the butler draw Gloria to one side. He was disturbed to note that the news was obviously bad, but she nodded and whispered instructions to him, sent The Philpot off and, composing herself, rejoined them.

Ainsley and Tubes were well into a somewhat less than perfect rendition of 'The Policeman's Song' from 'The Pirates of Penzance' when who should stride into their midst but none other than the Master of the House, Gregory Cartiledge himself.

If he could look less attractive than usual he now did. He appeared to be smaller than ever – probably due to a slight girth thinning – his ruddiness had been replaced with a bilious yellowy-grey, and he needed a shave. All this mess was wrapped in a crumpled suit and long-worn shirt.

"Gregory, how lovely to see you back. You know everyone, don't you, dear?" Gloria advanced on her husband and, mindful of her marriage vows and the Nuptial Agreement, pecked him for a micro-second on the cheek.

Gregory stared wildly around him. "What's this lot doing here? My champagne!" He advanced on one of the many bottles adorning the tables.

"They're here to welcome you home safely, luvvie. They've all been so very kind to me in my grief, whilst you were, er…"

"Banged-up?" volunteered Tubes.

"Yes indeed." She giggled then, with an effort, put on a concerned face. "Thank you, Tubes. And as soon as we heard you were on the way back, we felt a grand celebration was in order. Didn't we, dears?"

They all agreed with varying degrees of false enthusiasm.

"Now I feel we must leave you to your joyful reunion." Ainsley gathered his brood around him. "Gloria, may I say on behalf of all of us at Oldthorpe House, your courage, leadership and kindness throughout all the – er – trials that have had to be faced have been way beyond the call of duty. Lesley will, I know, want to talk to you personally at some other time."

"Leslie? Who's Leslie?" Imprisonment in a filthy South American cell hadn't improved Gregory's memory – or manners?

Gloria ignored the interruption. "Simmonds and the Rolls are at the door."

"ROLLS? What's the matter with the bus? There's a stop

up at the end of the drive." Blood was slowly returning to Gregory's bilious features and it was obvious that his spell in clink had more curdled than warmed his personal milk of human kindness.

Gloria went on unabashed, "And that little suitcase you brought, Lesley, is at the front door. I'll chat to you all probably tomorrow and you, Ainsley and Tubes can finish that lovely little song for me."

"Now look here..."

Further totally unnecessary comment from Gregory was cut short by a hand-shaking session as they all filed past him. Twenty minutes later, in the merriest of moods, they were back in Oldthorpe House, greeted by a very confused Sister Newbiggin.

There were a few loose ends to tie up. The Philpott was instructed to inform the Flaxton Chronicle that it would be unwise to print any story regarding Brigadier Lesley Bristowe until the next day when further news would be available. With relief Vernon Rogers, the editor, agreed, thereby saving himself the thankless task of trying to make something out of the nothing filed by his Reporter Dan Pinkerton.

Early the next morning the Desk Sergeant at Ipswich Police Station was handed an envelope by a middle-aged lady who disappeared before he could get her name or a good look at her. Phyllis Coombe didn't want to be late for work. On the envelope was written 'THE BRISTOWE CASE' and its contents, once viewed on the station's videotape machine, made the arrest of a certain Janglin' Joe Crutchley, when he was propelled in through the doors by unseen hands an hour later, a mere formality.

Even after all that tidying-up there was a twist to the tail of the story. Sister couldn't fathom why the display of silver trophies in the sitting room was rather thinner than it had been and, on questioning the residents, discovered that many belonging to the Cavaliers had been withdrawn for a variety of reasons.

They were all very vague regarding their disappearance. Major Basil's – including his Pig-Sticking Cup – were evidently now to be looked after by his sister in Bexley, Brigadier Ainsley's had gone to his Regimental Mess in Warminster; others had been sold or lent or stored. It was all most confusing and disturbing. In all, some twenty silver trophies were now gone from the shelves and the place looked sad and bare without them.

It had to be, though. That arch-burglar, known only to them as 'Fingers', didn't work for nothing …

11

" Ah Brigadier, all these Electoral Roll forms came in the post this morning. With Lisa away I wonder if you would be so kind and hand them round – or delegate someone to do it." Despite the July heat, Sister Newbiggin was bustling as usual.

Brigadier Ainsley lowered his newspaper, pleased that she obviously accepted his seniority. "If you so wish, Sister. Consider it done."

"Pardon? What was that, Brigadier?" Sister swung round with a frown on her face and saw Ainsley smiling at her.

"Oh not you, Brigadier. I was talking to Brigadier Lesley here. If she would be so kind."

"I'll do it at lunch, Sister. Just leave it to me." Lesley Bristowe took the pile of envelopes, thrust them into her handbag and resumed her reading. As her Times rose so Ainsley's was noisily folded. Then he stood up and strode from the sitting room.

No one seemed to notice and yet those few moments in the midst of a long, hot summer were, for Ainsley Bennington, nearly the final straw and would lead to all manner of ructions in the coming days.

The heat wasn't really suiting the residents of Oldthorpe House and their discomfort was compounded by the effect it was also having on the staff. Sister, so near boiling point at the best of times, boiled over and bubbled in the airless rooms as she fretted over the care of her charges.

Her temperature wasn't helped by Gregory Cartiledge's recent decision not to fill the Matron post for the foreseeable future. "Why pay for a matron when Sister Newbiggin can do the job for less?" he had barked at his wife. On top of this disappointment she also had to cope with the absence of Nurse Lisa with her sick father. It was only the presence of Lesley Bristowe who, as another woman, would understand her problems, that kept Sister sane and she increasingly came to rely on her calm efficiency.

The obvious repercussions of this arrangement were entirely lost on Sister, there being no place for subtlety or psychology in the Newbiggin mentality and, uncharacteristically, Lesley, who should have known better, failed to spot the effect of this behaviour – and the effect was to put the nose of Brigadier Ainsley Bennington seriously out of joint.

It was now three months since the monastic existence of the residents of Oldthorpe House had been shattered by the arrival in their midst of a female retired officer and, except for the shop-lifting drama, no major incident had occurred to cause concern amongst them. But insidiously the underlying mood of the place had changed from, to put it simply, relaxed mischievous anarchy to apparent ordered and controlled behaviour. 'Apparent' because, whilst it might have appeared to be so on the surface, the Cavaliers had in no way given up on their chosen path; they merely moved their war against the unnecessarily harsh rule of the owner, implemented by Sister Newbiggin, from the surface to underground. As such, the warfare had become subtle balloon-pricking rather than table-thumping and it was more often Sister's thoughtless behaviour, as in this latest Electoral Roll incident, that led to friction.

As for Brigadier Lesley, she found herself torn between the devil and the deep blue sea. Not approving of factions, she didn't wish to be labelled either a Roundhead or a Cavalier – although much preferring the company of the latter group – nor did she have any intention of aligning herself with the female management team. As a result she was in a form of limbo, in essence, a drifter. This was not an easy role to play at Oldthorpe and it was probably the effort of doing so – and a considerable effort it was proving to be – that dulled her awareness of the effect that Sister's attentions to her were having on Ainsley.

But Ainsley was no fool and being very aware that any explosion would seriously damage the very leadership position he was so determined to maintain he made himself bottle-up his hurt and frustration so that outwardly those around him saw little sign of his anger.

Or so he thought. But, of course, they did.

195

The two Cavaliers closest to him, Tubes Potter and Basil Reardon, whilst being aware of the darker mood of their friend, couldn't fathom what was causing it. They were no experts in psychology and accepted their lives and the lives of those around them very much at face value, but during their many visits to the pub over that long, hot early summer there were occasions when Ainsley's unaccustomed low spirits prompted questioning.

One afternoon near the end of July the three Cavaliers, having forsaken The Anchor, were squeezed into a corner of the very busy Cosy Cot Café. This sacrifice was made because they had persuaded Lucy Banbury to join them for some afternoon refreshment. The place was packed with visitors to Flaxton's seaside attractions but the manageress, strangely meeting them with a warmth they weren't expecting, had an extra table brought from the back and laid especially for them. Not only that, but Basil noticed that they were immediately served way ahead of others who were waiting. This he put down to the rightful seniority locals had over holiday-makers.

With the obligatory tea and tea-cakes before them it wasn't long before Tubes, as usual driving like a torpedo at its target, got matters off to a rollicking start.

"Ainsley you old rogue, it's no use suddenly being cheerful just because Lucy's here. With us these days you're a real misery-guts. Like a wet weekend in Margate."

"Margate? Why Margate?"

There it was again. That sharp, tetchy voice. So unlike the Ainsley of old.

"Steady, old man, steady." Tubes was having none of this. "No reason. I might just as well have said Bognor."

Basil drew heavily on his pipe, plunging those around him into a thick fog of tobacco smoke. "I met my first girl in Bognor." He managed to make the word 'Bognor' sound even more mournful than it warranted. "Well, actually she was pretty well my last girl as well."

Tubes sighed deeply and noisily. Poor old Basil. That was the trouble of course. Having him in one of his mournful moods was quite enough to cope with but Ainsley joining him was more than a chap could stand.

"Always merry, she was. Laughing away with her friends. They'd look at me whilst they were giggling – which was nice."

Tubes stared at Basil and was about to attempt to put him right regarding his staggering naivety, but in kindness decided not to.

"I have the most terrible memory of Bognor Regis." Lucy gave it it's full and proper title. "I was there with my sister. We'd gone for a week at the end of the war to try to forget for a few moments the decimation of our family in the preceding years. We stayed in a small boarding house near the beach, very cheap but clean."

Basil's affection for Lucy increased by the moment. It was typical that she should want them to understand every detail to ensure they saw the story in the right perspective.

"It was very difficult but we forced ourselves to have fun and on the first day we bought ourselves two smart bathing costumes and braved the icy waters. We thought we looked the bee's knees."

She gave a little laugh, her eyes fixed away from them onto the far wall of the café. Ainsley was about to say something but Basil stayed him with a small hand movement.

"Two forty-year-olds in our new white nylon bathers behaving like a couple of schoolgirls, splashing each other and then braving the cold and plunging down and pretending to swim. Of course we didn't; we'd never learnt how to."

Lucy clicked back to the present and gave each of them a quick look. They were surprised to notice that her face was delightfully pink with the trace of a blush on her cheeks. She was extraordinarily abandoned telling these men such intimacies but she was strangely compelled to do so. It was, she felt, time to become involved with this delightful family which had come into her life rather than stay forever on the sidelines.

"Nylon as a material was new then and I don't believe – in fact can't believe – that it had been tried and tested in swimsuits – certainly not white ones. We came out of the water together and made our way up the crowded beach. I remember being rather flattered at the glances we received from the men around us although, looking back, everyone seemed to stare at us."

"Not surprising, my dear." Tubes was stirring his tea rather fast and noisily. "Dashed handsome pair of girls like you."

Basil stopped the stirring with a firm hand. "That's enough of that I think, Tubes. Best let Lucy get on." He was finding the picture of it all strangely disturbing. Nice though...

Ainsley uncharacteristically said nothing and seemed to be miles away, staring at the counter at the rear of the shop.

"As we reached our deckchairs I had the shock of my life – in fact I nearly fainted. I was obviously dreaming the whole episode and the dream had turned into a nightmare."

Now their attention was riveted on her. No stirring or staring into the distance. They held their breaths. What terrible disaster had befallen the two sisters on that beach in Bognor Regis that had so traumatised Lucy and seared its memory into her brain?

Lucy's voice was now a whisper. The three of them had to sit forward to hear her over the buzz of chatter around them.

"My sister was naked. As the day she was born."

They didn't move. They could see there was more to come.

"I looked down – and so was I. My sister saw me and let out a squeal which, of course, attracted the attention of those who hadn't already seen us. Of course we grabbed our towels, and then all our things, and rushed from the beach and back to our digs. We were mortified and then, that evening, we packed our bags and rushed back home."

To their intense surprise Lucy started to giggle and this meant, to their great relief, they could do the same. Her giggle turned into a laugh and soon the other customers in the Cosy Cot became aware of this table of elderly people convulsed in paroxysms of near hysteria. Most unseemly.

"I'm a trifle lost on this one, Lucy." Tubes wiped tears from various parts of his beard. "Had they fallen off or something? The cossies?"

"It was the nylon, you see. White nylon immersed in water becomes transparent – at least it did in those days. I'd rather not try it now."

They didn't know what to say to that but each had a naughty little frisson of electricity rushing through them that they kept very much to themselves.

They sat in contented silence for a while and then Basil's

attention was diverted from diaphanous bathing costumes by a glance at Ainsley who had apparently totally taken leave of his senses. The man was staring into the distance with a stupid, some would say grotesque, expression on his face. A grin? Smile? Lear? Was it indigestion? Heartburn? All these questions darted through Basil's mind but before he could decide on any one answer the expression's creator leapt to his feet.

"More tea, I think."

Lucy shook her head. "Not for me, thank you, Brigadier. I have a Flower Arrangers' meeting at the church so must be off. I have really enjoyed this afternoon and you must forgive me for boring you with my memories but just to speak them out loud is a delightful novelty for me."

Basil and Tubes saw her off whilst Ainsley went to the counter for replenishments. The two of them wondered why he bothered; a trip to The Anchor couldn't be delayed for too long.

"Where did you meet your first lady friend, Tubes?" Basil, appearing through the smoke, seemed to be perking up.

"In the loft."

"Ah. Checking water pipes. I had to do that in winter. I was the only one who could squeeze through the hatch."

Again Tubes prepared a blistering comment but checked himself in time. Instead he did some more violent tea-stirring. "Fancy Dress. There were boxes of old clothes and my cousin and I decided ..." his voice died away. Such memories. "I saw a lot of her after that." He laughed, "In more ways than one."

Basil, blissfully unaware of the double entendre, just smiled. The only 'fancy dress' he'd ever put on was his first army uniform in the closing days of the Great War. 1918. He remembered it well. He was just 16 but had added on a couple of years at the recruitment office. His mother had cried but his father had just laughed. He'd never forgotten that laugh. Cruel, loud – and *at* him. It struck him now that he'd never heard his father laugh before – nor in the few years the old man had left to live.

For a while they sat silently, immersed in their contrasting thoughts, Tubes seeing a parade of beautiful girls who had flitted through his life and mentally popping them into wet white nylon bathing costumes, and Basil, that first splendid uniform – and his unsmiling father.

"Three teas." Ainsley set the metal tray down with a bang making the others jump, their minds jarred back to the noisy café.

Basil, to the others' relief, rested his pipe in the ashtray. "You took your time, old chap. Tubes was just telling me about his lady plumber. She evidently used to wear fancy dress."

Tubes, as so often happened, couldn't decide whether Basil was joking or not and, deciding to give him the benefit of the doubt, winked at him.

Basil was annoyed to find that he automatically winked back, and then quickly gulped at his tea. He pushed the cup away from him. "This tea's cold, Ainsley. You've been standing up there jawing again."

"Nonsense. Long queue. Had to wait my turn."

Basil saw that there was no queue and doubted there ever had been but Ainsley ploughed on now, seemingly, in the best of spirits.

"We three are mad, you know. Three hail and hearty men in the prime of their lives – well, I don't think Basil's ever tested his prime – and all we do is sit in this God-forsaken wilderness reading newspapers and magazines, ogling Nurse Lisa, goading Sister N and knocking back vast quantities of Adnams Best Bitter."

"And cold tea…" Basil felt that the point needed to be made again.

"Good for you, Basil. And cold tea. Always drank it out East." Ainsley noisily pushed back his chair on the tiled floor. "Multitude of uses." He ushered the others towards the door, gave a cheery wave and blew a kiss towards the counter whilst propelling his colleagues out onto the pavement.

No more than five minutes later, at their usual table in The Anchor with pints of the said Adnams finest brew in front of them, Basil leant through the familiar cloud of pipe smoke and said, "What uses?"

Ainsley and Tubes looked at each other and expelled a unison sigh. It's difficult when someone says something like that out of the blue. It makes you yet again fear for your – or their – sanity. There's enough of doing that anyway as 'handing in of dinner plate time' gets closer without having a chap reminding you that you – or he – or both is – or are – bonkers.

"Yes, indeed." Tubes felt a comment, any comment, might end a potentially confusing session with Basil before it really started. It was not to be.

"The trouble with you, Ainsley, is that you make wild statements without giving thought as to where they might lead. 'Good for you?' 'Cold tea?' 'Multitude of uses?' Go on, then, what uses?"

It wasn't these bursts of petulance that put them in fear of Basil, it was rather the simultaneous stoking of his already red-hot pipe which accompanied them.

Ainsley, whose thoughts had apparently been far away, swung into action. "The sepoys. Great soldiers. Fighting for King and Country. Rawalpindi. Got restless, you see. Poor show. Mutinous, some of 'em. Had to nip it in the bud. Corporal Tremlett came to me…"

"Not *the* Corporal Tremlett?" Basil briefly appeared in the smoke cloud.

"Eh?" Ainsley was confused.

"The one who saved your life in France in forty-four?"

Ainsley looked confused. Basil ploughed on, "Stuck his head up above the battlements. You told me."

Tubes found this whole conversation not only confusing but, in its absurdity, faintly aggravating. The sooner it was sorted out the better. He found a solution, "Must have been father and son. Both corporals. It happens."

Basil felt better. "Or uncle and nephew maybe."

"Will you both shut up."

These sudden mood changes of Ainsley's were a new and unpleasant challenge to his friends. There was an uncomfortable silence during which they each reduced pints to half-pints. Basil hated silences. He'd had more than enough of them during his childhood. He tried his gentle voice. "About the sepoys?"

Another silence then, like an indulgent parent, Ainsley was off.

"Restless. Corporal Tremlett…" he held up his hand to stifle any interruption, "no relation – came to me and warned me that a group of them was advancing on my bungalow. I was taking tea on the veranda at the time. They surged round the corner and this big chap came storming up to me. I rose slowly, as an officer would, and, grabbing the nearest object, crashed it down on his head. Shattered. Smithereens. Spewed its contents all over the place."

"Ainsley, that's revolting. For God's sake spare us the details." Tubes shuddered, "I've never liked the thought of brains at the best of times, but splattered…"

"What are you blathering about, man? The teapot. I grabbed it. It shattered. Tea everywhere. Corporal Tremlett took an age to gather up the pieces – and mop up."

'Amazing,' thought Basil.

'Rubbish,' thought Tubes.

"Did it quell the mutiny?" Basil liked a happy ending – and was rewarded with one.

"Just like that. No further trouble. Tea, you see. A multiple of uses." Ainsley could see that whilst Basil was apparently well satisfied Tubes most certainly was not. It was, he felt, time for a tactical withdrawal.

"Come on, you two. Dear Sister N calls. Oh Lord, dash it. Left my magazine in the Cosy Cot. Must get it. Costs a fortune. Load of rubbish. Who wants to know what's going on in the outside world anyway? See you chaps back in prison."

With that outpouring of incomprehensible rubbish he drained his glass and was off before the other two could say a word.

The bus ran slowly along the coast road delivering Tubes and Basil back to Oldthorpe House.

"It wasn't really the tea that quelled the riot, you know." Basil was a stickler for accuracy – rare in an artilleryman. "It was the teapot."

"It was, my dear naïve old chump, a load of poppy-cock. As if I haven't got my work cut out worrying about you, I've now got Ainsley on my mind. There's something wrong, I'm sure. Changes of mood. Miserable one minute, on a 'high' the next. I hope Sister hasn't been pumping too many pills into him."

Basil remained silent. There was still something disturbing

him, he knew the feeling of old. Something wasn't right. It came to him as they strolled into the driveway.

"But the tea wouldn't be cold, would it? It'd be scalding hot. I must ask Ainsley about it."

"I think it would be better if you didn't, old chum. Let sleeping Ainsley's lie," and then he added under his breath, "which he does so well…"

Lesley Bristowe licked the envelope, grimaced at the foul taste, and stuck it down. Then in a firm, clear hand she wrote the address of her niece and, with a further lick, added a first-class stamp. The whole operation was carried out with military precision as indeed it had to be. One pause and she would have torn the whole lot into little pieces; she knew she would; she'd done so half a dozen times already.

The letter had been difficult to write – more than difficult, nigh on impossible. Everything she had written, scored out, re-worded, re-phrased had been an anathema to her, a surrender of all her principles and values. However it was worded it read, both on and between the lines, as a plea for sanctuary, love and understanding.

She knew she could stay at Oldthorpe House no longer, seeing now that the whole idea had been flawed from the start, but in a way which had taken her by surprise. Whilst she'd been prepared for a male dominated environment, the nursing care hadn't been expected, nor as far as she was concerned, welcomed. She accepted that Sister Newbiggin had a job to do and, by all accounts, did it well but, to Lesley, the boot was very firmly on the wrong foot. Nursing care, fine: control, certainly not.

But that wasn't all. What made the situation ten times worse was that Sister had immediately marked her down as an ally in her crusade to subjugate the male residents whom she diagnosed as being, even at this latish stage in their lives, over-filled with nasty male hormones. She seemed totally unaware of the damage this strategy was causing not only to her own authority but also to Lesley's chances of being accepted amongst the men. And anyway, thought Lesley, the strategy was seriously flawed because no woman to her knowledge had ever been able to understand, let alone subjugate, male hormones.

And then there had been the terrible shop-lifting affair which, although entirely exonerated, had somehow made her dependent and vulnerable amongst her fellow residents and the staff. And lastly the men themselves, still treading on eggshells whenever she was anywhere near them.

So, she was beaten. Defeated. Three months of effort wasted. She had advanced, at first boldly, then hesitatingly across the battlefield and would now yield all that ground and retreat back to safety, the only safety available to her: her niece and husband and their three unruly children. It would be the first taste of defeat for Brigadier Lesley Bristowe – and the taste would be bitter. But – the decision was made.

Was it hell? She leapt up, grabbed the envelope and tore it into small pieces then, angrily screwing them up, sent them to join all their predecessors in the waste-paper basket.

At this low point in the lives of some of the Oldthorpe residents, Fate with a capital F took a hand. It was now mid July and the time was fast approaching for one of the great sporting events in the Oldthorpe House social calendar, the Annual Cricket Match. To be precise it was the only sporting event in which the residents took an exhausting, and in some cases, life-threatening part, others reaching them via the radio and television being more a drain on their wallets via the betting shops than their health.

The self-appointed President, Captain, Selector and one-man committee of the Oldthorpe House Cricket Team was, to no one's surprise, none other than Brigadier Ainsley Bennington.

Ainsley, by his own account, had had an illustrious career in the white flannels captaining, through his dizzy ascendancy in the Royal Tank Regiment, his Troop, Squadron and Regimental teams. He bowled a nifty leg-break and occasionally – as much to his surprise as the batsman's – managed to dislodge the bails. With his bat, through great application and concentration he tested fielders in areas where they – and he – least expected the ball to run. Even though his success at the higher level of the game was limited, amongst his peers at Oldthorpe he was king. However, as far as these peers were concerned, he was welcome to his crown, their only interest in cricket being of the sleep-in-front-of-the-television variety.

On hearing of it Gloria Cartiledge was immediately greatly in favour of this annual extravaganza and threw herself into the organising of it, reluctantly supported by Sister. She decided that her main input would be to prepare an enormous tea for the interval between innings. This would not only produce a far higher quality of food than usually emerged from the kitchen but also release the cook/chef, Clint Rogers/Jean-Paul, from his duties to join one of the teams. He was renowned for wielding a bat almost as recklessly as he did his trusty kitchen knife.

In the days prior to the match the garden was transformed into a miniature cricket ground; the lawn was mown to provide a fast outfield and the pitch itself shaved, rolled and watered to provide a surface as near to ideal for Ainsley's many types of bowling. In these vital cricketing matters he took personal charge and in keeping with his role as President, Captain and Selector, issued orders to all and sundry from the vantage point of a deckchair on the terrace.

The all and sundry who were most often co-opted for grounds-mens' duties were Tubes and Basil. Despite swearing not to be involved the following year they rarely escaped.

"I can trust you chaps. A true wicket. That's what we need." Ainsley would take a sip from his glass of lemon squash and smile on his sweating compatriots. "But remember our strengths. I like to bring the ball down full length just outside the off-stump, so if the surface is a little rough there, so be it…"

Freddy and Clarence were responsible for organising the boundary and deckchairs, but that was easier said than done because there was something about Clarence and the assembly of a deckchair that was totally incompatible. His gaunt body seemed to fold smoothly into its frame as he tussled with it so that they could neither be identified – nor prised – apart. In previous years it had been known for a saw to be used to separate the two of them, but this was only resorted to in extreme circumstances because of the fear of mistaking one for the other and ending up with a Clarence arm or leg dropping to the ground. This would seriously reduce his value as an umpire.

It will be seen that most of the preparation was done –

fairly unwillingly – by the Cavalier element of the residents. The Roundheads, in their posh front bedrooms, bided their time. Every year they attempted to have the match cancelled and every year their plea was rejected by Sister and her decision was now endorsed by an enthusiastic Gloria; the former on the grounds of health – it was the only exercise most of them had in the year – and the latter on the grounds of fun – why shouldn't the boys let their hair down once in a while?

That few of the residents saw the contest as fun was by the way; to them it was a manly joust of skill and dominance. Lesley Bristowe would better describe it as a battle of the hormones.

This year the preparation for the big day lifted Ainsley's spirits back to a level approaching his normal, dangerous self. The match would clearly be his opportunity to re-establish his now-disputed position as 'leader of the pack', and whilst he still followed his recent custom of disappearing into town most afternoons, he found time to take Tubes and Basil to the local recreation ground for a spot of secret practice. The result of this dedication to perfecting the finer points of this noblest of sports was immensely disappointing to the President, Captain and Selector, who spent much of the practice bullying his friends into at least trying to make contact between bat and ball. But it was to little avail. Tubes made the perfectly valid point that there was no room in a submarine for a cricket pitch and so the sport had passed him by and Basil insisted on batting with his pipe in his mouth and therefore couldn't see the bowler, let alone the ball, through the resulting smoke-screen.

But his team's lack of application was not the only cause for Ainsley's spirits to be sorely tested.

First there was 'the great ball controversy'. The gardening residents – mostly Roundheads – petitioned Sister for the replacement of the cricket ball with a tennis ball on the grounds of plant preservation. Ainsley, hormones rampant, was almost speechless with rage, hurling words like 'namby-pamby', 'girlie', 'lily-livered' and the like to anyone unfortunate enough to come into earshot.

Gloria, during one of her increasingly frequent visits, suggested a compromise with some old fruit netting from Cartiledge Towers which they stretched on canes around the flower beds.

Hot on that upheaval came the 'umpire dispute'. The Roundheads insisted that Clarence Cuthbert, zimmer supported, with dicky water-works, sight seriously impaired and well into his eighties, no longer possessed the credentials of your average cricket umpire. He also had the disadvantage of being totally partial in favour of one team and had, the previous year, adjudged two Roundheads 'leg-before-wicket' before the ball had even been bowled.

The Cavaliers were appalled to have the objection sustained by Sister and Gloria, who seemed to have formed themselves into a combination of the United Nations and the Court of Human Rights. There could be no appeal. Captain Cuthbert would have to join the ranks of spectators and remain entombed in his deckchair.

Finally, when Ainsley felt nothing more could be done to damage the match and its, or rather his, intended result came the biggest bombshell of all – SEX.

Gloria had the bright idea of incorporating women into the teams not, as the male hormoned members hoped, as liniment appliers, tea getters and white flannel pressers, but actually as players.

"You'll love it, dears," she announced to the women in her light bird-like way. "Give you all a chance to let your hair down and put some wind in your sails."

Sister wasn't sure. She wasn't sure at all. Hair down and wind in sails was better kept to the privacy of one's bedroom rather than aired in public. But secretly she rather liked the idea of playing; it could be fun – and it would be rather nice to rediscover fun.

As usual – and quite rightly as the owner's wife – Gloria prevailed, and an extremely grumpy President, Captain and Selector sat down in the summerhouse to pick the two teams, each of six men and, dammit, women. And then, blow the President, Captain and Selector, if dear old Gloria didn't pop in and plonk herself down opposite him.

"Here we are then, dearie. What fun. How do we do it? Names in a hat then choose the Captains?"

Ainsley was dumbfounded. He just stared at her.

"I've brought some snippets of paper…"

"Madam." This was the President speaking.

"Gloria, dearie. As you well know. I think you should captain one of the teams in recognition of all your hard work." She smiled so sweetly at him that he found himself smiling back.

"You are too kind." This was more the sarcasm of a Team Captain but it was totally lost on Gloria.

"That's right, dear. I'd love to take part but I think I'll be more use here in the pavilion with Crumb and the teapot."

Ainsley sometimes found conversations running away from him. He tried to re-establish control. "Traditionally we have the nucleus of two teams." The Selector had now taken over. "And if you feel we must augment them with, er, female passengers – I mean, players – then so be it. They are as follows."

Ainsley pushed a sheet of paper across the table. There were two columns:-

CAVALIERS	ROUNDHEADS
A. Bennington (capt)	R. Bellows (capt)
Tubes Potter	T Rickworth
B. Reardon	J. Drummond (wkt)
F. Foster (wkt)	P. Phelps
C. Rogers	

"Well done, dear. Most of the work done. Good to see Clint out of his kitchen for a change. Give us space to prepare the tea. Now then, Sister, Lisa and, of course, Brigadier Lesley. That'll put you up to six each. Who's for which?"

Gloria always spoke so fast that she tended to leave Ainsley somewhat behind and, it has to be said, floundering a little.

"Um." It was the best that the President, Captain and Selector could manage.

"My bits of paper, luvvie. Just the job. Now then." With tongue slightly protruding through her little lips, Gloria wrote and very slowly recited, "S-i-s-t-e-r. That's one. L-i-s-a. Another. And L-e-s-l-i-e. There."

Ainsley found himself mimicking Gloria, "L-e-s-l-e-y."

"Never mind, dear. She'll know who she is." She folded the pieces of paper. "No peeking now. Close your eyes."

Was this really happening? To a President? A Chairman? The Selector? Ainsley did as he was told. A little soft hand guided his to the three folded scraps.

"Your team first."

He selected one, opened his eyes and unscrewed the paper. "Sister. Oh good." He really couldn't make it sound anything other than Neville Chamberlain announcing the outbreak of war.

"Now Ronnie's team." Gloria was really enjoying herself. The same procedure.

"Lesley." Good, he thought. She'd have been a pain to captain.

"And that leaves Lisa for them as well. Wasn't that fun? Shall you tell them or shall I?"

"As Captain…" Ainsley rose majestically – and then sank, aware that the last thing he wanted to do was to tell the women anything regarding team selection. "As Captain, I would be grateful if you would, Gloria. They must be ready for combat at two o'clock sharp. It is then that we shall toss-up for first innings."

Gloria clapped her hands together gleefully. "Oh what jolly fun. I must join the kitchen brigade. Sandwiches, cakes, jelly and cream. Good luck, dearie. May the best team win." With that she scampered away across the lawn, Ainsley wincing as she invaded and crossed the pristine wicket.

"What does she mean? There's no question as to who will win. No question at all."

The weather forecast for East Anglia's coastal strip warned of heavy cloud, showers and a strong easterly wind blowing in from the sea, and so the sky was clear, the sun shone down and the air was calm and warm.

The 'Ground', as Ainsley re-christened the garden each annual Match Day, was a picture of festive fun and frivolity. Nurse Lisa and Phyllis Coombe had hung bunting and balloons over the summerhouse – or 'Pavilion', to which status it had been promoted for the duration of the match – deckchairs, one already entombing Clarence, surrounded the boundary which was marked out in dabs of white distemper; a sheet hung from a wall trellis as a sightscreen, and, looking rather menacing in the centre of the mown grass, stood the stumps, three at one end for the batsmen, one at the other for the bowler. As in beach cricket, only one batsman at a time would face the onslaught of the opposing Truman or Statham and if he – or she – tonked the ball into a neighbour's garden, then the umpire's finger would be raised and the culprit sent trudging the long eight-or-so yards back to the pavilion.

Ainsley won the toss – or, more accurately, probably won the toss; he scooped the coin up so quickly that no one other than him was sure, but there was no point in arguing and anyway the captain of the Roundheads hardly cared. The sooner it was all over, the better.

Ainsley elected to bat and, surprise of surprises, also elected to open the innings. There was a pause, during which the spectators dozed in the warm sunshine or chatted about anything other than cricket, and then A. Bennington (captain), as the half-dozen or so type-written scorecards announced him to be, appeared. It must be said that he was immaculately turned out – as a President, Captain and Selector would be. Pristine whiteness, sharp creases, blanco'd boots and pads, a multi-coloured cap from some Colonial cricket club now long defunct, thick batting gloves that had cost him far more than he could afford, and a gleaming linseed-oiled bat twirling in his hand. The Denis Compton of Thorpe Haven was marching out to do battle.

Gloria led the applause and, in deference to her position as the owner's wife, everyone around the boundary joined in enthusiastically.

Ainsley took guard. "Middle and leg please, umpire."

With minor adjustments to the pitch and then himself, he was ready. He adopted an ultra-correct stance and peered down the wicket. What on earth was happening? In the distance, up against the sheet hanging on the wall trellis he could just make out Ronnie Bellows, the opposing skipper, talking to – surely not? It was. Lesley Bristowe.

Before he could register what was going on, the umpire shouted "play" and the lady Brigadier came bounding in.

Lesley was ashamed of herself. All her competitive instincts said 'get him first ball', but her plan was to do just the opposite. Let

Ainsley pick up twenty or so runs and his confidence would return and, maybe, she could start to build a rapport with him. They could then chat about cricket as equals – she'd captained the Women's Royal Army Corps First Eleven for many seasons and had had an England trial – and then she'd be accepted amongst them and live happily ever after.

That was the plan but, like so many plans, it went hideously wrong right from the start.

Ainsley, mesmerised by the sight of a fast approaching Lesley, froze. He didn't see the gently lobbed ball as it arced its way towards him, a gift for the blindest of batsman, and only became aware of it as it shattered his wicket.

"Not ready," bellowed the President, Captain and Selector.

"I think I bowled a no-ball," pleaded Lesley to the umpire.

"Out," said the umpire and, to emphasise the point, raised his finger in dismissal.

No one moved. And then, very slowly, hunch-shouldered, Ainsley made his way back to the pavilion. As if the atmosphere wasn't charged enough Gloria, feeling everyone needed some encouragement, clapped enthusiastically and, as before, those around the boundary followed suit.

Ainsley did not reappear for the remainder of the Cavaliers' innings which, in some ways, was a pity because he was the only person on both teams to be wearing white, thereby giving a cricketing feel to the occasion.

Tubes, Basil, Freddy and Clint-the-cook knocked up fifty or so runs against a bowling attack depleted by the retirement of Lesley in utter confusion and desolation to the third-man boundary after her one and only over.

When the Roundheads batted she opened the innings with the firm intention of getting herself out quickly but, as often happens in such circumstances, it wasn't to be. The bowling was so innocuous that, to a first-class player, it just couldn't be ignored and, with the boundary only a few yards away, her fifty came up only half-an-hour after tea. Then at last, she managed to get herself out leaving her skipper to make the few runs required for an historic win.

Everyone was certain of one thing. It had been a marvellous afternoon, the best ever. Everyone, that is, except Ainsley and Lesley who, in their own totally opposite ways, had suffered an unmitigated disaster. They missed supper and went straight to their rooms and there, sitting at their respective dressing-tables, they started writing.

No one really missed the two of them that evening. There was no celebration they should be attending. The victorious Roundheads and, in all honesty, the other members of the defeated Cavaliers, treated the annual event as a bit of fun – and a chore – that warranted little attention once it was over. Tubes understood that Ainsley, particularly in his present strange mood, would want to lick his wounds in private and they all felt that Lesley, after her splendid innings, would want an early night.

Next morning Sister found Lesley sitting in the Residents' Lounge staring out of the French windows.

"Good morning, Brigadier. Bright and early this morning." She started her infuriating cushion pummelling. "Looking out on the scene of your triumphs? You did so well. The Roundheads will be proud of you – and serve those Cavaliers right."

Her pummelling had got dangerously close to Lesley who shot her arm out and stayed the violent action.

"Sister…"

"Oh do please call me Amelia." She was almost twittering. "All girls together. Good to put those men in their place. Fancy you being a top cricketer. Hiding your light under a bushel…" She'd moved on to rearranging the already arranged curtains.

"Sister, I must talk to you. You see, that's the trouble. Exactly that. Factions. It never works. It's wrong." The staccato sentences came tumbling out in a totally un-Lesley-like disorganised way. She got up. "I've written to my…"

At that moment they were frightened out of their lives by Father Christmas hurling himself into the room. Closer examination showed it to be the white bearded and whiskered Tubes dressed in a scarlet dressing-gown. Here he was, wild-eyed, doing an impression of Neville Chamberlain, waving a piece of paper above his head.

"He's done it. The chump. The idiot. Oh Ainsley, why? Why?" He dropped like Father Christmas's sack into an armchair.

This was definitely a Tubes in considerable anguish. They'd never seen him like this before, he was usually the most undemonstrative of men, and they knew that something must be terribly wrong. Lesley moved over to him and gently took the paper from his hand. She read it and then handed it to Sister.

I CANNOT TAKE COUNTRY LIFE ANYMORE AND HAVE DECIDED TO END IT FORTHWITH. THANK YOU FOR YOUR FRIENDSHIP. I'M SORRY IF THIS CAUSES ANY DISTRESS. AINSLEY BENNINGTON

"It was under my door. There when I got up." Tubes put his head in his hands. "Why? We could have talked it over. Damn it. It was only a game."

The last sentence froze Lesley. That there might be a connection between the cricket match and Ainsley's disappearance hadn't struck her. She had driven him to do it. Her selfishness. Thoughtlessness. She had made him an object of ridicule in front of everyone, both residents and staff.

Without a word she left the room and climbed the stairs to pack.

12

"He looks rather fuzzy." Police Constable Partington of the Flaxton-on-Sea Constabulary blew on the photograph as if doing so would transform it into a sharper image.

He, Tubes, Basil and Sister were squashed into Ainsley's bedroom, Tubes and Basil sitting uncomfortably on the bed which they both felt was rather like sitting on the poor man's coffin and Sister, white as a sheet, on the only chair. The policeman was poking around the drawers and cupboards and, remembering his very recent training, was using his pencil to gingerly explore their contents.

"Brigadier Bennington was in no way a fuzzy officer." Basil, at his haughty best, felt the honour of the army was at stake. "He was…"

"Is…" Tubes nudged his friend.

"Pardon?"

"Is, old man. Let's cling to the hope that he still is, rather than was."

Basil allowed his tenseness to get the better of him. "Please let me finish, Tubes. Sometimes I am in fear that your interruptions cloud the issue. As I was saying …"

"Like this photo." The policeman wiped it with a grubby finger. "Cloudy."

"He was − is − a fine, upstanding officer." Basil signalled that he had said his piece with a curt nod.

"Outstanding." Tubes added weight to his friend's testimonial.

"Up or out?" PC Partington pulled a black notebook from his breast pocket and prepared to write.

Sister sighed, "Does it really matter?"

"What's he blathering about, Tubes?" Basil knew a confused feeling when he had one; it seemed to invade him more and more these days.

The policeman looked at them all balefully.

"My notes must be precise in the event of them having to

be read out in court. Was this chap..." he flicked back through the pages, "Ainsley Bennington upstanding, as in straight like a poker, or outstanding as in looking a bit funny?" Seeing the confusion on their faces he decided to help even more. "I need to know, you see, so that we can issue a description."

Tubes was all for letting this inane conversation die but Basil, unsettled by this aggravating man, dived in again.

"He was both of those things but, if I may say so, I find your interpretations absurd."

The policeman looked as if he might have a little cry.

Basil dived on. "He was upstanding, that is, of the finest character and outstanding which is to say that the splendid man was..."

"Is," Tubes would have his say.

"SHUT UP TUBES." Basil grabbed at his friend who, surprised by this friendly fire, felt that in retaliation he might hit him. He'd accidentally hit a few chaps in his Torpedo Room in his time.

"Sorry, old fellow." Basil didn't know what had come over him to shout at dear old Tubes. "Carried away d'you see? Where was I? Oh yes, Brigadier Ainsley Bennington was – is – outstanding, that is to say head and shoulders above the rest."

Another curt nod. The policeman spoke at his slow speed of writing. "V-er-y tall."

"NO." Basil's yelp made them all jump but the policeman who had been putting all his mental energies into the difficult business of writing, looked up and dropped two bombshells that left the bed-sitters speechless, utterly speechless.

"How do you spell Brigadier?"

How could anyone reach a mature age – well, in this chap's case a moderately mature age – and not know how to spell an everyday word like Brigadier?

Sister, who had been far away contemplating the owner's wrath on being told of the loss of one of his residents, noted the stupefying effect the question was having on the two men and obligingly spelt it out for the policeman. Again he wrote laboriously, intoning the syllables whilst doing so. "Brig - a - dier."

Then he dropped the second bombshell – of even larger

calibre than the first.

"What is a Brig - a - dier?"

The men just gulped. Sister dived in again, this time with a simple explanation that left the policeman as befogged as he had been before. But now, with the formalities completed, real detection could be started.

"No better photos, then?" Another wipe of the fuzzy picture with an oily thumb which had only recently eased his bicycle chain back onto its sprockets. The fuzzy Ainsley dropped back into even greater obscurity.

"Can't understand it." Tubes felt misunderstood by both friend and foe. "He had a lot of albums. We all had to, er, were privileged to look through them frequently. Whole career, do you see?"

The policeman didn't. Tubes took the bicycle-oil-stained photo from him. "Must have fallen out of an album. A fine man. Born in 1899." He gently wiped it with his hanky in respect to his – hopefully temporarily – departed friend.

PC Partington did some adding up on his fingers, his face contorting as it struggled with some basic mental arithmetic. "That puts him in his seventies, doesn't it?" He wanted it to sound more a statement than a question but he was open to correction if necessary.

They nodded. Did he really need confirmation?

He whistled through his teeth. "They're losing them by then, you see – their marbles." He could tell that he wasn't carrying his audience with him but then, he reasoned, they were all probably as gaga as each other. They'd have to be for one of them to be named after the London Underground system.

He aggravatingly whistled through his teeth again. "Just wander off. Fall into a ditch. Under a train. Off a cliff…"

He saw the London Underground chap leaping up and retreated, automatically feeling for his whistle. He wasn't the first person to confuse the sight of an advancing white bristly, bearded, rampant Tubes with being attacked by a giant lavatory brush. He was further disturbed to find that his whistle had disappeared to some dark, fluffy corner of his jacket lining. He felt a caution would be in order.

"Now then, sir…"

"Don't 'now then sir' me, my man. Are you the best our inflated rates can afford? Brigadier Ainsley Bennington is as hale and hearty as any of us." The extra effort of this admonition caused Tubes to collapse in a fit of rasping coughing.

'And gaga,' thought the policeman...

Tubes recovered sufficiently to continue hoarsely, "And, despite his disappointment yesterday..."

"Bowled by a woman." Basil wanted to help. Always a dangerous sign, "First ball."

"How was that, sir?"

The policeman's cricketing expression was totally coincidental but was not lost on Tubes who added to the confusion by murmuring, "Not out."

Basil continued helping. "Eye off the ball, d'you see? And his stance was lower than usual." He picked up Ainsley's shining bat, unblemished by yesterday's brief journey to the wicket and now relegated to a corner of the room where it had obviously been thrown, and arranged himself at an imaginary wicket. "The back-swing would leave a gap..."

Sister had had quite, indeed more than, enough. "Thank you, Major Reardon. I don't think this is getting us anywhere. We require a search now, Constable. Of Thorpe Haven, Flaxton, East Anglia, the whole country if necessary." Her voice was rising steeply and those present, even the Flaxton Constabulary, knew that immediate action was required to replace words. "Here is a list from my files. The Brigadier's known contacts, next-of-kin – a nephew in the television industry up here – and those places he most frequently frequents."

Basil found the last two words intriguing and giggled nervously. This confirmed PC Partington's fear that both he and the Underground chap were indeed gaga.

Sister opened the door. "Off you go and FIND HIM. Get the note analysed expertly. Please God it doesn't mean suicide. He might just have gone back to the south." Partington found himself being propelled down the stairs. "He comes from London, you see. Hence his reference to the country. That's all it might mean."

PC Partington had not joined the Police Force to be chivvied, even by bossy nurses. He halted his exit through the front door by raising his hand as he had been taught to do when required to perform traffic duty.

"One moment, madam."

They all came to a halt in the hall. "This woman who balled him." Again he noted the gaga looks. He felt dangerously naked without his whistle in easy reach.

"BOWLED, man." Tubes had had more than enough. "BOWLED. Dear Lord, have you never watched cricket. You're a Englishman, for God's sake."

PC Partington drew himself up to his full five foot seven. "We, sir, are far too busy upholding the law to have time for fripperies. Now, about this woman?"

"It was I, Officer." Brigadier Lesley stood in the sitting room doorway. Her voice was calm and unusually soft. "It is I with whom you wish to speak. You see, I killed him."

There was no doubt that Lesley Bristowe was in a bad way. Having sent the representative of the Flaxton Constabulary on his way – they feared a serious skin complaint as he tore violently at his uniform jacket unaware that it was a vain attempt on his part to extricate his whistle – they all assembled in the lounge. The Roundheads, whilst deeply concerned for their recently lost colleague, maintained their usual silence but the Cavaliers, to whom Lesley had been drawn after considerable soul-searching were, as usual, most vociferous. They rightly saw Ainsley as one of their own and now closed ranks, gathering in a group around the fireplace. Basil had very firmly led Lesley to one of the armchairs where she sat forward on the front edge, bolt upright, twisting a handkerchief in her hands.

Tubes was, as usual, 'on the bridge'. "Lesley, old love…" It was unusual of him to use such endearing terms; they weren't a natural part of a submariner's vocabulary. "You really must stop torturing yourself, old girl".

There he went again. Lesley, whilst appreciating the sentiment, would have been happy with a little less of the 'old'.

He smiled down at her from his anchorage at the fireplace. "No more talk of killing, eh? That daft copper nearly took you in on the spot."

Squadron Leader Freddy described a stall turn with his

hand. "Probably get your old cell back."

Basil sighed. "Another landing with your undercarriage up. Well done, Freddy."

Tubes did a bit of up-and-downing on the balls of his feet; a sure sign that he was in command. "Ainsley hasn't been himself for some time. We all know that."

There was a rustling from deep down in a chair and Clarence popped into view. "We had a chap like that. At Epping. Nineteen forty-four. Got the wrong paybook. Thought he was being ordered to be someone else. So he did – and was. Only got his real name back at demob." With a contented feeling that he had contributed something useful to the conversation he sank back again into obscurity.

As so often happened after a Cuthbert utterance there was a short period of silence, not so much to digest his jewels of wisdom but rather to try to work out why he had bothered to utter them and where they'd been before he had. Lesley got things moving again.

"I only lobbed it at him. Slowly. A dolly."

"Seemed to fizz to me." Freddy still hadn't got his undercarriage down. "And over-arm. I thought girls bowled under-arm."

"My cousins…" Basil's female cousins had a lot to answer for.

"Will you all please SHUT UP." Tubes was finding the responsibilities of commanding this lot rather more than he could easily handle. "We are NOT, I repeat, NOT talking cricket here. The match had nothing to do with it or, if it did, it was only the final straw. Ainsley's been odd for ages. Look at his Cosy Cot Café fixation. Dragging us there for revolting tea…"

"Cold."

"Shut up, Basil – sorry old chap, but do please let me get on. Sloping off there on his own. Knocking back the Adnam's Best in The Anchor as if his life depended on it."

Lesley half rose. "Perhaps it did." They all looked her. "Perhaps he had some terrible illness."

"Sister would know. Nothing gets past Sister." Basil's pipe was at full throttle now, and the Roundheads, sitting silently around the room, began to lose sight of the smoke-enveloped

Cavaliers and felt it safe to drift off to their rooms.

"Sister never knew about my boil." The trembling voice came from somewhere in Clarence's armchair. "Nurse Lisa and I kept it a secret. She dressed it every morning." He struggled into view. "Because I couldn't reach it. It was on my…"

"PLEASE, Clarence." Tubes had had quite enough. "We will disperse and visit Ainsley's haunts. Lesley would you please take on the Café. Basil please check with Sister and the others to find if there are any other known ports of call he might have visited – chemists, etcetera, and check on them. Freddy stay here to field any incoming messages. I will cross-question the regulars and the landlord at The Anch…"

"I thought you might." Freddy looped-the-loop with his hand which finished in a smart salute.

Lesley shook her head, exasperated by his flippancy, but there were more important things to sort out. There was something that none of them had yet addressed. "What about the note?" It was the wording that worried, indeed frightened her more than anything else. "'Ending it forthwith'. 'Causing distress'. It sounds so – so final."

Again there was silence and then Tubes marched towards the door. "That's what we've got to find out. Any talk of, er, suicide? Running away? What was really distressing him?"

They all followed him out, Freddy, supporting Clarence, bringing up the rear.

"Even you didn't know about my boil, did you, Freddy?" The old man seemed well pleased with himself.

"Not even me, you old rascal. But then, it seems Freddy doesn't really know about anything of any importance."

With the men launched on their various missions Sister took Lesley upstairs to the privacy of her bedroom and having settled her in the only armchair, revealed her agitation by busily straightening her already straightened bed-clothes.

"It's so unlike him," she pummelled a pillow, "always so assured. Flippant, yes, but underneath it all – oh…" another pillow was sorted out, "if only the Cartiledges weren't away. Here I am trying to impress them with my ability to be Matron and it's one disaster after another."

Lesley was about to rebuke her for thinking of herself at a

time like this but decided it was not the moment. Instead she steered them back onto the Ainsley mystery.

"But what about all his photo albums? Where are they?"

She asked the question because she felt it so unlike Ainsley to have maybe destroyed his precious albums. In the few months she'd been at Oldthorpe he'd already taken her through them at least half a dozen times as he proudly pointed out obscure moments in his life that meant so much to him.

Sister paused in her frenzied pillow pummelling.

"There's one album he never showed you – or anybody – except me. One day when he and I were very low and, for some reason, found ourselves comforting each other."

She sat on the bed, for once still, and her voice was quieter and gentler than Lesley imagined it could ever be.

"He'd been married, you know. His wife was killed in the blitz. In London. He was abroad, I think. He told me about her and showed me photos of their wedding. Distraught. They were young, you see. Very much in love." She smiled, "I think his manner, you know, the bravado and silliness, it hides his loneliness – from himself and from us. And being sort of in command of the residents helps. Gives him a purpose." Then she quietly added, "Or gave."

"Ah." Lesley sat forward and tapped Sister's knee. Here was an opportunity too good to miss and Lesley intended to use it to its full advantage.

"This business of command, Sister. Something I feel we should discuss – and now is just the right moment."

The two of them settled down to an earnest chat before the Brigadier, with a lighter heart than she'd had for some considerable time, set off to trawl the town for information regarding the whereabouts of the missing Ainsley.

Against all her military training, Lesley left the house without an inkling of what her plan would be once she reached the centre of Flaxton. She knew that the police were meant to be 'making enquiries' but if PC Partington was anything to go by there couldn't be much hope of success from that direction. The other Cavaliers were visiting Ainsley's known haunts but, eager as they were, she didn't think much more than beer sampling would emerge from their investigations. There needed to be some blunt questioning, and now that a few matters had been amicably sorted out with Sister her mind was able to concentrate on doing just that.

She climbed down from the bus in Flaxton's High Street. There in front of her was the Cosy Cot Café. She smiled. Its popularity with her fellow Cavaliers was now clear: it was only half-a-dozen steps from the bus stop and not far down the street from a swinging sign showing a ship's anchor! With its tables sporting brightly embroidered cloths and the walls and shelves covered with old china, knick-knacks and photographs of old Flaxton, the Cosy Cot was indeed as cosy as any café could be.

Its problem today was that it was obviously the only cosy café in town and, as a result, there wasn't a single spare table. Lesley was about to leave and come back later when her attention was caught by the waving arm of a petite, prim lady sitting bolt upright on her own in a far corner. She immediately recognised her as Lucy Banbury with whom she shared a pew most Sundays at the Parish Church.

She had been introduced to Lucy by the Cavaliers who regularly attended 'Church Parade', somewhat to the dismay of the young Rector – they called him Padre – who knew that the culmination of every attendance would be a detailed and rather loud critique of his sermon carried out at the porch door as his flock were filing past. Their saving grace was that they sang lustily, particularly the Squadron Leader who had a delightful tenor voice, suggesting that at least some members of the congregation were actually enjoying themselves.

Lesley joined Lucy and in no time another pot of tea and a warm scone had been placed on the table.

Lucy was appalled to hear the news of the missing Ainsley. He had, she said, been in fine form when she had last seen him, which, by coincidence, had been here in the café. As she usually did she sat very still whilst Lesley told her all about the cricket match and the note, but as it became apparent that Lesley was distressed at what she saw as her involvement in his departure she put a hand on her arm.

"That, my dear, if I may say so, is utter rubbish."

Lesley hadn't been spoken to quite so firmly for many a

long year and it made her stop dead in her tracks.

Lucy went on in her firm, quiet voice, "We're speaking here of a man in his seventies, not a little rascal at school – although I agree that sometimes it is difficult to differentiate between the two with the Cavaliers."

Her smile relaxed Lesley but there was more to come. "I can't begin to count the number of occasions when my pupils had their noses put out of joint by just such a catastrophe as a first-ball duck or something similar. I have always been of the opinion that it conditioned them for so many similar occasions ahead of them in their adult lives and I'm quite sure that Ainsley was equally well prepared. No, there's something more to this than your excellent bowling."

Lesley was reassured by this logic but if it wasn't pique that had driven Ainsley to do something dreadful, what on earth was it?

"It's the note that really worries me." She brought an envelope out of her handbag on which she had copied down the bleak message.

"'I cannot take country life anymore and have decided to end it forthwith'. That's dreadful. So final. 'I'm sorry if this causes any distress'." She felt a lump rising in her throat and was somewhat surprised to note that Lucy, rather than sharing the emotion, appeared to be miles away.

When the bill for the tea was produced Lesley asked the waitress if they might have a quick word with the manageress but this, she was told, wouldn't be possible. Mavis had left. She had only been in Flaxton temporarily whilst she looked after her sick mother but now that the poor woman had died Mavis had gone back south to her folks. Lesley described Ainsley to her and they were surprised how quickly she recognised him. Oh yes, he obviously loved the place and would often stay on after they'd closed chattering to them all. They all had many a good laugh.

This just didn't sound like the rather austere, touching on the pompous, Ainsley that both Lesley and Lucy had got to know and they left the café feeling further from solving the mystery than when they had met.

So what now? Lesley had no answer to her own question.

Ainsley obviously got some comfort from Mavis but surely that wouldn't decide him to end it all; that he couldn't take life anymore. He was made of far sterner stuff than that and, as Sister, and now Lucy, had said, her arrival at Oldthorpe was surely hardly a suicide issue.

Should they go to The Anchor? Not yet. Tubes wouldn't be pleased to have his detection toes trodden on, and she knew that his enquiries would be long, detailed, and thirst making.

They were idly walking along the pavement when Lucy stopped in her tracks and asked an extraordinary question.

"Was the note in capitals or lower case?"

Lesley had to think for a moment. "As far as I can recall it was in capitals. Do you think it matters?"

"It well might. Does the name Sanjiv Patel mean anything to you?"

The questions were getting stranger by the minute. Wait a moment though, there was something about that name. She'd heard it before, quite often in fact, but in what context?

She felt Lucy's finger tapping her arm and followed her gaze up above the window of the shop.

SANJIV PATEL – Newsagents.

Of course. 'Sanjiv's got it wrong again.' 'Who ordered The Lady'? 'That Patel man's an idiot, I have the Daily Express, not the Daily Sport'. Sanjiv Patel, rather inefficient purveyor of newspapers and magazines to Oldthorpe House.

"Let's pop inside and have a word with Mr Patel." Lucy was already in the shop before she'd finished the sentence.

Two minutes later they rushed out scattering everyone in their path and, at an unseemly trot, made their way back to the Cosy Cot Café.

Nearly everyone was out and about when the telephone rang in the hall at Oldthorpe House. It was just bad luck that Clarence Cuthbert was emerging from the cloakroom at that moment and picked up the receiver.

"Oldthorpe House, home for retired…"

"Who's that?" The female voice was urgent and almost as loud as Clarence's.

"…officers of His Majesty's Forces."

There was a silence which, to Clarence, suggested that the conversation had come to an end but just before he unravelled the handset from his hearing aid the voice was back again.

"Is that you, Clarence?"

"Captain Clarence Cuthbert, Royal Signals, retired, speaking."

"It's me, Clarence, Lesley – and it's 'Her' not 'His'."

This was, of course, far too much for most hale and hearty people to handle, never mind an eighty-plus deaf and multi-infirm chap who longed to retrace his steps to the safety of the cloakroom. Lesley wished she'd left the sex of the Sovereign in abeyance until later.

"Please get Sister, Clarence."

The old man was no fool and, despite his infirmities, he could handle the telephone as well as anyone. After all, had he not been a Royal Signals Officer?

"Which would you like me to fetch first? Clarence Lesley or Sister Clarence? And I have to tell you, madam, that I fear you have the wrong number because we have neither living here and therefore whichever you choose first I cannot get them for you." Clarence was really proud of what had been his longest sentence for quite some time.

Lesley tried to keep her voice sounding pleasant which wasn't easy. "I've got to go, the train's coming in. Tell Sister I'll phone later." And with that the instrument went dead.

Clarence shuffled back to the cloakroom, the whole experience having badly knocked his equilibrium. A few moments later, much relieved, he had forgotten the unsettling phone call had ever taken place.

The evening came and with it a highly distraught Sister. She banged around the kitchen tidying away everything in sight including, much to the fury of chef Jean-Paul, the cutlery and crockery which he was using to prepare supper. He, dodging around and under her flailing arms, was glad to have his ever-faithful knife on hand to protect himself should she finally 'flip her lid' – more a Clint Rogers expression than his Gallic alter-ego.

"Where is she?" Sister hurled the challenge at Lisa who, deciding to reorganise the drugs cupboard rather than watch

Sister sparring with Jean-Paul, replied as best she could.

"Brigadier Bristowe left after your meeting with her in your room."

It was a simple, factual answer that incurred something approaching a squeal from Sister.

"I KNOW. I SENT HER OUT. But where is she NOW?"

"Still out?" Jean-Paul's observation was a mistake. He would have done better to have let the ladies have their little chat whilst he continued his culinary pursuits. Sister advanced on him causing him to retire with his back to the sink, his knife held like a ceremonial sword before him. She literally brushed him aside and violently washed a clean saucepan she'd swept up from the table. Her voice moved with ease from hectoring to grumbling. "Ever since Matron left six months ago it's been one disaster after another."

"It wasn't much better when she was here..." Jean-Paul thought he might be helping – but evidently not.

"No, indeed. WHAT?" The saucepan looked far more dangerous than the knife.

"Oh Sister, PLEASE." Lisa turned and stamped her foot. "We know it's rotten and the least Brigadier Lesley could have done is ring but you must trust her. She's a grown woman for heaven's sake. Much more able to look after herself than the men – and they're all safely back."

"Except what's-his-name." Jean-Paul obviously wanted to die, crushed to pulp by a stainless steel saucepan. He was saved, not by the bell, but by a perfunctory knock on the door and the hand of Squadron Leader Freddy flying in, followed by its owner.

"Getting supper? How nice. Lesley's just phoned. You won't have heard it ringing because of all the racket you were making so I took the call."

Sister rushed at Freddy as if to enact a mid-air collision and he banked steeply to port.

"Don't let her hang up," she fired in a rapid burst at him.

"She's hung."

For a moment Sister had a vision of a body and a noose. "WHAT DO YOU MEAN, HUNG?" If possible, this was yelled louder than anything that had gone before.

Freddy's sweet, helpful, reply was in stark contrast. "Hung up, Sister. That's what she's done. She was in a rush. Said, 'Not to worry. All's well. See you tomorrow. Here's the taxi'."

"HERE'S THE TAXI?" It seemed the simplest of phrases was causing Sister apoplexy.

"That's the ticket. Supper nearly ready?"

There were times when the bravest of pilots sought cloud cover to regroup and this seemed to be one of those moments. The three occupants of the kitchen were staring at a closed door.

Only one person spent anything approaching a peaceful night in Oldthorpe House – and even he – Captain Clarence Cuthbert – had his punctuated by the usual frequent visits to the loo. The others were plagued by every type of imagining concerning the fate of Ainsley Bennington and, with the exaggerated fears that darkness brings, they saw his lifeless corpse, a prey to creatures of the night, in any number of bizarre settings.

Sister's aspirins were no help. She had sacked Nurse Lisa for refusing to hand over the key to the drugs cupboard and then quickly reinstated her. Such was her state that she knew she would have taken an overdose of something, not to kill herself but to try to get some sleep before the dreaded morrow.

All night she tossed and turned. For her it would obviously be a matter of resignation. As Sister in charge of an Old People's Home it was unforgivable to lose any one of her charges, let alone two, and the Inquiry and subsequent publicity didn't bear thinking about. And the next-of-kin? The police? Could – would – she be charged with manslaughter? Prison? As always happens at times of crisis, as the night wore on, her thoughts became blacker and blacker and, with passing, more surreal. Eventually, exhausted, she slept.

The said morrow seemed to take a devil of a long time coming but, as dreaded, it came. Breakfast was sombre. Everyone knew that today would be the day of reckoning and so moved silently from place to place not daring to look at, much less speak to, each other.

Then the telephone rang.

As he spent most of his day travelling to and from the

cloakroom it was perhaps no coincidence that it was Clarence who was again passing the instrument and who picked it up.

"Oldthorpe House, home for retired officers of…"

"Don't touch it." Sister was hurtling downstairs.

"Right you are," said Clarence most affably – and replaced the receiver.

Sister sat on the bottom step, put her head in her hands, and burst into tears. Clarence, fearful of women even when they weren't crying, padded on into the lounge mouthing 'migraine – usual problem' to Basil who brushed past him and stood awkwardly in front of her. He wanted to put his arm around her shoulder and comfort her but he didn't know how to.

Lisa came to the rescue and led her gently upstairs. "If that phone rings again, Basil," she said over her shoulder, "you or Tubes answer it."

But it didn't.

At 10.48 a.m. precisely, Lesley Bristowe and a very sheepish Ainsley Bennington marched in through the front door.

"Hello? We're back. Where are you all?" Lesley's voice was at its most commanding and the troops quickly fell in on parade in the hall. As they shook the four Brigadier hands and slapped any back in easy reach they threw friendly and, mainly from the Cavaliers, somewhat doubtfully worded salutations at their long-lost colleague. And then the domino effect clicked in as first one, then another, noticed Sister, at her most starched, descending the stairs followed by a worried looking Nurse Lisa. There will always be an end domino and, in this case, it was Tubes whose voice was the last to be heard by his now-silent companions.

"…been, you old bugger?" Then he, too, was silent.

They all waited for the earthquake, eruption, ground-zero melt-down, call it what you will. One thing was certain, it was all going to be very unpleasant.

Then to their utter staggering amazement they heard Brigadier Lesley's brisk but friendly voice, one that commanded immediate obedience, saying, "Ah, there you are, Sister. And here we are, safe and well. Perhaps you would be so kind as to arrange tea for Brigadier Bennington in his room. He is a trifle weary. Don't bother about food, we had breakfast on the train."

Sadly no one had a pin to drop and so the theory could not be tested but sound, movement and, to a great extent, breathing, were suspended for what seemed an age. And then, as they all watched in disbelief, Sister smiled a sad, defeated smile and went into the kitchen.

Over the next hour Lesley briefed Sister and Lisa on the outline of what had happened. Ainsley, she said, had frankly had enough of what he saw as demotion by Sister, causing the eroding of his position as leader in the eyes of the residents – a belief which she had assured him was completely unfounded. But, as is human nature, one little niggle begat a bigger one and so the snowball grew until its effect was out of all proportion to its substance.

So he had gone off for a while but now was back in a far more contented frame of mind. He would, Lesley assured them, apologise in due course for the distress he had caused.

Acknowledging that the relief of having him, indeed, both of them back in one piece was enough, Sister was happy to accept this but she did feel – and in the new climate she picked her words carefully – that Lesley might have kept her informed of the retrieval operation.

"I tried to reach you three times, Sister. Each time with a train or taxi waiting to leave. First there was Clarence…"

"Say no more, Brigadier." Sister smiled. "Telephones and Captain Cuthbert do not connect."

"Then Freddy, I hope, took a simple message from me – although how it reached you is anybody's guess. And then Clarence hung up on me just as I was about to ask for you."

"Yes, well. What a pity." That was the best Sister could do in the circumstances. "But there's a lot more I need to know."

"In time, Sister. When Ainsley's ready he'll tell you all about it himself."

Sister had to make do with that. In the past she would have been more insistent but she was so relieved to have a full complement of her charges together again under one roof that she wisely decided to bide her time before seeking a more detailed explanation.

"G and T for you, Lesley and you, dear Lucy and one for Clarence. And pints for us." Tubes settled himself at the small table in The Anchor and peered at the two ladies through a cloud of bluish Basil pipe smoke.

Lesley had summoned the Cavaliers, less the sleeping Ainsley, to join her for a thorough debriefing session at midday having told Sister that they would like a late luncheon at 1.30 p.m. it being a special celebration to mark the wanderer's return. She was quickly into her stride.

"Let me say straight away that we owe the solving of the mystery and thereby the safe return of Ainsley totally to Lucy."

Lucy attempted to interrupt but, for once, a Brigadier outranked a Headmistress.

"It all started in the Cosy Cot Café. Poor Ainsley." Lesley sounded sad. "It had all been too much for him. And my wretched donkey-drop ball was the last straw. He so wanted to show us all that he was still a force to be reckoned with and the cricket field offered the best chance. And he just stood there and let it slowly bounce and hit the bails."

They waited obediently as Lesley sipped her drink and, wishing to please her, they did the same. When she was ready she continued.

"But our Ainsley Bennington had a secret weapon: Mavis."

They sat forward and such was the impact of the statement that Basil's pipe was placed in an ashtray to cool down.

"She was working part-time as the manageress in the café…"

Tubes gasped. "Good Lord. The never-ending cups of tea. Staring gooey-eyed. Grinning. It was at her! We thought he'd flipped."

"Tubes, please. We'll never get back to lunch if you go on like this." Lesley sat back and now there was a catch in her voice. "They were both lonely. Mavis was away from home, caring for her dying mother up here and she took this part-time job just for company. She loved company. And along came Ainsley – and you lot. They got to know each other. Kindred spirits really. They just, er, clicked. That's the word. He showed her his albums of photographs. They'd hold hands. The occasional little kiss. And – and this was at the root of all the kerfuffle – she said that if ever he needed it there would always be a room in her house whatever the circumstances. They were her words and Ainsley managed to misinterpret them masterfully. She gave him her address and, to him, the inference was obvious."

It was time for more drinks and a pit-stop for Clarence. It was all done in a rush – which was never a good idea as far as fly-buttons were concerned – because there was still much to be explained.

"Ainsley went to his room after the cricket match in a state of great despair. His ignominy at having been bowled first ball by me wasn't helped by him having had a sad parting with Mavis the previous day. Her mother having died she was off back home. All in all, everything had gone wrong and his spirits were at a low ebb. So, on an impulse, he packed pyjamas, a spare tooth brush and his beloved photo albums in a carrier bag, sneaked out of the house whilst we were at supper, and took the night train to London where he changed stations and chugged to his beloved Mavis in Margate."

"MARGATE? Good God." Tubes took a gulp of beer. "He was angry with us when we mentioned Margate."

Basil nodded. "Probably thought we were on to him. Go on, Lesley."

Tubes clapped his hands together. "Don't tell us that dear old Ainsley got up to a bit of mischief in Margate?"

"What happened?" Basil started a pipe refill.

Lesley was becoming annoyed at the constant interruptions. "He arrived at the house and surprised her out of her life. He was shown into the front room – and introduced to her husband."

"Her HUSBAND?"

"Her husband, yes. You see, it was a Boarding House. They gave him a slap-up meal and told him he could stay as long as he liked. No charge. She thought she'd told him that she ran a sort of B&B – she probably had, but he'd missed it – and she'd meant what she'd said. Even if there were no vacancies – that is, 'whatever the circumstances' – there would always be a room for him."

They sat quietly for a moment. Basil lit his pipe again and

they waited until the familiar smoke-screen engulfed them all.

"Poor Ainsley. What did he do?"

"He couldn't think what to do. He couldn't come back here with his tail between his legs and face the ridicule – and Sister's wrath – and the prevailing atmosphere at Oldthorpe. He was flummoxed. And then there I was and…" Lesley blushed rather attractively, "he flung his arms around my neck and – and was so pleased to see me."

"Plonked one on you, I bet." Freddy was nodding vigorously and it was Clarence of all people who crash-landed his flying arm with his stick.

"He did, actually, yes. But only, of course, through relief."

"Of course."

"We had a long talk in which I reassured him that, according to the Army List, he was – is – the senior of the two of us and, having sorted out a lot of things, we then started back. And that's really it."

"Is it? There are still mysteries to be solved." Basil was a stickler for detail.

Tubes gulped down a prodigious quantity of Adnams and wiped his white beard with the back of his hand; a sure sign that he was distracted. "But the wretched note. That's what caused all the trouble. 'Can't take life anymore'. 'End it forthwith'. 'Distress'. How could he do such a thing to us?"

Lesley directed their gaze to Lucy. "That's the really clever part and it was, of course, Lucy who solved the puzzle."

Lucy shook her head. "No really, Lesley. Not at all. It was just the wording of the note. It seemed clumsy to me. I would have given it only two or three out of ten."

They all smiled but were none the wiser. She went on.

"And once I'd established that it was written in capitals it completely changed its sense. You see, it was quite a natural mistake. Many of us have done – or nearly done – the same thing."

They looked at her. It was all far too much to comprehend.

"When things became difficult at Oldthorpe he saw it as synonymous with living in the country. He used to take the Country Life magazine…"

"We all enjoyed it. Good value."

"In the mood he was in that evening he saw it as everything that was wrong with his life. So, as he'd decided to leave anyway and start a new life with Mavis, he cancelled it. He wrote a note to his good Indian friend, the newsagent, Sanjiv Patel, with whom he'd had many a long cricketing discussion and posted it to him at the railway station that evening. Then before he left Oldthorpe he slipped another note under your door, Tubes. It said – would you please, Lesley?"

Lesley pulled a sheet of paper from her handbag and read the note to them,

SORRY TO DO THIS TO YOU CHAPS.
ALL TOO MUCH. NEED A BREAK.
OFF TO MAVIS IN MARGATE.
WILL CONTACT SOON.
AINSLEY

"No, it didn't." Tubes was having none of this. "You know what it said."

Lucy took no notice of the interruption.

"We went to see Mr Patel and asked him about Ainsley. He couldn't help at first and then the Christian name clicked – he'd only known him, you see, as 'Mr Bennington'. He remembered an incomprehensible letter he'd received bearing the name 'Ainsley'."

"You don't mean?…

"I certainly do. Wrong envelopes. You got the letter cancelling Country Life, Mr Patel got the one intended for you."

The awed silence was broken by Clarence. "I got a letter once from a girl in Epping. But she didn't mean it either."

"Lucy Banbury – and Lesley Bristowe, we salute you." Basil got to his feet and the others did the same, then they threw their arms up, hands to their foreheads, in perfect naval, military and air force salutes.

In the embarrassment that overwhelmed Lucy and Lesley – and everyone else in the bar – a familiar voice invaded the respectful silence.

"Hello, chaps and ladies. My round I think."

When, eventually, calm was restored and Ainsley had settled amongst them, they were ashamed to lapse into an embarrassed silence. Ainsley, in the finest of spirits, rubbed his hands together. "Have the amazing Holmes and Watson told you?"

They murmured, "Yes," and studied their fingernails and anything else that was near at hand.

He took an enormous swig and grinned at them. "We should all have known, shouldn't we? Missed it in the heat of the moment."

They looked at him, at Lesley, at Lucy and back to their fingernails. The terrible experience had obviously unhinged the poor fellow.

"A grave error." Tubes felt it best to keep the conversation moving towards something, but heaven knew what.

Ainsley banged the table with glee setting the glasses rattling, "So I was not out. As far as the scoreboard was concerned I never batted. And the Roundheads didn't win. Not that we're going to tell them. Lesley feels it will be better to let things rest. Keep the peace. Isn't she marvellous?"

Before more damage could be done, Lesley chipped in, "First ball of a match, you see. The umpire must tell the batsman the type of bowling he is to receive. And whether left or right arm. And, er, the sex of the bowler."

There was a murmur which she cut off with a raised hand. "Otherwise it's a no-ball. Rules of cricket, you see."

There was a respectful silence. Who would argue with that? Freddy Foster, of course, would.

"Are you sure…?" The heel of a strong, female brogue shoe came down expertly on his polished toe-cap.

The landing was heavy, but all he managed was, "Ow!"

13

"Where'er you walk
Cool gales shall fan the glade,
Trees, where you sit ..."

Nurse Lisa came out of her bedroom and saw Captain
Clarence lift his zimmer into battering-ram position and
bash its four feet into the bathroom door. The physical assault,
which almost knocked the old man over, was accompanied by
his quivering voice.

"For the Lord's sake, Freddy, stop that infernal din. It gives
a chap a headache."

The rubber bungs on each zimmer leg muffled most of the
noise of impact but it was enough to halt Squadron Leader
Freddy's splendid rendition of Handel's well-known aria and
substitute the next phrase for a laugh.

"Miserable old devil," he shouted. "You had a good voice
once. It's meant to be a duet. Come on in and sing the other line."

Nurse Lisa giggled. "Really, Squadron-Leader. Two in a
bathroom?"

There was a splash. "I could transpose it for a soprano,
Lisa," he shouted through the door. "Anything to oblige."

"That's quite enough of that, thank you." She giggled again
and caught up with Clarence, helping him down the stairs. "He's
got a lovely voice, hasn't he?"

"Humph," was all she got in reply as the old man zimmered
his way into the downstairs cloakroom.

Freddy, his left hand now in the guise of a flying boat
brought it in to a perfect landing on the surface of the warm,
soapy water despite a number of man-made and physical
obstacles.

"Where'er you tread,
The blushing flowers shall rise,
And all things flourish ..."

His tenor voice filled the house with a sweet sound. Lisa paused in the hall. "We need this," she thought. "Poor old Oldthorpe House needs this. A bit of gentleness, warmth – love."

The singing reached into the sitting room where, having a somewhat different effect on its inhabitants, one of them turned up the telly to help them hear the football results.

It had been a quiet few weeks since Brigadier Ainsley Bennington's return. Now into September, the evenings had drawn in and this rather suited the residents. Getting older seemed to fit better with chairs pulled up to the fire and evenings dozing in front of the TV. Shorter days provided a perfect excuse for less activity or too much conscious thinking about what had been and what, sooner rather than later, would be.

Few of them remembered Ainsley's recent troubles or, in fact, any of the embarrassing episodes that befell them from time to time. It wasn't that they didn't care for each other; as they so often proved, that was far from being so. It was more that, whilst the owners and staff believed that they all existed in close comradeship they were, in fact, a group of individuals tightly wrapped in their own private lives, rarely sharing them until forced by circumstances to do so and then, quickly, scuttling back into the safety of their own worlds. Sister Newbiggin and her team would have been surprised and saddened to realize this and, in a way, it was from here that the underlying tensions emanated. As the staff, through an explosive mixture of bullying and cajoling, false cheerfulness and often none too subtle persuasion, tried to mould the residents into a compliant group, they pulled further apart.

This was not ground-breaking psychology: this unwilling herding into groups happened on frequent occasions in most people's lives from their first birthday party onwards. And it was happening now, again, here in Oldthorpe House. The down side to these private worlds spinning in this smoke-laden, cabbage-scented atmosphere was that no one saw the signs – well, not until it was nearly too late. Self-absorption burnt up all the fuel that these elderly people could generate in each waking session and, until two or more worlds collided, life moved inexorably on.

This was where the staff could – or should – be of most help. Nurse Lisa was a far better judge of atmosphere and mood than Sister, partly because, with less responsibility, she didn't fuss so much. But it was also due to her closeness to each resident. As she gently ministered to them, they felt they could confide in her knowing that their secrets would be safe.

So it was that, despite a determination to tell no one, Captain Clarence Cuthbert, during an embrocation session, gruffly blurted out to Lisa all the pent-up anger and frustration that had been eating into him for the past fortnight.

She had known that something was wrong from the feel of his skin. She knew others would scoff at the idea but there it was. Where normally it was cool and almost silky in its old age, she was now finding it prickly hot and rough as she rubbed in the soothing ointment. And then there was his manner; tense and sharp. His comments, less kind to her than usual, found fault in any and everything. In such a taciturn man it was hardly surprising that nobody else noticed the change. But Lisa did.

"You can tell me, Clarence, you know. Any time. Whenever you feel like it." She spoke softly.

He was quiet for a while and then, with Lisa sitting beside him on his bed, her arm around his thin shaking shoulders, he told her.

"Don't get old, Lisa. Pack it all in before it grabs you. Old age. We never think it'll happen, see? I felt young way beyond my time. Until things started to go wrong. Bones. Innards. No point in going on."

Lisa stroked his arm. "Come on now, Clarence. We've often had this chat. We've agreed not to feel like this. D'you remember? When my dad died? You helped me then. Every day, every hour counts, you said. Remember?"

"They've told me I can't go. On my own. Too much responsibility." Clarence banged his bony fist into the palm of his other hand. "No grant, you see. Left it too late. That's what they said." He pulled away from Lisa and pushed himself up onto his zimmer. "What do they mean, 'left it too late'? It's because it's almost too late that I must go. It's expected." He sank down again, elbows on knees, head in his hands. "It's expected, d'you see? I should have gone before. And now it's

237

too late."

It took another half hour for the full story to come out. 1917. Passchendaele. The northern Flanders landscape a sea of mud. A war of attrition, yards gained, yards lost – at a cost of over a quarter of a million lives. So many never found, never buried. But their names lived on, cut into the stonework of the Menin Gate at Ypres in Belgium. More than fifty thousand of them with no known graves remembered there.

"Charlie Parfitt, Reg Spittalfield, Bob Symes – and me, Clarence Cuthbert. Joined up together. The East Essex Yeomanry. 1914. Stayed together through it all. Like brothers, d'you see? Blood brothers. Plenty of that around us. Blood. And then there we were, bogged down – literally bogged down in Flanders. Huh. 'They shall grow not old...' They bloody well didn't – sorry, lass, my mistake."

Lisa just held him, gently rocking with him. She knew all about it, of course. Intoned at her by her bored history teacher as if he were reading out the times of trains. But hearing it here from Clarence was almost living it. And he was so sad. Sad and bitter. Deep down he must have been like this for the past fifty and more years.

"The three of them copped it. I sometimes wish I had too."

She squeezed his hand. So inadequate, but she realised that nothing to do with this could be adequate. In this comfortable world it was all beyond the limits of human feelings.

"When it was all over the Belgians built this giant gateway. Like Marble Arch. With their names cut into the stonework."

His eyes opened wide like a small child's.

"D'you know, they sound the Last Post every evening, the Belgians do. Without fail. I always said I'd go – but somehow never wanted to. Frightened, I suppose. Ghosts. But now I saw this advert in the Signals magazine. A pilgrimage. Hundred pounds. Huh. As if..."

Clarence moved over to the window and looked out, embarrassed that he was talking about money to someone else, a thing he never did.

"So I went for a grant." He swung round. "No chance. Too infirm." His voice was louder, bitter now. "Too risky. Not eligible. Letter last week." He picked it up from the table and his shaking hands ripped it out of its envelope. "Due to insurance considerations," he read, "it will not be possible." Violently he tore it into pieces and let them fall.

Lisa watched the fragments drift down. It reminded her of the poppies in the Albert Hall: poppies in Flanders' fields... Clarence marched his zimmer towards the door. He turned and in a hard voice growled, "And now it's too late, d'you see? So that's that."

This wasn't an easy one to sort out. Lisa sat at the kitchen table that evening with a mug of cocoa. The house was quiet, chef Clint/Jean-Paul had cleared up and retired to his quarters above the garage and the residents were settling down to an evening's telly before bed.

Sister, exhausted, had gone to her room with her usual aspirins and a good book. Lisa was sure that there was something wrong with her as well. She seemed withdrawn and preoccupied. Probably the business of promotion to matron. It would be good to get that settled one way or another.

She pulled her thoughts back to poor old Clarence. What could be done? The devil of it was that he would countenance no question of financial help from anyone. Apart from the shame of accepting charity, he knew that all the residents in Oldthorpe House existed on totally inadequate incomes and if he were to go to Belgium someone would have to accompany him. That would mean over two hundred pounds for the trip if you included expenses. Impossible.

A secret donor? Gloria, the owner's wife? She'd arrange it like a shot but Clarence would insist on knowing where the money came from. Lie? No, not her or anybody's style. Well, not the sort of lying that would be needed here.

No gift accepted and no crafty subterfuge equals no money. Lisa sighed. This was one for tomorrow, but it had better be sorted out then. She feared for Captain Clarence's survival unless something could be done. He was frail enough as it was without this anger filling his waking hours – and she knew that the anger was mainly directed at himself. He'd left it too long, found every excuse to put off the traumatic day when he would face the names of his old mates on the stone walls of the Menin gate. But before he died he was determined to atone for his weakness one way or another.

How? Heaven alone knew. Lisa drained her mug, washed it under the tap and with a deep sigh prepared for the nightly ritual of pills, potions and the tucking in of those of her charges who were infirm.

And that very much included Captain Clarence Cuthbert.

Activity early the next morning centred around the dining-room which, due to the beneficence of Gloria Cartiledge, was now re-christened 'The Dining and Recreation Room' which made everybody outwardly feel much better even if inwardly the degree of indigestion had hardly changed.

During the past month Gloria had arranged for the transfer of an upright piano and a table-tennis table from deep within the bowels of Cartiledge Towers to Oldthorpe House. This was done without her husband's knowledge, there being, she wisely reasoned, no point in having a flaming row when it could be avoided – and anyway she doubted he even knew the two artefacts even existed.

She had also considered transferring the billiard table but as he'd been known to try to impress his doubtful clients with a frame or two, usually resulting in a split cloth, and the rather more compelling argument that they wouldn't be able to get it into Oldthorpe without chopping it up she postponed the venture to another time.

Nurse Lisa heard the piano and Squadron Leader Freddy's delightful singing as she came downstairs at 7.30 that morning. The Dining and Recreation Room filled the lower floor of one of the rear wings. At its near end were the eight tables, closer together now to leave the rear half of the room free for wild ping-pong sessions and what Gloria described as 'Musical Soirées' – which was probably setting the sights a little high.

But Freddy Foster was an exception. Although his colleagues knew he had a fine voice he'd never told them that his early life had revolved around music. As a young lad he had quickly graduated from church to cathedral choir and was to make music his career if Adolf Hitler hadn't intervened.

Lisa just stood at the door, watching and listening. It was a homely sight. Freddy at the piano, oblivious to everything around him, and Phyllis Coombe – dear Crumb – laying breakfast happily humming not quite along with him. Lisa was pretty sure hers was a completely different tune and definitely in a rival key.

Phyllis looked up and saw her. "In't he lovely? Like a nightingale. I just love singing along with him."

Lisa smiled. She doubted if Freddy would share the sentiment but lovely or not she had something that needed Freddy's more urgent attention than coaxing Maud to come into the garden. Maud would have to wait.

As any music-lover would, she waited until Freddy had reached the end of the verse and then tapped him on the shoulder. He jumped, saw her, smiled and did a crash-landing arpeggio up the length of the keyboard. When the piano had finished registering its pain, the resulting silence was only challenged by Crumb's continued humming – and it was quite a challenge.

"Nurse Lisa. You are an answer to an Ainsley prayer." Freddy pointed up to the ceiling. "He's already twice jumped out of bed and practised an excellent tap-dance routine on his floorboards. I think Fred Astaire might have judged it rather heavy-footed."

She smiled. "Can we nip to the sitting room for a moment, Squadron Leader? There's something very delicate I need to discuss with you."

Of course it was a mistake. Lisa still hadn't mastered the male penchant for sexual innuendo and got caught out time and time again.

"Nurse Roberts." Freddy rose from the piano stool and gave her a monstrous wink. "I thought you'd never ask." He gave her his arm and led her towards the door. She, refusing the offer, followed him, smiling and shaking her head.

Freddy called over his shoulder, "Keep the home fires burning, Crumb. We may be some time."

"Take all the time you need, luvvies," Phyllis interpolated into her humming. "No rush."

Twenty minutes or so later the two of them were back. Lisa

noted that Crumb was still humming the same discordant tune but was now doing so whilst dusting the piano. Freddy gently moved her to one side and sat again on the stool.

> "Come into the garden, Maud,
> For the black bat night has flown…"

"What's a black bat night when it's at home, luvvie?" The hummer needed information for future hums.

"Ask Alfred, Lord Tennyson, Crumb. He wrote it."

"Did he now?" She hummed aimlessly. "What room's he in then?"

Above there was another bout of hob-nailed tap-dancing.

Freddy waited until after breakfast and then, having completed the ritual of wiping Clarence down and helping him up, coupled him again to his zimmer and led him towards the garden door. The old man, noting the unusual darkness for a September morning and the start of a lashing shower of rain hung back.

"I've had enough mud for a lifetime, thank you Freddy," he growled. "The coffin will be here soon enough."

That was the trouble with Oldthorpe, thought Freddy. Nowhere for a private chat other than the bedrooms and they were out of bounds during muck-out times.

"Rather fun, don't you think? The new summerhouse? Warm and snug with the rain lashing on the roof." He saw the look on Clarence's face and could only add a weak, "don't you know?"

"No I don't, you idiot. Rare altitudes have finally got to you, Freddy Foster. Looping-the-loop up there. Showing off. Dislodged your brain at last." Clarence held up an admonishing finger. "We've all seen it happening for some time."

Normally such a comment so near, he feared, the mark, would have made Freddy a very angry man but not now, not with the news that Lisa had divulged to him. Somehow he had to get Clarence to tell him all about it and then, maybe, something could be done. But what, heaven alone knew.

Then the said brain had a wave. Just like that. His hand made one of its many perfect landings on Clarence's arm as he leant across to whisper in the old man's ear. "I've got a bit of a problem, old chap. You're my closest here. I'd much appreciate your help. Sitting room's filling up, d'you see?"

In next to no time they were in the summerhouse, the rain, as predicted, beating on the roof. Each shook out the umbrellas that they had hastily grabbed from the hall.

Clarence looked around the bare wooden walls. "Dug-outs. Only smarter wood." His voice was so mournful. "Officers only, of course. We had the trenches." He ran his hand over the varnished surface. "Perhaps that's why I became one in the next show. Officer, that is." He swung round and motioned Freddy to a garden chair. "Well, old man. Spit it out."

Freddy was speechless. Nonplussed. He felt that he'd been damned clever with his ruse to get Clarence to the privacy of the summerhouse but it was asking a bit much to expect him to know what to do next.

And then, for the second time in next to no time, another inspiration hit him and he was burbling away long before he knew what he was saying.

"I'm in love," went the burble, "with – er – let me see – er – Lisa. Er – Nurse Lisa," he added should there be any confusion.

Clarence sat down heavily on one of the wooden chairs. Freddy would have been obliged if he'd taken his usual lengthy time to do so although he doubted if even that would be long enough for him to plan his next move. Perhaps he could water down his fictitious passion for Lisa just a bit. He mumbled, "Well, sort of."

"How much 'sort of'?" The old man could be so infuriating at times.

"Er, sort of, sort of." By the look Clarence gave him his elucidation of the degree of love hadn't helped much.

"And does she reciprocate?"

For a moment Freddy was seriously confused, seeing the verb in a rather doubtful light. He fell back on a short word – more a sound really – that had often helped him when closely questioned before.

"Er…"

How many times had schoolmasters jocularly responded to

this total mental switch-off of his brain with, "Ah, Foster, to err is human – but in your case…"

As the wooden hut fought the storm to stay in one piece the best they could do at this point was just stare at each other, and then a Divine Being stepped into the ever-widening chasm and whispered in Clarence's ear precisely what needed to be said.

"You think you've got problems. They're nothing compared with some of us. Grow up Freddie. Be your age. We're all in love with Lisa – but not in *love*, you chump. It's all that singing you do. They're all about love, those songs. Quite bent your brain."

It was one of Clarence's longest ever speeches and might, at another time, have earned him a spirited response from Freddy, but on this occasion it did just the opposite. The airman did a stall turn with his left hand and then caused a mid-air collision by clapping both hands as if in jubilation.

With a seraphic smile – appropriate to an ex-choirboy – he said, "What problems have *you* got, Clarence?" and then, rather too smoothly, "can I be of some help?"

Sister Newbiggin put her head around the kitchen door and noted with satisfaction that the morning regime was running smoothly. The chef was preparing lunch with his symbol of authority, the unnecessarily large knife, murdering an unidentifiable portion of cow, Nurse Lisa was checking the contents of her drugs cupboard and Mrs Coombe was out in the pantry mopping the floor, the bare-walled room amplifying her humming to horrifying proportions.

"Just popping out for an hour, Lisa. Won't be long," Sister shouted above the noise.

The three of them stopped and, in perfect unison, did a double-take at the sight of Sister with a mackintosh wrapped closely around her, the collar done up to the neck, and a terrible rain hat pulled well down and overlapping it. She appeared to be dressed for a North Sea fishing trip.

What did she look like? An image of the poor old soul who sat begging in the railway station entrance was the best Lisa could do, but before there could be any reaction from the tableau Sister was gone.

Standing in the pouring rain on a street corner in the less salubrious part of Flaxton-on-Sea, Sister Newbiggin felt very exposed despite the waterproof camouflage. She was hating this. It had never been in her mind to put herself through such anguish and humiliation and it was only the force of circumstances that had made her take this terrible decision and submit herself to the demands of – she checked the name again – Mr Horace Middleton. Glancing at her watch she saw that the wretched man was well overdue. Twice she moved away, each time experiencing that mixture of relief and guilt at escaping an ordeal that would eventually have to be faced.

At last a car pulled up at the curb. A podgy hand stretched across and lowered the passenger window revealing a puffy florid face which adjusted itself into a sickly grin exposing a set of teeth that had, even a long time ago, seen better days.

"Amelia?"

It annoyed her that the voice was friendly – and how dare he presume to use her Christian name?

"Mrs Newbiggin, Mr Middleton. And you're late." She felt she had to set the rules of engagement right at the start. He may well be able to assume a dominant position in the ordeal to come but whilst she still had some vestige of independence she would see that the correct proprieties were observed. Christian names and unpunctuality were not to be tolerated.

"Sorry, love…"

Things were getting no better.

"Pop in and let's get down to it."

With a sigh of utter hopelessness and resignation, Sister Amelia Newbiggin, her uniform camouflaged by the dreadful raincoat, lowered herself into the passenger seat, far too close to Mr Middleton for comfort, and submitted herself to her first driving lesson.

Back in the Oldthorpe summerhouse Freddy sat spellbound. It was uncanny how the story of the terrible battles that ebbed and flowed in the waterlogged fields of Flanders was enhanced by the setting in which it was told, quietly and hesitantly, by Clarence. The wind howled and whistled around the wooden building, the rain lashed at its windows, and had the door suddenly burst open and a platoon of bedraggled, exhausted soldiers fallen in it would hardly have surprised him.

When the story was done, the two of them sat for a while letting the elements do their worst on the outside of their dugout. Freddy knew he would have to leave it to Clarence to introduce the pilgrimage problem but there seemed to be no sign of it happening. It would need a nudge. He was well aware of his outstanding ability to land with his undercarriage up so unaccustomed subtlety would be needed here. He composed several verbal nudges and discarded all of them as being too forthright. Heaven knows what they were when judged against his ultimate choice.

"So, what's the problem?"

Clarence felt that a battle that had cost tens of thousands of lives to gain a few hundred yards of territory and been fought in the most appalling conditions that the elements could devise was probably problem enough. He picked his words carefully.

"Problem, you stupid idiot? Problem? What the hell do you mean, problem?"

At any other time Freddy would have walked away but this wasn't the Clarence he knew.

"It's all right, old friend." His voice could only just be heard above the onslaught of the weather on the wooden building. "You told me all this because something's wrong and I want to know how – if – I can help."

That was enough to trigger the pilgrimage end of the story. Clarence got up to tell it and, unable to look his friend in the eye, clattered around the summerhouse using his zimmer to batter his way through his fury and disappointment at the outcome.

Knowing all about it already allowed Freddy to let his mind drift into the search for a solution that would be acceptable to Clarence. No charity, no borrowing, so really no hope. What they needed was a windfall; a dollop of cash dropping, as it were, into their lap. What could they win – and how? Freddy stretched his mind over the skills of the Oldthorpe residents and found it a sadly un-stretching exercise. Crossword competitions? Sports quizzes? Gardening? A touch of topiary? One of the Roundheads was evidently a dab hand at flower arranging? Hopeless, quite hopeless.

Clarence was coming to the end of his story. "I just want to be near them again, you see. Even if it's only to see their names. To be near them again. The last time we were together we were huddled in the water – the trench was filling up. We couldn't wait to get out of it but we knew what would happen when we did. We just sat there, humming. Would you believe it? Humming!" His voice broke and, rocking, he half hummed, half croaked the words that took him back sixty or so years to the hell of Passchendaele.

"Roses are blooming in Picardy,
mm, mm, mm…"

His heart, already strained almost to its limits, missed yet another beat as Freddy suddenly jumped up and clapped him on the back.

"Fear not, Clarence. Salvation is at hand. Leave it all to me."

And with that he was gone.

Clarence made his slow way back to the house, the rain bouncing off his umbrella as he tried with little success to steer the zimmer one-handed. Freddy would be disappointed to know that, even after all his efforts, the old man now felt more disheartened than ever. 'Fear not'? 'Leave it all to him'? That, thought Clarence, puts the final nail in the pilgrimage coffin.

The little car, sporting a large 'L' sign on its roof and the legend ' THE HORACE MIDDLETON DRIVING ACADEMY' was parked on a bit of waste ground safely off the road.

"You will, of course, know about the three pedals?" Mr Middleton, having had a more-or-less fruitless 'Let's get to know each other' chat with his new pupil, decided to get down to work. Most of those who came to him were youngsters eager to get behind the wheel and emulate Stirling Moss. They knew as much – and more – about cars than he'd ever know but now he had a rare challenge, a middle-aged woman who, it appeared, not only knew nothing about them – but didn't want to! What on earth was she doing here?

Sister Newbiggin, having set her instructor even further back on his heels by assuring him that she knew nothing about car pedals, cursed for the umpteenth time the cause of all this unwelcomed drama. And the cause was, very uncharacteristically, none other than Gloria Cartiledge.

She had arrived on one of her bustling visits full of cheerfulness and enthusiasm bearing little gifts for everybody and obviously bursting with good ideas. She couldn't wait to get Sister on her own and tell her the amazing news that Oldthorpe House was to become the proud owner of a brand new minibus!

She didn't mention – hardly needed to – what a battle she'd had with her husband Gregory over this idea, but once he was convinced that the publicity of such a generous gesture would propel him up another rung on the knighthood ladder, he set his team of overworked accountants at CARTILEDGE WORLD ARMAMENTS onto devising a scheme whereby its costs would be borne by others and he'd receive a healthy tax rebate.

Gloria impressed on Sister that this gift was to be kept secret until it was delivered – she loved surprises – and then dropped the bombshell: Sister and Lisa would be the registered drivers. It never struck her that maybe one, other, or both couldn't drive. As it happened, Lisa could, but Sister Newbiggin had never wanted, nor ever seen a need to.

She was far too proud to admit this to Gloria – apart from anything else it could damage her chances of becoming matron – so, with a very heavy heart, she had secretly sought the services of a Flaxton driving school.

So here she was, gazing between her knees at the three staggeringly uninteresting lumps of rubber-covered metal down by her feet.

"What do you do then, love?" Mr Middleton asked, eyeing the all-enveloping mackintosh and rain hat.

"Less of the 'love', thank you, Mr Middleton. Eyes on the road."

As they hadn't as yet reached the road from the driveway in which the opening battle between her and the internal combustion engine had taken place, the command was somewhat superfluous. Horace Middleton realized that he'd been landed with 'one of those'. The older they got, the less co-ordination they had. With this one, though, the driving theory was as good as any bright youngster. With very few errors she had rattled through the Highway Code questions with an authority that left him feeling it was he who was being examined. Now he could get his own back with a bit of brutal practical instruction.

"Make sure you're in neutral."

"I beg your pardon?"

"Neutral, dear – sorry, madam." He waggled the gear lever. "It is."

"Then there is no need for me to check it, is there Mr Middleton? I am happy to take your word for it, you being the expert."

He noted that she seemed to be talking through somewhat pursed lips.

"As the driver, madam, it is up to you to waggle it – that is, the gear lever." He could purse as well as the next person.

From thereon, things – not the car, thank goodness – went rapidly downhill.

"Depress the clutch. Select first gear, check the mirror, look over your shoulder, e-e-e-ase the clutch out as you de-e-e-press the accelerator." Nothing happened. He expected – rather hoped for – a violent jolt and a stalled engine. Nothing.

"Should we not have the engine making a noise, Mr Middleton?"

This had never happened to him before; not in his thirty or more years of instructing. This woman flustered him and already seemed to have him completely in her control. He lunged across her and feeling for the ignition key on the steering column, switched it on. The starter motor surged.

"Push on the accelerator," he shouted, his head almost in her lap.

"Which is that? Please remind me, Mr Middleton."

"The right hand one, madam," he yelled loudly.

In her efforts to lift him from his unseemly position she inadvertently jammed his head against the steering wheel.

For a small car it was a very loud horn. This, coupled with a thrust to the floor by her right foot causing the engine to exceed six thousand revs a minute, turned the vehicle into a shaking, vibrating, shrieking and, it appeared, shortly disintegrating mechanical monster.

In this quiet suburban road it was remarkable how quickly a crowd could gather. People emerged from their houses, cyclists wobbled to a stop and, seeing a crowd gathering, the local bus pulled to a halt to provide its passengers with a rare bit of entertainment.

What they all saw was a man with his head evidently jammed into the lap of a woman driver who appeared to be wrestling with him and sounding the horn in alarm.

As with most British bystanders, they did just that until two burly men decided to be heroes and wrenched the passenger door open. Still with the engine screaming in pain, Mr Middleton was pulled from the vehicle and none-too-gently spread-eagled across the bonnet.

Order was eventually restored and, once everything had calmed down, as if on cue, a policeman cycled up and began to create chaos all over again.

The 'Learner' sign on the roof of the car helped poor Horace Middleton to avoid being charged with attempted rape – the young policeman was at that over-zealous stage in his new career – and, as the crowds dispersed, the hapless instructor and his student parted company for what turned out to be the first and last time.

Sister climbed on the bus receiving commiserations regarding the lustfulness of men from the women shoppers and the hapless Middleton drove very slowly and shakily back to his home.

He wondered whether it was time to make a career change.

Things were a trifle edgy that evening at Oldthorpe. The residents, well aware of the cycles of drama that descended on them from time to time, felt the distinct signs that another was on its way. It was the lull before the storm, the silent stillness before thunder and lightning and, instinctively, they braced themselves.

The actual storm had raged unabated all day. Record levels of rain had fallen and Sister, evidently in a very flustered state, had brought her fair share of it in with her when she returned in mid afternoon. One saving grace was that the mackintosh and rain hat had done all she had asked of them by not only keeping her dry but also disguising her from the prying – possibly even lustful – eyes of the wretched Mr Middleton.

'Fear not. Salvation is at hand. Leave it all to me.' Freddy

250

Foster was now fretting. It was all very well to have said such a thing to Clarence in the summerhouse and it was equally splendid that he had meant it and, indeed, did have a plan that could bring salvation to the old man – but how to put the plan into action, that was the question?

All his years of military training now came to his assistance. The answer was simple: tell someone senior to him and hand him the problem.

The obvious candidate was Brigadier Ainsley and so he did just that, having for security's sake dragged the poor man through the torrential rain back to the site of the original confession, the summerhouse.

A soaking wet Ainsley was frankly amazed, not only by this new, assured Freddy whom he had never seen before, but also by the extraordinary solution which he suggested for raising funds to get Clarence to Ypres with his comrades.

They agreed that as the plan involved most of the residents it would be necessary to get them together and tell them all about it and so after supper, at his request, everyone gathered at the recreation end of the dining room. It wasn't too much of an effort because all they had to do was carry their chairs a few yards from the tables to around the piano and most of them managed it without mishap.

Knowing that Clarence would rebuff any assistance and be livid that his story, told in total confidence to Lisa that morning, was now to be shared with everyone only a few hours later, a small piece of subterfuge had been employed. Before the announcement of the meeting Lisa persuaded Clarence that, having a bit of a chill caused by sitting in a damp summerhouse during one of the worst September storms on record, he should retire early with a hot water bottle. On being assured that this included an extra long embrocation session administered by her, he readily agreed.

Down in the Dining and Recreation Room, for the fourth time, the horrors of Passchendaele were recounted but now, with Ainsley's past study of the campaign, in even more ghastly detail. The audience sat spellbound. His presentation was masterful and by its end there was no one in any doubt about the need, somehow, to get Clarence to Ypres to 'privately commune', as Ainsley put it, with his fallen comrades before he, too, would join them. But how?

Now Freddy took over, but a very different Freddy from the one they were accustomed to. The light, lackadaisical air was gone and his left hand remained firmly grounded. He was going to talk about something of which he was, in this group, the acknowledged master: music.

He had escaped to Flaxton-on-Sea that afternoon and made two calls, first to the Council Offices and then to his old friend Mr Templar at the music shop.

"Gentlemen."

Brigadier Lesley cleared her throat rather loudly. This was not a good start.

"Sorry. Gentlemen and Lesley."

The throat clearing became almost a gargle.

"I, er, mean, Lesley and Gentlemen. Sorry."

"Get on with it, old fruit. They'll be wanting to lay breakfast soon." The general wave of amused agreement was silenced by one look from Ainsley.

"In one month's time – October the fifteenth to be precise – the Annual Flaxton Arts Festival, which takes place every year..."

"It would."

"Sssh."

"...takes place here in Flaxton..."

"It would."

"Will you shut up?" Ainsley heartily agreed with the barracker but they'd never get to 'Match of the Day' at this rate.

"...and I have entered us."

That silenced the barracker. They all just stared at Freddy. So he *was* mad after all.

"The Mixed Choirs category. A minimum of twelve people in each choir. It's a competition, you see. AND – here's the best bit, the first prize is three hundred pounds. And the second prize which, of course, doesn't interest us, is two hundred pounds. What do you think about that then?"

No one thought about that in any way, shape or form. They just stared at him – and wondered whether Ipswich Town had scored a goal at last.

Freddy was totally unabashed and unaware of the deep depths of disinterest wafting from his audience.

"Twelve of us. I've heard you all sing and I know already of at least ten of us who have good, true voices. All we have to do is practice singing together, incorporate tone and texture, blending, expression – and we're on a winner."

"Is that all?" There seemed to be rather more mirth than genuine consideration of the proposition amongst the audience.

"There's something else we'll have to do, Freddy."

"What's that, old boy?"

"Learn to sing polite words instead of rude ones." The laughter really wasn't helping and at last Freddy became conscious of it.

"I mean this, you know. And even if it has to be just me and Lisa – she's offered to join in – we'll enter and win and, because it comes from none of our pockets, Clarence will agree to its use to get him and a helper to Belgium. I'm sure of that."

His sincerity worked. The mood changed, and in no time all but a small number who felt they just couldn't take part had agreed to private auditions with Freddy the next day.

"What about the top lines, Freddy?" Ainsley had done a fair bit of singing in his time and knew about these things. "We can't expect Lesley and Lisa to represent the sopranos and altos on their own."

"Bring in the others," said Lesley. "Why not? Sister, – even Crumb. What do you need, Freddy, four or five sops, two or three altos, two tenors, two or three basses? That will give you your twelve. Same strength as the last choir I was in. Garrison Church, Catterick."

This was going better than Freddy's wildest dreams. He could almost feel the sixty crisp five-pound notes in his hand already.

As they moved towards the lounge they were all, it seemed to Ainsley, in an excellent frame of mind and it struck him that it was probably because, for once, they were pulling together in a common cause. Well done, Freddy.

They all dropped into armchairs and one of them switched on the television.

Damn. Ipswich Town had lost again.

14

There was now going to be a month of hard work ahead for Freddy and his singers. The morning following the meeting he embarked on the ticklish job of auditioning his fellow residents for a place in the Choir. Ticklish because, as with all auditions, each applicant came in bearing a confusing mixture of embarrassment, apprehension, inadequacy and humiliation coupled with a strong desire not to be there in the first place. But as they were submitting themselves to probable ridicule for Clarence's sake they supposed it was worth it.

Brigadier Ainsley was first in. Whilst the art of pitching a note to match that played on the piano was for him slightly hit or miss – "Try hitting another one, Freddy. See if you can get closer to me" – his fine baritone voice, even without the aid of alcoholic stimulus, made him a certainty in the bass section.

Tubes followed, projected into the room by a firm shove from Ainsley. Singing was a bit of a mystery as far as he was concerned. There hadn't been much singing in submarines, any group effort generally resulting in a loud, echoing, metallic roar which would have been picked up by enemy hydrophones many nautical miles away. So, apart from the odd ditty in the bath as he played with his submarine-like loofahs, Tubes was a stranger to tonic sol-fa and all that it stood for. The only tonic he was aware of was used, a splash at a time, to enhance gin.

"Let's try a scale, old boy." Freddy had given up on the 'humming a note' challenge.

"Why not, Freddy. You're the musician. Off you go."

"I'll give you a note and you 'la' your way up the scale."

"Bit of a disadvantage there, old chum. You've got the piano to help you. Much better you do that sort of thing, d'you see? We singers will just follow along and it'll be fine." Tubes's confidence stoked by the depth of his musical ignorance was amazing.

"Tubes, we'll get nowhere unless you do as I say."

"Oh, like that is it? Command already gone to your head. Now look here…"

He got no further. With a crashing C major chord down at the bass end of the keyboard Freddy arpeggioed his way to the top-most note, removed his foot from the loud pedal and said, very quietly, "It would be really nice to have you on board, Tubes. You are, after all, a Cavalier and, as such, a close friend of dear old Clarence. But to blend, harmonize, sing in a group, you must be able to pitch a note. All right?"

The last words were said with a sickly sweetness and in stark contrast to the gruff reply.

"Get on with it then."

"Thank you. Here is a scale." Freddy played the eight ascending notes loudly and clearly and then the first one again. "Would you be so kind as to la or hum – or grunt that scale for me?"

It really wasn't too bad. The notes more or less complimented each other in the musical form of a scale even if Tubes started some distance away from where Freddy had indicated.

With a sigh the Musical Director of the Oldthorpe Choir played a G.

"What about that one?"

"Fine by me, if that's the one you've chosen."

There was a pause.

"Would you sing it for me, then?"

"Rather not, actually. Piano seems a bit out of tune – or you're pressing the wrong jobs. Tell you what, you do the notes bit and we'll sing the songs. Much the best thing. Is that the time? Must dash."

Tubes was out of the room faster than a torpedo, leaving Freddy to mark him down as a 'possible' if all the other men were struck down by bubonic plague on the day of the competition.

It came as a considerable shock to see that the next applicant was preceded by a zimmer frame. It hadn't struck him that Clarence would know what they were all up to, even if why they were doing it was a secret. A branch of the Huddersfield Choral Society, however dissimilar, in his dining room would eventually arouse even his curiosity!

Now he clattered down the length of the room to the piano. As Freddy watched in what was best described as a stall turn, the old man punched a bony finger onto a lower key and, choosing a completely different one, was off in a quavering but surprisingly strong voice.

"I'll be there, I'll be there,
In the little harness room across the square..."

"Clarence!" Freddy knew this one and feared propriety was about to be breached.

"When they're leading the horses to water..."

"CLARENCE!"

"I'll be kissing the Colonel's daughter..."

"Phew!"

"In the little harness room across the square."

Across the courtyard they heard applause. A glance showed Jean-Paul at the window waving his knife in the air and Nurse Lisa clapping enthusiastically.

"Am I in then, Freddy?" Clarence plonked himself onto a chair.

Freddy found his voice, "Don't you think it might all be a bit strenuous for you, old chap?"

"Strenuous? Strenuous? You young pups don't know the meaning of the word. I know another verse." Clarence stood up and, with the help of the zimmer, adopted an operatic pose.

"So do I, thank you, Clarence. And I think not. You'll have poor Lisa blushing."

"She's lovely when she blushes." Clarence stared above his audience into the distance. "She's lovely anyway." He banged his zimmer. "Am I in?"

"Yes, Clarence," Freddy sounded rather defeated, "you're in. But very quietly. I need a whispering bass, do you see? And you're just the ticket."

By lunchtime he had four 'more-or-less' basses and a couple of tenors to sing the line with him.

The afternoon with the women proved no less exhausting – or perhaps the word traumatic was a better description. It started well enough with Nurse Lisa and Mrs Braithwaite (who came in each day to do the dishes) displaying much beauty of tone and enthusiasm as sopranos. Then a slightly tetchy and distracted Sister came in, sat down and went through a series of jerks and hand waving which only a connoisseur of motoring law would have been able to identify. Having checked her rear-view mirror, she waggled the gear lever, looked over her shoulder, depressed the clutch and, with smooth pressure on the accelerator – looked up and blinked.

"Well, Squadron Leader. Here we are then. And you of all people our resident musician. We are indeed fortunate. I have not sung in a choir since my Grammar School days – which, of course..." she added quickly, "is not so very long ago. I remember attending concerts where the great Sir John Barbirolli was the conductor."

"That's going back a while." The undercarriage was up again.

"It most certainly is not!" Sister was outraged. "I was only a very young child. Now..." before the subject could be developed, "what do you wish of me?"

Very little, thought Freddy but, for once, he kept it to himself. He hadn't been looking forward to this session. Had he known the fate of poor Horace Middleton he would probably have just let Sister join the sopranos without an audition but word would have got around. There could be no favouritism, so he took a deep breath and launched in.

To his great surprise Sister did all that was required of her and he was so carried away that he led on to the art of breathing correctly – so important in singing.

"What's the first thing you need to do, Sister?"

The reply was instant.

"Check the gears are in neutral and the handbrake is on."

Freddy, aware that much good work could be undone in a second, merely nodded and inked her in alongside Lisa and Mrs Braithwaite. The soprano line was filling up nicely.

Brigadier Lesley literally burst into the room. For her, this whole choir business was a heaven-sent opportunity to get back into some semblance of a creative life. Why on earth hadn't she thought of it? But full marks to Freddy who, to her shame, she had labelled a lightweight, proving yet again how deceptive appearances could be.

Now she drew on all the skills that had marked her out from her earliest schooldays and through an illustrious army career and gave Freddy the works. Her strong voice, which had in its time taken many opposing games teams apart and maintained strict discipline amongst her troops, now provided a complete alto line for the Oldthorpe Choir. Gladys Ripley, Constance Shacklock and Kathleen Ferrier all rolled into one! It was a true, accurate sound and it made Freddy almost weep with pleasure. No one at Oldthorpe had experienced this Lesley Bristowe but it seemed that, thanks to Freddy, from now on they would.

Well satisfied with his day's work, Freddy packed his music away and prepared to go to his room to start preparing the two items they would present to the judges. Allowing for the limited choice of singers available to him, he reckoned that with hard work a balanced choir would emerge and, with the average standard of competition from the surrounding East Anglian area that they would be up against, he saw no reason why they shouldn't have a good chance of winning.

"Here I am, luvvie. Sorry to be late. My Albert's had another brush with the fuzz. Mistaken identity. He'll be out by tomorrow."

Freddy froze. He'd forgotten Phyllis – well, he'd forgotten that she might decide to audition, he hadn't forgotten the terrible humming noises she emitted when he was practicing. It reminded him of the sound German bombers made in the last war. Whenever she hummed he wanted to scramble and shoot her down.

"Hello, Crumb. We're all right if you'd rather not." His left hand was back to its old tricks again. It hedge-hopped above the keyboard.

"Bless you, dearie. I wouldn't let you down. I'm here to help."

Not auditioning would help, thought Freddie, but before he could say it, or preferably something kinder, the Luftwaffe started another bombing run as she hummed her way through the business of setting the chairs in a neat row. It was strange, although the noise was terrible it actually was more or less in tune!

The humming paused whilst Phyllis matched Sister's lip-pursing skill.

"Mrs Braithwaite in then?" She regarded dish washing as at least one rung below dusting, polishing and hoovering on the skilled trade ladder.

"A fine voice," said Freddy, and added craftily, "completes a very full soprano line."

"Does she indeed?" The pursing had not relaxed. "Many's the duet we've sung in the kitchen. Tom and Jerry. Marks and Spencer. One can't do without the other. I've sung since I was a tiddler."

Freddy, with unaccustomed tact, wisely decided that no answer was better than anything he could think up so he busied himself arranging his music whilst Phyllis took her bombers on a quick and noisy sortie around the room.

"Have you got a pencil, Crumb?" He'd need one for his music.

"Sorry, dearie. I use a duster."

It probably wasn't meant to be sarcastic.

"Back in a jiff." He took off at great speed out of the room, anything to buy a little time before the moment of truth. It was dashed difficult. The last thing any of them wanted was to upset Phyllis who was a breath of fresh air in the Oldthorpe household, but if her singing voice emerged with anything like the same guttural growl as her humming it would spell disaster for the choir. Anyway, he didn't need another singer; he had the minimum of twelve and that, he felt, was quite sufficient to work with – or, more precisely, on.

Searching his room for a pencil, it struck him that this was as enormous a challenge as the first time he'd climbed into a Spitfire's cockpit. Never volunteer for anything was the service motto and he'd done just that. Not only did he have to mould a disparate group of semi-enthusiastic volunteers into a prize-winning choir, he also had to conduct, accompany on the piano and provide a principal singing voice.

He'd chosen contrasting songs for their repertoire: 'Passing By' and a Beatles hit to set the audience giggling – and, he hoped, the judges – 'When I'm Sixty-four'. He felt a mix of Henry Purcell and Lennon/McCartney would provide a suitable contrast to demonstrate what skills he could create in four weeks.

Quietly whistling 'Passing By' as he sauntered down the stairs, he automatically adjusted the key to match the piano and then stopped dead in the hall. The piano? What in blazes was going on? It was in no way an error-free performance, but it wasn't a long way off one. The pianist was obviously rusty but it was nothing that a bit of practice wouldn't put right.

He stood at the door and just stared – at the back of Phyllis, perched on the piano stool, leaning forward with her face only a few inches from the music, still humming atrociously as she picked her way carefully through the notes.

He moved alongside her and she stopped.

"Sorry, luvvie. Couldn't resist it." She rattled through a few chords. "Better than ours at 'ome. Albert's poured a lot of beer in it. Can't do it any good in the long run. This one's a beauty, though."

At a stroke, two of Freddy's most pressing problems were solved. He had an accompanist and was saved rejecting Phyllis as a singer.

"I started when I was a nipper. I tried to get into the choir but for some reason they put me down for the piano." Phyllis launched into 'When I'm Sixty-four' with considerable abandon, aimlessly humming at the same time. It was, thought Freddy, a remarkable, if excruciating, feat.

"It's that hum, Crumb." Freddy could never leave well alone. "It sounds like a squadron of German bombers."

There was a pause which neither Lennon nor McCartney had written into the music followed by a jolly cackle.

"Oh, Squadron Leader. What a joke. You have such a way with words."

Things rolled on fairly smoothly over the next couple of weeks. The group of reluctant enthusiasts now known as the Oldthorpe Choir started to resemble something approaching a musical ensemble and Sister, with increasing enthusiasm, was mastering all matters mechanical in getting a car to behave as if it were one of her patients; in other words, obey her. Time was short. Not only did she need to pass the ordinary driving test, but that was to be followed by a further even more stringent examination to ensure her fitness to drive a vehicle carrying passengers. Honour was at stake, and whilst the Newbiggin parents had never set their sights on their favourite daughter becoming a fully qualified bus driver, if that's what she wanted, so be it.

The secret of the driving lessons was eventually revealed to all via the journalistic skills of the editor of the Flaxton Chronicle, doubling in these hard times as chief reporter, in what was undoubtedly a major incident in this usually sleepy seaside town that resulted in the gutting by fire of a second floor flat, the rescue of its occupants, a family of four, by turntable ladder – four fire appliances attended – a vehicle pile-up sending five people to hospital, a dented police car and a lot of hurt pride.

On a technical point it could be argued that Sister Newbiggin was at the root of the sequence of events, maybe even the cause, but whilst blame was rightly placed elsewhere, she was left with a fair bit of explaining to do.

The lesson had gone extremely well. Moira Moon, who had filled the void left by the shattered Horace Middleton, had finished her instruction and asked Sister to carefully propel the car along Church Street towards her Driving School premises.

In her subsequent statement to the police, Sister mentioned observing, as she had been taught to do, two slightly unusual hazards. She saw ahead of her a group of bearded men dressed in long white robes sporting boards slung over their shoulders announcing THE END OF THE WORLD IS NIGH, who, aware that there was little time left, were risking life and limb by jay-walking across the road trying to get passers-by to join them and, presumably, thereby prove that in their particular case the prophecy was correct. She also noted a man up a ladder working on an upstairs window.

Her teaching had taught her that this was the moment to slow down and give both the ladder and the prophets of doom a wide berth, and so she did by using every available limb to de-clutch and apply the footbrake, indicate that she was slowing down and pulling out slightly with the correct hand signals, steer the required course, and look in her rear-view mirror. This was a feat not only totally beyond her just a fortnight previously, but also way beyond anything she had done since.

At this moment a large black saloon with a far too powerful engine screeched round the corner behind the learner car and bore down on them at enormous speed, followed by a police car with siren blaring. Seeing Sister pulling out to avoid the hazards ahead, the driver of the saloon pulled onto the wrong side of the road to overtake, as did the police.

The man up the ladder, blow-torching paint from a window frame, had a grandstand view, as his statement, which dovetailed splendidly with Sister's, graphically described. In a nutshell, the saloon hit a parked lorry, the police car hit the saloon and Sister Amelia ran gently, almost elegantly, into the back of the police car.

Sister, instantly reverting to her chosen profession, was quickly out and, having checked that the policemen were physically unhurt except for their feelings, rushed to the mangled saloon where the driver, a young man, was jammed semi-conscious behind the steering wheel.

"Were you driving the car that hit us, Miss?" The police liked to get their priorities right.

The young man opened his eyes to hear Sister say, "I'm a learner, constable."

"Gawd help me," groaned the young man seeing her nurse's uniform, "can't you find a real one? I'm feeling real groggy." With that he lapsed back into semi-consciousness.

The demonstrators were now all around the car in their weird Druid outfits. Their leader peered over Sister's shoulder, his long beard tickling her neck.

"Is he dead?" he asked, clicking his teeth. "He might have waited for us. We only said it was nigh." His colleagues murmured agreement.

The young man opened his eyes again and now saw, instead of Sister, a face complete with biblical beard and the board inscribed with its note of finality. "Sweet Jesus," he said, and his eyes closed again.

The policeman looked sternly at the white robed and bearded man. "Does he know you, Sir?"

Sister didn't know whether to laugh or cry but she was saved needing to make a choice by the arrival of the Fire Brigade.

Whilst the painter up the ladder had indeed had a grandstand view of the chaos developing below him, his blowtorch had diverted itself from the window frame and found much better combustible material in the curtains. He thought things were warming up nicely but didn't bother to find out why until the sound of crackling and breaking glass made him glance round and see the whole room merrily ablaze. Through the smoke appeared a man, a woman and two children all of whom, he reported later, were coughing up smoke and seemed to be very upset.

It was going to take a very long time to sort out but there was no doubt where it was all going to end. The young man, once out of hospital, would be charged with 'taking away a motor vehicle without the owner's consent' and given a caution, lots of Insurance Companies would fight over who should pay what and, of course, lots of solicitors would become ever richer.

Meanwhile Sister Newbiggin returned to Oldthorpe House to a hero's welcome. The Chronicle, covering its biggest home-grown story for many a long month, was full of praise for her medical assistance at the accident scene, particularly when editor-cum-chief-reporter Vernon Rogers, who had recently been fined for speeding, noted that, 'the police car had stopped suddenly causing a collision with the nurse's vehicle'.

Everyone at Oldthorpe was thrilled, though why she should want to learn to drive at her age was a mystery – and would remain so for the foreseeable future.

On the musical front things were going far from smoothly for Freddy. He was finding that coaxing a dozen larynxes to provide a more or less harmonious blend of sound was infinitely more challenging than chasing a few Messerschmitts around the skies. As for turning his friends into an award-winning choir, that was apparently attempting the impossible.

"Can I have a little less from the basses, please?"

"Which basses?" barked Ainsley who felt that his contribution was just about right. But he knew who it was who needed to shut up a bit. He stared meaningfully at Clarence.

"I'm hardly making any sound as it is."

It was true. Clarence's volume had already been turned down to almost zero by Freddy but still his tremulous growl broke through his bass companions.

"Maybe a little less, Clarence old chap. If you would be so kind."

Freddy had found that adopting a fair dollop of obsequiousness in his dealings with his reluctant choristers generally avoided huffy walk-outs which, in turn, led to time wasted in cajoling and pleading afterwards. If only he could tell Clarence that they were doing – enduring – all this for him, but of course he couldn't. The old man, still smarting from his rejection by the pilgrimage group, would blow up, refuse their gesture and that would be that. Clarence obediently moved to whispering mode, but still the growl broke through.

"Open your mouths, ladies, please." Even Sister, since her pivotal role in the 'Church Street Catastrophe', had clammed up. Having provided the strongest soprano voice – nothing surprising in that – she now seemed uncharacteristically withdrawn.

Freddy's struggle with his singers wasn't his only challenge. There was also the matter of Phyllis and her humming. Try as he would, he couldn't stop her making the dreadful discordant noises whilst she was quite ably playing the piano. But she would have none of it.

"You're imagining it, luvvie. It's probably all that Spitfire racket in your ears. Bound to affect them."

The choir suggested many solutions from a bit of sticky tape to a diver's helmet, but in the end it was Clarence of all people who came up with the solution, thanks to his trusty tape recorder. By rigging the microphone around Phyllis's neck and headphones over her ears, even she became aware of the terrible noise she was making and worked hard at stifling it. Quite often it worked, but you never knew when the squadron of German Bombers would rev up again, usually during the quiet passages of the songs.

Despite all the ructions the singers were quite enjoying themselves. The nightly practices made them all aware of the aimless lives they'd been leading and, whilst Freddy could still be his old infuriating self and needed a fair bit of regular goading to keep him down to size, they were secretly immensely impressed with both his musicianship and dedication to the challenge he had created for them all.

For fun they put together a list of translations of his assessments of their efforts.

Quite good = Lord above. Can't they hear how awful it is?

Interesting = Terrible

It's coming on = Why did I ever get myself into this?

Not a bad start = Is there a cancellation fee?

...and many more.

He was, of course, trying to encourage them but they knew only too well that the mountain ahead was almost unclimbable.

They were sent details of the competition evening and told that it would take place before a packed audience in the Victory Hall in the presence of the Mayor and Mayoress and the entire Flaxton-on-Sea Council. It was to be a 'Gala Evening' and one that, the blurb assured its readers, would be unforgettable. That's exactly what the Oldthorpe Choir feared! They saw that they were up against various Church Choirs, the Police Choir and even a Fire Brigade Choir. Sister hoped she wouldn't be recognised by either of the latter two.

So it would be Oldthorpe versus eight other choirs, most of them with years of experience behind them. If there was one event in their long lives that would never be forgotten, this was going to be it.

One important break in the intense preparations was the news that Sister had passed her driving test with flying colours. It was extraordinary how bottles of all sorts of alcoholic liquid appeared from unknown bedrooms to create a bar on the sideboard in the dining room.

Gloria Cartiledge popped in with a crate or two, and in no time all apprehensions and fears of the coming competition were drowned in an impromptu celebration. So well did the liquor flow that the Oldthorpe Choir suddenly found itself called upon to give its first-ever performance before a live audience – the few non-choir residents and Gloria – and received a rapturous ovation. It struck Freddy that if they could lace the judges' tea with the same quantities of jungle juice they'd all consumed, they might just stand a chance.

The start of October and the final fortnight saw a frenzy of preparation as the choir practised well into the night. As with all things musical sometimes it surged ahead, sometimes it dropped back alarmingly. Tempers frayed and snapped, there were resignations and rejoinings, harsh words and warm praise. The whole pot of extreme emotions bubbled as, imperceptibly, the group settled into a fairly finely-tuned, well blended group of singers. Three nights before the competition Freddy announced that they were as ready as they would ever be.

And then, the following night, disaster struck. It was just a little virus; similar to the innumerable ones that had preceded it into Oldthorpe House over the years and, in a matter of a week or so, been defeated. But to add insult to injury this little demon went, literally, for the throat.

Sister ordered immediate segregation of all choir members. They were urged to stay in their rooms and mix with no one, meals were brought to them, they were to speak as little as possible and vast quantities of gargle and throat medicaments were thrust upon them. Oldthorpe was on a war footing.

With rehearsals now impossible Freddy fretted in his room receiving almost hourly bulletins from Nurse Lisa on the present state of his singers. The most serious casualty was Brigadier Ainsley, the undisputed bastion of the basses. With one day to go he had no voice at all. Mrs Braithwaite, of the dishwashing, was in a similar state and was excused all duties and put to rest in the sick bay. Others complained of dry throats but could still raise a passable musical scale in the privacy of their own quarters.

As the reports came in Freddy juggled with his team. Before the bug struck he had decided to gently move Clarence from a singing – or growling – role into, maybe, the lozenge dispenser or something similar. Now he realized that this luxury might be denied him. The rules stated a minimum of twelve singers so, if Ainsley didn't recover his voice in time, Clarence might have to stand – or stoop – in the basses under the strictest instructions to mouth the words in total, absolute, unequivocal silence.

Taking stock, the situation was just about tenable. One other bass was confined to bed speechless, but through the sterling work of Sister and Nurse Lisa, it now appeared that Ainsley would recover to roughly half volume level.

In the wake of that encouraging news came another blow. Lesley, anchor of the altos, woke on the Festival morning with a voice which appeared to be heading towards protracted silence. She was only able to whisper the required notes. It was she herself who had the brainwave: Lucy Banbury. She knew from sitting next to her in church that she had a true, if rather quiet voice and had let slip that she had over many years trained her school choirs.

After consultation with the others a phone call quickly secured her services in the altos but Lucy could see a difficulty that, in their haste, they had all overlooked: she wasn't anything to do with Oldthorpe House and the rules decreed that she had to be.

Now it was Sister's turn to weigh in with the answer. Did Lucy have a driving licence? Yes she did, although it hadn't been called upon for two decades or more. In no time she was co-opted into Reserve Minibus Driver. So that problem was solved – but only on the understanding that she could report sick if ever there was a need for her services in that direction.

"Who's going to make up the numbers, maestro?" Ainsley was saving his voice by watching a football match on the telly.

Freddy, sitting as far away from the noisy screen as possible, looked up from his music score. "We're all right now we've got Lucy on board. Stop talking, Ainsley, for heaven's sake. Sister should have gagged you."

"You're not all right actually, old boy. If you do your sums, which I accept is something few Raf types can do accurately, you'll find that even with the halt and lame we only muster eleven."

Freddy sighed and, to humour his muted bass, did a quick calculation, then a slower one, and then, using his fingers, a slower one still. However hard he tried he could only make the total eleven. Ainsley, damn him, was right.

The maestro zoomed to the door and collided with Tubes which caused him to drop his music.

"What's the score?" Tubes made for the telly.

"Passing By," said Freddy picking up the pages of music.

"Two nil," said Ainsley without taking his eyes off the screen.

Freddy leapt up the stairs two at a time. His target was the three Roundheads who were not members of the Oldthorpe Choir. One had failed his audition being totally and absolutely tone deaf, another had refused to even countenance the idea of standing on a stage and making a fool of himself and the third had promised Freddy that he would be violently sick if asked to sing in public.

But desperate times called for desperate measures. Even if none of them sang they could at least stand there and open and close their mouths like the fish out of water they would be. The vital thing was to make up the numbers to twelve.

Freddy's first call was on the tone-deaf Roundhead. Having announced himself, he was hurt that the door was only opened a couple of inches.

"Ah, old fruit. Watcher. Yes. Well…"

It seemed a good start to him. There was a pause. No response.

"Fairly desperate old chap actually. I know I failed you at your audition but this is an emergency. Frankly I'll take anyone however ghastly their voice is…"

He was surprised and hurt that the door was firmly closed in his face. So much for comradeship. Shaking his head in sorrow at the brusqueness of some people he moved on to his next quarry.

It was extraordinary. Again the door was only opened to a sliver and one baleful eye stared at him, unblinking. Freddy was beginning to lose his nerve which, to a man so totally lacking in subtlety, was a dangerous condition to be in.

"Ah, well, here it is."

This variant on his previous opening salvo created a more robust response: the door closed instantly. Now he had to shout through the thick wood.

"I've been thinking of you, do you see. One of the best voices in the house. I've always said so. A bit loud maybe so it'll be best if you don't sing at all. Just stand there and mouth everything. Much better all round."

He stood there confident that the door would open and his problem would be solved. What was that? Surely not. Not the language of an officer and gentleman. Too long spent with the troops. Poor show. Wouldn't want him mouthing that at the

Mayor and Mayoress.

One last hope: the Roundhead who promised to vomit if he found himself standing on a stage. Freddy was sure he wouldn't but Sister could always bring along some bags and he'd be in the back row anyway.

Knock knock. This was uncanny. Again one eye peered at him through the narrow slit. This called for very careful handling.

"I've tried everyone with the smallest semblance of singing ability but to no avail, and now I'm down to you…"

Freddy made his way downstairs a defeated maestro. How could they do this to him? At this late stage there was only one thing to do and, with a very heavy heart, he did it; Clarence would, after all, have to make up the numbers.

Upstairs the three Roundheads came out onto the landing. They had followed the events of the past day, done their counting and rightly guessed what Freddy's tactics would be. They smiled at each other. Their planned counter-measures had proved totally successful…

By the time the Oldthorpe Choir left for the Victory Hall they could be said to be firing on at least two of their four cylinders. On entering the auditorium they looked around nervously and saw that it was filling with an excited, chattering crowd of happy people. The only miserable faces seemed to be theirs. With whatever confidence they still had in them, they made for a block of seats reserved near the front for the competing singers.

None of the other choirs had yet arrived. Being seasoned performers who knew the ropes, they would employ well proven tactics and march in near the start, receive a wild ovation from their supporters who by then would be in their seats near the back of the hall, and so be well charged up to do battle.

No one knew the Oldthorpe people and, as yet, they had no supporters. They appeared as a strange mixture of regimental blazers and dresses of every colour and design; a mixed bunch in every sense of the word. Phyllis looked amazing. She had dressed as she felt an accompanist would dress, in a long velvet evening gown in royal blue trimmed with matching lace, long white gloves which she would ceremoniously remove very slowly before playing and a mass of jangling jewelry. On her head was a rather over-grand tiara. Having told Albert and George about her preferred outfit for the great occasion she had not been in the least surprised that they had come home after their night shift with exactly what she had described to them. They'd evidently found the whole ensemble in a dustbin somewhere in town, bless them. Only a column inch in the Flaxton Chronicle was given over to a raid on the 'Nearly-Nu' shop reporting that nothing of value had been stolen.

In the Hall the Oldthorpe Choir watched in growing dismay as their rivals came in to cheers and stamping which, well practiced in the art of performance, they acknowledged with grins and waves into the semi-darkness behind them. With a shock Freddy and his singers realized that all the other competitors were in matching outfits!

A very large, be-baubled woman turned and hissed, "You're in the choir seats. Reserved for performers." It was a mistake to hiss it within a few inches of the face of Lesley.

"Brigadier Lesley Bristowe. Oldthorpe Choir. Sit down please, you are blocking my view."

The woman sat – but not without an audible humph.

Gloria Cartiledge, who was with them as Chief Supporter, sniffed. "Obviously all shopped at the same frock shop."

Her voice carried sufficiently far to receive a unison turning of angry heads in front of her, and a welcome burst of laughter and clapping from behind. It had, Freddy thought glumly, all got off to a very bad start.

Everyone stood as the Mayor, his good lady Mayoress, and the Council traipsed to the front row and settled noisily and, it appeared, rather reluctantly into their seats and then the 'Grand Gala Evening' got down to business.

To the Oldthorpe Choir it was all a blur. People spoke, stage lights went up and down, music played loudly, softly, the audience laughed, groaned and applauded. It was excruciating to know that they would have to endure this torture for an hour or more before the climax of the evening, the Choir Competition. They now feared that this would be for them their moment of execution.

For a moment they were jerked back to reality by Freddy

easing his way diffidently along the row and moving up to the stage. Oh Lord, was it them already?

Thank the Lord it wasn't. Freddy, to avoid adding to their fears, hadn't told them that he had entered for the solo voice competition and now here he was, their funny old Freddy, standing in a spotlight and giving a perfect rendering of two tenor arias to a rapt, appreciative audience.

The applause was deafening; more, they were sure, than for any other performer so far. On a cue from Gloria, who was almost beside herself with pride, they all stood and cheered him back to his seat. Freddy, unused to any crowd reaction other than derision, was so overcome that he treated the audience to a loop-the-loop with his left hand and retreated into the safety of his seat.

For a moment they all felt better and it was noticeable that the choirs around them were treating them with a new respect. Here was a singer well ahead of anything they could produce from their ranks.

But the reprieve was short-lived. One by one the choirs marched up and assembled smartly into rows, their neatly pressed uniforms conveying a clear message of precision, order and competence. As one group gave way to another the Oldthorpes had to accept that the opposition choirs were all good, some very good, and that even without their croaky throats they would be hard pressed to match, let alone beat, their rivals.

Another advantage was that all the other choirs had conductors, some of whom used the 'St Vitus Dance' technique whilst others proffered a languid wave in various directions. Whichever, they gave their groups confidence and at least a rough indication of when and where not to sing.

Oldthorpe had no such luxury. Their conductor was in the tenor ranks – and their leading singer. But Freddy had already foreseen this and arranged the choir in a semicircle where they could all see him and gain some confidence by singing as much to each other as to the audience. What none of them realised at the time was how attractive and novel this arrangement was to both the audience and the judges – and how pleasantly different they looked in their smart individual outfits.

'Passing By' went splendidly, the gentle music and words drifting like a wave over the audience who, relieved to be

271

released from a string of boisterous Gilbert and Sullivan choruses blasted at them by coppers and firemen, gave the choir generous applause.

Freddy took Phyllis's hand and raised her from the piano and she gave an elaborate curtsy that she had practiced whilst plugging in the vacuum cleaner – it looked rather as if she was doing so now – and, when upright again, went through the lengthy business of putting on her white gloves. Then she sat down and went through the slightly lengthier business of taking them off again.

With renewed confidence they embarked on Lennon and McCartney's 'When I'm Sixty-four' which created the intended ripple of laughter amongst the audience who noted that many of the singers were already way beyond it.

A note on the music required them to sing it with 'verve and humour' and, with a bit of unison swaying, they certainly did! It was near the end of the second of the two verses that things started to go wrong. At first none of them, not even Freddy, could identify the cause, then Ainsley, his voice blending far better with the others now that it was forcibly reduced to half volume, spotted it.

Clarence!

Having, as instructed, remained virtually silent through the pieces to date, something inside him sparked – or clicked – or exploded. Whatever it was, his grunting dynamo was activated and, with gathering speed, it lifted in volume and transmogrified into strangulated words and approximation of musical notes until he was contributing as much noise as any of them – and rather more than most.

Ainsley did all he could. He tugged at the old man, punched his arm, biffed him on the shoulder, but to absolutely no avail. Clarence was blissfully in his own world, caught up by the excitement of it all. He saw none of the twenty-two anguished eyes staring at him, nor felt the blows of his furious fellow bass.

"Will you need me, will you feed me,
When I'm sixty-four?
SIXTY-FOUR"

The capitals were Clarence, who finished in a grunting fortissimo all on his own a good musical bar after everyone else.

Amazingly, the audience loved it! It had seen the antics as Ainsley tried to apparently exterminate his zimmered companion, had noted Freddy's despaired waving to try to shut him up, and couldn't miss hearing the rising boom of the foghorn as it reached and then overwhelmed the other singers.

It suddenly struck the choir that the audience – except of course, for protocol reasons, the Mayor and his good lady Mayoress – was standing, applauding wildly and stamping its feet. The choir didn't realize that their wild antics were being seen as part of the performance!

In some confusion they made their way back to their seats and now came the terrible wait. The judges retired to deliberate and the audience was released to stretch legs and increase the bar takings.

It was strange. Whilst the other choirs joked and drank, obviously finding the whole tense event a bit of good fun, the Oldthorpes stood around in embarrassed silence not knowing what to say or do. Clarence, in total ignorance of his virtuoso performance, went on one of his frequent visits and then sat down and had a snooze; he wasn't used to such exertion and late nights. His fellow choir members looked down at the sleeping figure, his head resting on his faithful zimmer, and felt a strange mixture of fury and love for their eighty-four-year-old friend who had probably ruined everything – and for whom they had set out on this exhausting adventure in the first place.

The bell summoned them back to their seats. Freddy prepared them for the worst. He knew that they had blown it but in the true spirit of Oldthorpe – which, in all honesty, hadn't yet been tested in such trying circumstances – he reminded them to be magnanimous in defeat. They would grit their teeth and applaud the damned winners.

The judges made their way onto the stage, earnest and unctuous as befitted citizens burdened with such heavy responsibilities. Freddy was amazed to see that there were seven of them, but heartened that one was his friend Mr Templar from the music shop who gave him a sad smile.

Then the compère invited the Mayor and his good lady Mayoress to join them on stage and, at last, with much shuffling for prominent position, all was ready.

"We have been set a Herculean task this evening," the Chairman of the judges was enjoying his moment.

"Get on with it, man," growled Clarence, back in his whispering mode.

"The contestants will, of course, be fresh in your memories, despite time spent tippling in the bar…" pause for belated, sporadic laughter, "which, I have to say we judges could not indulge in due to …"

"Your Herculean task?" Clarence's growl was now loud enough to reach the stage.

"Exactly." The penetrating stare in the Oldthorpe direction was no match for the thirteen flashed back at him.

"So without more ado…"

Freddy clamped his hand over Clarence's mouth. For two pins he would have pinched his nose shut as well.

"The winner of this year's Flaxton-on-Sea Choir Competition and a cheque for three hundred pounds, yes, three hundred pounds, is…" there was much scanning of his clipboard, "the Flaxton-on-Sea Fire Brigade Choir."

The audience was suitably pleased. It was difficult to better Gilbert and Sullivan and the chosen choruses had certainly been delivered with spirit even if Freddy felt that a certain finesse was lacking. Judging by his expression it had not been Mr Templar's choice.

"And the runner-up is… St John's Church Choir."

Now the audience was less pleased. A worthy performance, yes, but no fun. All very earnest. It had obviously not been Mr Templar's choice either.

The dreadful woman in front of Brigadier Lesley rose, gave the Oldthorpes a triumphant smirk and eased along the row to go up and receive the two-hundred pound cheque from the Mayor.

As she reached the aisle Ainsley whispered to her, "Your zip's undone, madam," and had much pleasure seeing her contortions with her hands fumbling behind her as she moved down the aisle. Her triumphant moment on stage was ruined by the fear that petticoat and bra straps – maybe even worse – were being viewed by the assembled multitude – and the Flaxton Chronicle photographer.

The Chairman moved importantly forward and cleared his throat. "We are introducing a third prize of one hundred pounds donated by a local trader for a new category of 'Most Promising Newcomer'. Three entries tonight were eligible and it is our unanimous choice that the winner in this category should be 'The Oldthorpe Choir' for their blend of musicianship and entertainment."

The audience loved it. Freddy made his way to the stage in a daze and received a special wink from Mr Templar which was quickly followed by a very wet kiss from the good Lady Mayoress.

All three choirs were brought up to the stage and then the winners gave another battering to Gilbert and Sullivan and the evening moved into its closing stages.

One hundred pounds. Freddy's euphoria quickly died. His plan had failed. After all that work. He sat amongst his friends in the dim auditorium realizing that the one time he had – and probably ever would have – the privilege of leading his fellow residents and staff in a worthy venture, he had not come up to scratch. Silly old Freddy Foster had proved to be just that. Damn.

"Freddy. Freddy." He was being nudged by Lesley and Ainsley.

"Well done, old chap. Well done. Up you go. You jolly well deserve it."

"What?"

"First prize in the Solo Section. Weren't you listening?"

Up he went again. This time the audience rose to him. They stamped their feet and shouted. Another wet kiss, and then he was back amongst his friends, his back sore from the slaps he'd received as he came up the aisle.

In the darkness he opened the envelope. Two hundred pounds! It had worked. IT HAD WORKED.

It was like receiving the Distinguished Flying Cross from the King all over again. Only then his proud parents had been alive to see it.

No one slept much that night. Even Clarence, who needed a lot of beauty sleep, didn't get his embrocation rub from Nurse Lisa until after midnight.

The next morning Gloria Cartiledge arrived whilst they were all still eating breakfast. She chivvied them on and then, as soon as they had finished, herded them down to the piano end of the room and made a little speech in praise of their amazing achievement in the competition. Then she brought Freddy to the front and invited him to explain to Clarence the connection between his establishment of the choir and the financing of the old man's pilgrimage.

"I don't know what to say..." The old man's voice quivered even more than usual.

"Just grunt then, old boy." Ainsley couldn't resist it. When the laughter had died down, Clarence went on as if he hadn't noticed the interruption. He told them about Passchendaele and Charlie Parfitt and Reg Spittalfield and Bob Symes, and his shame at not being able to pay his last respects to them. Even though they had only recently heard the dreadful story of the battle from Ainsley, his account of the pointless waste of thousands of lives in the most terrible conditions imaginable, graphic though it was, couldn't begin to match what they were hearing from the old man himself. They sat spellbound as he haltingly whispered his memories of being there amidst the carnage.

When he had at last finished there was silence, no movement whatsoever. It was not the moment for applause, indeed anything other than a respectful silence.

Gloria gently broke the spell. "Now then, dears; everyone out to the front. We've got a surprise for you."

Out they trooped and saw Gloria signal down the road. Mystified they waited and then, very gingerly, a large white minibus bearing the legend 'OLDTHORPE HOUSE' squeezed in through the gate. At the wheel was an apparently petrified Sister.

Freddy's nose was only slightly put out of joint by Clarence's request that Nurse Lisa should accompany him to the Menin Gate in Belgium. Clarence's nose was decidedly more disjointed by Sister's veto of the jolly idea due to any number of reasons, the fact that she couldn't run Oldthorpe without her nurse being the least of them. So Freddy would go instead, having had a crash course in embrocation application and certain unmentionable medical matters. It seemed to him a curious reward for his choir work, but deep down he was thrilled at the idea.

All the Cavaliers piled into the minibus to see the two of them off on their train trip to London where they were to join the Pilgrimage group. Clarence was very quiet and, respecting his privacy at a time like this, they sat in silence as Sister gingerly guided the vehicle towards the railway station. Speech would have been difficult anyway because all her passengers seemed to be holding their breaths, tightly gripping the seat rails in front of them as the bus crawled along the empty roads. Every now and then they looked at Clarence, fearful that this emotionally charged adventure might already be proving too much for him.

Then he stirred and, as one, they smiled at him ready to offer any reassurance that might help.

"I was glad we got that second song right."

They stiffened.

"I could tell it was all going wrong and came in in the nick of time. Anyway, all's well that ends well."

Then he was off in an unusually loud tremulous voice, rocking from side to side on the seat.

"Will you need me, will you feed me,
When I'm sixty-four?"

With one voice the bus-load roared, "SIXTY-FOUR," and then they all fell about in hysterics – all, that is, except for Clarence. What on earth were the idiots laughing at?

15

The November week during which Clarence and Freddy invaded Belgium on their pilgrimage caused many and varied reactions in Oldthorpe House. The nursing staff found their workload considerably reduced, the Roundheads breathed a collective sigh of relief at the unaccustomed peace around the place and the Cavaliers worried both at Freddy's ability to handle the mission and at Clarence's ability to create chaos out of order. The house itself also noticed a difference, the lavatory cisterns receiving far less battering than usual.

The only event of any note since the Arts Festival was the appointment of yet another member of the support staff. At Gloria's insistence – she had to remind her dear Gregory of the Nuptial Agreement – a gardener arrived, an engagement which, to her dismay, caused ructions amongst the Roundheads who had taken as their own preserve maintenance of the lawn and flowerbeds. A compromise was reached with Mr Griffin's green fingers being restricted to the large, unkempt vegetable garden below the lawn. The distant hope was that Oldthorpe might eat some of its own produce.

On a fine, crisp morning during that week Lesley, Ainsley, Tubes and Basil, well wrapped up, were comfortably ensconced in wicker chairs in the summerhouse away from hoovers and bed-making.

After a while Basil stirred. "I thought a lot about Clarence at the Remembrance Service yesterday."

"Poor old Ypres. As if it hasn't been through enough already." Ainsley performed an elaborate stretch that challenged every precarious joint in his body as well as the chair's wickerwork.

Tubes, who enjoyed a gentle stroking of his beard in the morning, now augmented the ritual by sucking the remnants of bacon and eggs from its accompanying moustache. He nodded.

"Destroyed, decimated in both world wars, and now it has

to face the onslaught of Freddy and Clarence. Life can be so unfair."

The stroking continued.

It was quite strange, noted Lesley, how these three close friends tended to speak one after the other, none coming back into the conversation until the third had had his say. She'd noticed it before and now looked at Basil knowing that he'd speak next.

He did – but it might have been as well if he hadn't bothered.

"I wonder what the lavs are like over there now. When I left in forty-five they only had holes in the ground." He took an enormous draw on his pipe probably hoping that a cloud of Old Holborn tobacco would expunge the vision. "We used to have to…"

Lesley coughed loudly – helped by the smoke. Basil took the hint.

"I say, Lesley old thing. Really do apologise. Completely forgotten you were here. Thousand pardons."

Basil had, thought Lesley, a rare skill of veiling an apology with an unintended insult. They sat in silence for a while, deep in their own thoughts, the men contemplating Clarence coming to terms, or more likely not coming to terms, with continental plumbing which created visions too horrible to contemplate, whilst Lesley's mind dwelt in purer pastures as she imagined the old man reunited with the names of his three old chums inscribed on the walls of the Menin Gate.

The quietness was suddenly shattered by a police siren as it and its accompanying car sped through Thorpe Haven. Ainsley stretched again and broke the silence.

"I was chased once."

"I doubt that the verb had a 't' in it," Lesley said wryly, sitting back and chuckling at her joke which had drifted way above the heads of her companions.

Ainsley ploughed on. "Egypt, fifties. Canal Zone. Fayed to Ismailia. We were guarding an ammunition dump. Corporal Tremlett was driving."

"That man certainly gets around." Tubes saw another unlikely story on the way. "Did he never leave your side?"

279

"I had a dog like that once," Basil drew deeply on his pipe and blew another mushroom cloud of smoke up to the summerhouse roof. The others noted that the cloud ceiling was descending rapidly. "Found it wandering along the road in an Italian village..." he added distractedly, "somewhere. 1944. I adopted him – or rather he adopted me. Called him Fido."

"That was original, Basil. Any reason?" Lesley liked dogs but felt that the names they were given often let them down.

"It's the only dog's name I knew at the time and it sounded Italian so I was sure it would understand."

They sometimes despaired of Basil; quite often, actually.

"He came with me – everywhere – never left my side. Right up to Monte Cassino. Tragic actually."

"He was killed?"

"Had puppies. Extraordinary."

There was a silence. There seemed nothing to say. The cloud ceiling dropped a fraction and Tubes opened more windows. Crisp winter air was infinitely preferably to an over-supply of Old Holborn. It struck him how preferable life would have been in submarines if they'd had opening windows.

"Do you want to hear about the chase or not?"

Ainsley was getting grumpy. They would have liked to take a vote on the answer to that question but Basil decided on a diversionary move.

"What relation was this Tremlett to the other two – if he wasn't the same chap?"

Ainsley moved from grumpy to testy. "Does it really matter?"

"It probably does – or did – to him – or them." Tubes sensed that his friend was splendidly manoeuvring himself into a corner. A nudge or two might help. "If the three of them were different Tremletts, they would be interested to know if they were related." He winked at Lesley.

"Whether they were related or not is unimportant." Ainsley had nearly had enough of all this. He feared that his friends were being unduly influenced by all those rubbishy chat shows that were now all the vogue on television. He fired what he hoped was a closing salvo; "Anyway, there are millions of Tremletts in this world so it's highly unlikely that they were related. Now, about this chase…"

"Hardly millions, old boy," Basil's puff brought the cloud ceiling even lower.

"What?"

"I doubt if there are many Russian Tremletts."

"Or Hungarian," volunteered Tubes.

"Or Chinese," Lesley joined in.

"Or…" Basil's turn.

"Right." Ainsley jumped from his chair. "Right. I shall go and do the crossword again. You're all obviously…"

Lesley laid a hand on his arm and purred, "Sit down, dear Ainsley, and tell me the time when you were chaste." She emphasised the 't' but the subtlety was luckily missed on Ainsley.

"Yes, well, right, Lesley. As least you appreciate my efforts to lift the boredom of our lives…"

"To new heights," muttered Tubes. He was relishing all this and lay back, eyes closed, his hands clasped across his ample chest.

Ainsley swung around to him, "What was that?"

"Or Outer Mongolia." Basil was still Tremletting.

Lesley moved in quickly, "Egypt, Ainsley. That's where you were, wasn't it? With the third Tremlett." She wished she'd left out 'the third' bit but Ainsley, now given clearance, was off.

"No military vehicle to travel alone. That was the order. Ambushed, you see? Then the wo…, er, Egyptians scattered the bits they'd cut off you over an amazingly wide area."

Tubes opened his eyes, "I wonder what Jean-Paul has for our lunch today?"

They all gulped, some more noisily than others. Ainsley hadn't understood the interruption and ploughed on.

"I'd been to a Mess 'do' in Fayed. It was midnight. Corporal Tremlett was my driver."

"I doubt if even Wales has many Tremletts," Basil would never learn.

Ainsley managed to continue but through tightly clenched teeth.

"He and I sat in our jeep outside the camp waiting for another vehicle to pass by so that we could go up the canal road in convoy. They never attacked convoys…"

"Too many bits to dispose of?" Tubes wanted to help with the detail.

"Nothing came. After ten minutes or so I said to Tremlett…"

"Och, aye the noo…" another wink all round from Tubes.

"How did you know he was Scottish?"

They just stared at him.

"So I said 'We'll go it alone. Put your foot down'." Ainsley nodded in satisfaction at the memory. "Pitch dark. We really moved. And then Tremlett said…"

"Och…"

"Sssh," Lesley felt there'd been enough Ainsley baiting.

"We're being chased."

"I'm so glad," said Tubes with a wicked grin at the others. "Two chaps together. Much the best thing."

Ainsley, his mind reliving what was evidently an exciting episode during his posting in Egypt's Canal Zone, again missed the point. "And we were – being chased. I could see these vehicle lights behind us. They'd get closer, I'd urge Tremlett to go faster, and they'd drop back, and then get closer again. 'Faster', I'd order Tremlett…"

"How long will this go on, old boy? Only with Christmas just six or so weeks away…"

"I got out my revolver and with shaking hands…"

"Too much port probably…"

"Loaded it. If Tremlett and I were to finish up…"

"In little pieces…"

"Dead, then we'd go down fighting."

Symbolically the smoke cloud ceiling now hovered only a few inches above their heads. Tubes and Basil, exhausted from what they saw as their witty interruptions, waited with Lesley for the stupendous climax to this amazingly boring story.

"We pulled away again…"

"Oh God…"

"And reached the high gates of the ammunition dump well clear of our pursuer. 'Open the gates', I yelled out to the sentries. 'It is I, your commander'."

"I bet you didn't say, 'It is I'. I won't believe it, Ainsley," chuckled Lesley, joining the doubters.

"The gates opened and we swung in. Gates closed. Engine off. Lights out. Only the sound of our heavy breathing…"

"No bagpipes?"

"…disturbed the silence of that Egyptian night."

There was no doubt about it, whatever rubbish he was uttering, Ainsley had a way with words.

"We heard the other vehicle approaching. It would, we were sure, speed past keen to get at us, but seeing the sentries on the gate, IT STOPPED."

Now they sat forward. Would there be carnage? A hail of bullets? Would a stray one hit some of the stored ammunition? A mighty explosion? The Suez Canal breached? The possibilities were endless – but unlikely. Ainsley appeared relatively unscarred and, except after a long session in The Anchor, walked fairly normally.

"We heard a voice in the dark."

Basil nodded. "Those Egyptians can sound very excited; yelling and screaming. The sentries must have been petrified."

"I think he came from Oxfordshire. Beautiful diction. Like me really. Obviously an officer."

They had no trouble looking confused.

" 'Did you see a vehicle go past', the voice said. 'I've been trying to keep up with it. A convoy, do you see? And now he's gorn'."

"Gorn? Must have been a Guards chap."

For a few moments there was silence; one of those awful silences when the audience waits for the punch line that has already been delivered. Then Lesley stood up.

"Do you mean that we have sat here, overhung with Basil's smokescreen, to listen to…"

"That was terrible, Ainsley," Basil felt cheated.

Ainsley, convulsed in laughter, nodded and, gurgling through his hysterics, managed, "It certainly was, old chap. Y'see this chap was trying to keep up with us to make a convoy and WE WERE TRYING TO GET AWAY FROM HIM."

The end of this totally unnecessary explanation became a strangulated screech as Ainsley, desperately wiping the tears from his eyes, sank back into his chair. The others stared at the shaking jelly wobbling with delight deep in his wickerwork and then looked at each other. He saw the concern on their faces and, quickly composing himself, sat forward, aware that something more needed to be said if they were to share his delight at the story.

"Poor old Tremlett. He was never the same again."

Tubes nodded.

"Probably as well, really. If he wasn't the same he wouldn't be confused with all the other Tremletts."

It was at moments like this, at the end of a brief spark of harmless banter, that the Oldthorpe residents subsided into a period of total silence.

The whole banter business was automatic; unintentionally initiated by anyone at random, carried through with an innate raconteur's skills, and punctuated with wicked asides, sparked by brains that, in their time, had been razor sharp. But at this stage in their lives these bouts of verbal jousting were mentally tiring, and refuelling was best done in the privacy of their own thoughts.

So now the four of them sat contentedly in a relaxing state of suspended animation. Familiar sounds were neutralised by their brains and discarded as unheard: Sister's strident voice disapproving of something or anything, the sound of ping-pong ball pinging on ping-pong bat, a disembodied curse caused by an arthritic joint, a football score or, when a certain resident was residing, the comforting swish of a lavatory cistern emptying.

"For the last time, NO; and stop pestering me."

The voice had come through the rear wooden wall of the summerhouse and was undoubtedly that of Nurse Lisa. They all sat forward, back to reality with a bump.

"Why do you go on and on? It's so unfair." Lisa's voice broke, "I've told you a million times to leave – me – alone. STOP IT."

There was a sound of scuffling and the men began to get up from their chairs but Lesley ushered them back and put her finger to her lips for silence. They settled back quietly but reluctantly. If Nurse Lisa were in trouble they'd soon sort out the bounder.

They heard a gruff voice receding, but couldn't identify it. One thing was clear though, the man was obviously angry.

"NO. For the last time no." Again Lisa's voice broke. "Can't you understand? I want nothing more to do with you. You're – you're – a dirty old man. Never speak to me again."

Footsteps ran past the summerhouse and they saw through the open doors their very own Lisa, wiping her eyes and then smoothing down her uniform, crossing the lawn towards the back door. On reaching it she stopped, touched her hair to capture the loose strands, gave herself a little shake, took a deep breath and marched in.

"We should have helped her, you know," Basil drew on his dead pipe and banged its contents into the ashtray. As if surprised by this rare occurrence the smoke cloud drifted away.

Lesley shook her head, "Much better not at this stage, Basil. A woman is embarrassed enough at a moment like that without finding she has an audience, however willing they may be to help."

"Who was he, though?" Tubes pulled at his beard, a sure sign to the others that he was about to explode – which he then did, leaping up and rushing out and round the side of the building.

Ainsley called after him. "Come back, Tubes. He'll have long gone now. Lesley's right, we'll tackle this with a bit of stealth." He was thoughtful. "A dirty old man?"

"Could be any of us." Basil's pipe pointed in all directions.

"Basil! What are you saying?" Lesley was shocked.

"Sorry, Lesley. I was thinking of the 'old'. Damn it, if she was my daughter…"

Lesley nodded. "I'm sure you'd tell us if she was."

The trouble with Brigadier Lesley was that you couldn't tell when she was teasing you. She stood up, serious now. "But the others? Keep your eyes open. I'll see if I can find an opportune moment to speak to Lisa."

As they left Ainsley darted back and, quickly checking the chairs and table, collected the ashtray. One burnt out summerhouse a year was quite enough.

The rest of the day, between the essential duties of eating, dozing and studying the state of the world through correspondents representing newspapers of every political colour and persuasion, was spent by the four of them in amateur detection. Agatha Christie, indeed any sleuth worth his or her salt would have got the case cleared up and the villain confessed and in a dank cell by bedtime but, sadly, not the Cavaliers. Many skills had they developed and honed to perfection in their long lives but subtlety in surveillance was not one of them.

Ainsley, Tubes and Basil, leering surreptitiously at all their colleagues, discovered a disturbing fact: all of them 'eyed' Nurse Lisa whenever she mingled amongst them! As soon as she came into the room, or pitter-pattered up or down the stairs, or just popped her head around the door, they moved into 'eyeing' mode. They would apparently continue to do whatever it was they had been doing before their in-built radar detected a 'Lisa presence' whilst their eyes, cast down to avoid detection, peered at her.

Lesley resorted to nothing so crude as leering. She didn't have to because she was blessed with that in-built commodity, infuriating to all men, feminine intuition. She could 'feel the atmosphere', it's moods and changing nuances and tell when something – a word, a look, a flick of an eyelid, anything – was out of the ordinary. Her surveillance noted that there were no such signs from her fellow residents although, like her three colleagues, she was startled to discover the effect Lisa apparently had on them.

Over the next few days she wrestled with the problem of tackling the nurse regarding her unwelcome suitor, but with her military training knew that no direct approach was possible. Sister Newbiggin had Lisa in her charge and any interference would certainly be improper.

She would have to bide her time and hope an opportunity would present itself.

Basil and Tubes stood fretting at the bus-stop outside Oldthorpe House in Harbour Road. The late bus was later than ever. It had earned that nickname in Oldthorpe House because never, ever, was it on time and to people to whom punctuality had been the cornerstone of their disciplined lives, this was an enigma they couldn't understand or condone.

But it wasn't only its lateness that was causing them to fret; it was what lay ahead once it arrived: the driver. This early afternoon service was usually manned by, in their eyes – and probably even his mother's – a young, gangling, drooping, pimply youth with a wide variety of skin complaints and a most unpleasant manner to match.

As with most elderly people what was even worse to Basil and Tubes was the doubling up of the man's roles as driver and conductor. When they had gone off to war there had been two chaps to a bus.

"Do you know what I think?" Basil's pipe was well stoked up again.

"Very rarely, old boy. In fact there are times when I wonder if you really know what you think." Tubes hoped that this might end the conversation. It was too cold to chat; it meant lowering his muffler.

The question having been rhetorical, Basil ploughed on regardless.

"Perhaps all bus drivers were recruited for their unpleasantness. It's just that we never met them, d'you see? Tucked away in their own sealed-off compartments."

Tubes allowed himself a cautious but doubtful, "Yes."

"It's just that we were never introduced to them. D'you remember that chap? What was his name?"

Tubes looked at Basil. There were times when he despaired of his old friend. Perhaps too much tobacco smoke was kippering him.

Basil ploughed on, "Looked like that Elvis singer chappie. Wriggled a lot. Ants in his pants. You know who I mean."

"Basil, old chap. Would you like to pop back for a little lie down?"

"Lie down? What are you on about? Try to keep up, Tubes. In court. The driver with the stupid hair cut."

At last Tubes got the drift, something naval men were good at. Basil, as obtusely as possible, was remembering last January's great bus-stop protest and his trial for 'causing an obstruction on the highway'. Now he felt in a position to fill in a few more details.

"Seymour. Pretended he was that Presley fellow. A nasty piece of work. Glad he's disappeared from our route."

He glanced at Basil, expecting, maybe, a brief nod and was horrified to see his friend obviously in the last stages of collapse. Basil was swaying like a very old willow in a howling gale. Coupled with this disturbing motion was an apparent scratching of his stomach – something not even Artillery Officers did in public – and a weird humming made weirder by being emitted through teeth clenching his billowing pipe. Tubes felt he might again need the mattress that had served so well in the protest.

"My dear chap…"

Basil jerked back into the real world and compensated for his strange behaviour by standing to attention. Something Artillery Officers were jolly good at.

"Yes, well," he mumbled. "Seen them doing it on that ghastly Pop-of-the-Tops programme. Disgusting." Then he fell into an embarrassed silence. But not for long. The silence made him more embarrassed than ever. He looked at his watch and stamped his feet in frustration.

"Double marking time won't help, old man." Tubes, happier with stamped feet than gaga gyrations, stood, legs apart, as if at the controls in his torpedo room. "Better to conserve your energy for the forthcoming engagement with the enemy. Action stations. Here it is."

The bus, in hands obviously unsympathetic to the internal combustion engine, jerked to a stop. Basil, delighted to change the subject, took up his friend's allusion to a wartime battle and fired the opening salvo.

"You're very late today."

The trouble with firing salvos at bus driver/conductors is that the rounds rarely hit their target. Tubes would suggest that this experience should be nothing new to an artilleryman but that was just inter-service rivalry.

The driver, totally ignoring the rebuke, adopted a well-rehearsed and often used confrontational stare and launched into the attack.

"Come on. Come on."

The two warriors saw this as a statement rather than an

answer and registered it as a 'miss'.

"Why are you always late?" Basil struggled up the steep steps. His own personal supply of shrapnel, lodged deeply inside him, objecting to the effort.

The stare intensified.

"Where to?"

Another 'miss' but the question was wrapped deeply in an angry sigh.

"Not the way you're proposing to go."

Tubes had fired his first torpedo. The nearest to a 'hit' so far.

"Eh?"

"Your destination board says 'Loxton'. I would hazard a guess that you've just come from there."

When in doubt the stare had learned to repeat itself.

"Where to?" The accompanying sigh was now joined by a descending cadence of resignation.

Tubes took aim again. "It should say 'Flaxton Bus Station'." His finger hovered over the 'fire' button. Basil, noting signs of impatience amongst the three passengers already in the driver's tender care, moved things on.

"Two OAP returns to Flaxton High Street, please."

Tubes, on the lower step with his head unnaturally close to Basil's behind noted that the chap's rear trouser creases could be more symmetrical. There seemed little more to note at that moment. Re-engagement would have to wait until he could confront the smug little bounder protectively tucked in his driving seat.

"Cards?"

Basil had the insane desire to suggest Bridge but felt it might be lost on the man. Salvo followed salvo. There were no hits and each side retired with only pride dented but Tubes, now squashed alongside Basil in a front seat, hadn't finished yet, not by a long white whisker.

"Why don't you wind on your destination board so that it actually shows where you're going?"

This totally reasonable request was met by a loud and angry sigh and a renewed grating of the gear box as the driver punched it back into neutral. The man knew that a round had at last hit its target. It was company regulations: the correct destination must be displayed on the vehicle at all times. Even more important than that was the stark fact that he needed to keep this job that he was so ill-equipped to have.

With another even louder sigh, this time followed by a series of petulant 'clucks', he flung open the little gate dividing his private driving domain from the common, even muckier one reserved for the unfortunate passengers and stood up to reach the handle which, turned like a clock key, wound the canvas roll of destinations from one spindle to the other.

Basil and Tubes sat there, both rather embarrassed that this necessary admonishment had been administered in front of an, albeit supportive, audience. All the regulars disliked, and many feared the nasty little man.

Fear was certainly not in the warriors' minds though. They were far away, Basil thinking back to bus conductors of his youth: bell-punches and wooden ticket boards laden with packs of different coloured tickets, penny beige, three-ha-penny white... Tubes was thinking more in the present; scruffy man, scruffy navy blue uniform and, as he stretched up to turn the destination handle, he noted that the man was wearing WHITE socks which, judging by the different coloured rings on them, were not even a pair!

The bus eventually pulled away but even the violent jerk didn't disturb their thoughts. There was much that needed discussing in the Flaxton promenade shelter before suitable refreshments in the Cosy Cot Café and then The Anchor. A busy time ahead.

Late afternoon in the Oldthorpe kitchen, and 'popping and pouring' time for Nurse Lisa. She was providing half of the domestic scene as she stood at the dresser popping a pill into this little glass, pouring a potion into the next one and so on, measuring out the evening medicaments for those residents in need of varying degrees of help through the coming night.

Chef Jean-Paul was now safely out of the way, his lunch-time culinary skills, for what they were, exhausted through supplying mounds of shepherd's pie, cabbage, soggy potatoes, stewed apples and custard to his captive clientele. However much Sister Newbiggin remonstrated with him he slavishly adhered to his old granny's maxim that, rather than going through life on an empty stomach, you should spend it with something resembling a household brick lodged inside you.

In this lull between lunch and supper, when the survival of fifteen internal digestive systems would be put to the test yet again, Jean-Paul, in his real-life image of Clint Rogers, was down at the local fish and chip shop getting a proper meal inside him whilst he chatted-up the local Flaxton nymphs.

The other half of the domestic scene in the kitchen that afternoon was provided by Phyllis Coombe who, having proved her skills in the dusting and silver-cleaning department, had recently been promoted to chief ironer as well. She loved ironing. Her Albert's and George's clothes were often ironed then re-ironed, her curtains were ironed, in fact every inch of fabric in her home was ironed and, her husband and son feared, if they stood still long enough they'd have a sharp crease in them in no time at all. Phyllis hummed tunelessly to herself as she stroked her way through the previous day's washing. Nothing escaped. Even vests and underpants received her loving attention.

Augmenting the humming was a rhythmic slurping sound from the scullery where the gardener, Charlie Griffin, was taking his tea break via a saucer. All in all the duet of dreadful sounds would have tested the calmest of listeners but Nurse Lisa wasn't calm, she wasn't calm at all. She banged medicine bottles and pill boxes from cupboard to table and back again, crashed beakers and glasses onto her trolley, scraped chairs across the highly polished floor and generally signalled to those present that she was a very angry nurse and it was best for them to give her a wide berth.

The diplomatic thing to do would be to ignore the storm until it died down and then see if help could be provided but Phyllis Coombe had never studied or even considered diplomacy; it just wouldn't work in her own household. So she charged in, head first.

"Trouble, dearie?"

"Trouble? Me? Trouble? Oh no, certainly not. Not trouble, just anger. Fury really." Lisa held up a bottle containing a dark, noxious-looking liquid and shook it violently. "I'd just like to kill someone, that's all."

"That's all right then, isn't it."

Phyllis went into the scullery and, shifting the gardener out of the way, collected another pile of clothes from the top of the washing machine.

"Let me know if I can help. I've often thought of sorting out Albert – and George bless 'im. Drop of cyanide in their tea. But the mood soon passes." She pressed a neat crease into another pair of underpants and smiled. "I wouldn't know where to get the cyanide anyway."

Lisa giggled. "Oh, Crumb, bless you. You're a real tonic." She pushed her pill-laden trolley to the door. "Good idea that. Cyanide. I'll have a search through the drug cupboard. You never know."

Phyllis paused in mid-excruciating hum as the door closed. Had she been wise, she wondered, to joke about cyanide? She didn't want Lisa doing anything silly.

Resting in Flaxton's promenade shelter wasn't proving much of a success. The skirmish with the bus driver/conductor had left Basil and Tubes unaccountably depressed. Like so many wartime battles, no side had gained any advantage although, deep down, they feared the wretched man had got the better of them because the ride along the bumpy coast road into Flaxton had been a nightmare. Either he was in a desperate hurry or, more likely, he wanted to show his reluctant passengers who was in the best position to have the last laugh.

Despite some frantic ringing of the bell by Tubes, the driver hadn't stopped at the promenade but had taken them all on to the High Street where, to the old soldiers' surprise, their fellow passengers had given them less than warm looks as they dispersed rubbing aching and bruised limbs. Hence the depression.

It would have helped if Lucy Banbury had looked in to the shelter and shared the hard wooden seat with them. She was quite used to sorting out sulking boys but was obviously detained, probably on Church business either with The Guild of St Helena, in which she was now something pretty grand, or the

Flower Committee.

Matters weren't improved by Tubes telling Basil that, as he was out of cash, funding in the café and pub would be down to him. With Basil himself going through a lean financial time his friend's solution was hit firmly on the head. The answer was simple: a trip to the bank on the way to the two watering holes. So off they set.

Basil could tell it was going to go on being one of those days. They were met at the door by a man so young that he was obviously on the first rung of a banking career ladder. He looked pointedly at his watch and greeted his last customers of the day with, "Two minutes to go. You're lucky. Just about to close the doors."

Despite the engagement on the bus Basil still had some fight in him.

"You too will be lucky if I continue to maintain my account with your bank, young man."

It was a stiff and extremely pompous reply which Tubes was sure his friend would regret later but at the moment there was no quarter to be given: fire was met with fire. Basil, for his part, hoped the youngster was unaware of the rocky condition of his overdraft facility.

With only one teller on duty Tubes joined the short queue whilst Basil glanced through some leaflets offering good financial returns on his non-existent investments. The first sign that their day was going to get worse long before it got better was the sight of the young man on door duty sprawling at their feet followed by a cacophony of yelling coming from behind them. Later, trying to analyse the events for the police, Basil and Tubes thought that the yells included simultaneously –

"Don't turn round."

"Hit the floor."

"This is a hold-up."

"We've got guns."

Tubes was having none of this; he hadn't fought in two world wars to be bullied by a load of louts, so he swung round, only to be sent sprawling from a sharp clout on his arm delivered by a giant wearing a boiler suit and balaclava. Despite the pain he was surprised to note that he had fallen neatly between the young man and Basil.

"We haven't fought in two world wars…" snarled Tubes.

"…to be killed by a bunch of thugs," continued Basil who turned his head towards the shaking young employee who's banking ladder had temporarily collapsed. "Perhaps you could tell them that the bank's closed."

"Shurrup you." It was a voice from way above them.

Basil received a none-too-gentle kick but stayed an attempt by Tubes to retaliate. "Quietly, old chap. The moment will come."

The raid seemed to be taking its traditional course. Bags were being filled by the terrified teller and the manager, whilst the raiders hovered around seemingly as nervous as the little group of customers lying prone on the floor. Probably due to the number of bank robberies shown in films and on television everyone seemed quite at home with the unfolding events and would have been disappointed if they had taken any unusual direction. The victims knew what was expected of them and the raiders had obviously used the graphic images beamed to them by the media as a very comprehensive instruction manual.

"Close yer eyes."

That's better, thought Tubes. They'd forgotten that one. Still feeling thoroughly uncooperative he didn't, and noted that he was within a few inches of a pair of rather smelly shoes above which rose a short, unprepossessing body which seemed to be shaking more than its victims. Fastidious to the last he noted that the boiler suit didn't fit, being actually too small for its small wearer.

"No one move, right? For five minutes."

"Ten. Better be ten. There might be 'eavy traffic."

"Shut up. Right? Just shut up. I've go' it all worked out."

A third voice. "Split the diff'rance eh? Seven."

"Seven ain't splittin' it."

"Just shu' up. Right?" – a pause – doubtfully, "Eight then."

"Still ain't splittin' it. It…"

Tubes groaned loudly causing the raiders to jump. "How about telling us to stay like this until we hear you drive away?"

"Good thinkin'. Right."

It might be assumed that Tubes would receive a pat on the

head for this welcomed help in solving what was proving to be the most ticklish part of the whole operation but, thugs being thugs, all he got was a kick in the ribs.

It became very quiet. No one had heard the robbers leave and they were obviously jolly good at doing so silently. Tubes felt that they must have practiced it time and time again. He enjoyed the vision of them endlessly tip-toeing backwards out of one of their mother's kitchens to get the footwork absolutely right.

Basil got up and dusted himself down. For a bank charging him such exorbitant interest on his overdraft he felt it should be able to afford a bit of Crumb-like hoovering now and again.

"Shall I lock up now, Mr Beavis? It's well after three-thirty."

The banality of the young man's question was lost on the manager but it snapped him out of his hypnotic state and he leapt at the phone which, of course, didn't work, it's wires having been pulled from the wall.

"Run down to the police station and ask them to look in please, Drew. Explain that we have experienced an armed robbery and would they attend fairly speedily."

Just like their letters to me, thought Basil. They never use one simple word when two complicated ones will do.

As it turned out nothing was done speedily and by the time the entire Flaxton-on-Sea Police Force, shortly followed by the Flaxton Chronicle in the person of its editor, Vernon Rogers (doubling as crime reporter) had trudged over every available inch of floor space in the bank, there was precious little left for the forensic boys of Ipswich CID.

Basil and Tubes returned to Oldthorpe House to be admonished by Sister for missing supper and told the exciting news by the resident telly watchers that there had been a raid on Flaxton's only bank. They felt that tomorrow would be soon enough, after a good night's sleep, to bask in the glory of their involvement in a story that might actually make a small paragraph in their beloved Telegraph and Times newspapers.

But Tubes didn't sleep well. Something was niggling him: a detail about the raid that had lodged itself in a hidden recess of his mind. Try as he would he couldn't retrieve it.

Maybe tomorrow…

The next morning saw an unaccustomed burst of chatter over breakfast as the residents requested a detailed account of the bank raid which Basil willingly provided. Because he'd spent the entire time prone on the dusty floor his account had to be somewhat embellished and, with years of study behind him, he selected the better television and film moments and popped them in.

Tubes remained strangely silent. His friends feared that, in that he had probably never experienced a bank raid in a submarine, it might have all been too much for him.

Later, having studied the national newspapers, the main bone of contention amongst the residents was the lack of any mention of this world-shattering outrage within their pages. Judging by the amount of time and effort Flaxton Chronicle's Vernon Rogers put into his on-the-spot reporting, there would be plenty of local coverage, but why was not the British nation as a whole being informed? The more gifted 'letters-to-the editor' residents were quick to put pen to paper. They felt a good dressing-down was required.

"How did it feel to have the muzzle of a gun in the back of your neck again?"

This question to Basil was a tricky one to handle. He used his usual delaying tactic and re-lit his pipe as he considered an answer that, whilst not actually telling a lie, would not reveal that on this occasion no gun touched any part of him nor, throughout his career, ever had. He blew out a cloud of smoke and smiled bravely.

"No one likes a gun to his neck. We remained perfectly calm."

Basil, emulating the skills displayed in the non-answering of questions by politicians on the television, fielded every question, brushing them aside and making reassuring statements. He was in sparkling form.

Tubes was still silent. His colleagues respected it, noting that even those trained to the highest standards of the Senior Service could, at times, throw a wobbly.

That afternoon the usual drill was taking its course in the Oldthorpe kitchen. Lisa busy with her medicines, Phyllis doing that day's ironing and Sister rushing about being terribly busy, although at what was hard to define.

Lisa seemed a trifle more cheerful. Unbeknownst to any of them, she had finally sorted out her unwanted admirer who had been demanding of her far more than she was willing to give. She had been brutal in her dismissal of him because it was the only way to detach his crab-like claws from her, but it was now done and the relief was enormous.

So the scene was rather as it had been the previous day. Medicine sorting by a happier Lisa, ironing by a humming Phyllis, tea slurping by Mr Griffin, and Sister popping in and out like sudden gale-force gusts of wind blowing through an open window.

It was a surprise when Brigadier Lesley popped her head around the door. Seeing only Lisa and Phyllis, she came in. She'd heard Sister bounding about upstairs and this seemed an ideal moment to see what she could do to help Lisa. Maybe she could take her into the garden for a little chat.

"Hello Brigand, luvvie. Cuppa tea?" Phyllis hummed her way to the dresser for another cup and saucer.

"Thank you, Crumb, but no. I was wondering if you would spare me a moment or two, Lisa?"

"I bin robbed."

The calm was shattered by the simultaneous arrival in the kitchen of Sister from the hall and Mr Griffin holding aloft a battered and obviously empty purse. He was shaking it to make its emptiness even more evident.

When order had been relatively restored, Sister sent Mr Griffin back to the scullery to check the pockets of his overcoat again.

"It was there this mornin'. I checked."

"How much?" Lesley moved into the command mode.

"Roughly how much, Mr Griffin?" Sister wished to be in charge.

"It won't have been there if it's not there now. The very idea." Phyllis smelt trouble. She knew all about things missing and mysteriously found through her long association with hubby George.

"It was there and someone's took it. Twenty-five pound. Five fivers. I want the police."

Sister stiffened. Surely not another police investigation? Elevation to Matron seemed to be drifting further and further away.

"I'm sure we can sort this out amongst ourselves." Sister's tone bordered on desperation.

"Of course." Lesley was back in command. "Anyone come or gone since the gardener hung his coat there this morning?"

Phyllis shook her head. "I've been around all the morning, love. No one."

"Then it's simple. Everyone empties their bags and pockets and if, Mr Griffin, as seems likely, your money isn't there, then you've been mistaken and you didn't bring it with you this morning. Q.E.D."

Phyllis looked around. Who was the Brigand calling Edie and why should she queue?

Mr Griffin nodded enthusiastically. "You're right, Missus. I've shown you me purse and it's empty." He shook it to make the point yet again. "It's you three now." He pointed at Sister, Lisa and Phyllis.

All three had their handbags piled on the corner of the dresser. Self-consciously, one by one, they emptied the contents onto the table. Sister would have refused, but the thought of the police and her promised elevation made her bite on the bullet.

"I have about two pounds in notes and coins in my purse," she said tightly and tipped the contents onto the table. So it proved to be. She quickly gathered them up, feeling that she had stripped naked in front of them.

"I don't expect I've even got that unless my Albert popped something in. Sometimes there's a hundred or two which he's looking after for a friend, but it's soon taken back again." Phyllis counted out the money. "Four pounds seventy-eight p. That's it. I still can't get used to this decimal stuff."

Lisa opened her bag and, like Sister, felt deeply embarrassed as she tipped its contents onto the table.

"I've got about three pounds left 'til pay day."

She turned her purse upside down. Out dropped three pound notes – and five crisp fivers.

The stunned silence was broken by Lisa dashing from the kitchen. They could hear her sobbing as she rushed upstairs and slammed her bedroom door.

Sister found her voice. "She'll have to be suspended." She sighed. "A full investigation. I can't believe it."

Lesley's voice was hard. "Neither can I," was all she said.

The last drama of the day occurred at about 11p.m. as Oldthorpe House settled down for the night. Because of a strict imposition of secrecy on the events in the kitchen no one knew of Lisa's plight and it was assumed that she'd retired unwell to her room. Neither did they know that Lesley had gone up and spent some time with her.

So bedtime thoughts were still very much on the bank robbery which had, in Basil's capable hands, grown somewhat in scale and dramatic incident.

Tubes slowly undressed, his mind still plagued by the hidden image of something during the robbery that had triggered a question that needed answering. It was, his mind told him, a desperately important question – but what?

He sat on his bed, pulled off his socks and swivelled under the bedclothes.

There it was! Yes, there it most certainly was.

"Got him." Then he kicked back the blankets and padded his way down the landing to Basil's room.

16

Those who knew Tubes Potter well would have feared for his sanity had they been near the bus stop at eight-thirty the next morning. There he was, wide awake, sprightly and obviously keen to get on with whatever it was he needed to get on with. By the time the rest of Oldthorpe had gone through the laborious business of getting up, having breakfast and settling to some non-energetic exercise he was back amongst them, his mission, a trip to Flaxton-on-Sea's toyshop, accomplished.

And then even more madness. At half-past eleven he was at the bus stop again, this time with Basil, waiting for their usual bus into Flaxton – the 'late bus' – which would in all probability be driven by its nasty little regular driver.

On its jerky arrival they climbed aboard, but now the usual procedure took a new direction. As Tubes handed over the money for his ticket, he grabbed the driver's wrist and clamped half a pair of child's toy handcuffs on it and the other half on the metal handrail. At the same time he announced in true torpedo room fortissimo, "James Wendle, I am making a citizen's arrest in connection with yesterday's bank robbery."

To the passengers on the bus it was now evident that they had a madman on board. They sat, leaning into the aisle for a better view of this strange, improbable scene being acted out at the front of the bus.

Basil, wishing to make some contribution, leant over and took the key from the ignition and the bus subsided into unjuddering quietness. With a flourish he dropped the key into his trouser pocket, the effect being somewhat ruined by it falling with a clatter through a hole and down via his trouser leg onto the metal floor.

The next moment was even more unexpected.

"I'm not James Wendle. I'm Mickey Drewett. So undo these and I can sue you for wrongful arrest, mate." The driver tugged at the handcuffs.

Still under full steam Tubes was not to be put off by such

poor evasive tactics. "They said at the bus station your name's James ..."

He got no further. With another giant tug the chain between the cuffs gave way and the driver jumped up. This so surprised Tubes that he stepped back onto Basil's toe. Basil tried an 'ouch' but it was drowned by the little driver's agitated shouting.

"He's on the other bus. If you want to arrest him he'll be along in an hour. Get off"

"It's you I want to arrest." Tubes realised how silly it sounded as he said it.

"How can it be? You've just said you were arresting ..."

"They gave me the wrong name."

"Could we move on, please?"

Basil jumped as the voice boomed from just behind his right ear. A large woman eyed him suspiciously. Judging by the nodding and clucking behind her she had appointed herself as passenger spokesperson and obviously had their full support because her question was now augmented with mutterings that both Tubes and Basil easily recognised as discontentment, not, as they would have thought, towards the driver, but them.

"Key."

The driver held out his hand and Tubes, aware that a tactical – but temporary – withdrawal was necessary, handed over the handcuffs key. This was all going wrong. He felt rather sick.

"Not that one. I'm keeping this cuff on for evidence. Ignition key."

Basil found it in his unholey pocket and, at a nod from Tubes, handed it over. The bus burst into rattling life.

"Off. Next bus is Jimmy Wendle's. He'll enjoy you arresting him as a bank robber."

"Now look here..." Tubes got no further.

"Off."

It wasn't the driver's command this time but the stentorian voice of the large woman backed by energetic nodding from her fellow passengers.

The bus jerked away firing, as a final salvo, a burst of foul diesel exhaust all over them.

They stood silently at the bus stop.

"He was agitated, you know." Basil was urgently filling his pipe. "Far more agitated than he would be if he was innocent."

Tubes looked at his watch. "He's not innocent. Did you notice his socks?"

With the morning having so far been an unmitigated disaster it was kind of providence to reward Tubes and Basil with at least one stroke of good luck. A car drew up at the bus stop and in no time a kind motorist was driving them towards Flaxton Police Station.

Basil was pleased that the lady driver had not known the words of the jolly naval ditty that Tubes was humming to himself as they sped along. He was surprised that his friend was in such good spirits having, he felt, made an ass of himself on the bus.

Tubes, on the other hand, had seen the episode merely as an opening skirmish and now, with some difficulty, he galvanised the local police force into at least a small degree of activity.

"It's his socks, you see."

"His socks, sir?"

"Yes, his socks."

The policeman managed a raised eyebrow accompanied by an enquiring silence. Basil, who had learnt the significance of these articles of the driver's clothing when Tubes had looked into his bedroom the previous evening, nodded enthusiastically.

"White, d'you see?"

No response. The eyebrow remained raised.

Basil nodded again. "Dirty white." Why on earth couldn't the policeman understand?

"A lot of people wear dirty white socks, sir. My son ..."

Tubes really didn't want to know. "Not a pair. A red and a black ring on one, a single red ring on the other." He urgently tapped the counter. "How many people wear those?"

Basil felt that his friend sounded a little too triumphant but Tubes would not be deterred and, at his insistence, a detective was found.

"It was when I was tumbling into bed, d'you see?"

"Tumbling in bed." The detective wrote slowly, repeating out loud each word.

Tubes nodded but Basil saw trouble ahead.

"Tumbling *into* bed, officer. Very different."

"Very good, sir. If you say so." He crossed out the sentence and tried again even more slowly. Tubes waited impatiently.

"Took my socks off."

"Before or after the tumble, sir?"

Thankfully Tubes ignored the question and ploughed on.

"When I was on the floor in the bank I saw these feet in front of my face. Wearing these odd socks. It didn't register at the time but when I was getting into bed I remembered. They were the same unmatched pair that I'd seen the bus driver wearing that morning."

Tubes had loudly tapped out each syllable on the counter top as he revealed the last incriminating sentence, but rather than impressing its importance on the detective the tapping drowned the words so it took a little while for him to unravel the bed, the bus, the bank floor and the socks, particularly as Basil's efforts to help only confused the man even more.

The detective had seen this happen time and time again. Civilians reckoning they were policemen. He blamed the telly. But in real life it wasn't like that at all, it was painstaking work, calling on an intelligence way beyond the brains of ordinary human beings. He decided to demonstrate to these old geezers how the razor-sharp mind of a detective operated.

"You think this bus driver lent his socks to the bank robber? Why would he do that then?"

He took their nonplussed silence to suggest that they were struck dumb by his brilliance. It was a mistake. Tubes pressed the fire button and boomed, "Are you sure you're up to this? Would it not be a good idea to bring in a rather more experienced officer?"

"I must warn you, sir, that intimidating a police officer is a criminal offence. I may have to arrest you…" and then, realizing that he had absolutely no grounds for so doing and had confused 'intimidating' with 'imitating', added weakly, "or something."

He was right in one thing: it certainly didn't happen like this on the telly.

At last, through more patient, if slightly confusing explanations from Basil, a glimmer of light emerged at the end of the detective's dark tunnel and the police force galvanised itself into action. Michael Drewett was hauled from his bus canteen and brought in for questioning.

Statements were taken from all three of them – Basil's was quickly torn up because all he had to say was what Tubes had told him having noticed nothing himself – and then they were released whilst the police force 'considered its verdict'.

After a lengthy session in The Anchor, Tubes and Basil returned to the police station to be told that, far from being incarcerated in a damp cell, Mr Michael Drewett had been released 'pending further investigations'. The desk sergeant added confidentially, "He says he was in the cinema all afternoon. 'The Italian Job'. Grand film. Have you seen it?"

Basil had, but it didn't make either of them feel any better.

On their way to the bus they called in at the cinema in the vain hope that the manager would tell them that the Michael Caine epic hadn't been shown the previous afternoon, but it was not to be. Disappointment was piling upon disappointment at the end of this disappointing day. The manager confirmed that the film had been shown, it ran from 2 p.m. to just after 3.30, he had seen the small scruffy bus driver arrive – the chap had dropped his money on the floor and he, himself, had helped him pick it up. Even worse, no one left during the show – he knew because he'd been in the foyer throughout and, no, an alarm would go off if any other exit were used.

So, their prime suspect had been in the cinema when the robbery took place. The verdict was unanimous: Tubes had got it all horribly wrong.

And that, seemingly, was that.

It was to be a troubled night for quite a few of the Oldthorpe clan. Tubes fumed at the peppering he had received from all sides, so much so that as he and Basil made their way slowly upstairs he turned on his friend.

"Under fire from all directions. Poor show. Even you, Basil."

"Maybe you are just a little hasty at times don't you think, old man?"

"Only way I know. Press the button, the torpedo fires. Bang!"

"But you missed."

A wink appeared from somewhere within the white whiskers. "Not up to me d'you see. Not my fault if the skipper has the submarine pointing in the wrong direction." And with that he gave a small bow, went into his bedroom and shut the door.

Going to his own room Basil realized that he was now more confused than ever, but this wasn't a particularly unusual state for him to be in so it didn't trouble him. With well-practiced abandon he jettisoned clothes around the room and, more or less staggering into bed, was in no time fast a-snoring-sleep.

On the other front, Sister, Lesley and poor Lisa tossed and turned in their beds searching for a solution to the problem of Mr Griffin and his confounded five fivers. After some very close questioning Lisa had at last confided in Lesley that her unwanted suitor was the wretched gardener. There was no doubt that, unrequited in love, he had put his money in her purse to incriminate her and, he expected, have her dismissed – maybe even charged with robbery. It was an unspeakable thing to do but proving it, short of threatening to irrigate him with one of his own garden forks, would be nigh on impossible.

But by the morning Lesley had worked out the solution; she had decided to call on Moses for a bit of help. 'Eye for eye, tooth for tooth, hand for hand, foot for foot'. In other words, give Mr Griffin a taste of his own medicine.

Her first step was to brief Sister who, as she feared, immediately vetoed the plan as unworkable. Lesley had foreseen this and telephoned Gloria Cartiledge who vetoed Sister's veto and also agreed to have Lisa at Cartiledge Towers for a few days until the dust had settled. She also obliged in another direction.

Last to be drawn into the plot was Phyllis Coombe.

"Do you want the boys to work him over?"

Lesley felt that that would certainly be the best and quickest way but she was aiming at a little more refinement. She gave Phyllis her instructions.

"Oh, lovely, Brigand." She clapped her hands gleefully. "Just leave it to me. I'll get Albert and George sorted. It'll be a doddle."

For the third day running the late afternoon activity in Oldthorpe's kitchen took the usual form but with one difference: whilst Phyllis hummed her way through a pile of ironing and Mr Griffin the gardener slurped his tea, 'pills and potions' was being handled by Sister in Lisa's absence.

"I want justice, right?" Mr Griffin paused in his slurping and advanced into the kitchen.

"Oh, you'll get it right enough, dear. Don't you fret." Phyllis enjoyed the double entendre – even if she wouldn't have known it was one.

"Back into the scullery if you will, Mr Griffin. I want no muddy boots in here." Sister, already miffed at being countermanded yet again by Gloria Cartiledge, was seething with suppressed rage at the gardener's wicked ploy to get Lisa sacked. She forced herself to go on, calmly, "Nurse Roberts has been suspended during the investigation regarding the alleged theft. There will shortly be an outcome."

How true, thought Phyllis. Right, time for action.

"Bring me in that pile of clean washing, Charlie, there's a love."

The gardener carried a bundle of white garments into the kitchen and plonked them on the table and, with a defiant stare at Sister, clumped out again.

"Not these, dearie. They're Lisa's undies. She'll do her own. The other pile." Phyllis resumed the terrible humming accompaniment to her ironing.

Charlie Griffin looked around the pantry, "There ain't no more."

Sister's voice reached her strident level. "Come and take these back please, Mr Griffin. They're cluttering up the table."

The gardener considered a suitable reply that would include all his feelings towards women in general and this Oldthorpe lot in particular but restricted himself to an angry sucking in of breath and an expelled "humph." He sauntered in, dragging his boots to make the maximum mess, picked up the white bundle of bras and knickers and dragged out again. Having dropped them carelessly on the washing machine he stormed out, slamming the back door.

Sister and Phyllis looked at each other. So far, so good.

"You'll never make it. Much too fat. Not like the other bloke."

Basil, startled, lifted his head suddenly and banged it on the window frame.

The man, who was leaning out of his window in the house opposite the side wall of Flaxton's cinema went on conversationally, "What's up with that film then?"

Basil withdrew his head into the 'gents' and crept into the darkness of the auditorium. As the red, white and blue Minis hurtled around Rome on the screen, exhorted to ever greater recklessness by Michael Caine, he felt his way down the slope to the exit and out through the foyer.

The cinema manager looked up from chewing a Mars Bar. "You're the first person to leave during the film this week. And at the most exciting bit."

Basil smiled weakly and rushed along the pavement and up the side alley. There was the 'gents' window and, opposite, the window where the man had been.

"I say!"

"Hello again." The man reappeared and eyed Basil and then the small window. "You never got out through that?"

"Came round." Basil didn't want to waste time on all this. "What other bloke?"

It must be said that when the Flaxton-on-Sea Police Force wanted to move quickly, it could. Half an hour later Michael Drewett had been hauled from the bus depot canteen and, after some more questioning, was detained on 'suspicion of involvement in a bank robbery'.

Basil, who had no qualms regarding solitary drinking, made his way to The Anchor for a well-earned pint or two.

Things moved swiftly on both fronts the next day. The Flaxton Bus Company advertised for a replacement driver/conductor for its 'late bus' as soon as it became apparent that Michael Drewett would probably be unavailable for some considerable time. He had 'coughed' mightily once the full weight of evidence was listed and read slowly to him by the slow detective:

-Tubes had seen his odd socks both on the bus and in the bank.

-A man had observed a small chap climbing out of the 'gents' window at two-thirty on the afternoon of the raid and noticed that he was incongruously wearing white socks under a blue suit.

-Dust from the soles of his shoes matched that on the floor of the
bank.

-A set of dungarees and a balaclava had been found in his lodgings.

So it was a triumphant band of Cavaliers who sat at their table in The Anchor for a high spirited lunchtime celebration.

"What made you suspect that he had climbed out of the 'gents' window?"

Ainsley directed the question at a thick cloud of pipe smoke. Basil blew a small hole in it and smiled at his friend.

"Deduction, my dear Ainsley." He was enjoying this. Not often was he the centre of attention. "I endured the journey into Flaxton on Drewett's bus and once I realised he hadn't recognized me I followed him from the bus station to The Pier Head Tavern."

Tubes was confused. "How come he didn't recognize you? You were very unkind to him yesterday."

Basil couldn't believe it. *He* was unkind? Right, so be it.

"If you must know, Tubes, he did recognize me but I was sparing your feelings." Basil, when hurt, was quite forceful and could pull himself up to quite a height even when sitting down. "Once I assured him that I was the innocent party and had been under your bullying influence he forgave me and let me on the bus."

Tubes decided to sulk. Lesley, as she so often did these days, poured oil on the approaching troubled waters.

"You've both been very brave and clever. Don't spoil it. Do go on, Basil. You're in the public house with the driver."

"I bought him a beer."

Tubes exploded, "You bought..."

"Oh yes. We got chatting about the film. He had been very impressed with Michael Caine's planning for the robbery..."

Ainsley nodded. "He'd know. He'd just done the same himself."

"But I noticed that when it came to the three Minis' car chase and the coach teetering on the cliff edge at the end he obviously didn't know what I was talking about."

Tubes lifted himself out of his sulk. "So he'd only seen the first half of the film. Well done, old man."

"It was only a guess. So I went to see it – for about the fifth time. If Drewett hadn't left through the foyer or any other exit he either got out some other way – or he wasn't our man. The 'gents' was the only answer. Just before the car chase I went in and saw the window open. It was small, but so is our villain. I left the cinema at half past two – as he obviously did. It would have left plenty of time for him to dress in the gear and join his accomplices. So that was that. I went back to the police station and they did the rest."

Lesley summed it up neatly. "Trousers too short in the leg. That was his downfall." She hated untidy men.

Basil, whose clothes often appeared to have been thrown on him haphazardly, nodded. "Slovenly."

Ainsley sat forward. Something important was coming. "I remember Corporal Tremlett…"

Time for swift action. Tubes leapt up. "Another round, I think."

Basil was overwhelmed both by the congratulations poured upon him by his fellow Cavaliers and the Adnams Best Bitter they poured into him. As a final gesture of solidarity they matched him drink for drink and then, pooling their remaining meagre resources, hired a taxicab to take them back to Oldthorpe House.

Whilst Oldthorpe slept that night there was still some outstanding business to attend to regarding Lisa's dilemma and this was put into the capable and well gloved hands of the male members of the Coombe family, Albert and George.

The following morning the next stage of Brigadier Lesley's plan to metaphorically irrigate the gardener with his own fork got under way.

As arranged, Lisa returned, the Cartiledge Rolls having dropped her at the end of the road. After a quick briefing she sailed into the kitchen whilst Mr Griffin was slurping his elevenses and made straight for the scullery. Brushing aside the gardener she looked around and then called back to Phyllis, "Have you put my washing away, Crumb?"

"No luvvie. It's still there on top of the washing machine."

"It's not, love. There's nothing here."

Phyllis came to the door. "That's odd. It was there yesterday. No one will have moved it." She looked at Mr Griffin. "Have you seen it, Charlie?"

"Her smalls? Someone's moved 'em."

Lisa blushed. This was terrible. Could there be no other way?

On cue Sister joined them. "No one else comes in here. One of you must have moved them. Are you sure they were there, Mrs Coombe?"

Phyllis nodded. "Right next to Charlie there. I took them out of the machine."

All three women now stared silently at the gardener. There wasn't a man alive who wouldn't wilt under their piercing gaze. The implication was obvious.

"You don't think I pinched 'em? What would I do with Lisa's pants and bras?"

"What indeed." It was one of Sister's driest of dry retorts. "And how did you know the pile of washing contained Nurse Roberts's – er – underclothing?"

All this was too much for Lisa. For the second time in a few days she rushed from the kitchen and up to her bedroom.

Phyllis gave the gardener the sort of look she usually reserved for Albert when he had erred and strayed off course. "I've read about people who pinch girls' undies off washing lines."

"Now look 'ere..."

"No, Mr Griffin, you look here." Sister assumed one of her best bristles. "I'm sure there's nothing in it but you'll understand that the loss requires investigating. Go about your gardening and we'll soon have the matter cleared up."

At midday the gardener was summoned back to the kitchen where he found Sister and Phyllis standing behind a very imposing stranger who was sitting at the table, notebook at the ready.

"Charles Edward Griffin?"

He nodded. The last time he'd heard his name in full, spoken in such stentorian tones, was when he was sent down for petty larceny.

"I am Detective Sergeant Ridgeway. I am here to investigate the theft of a number of items of ladies underwear, namely…"

He was interrupted by a loud cough from Sister.

"Er, right. We will list the items later. They are the property of one Miss Lisa Roberts who resides here. Do you know her?"

Not as well as he'd wanted to. Charlie Griffin knew that something was going terribly wrong. He was sure all this was a dream but, try as he might, he couldn't wake himself from it. Like most law-breakers he was totally lost when accused of something he didn't do. He managed a hoarse whisper.

"Course I knows 'er. She's the nurse 'ere."

The Sergeant stood up, pocketed his notebook and said briskly, "You won't mind if we look around will you? The garden shed, your house, that sort of thing."

The gardener was now becoming thoroughly confused and found himself nodding. After all, he had nothing to hide, but with a police record for burglary that he had not divulged to his employer the sooner this nonsense was cleared up the better. Then he'd demand an apology – he'd enjoy Sister Nasty Newbiggin's embarrassment – and a substantial wad of notes to settle the matter out of court and after that a bit of blackmail to get Lisa where he wanted her. Yes, this might work very well in his favour…

But it didn't. Detective Sergeant Ridgeway accompanied the gardener to his house and a thorough search revealed the missing bundle of Lisa's underwear.

He was struck dumb: utterly speechless. It would be fair to say that never, throughout the rest of his life, would he be able to explain even to himself how the clothes came to be there. But the Sergeant was not willing to give him that length of time or, in fact, any time at all. Statements needed to be taken and with that in mind they returned to Oldthorpe House, the Sergeant in silence and the accused loudly protesting his innocence.

The investigation reconvened in the kitchen.

"I shall, of course, have to take you down to the station. There your fingerprints will be taken and we shall compare them with those on the retrieved garments. Should they match you will, of course, be charged."

"Of course they'll match," said the gardener desperately. "I was made to carry 'er washing into the kitchen yesterday. By them." He pointed at Phyllis and Sister.

"Ooh, how can you, Charlie Griffin? The very idea. Asking you to touch Lisa's undies."

Sister said nothing. If Phyllis was able to lie, fine, but she was not. Still, it was good to see Brigadier Lesley's little plan working so well.

The gardener began to fear not so much for his sanity but rather the sanity of these weird women. He had what he thought was a brainwave. "You check 'em. They'll be other fingerprints too – of whoever planted them in my 'ouse."

Not if Albert and George obeyed orders and wore gloves there won't, thought Phyllis.

"I don't want to press charges." Lisa felt close to tears. "Provided Mr Griffin withdraws any suggestion that I took his beastly money I'll let bygones be bygones. But I want him to go away, leave the area. I never want to see him again."

"And so say all of us, dearie." Phyllis put an arm around her shoulder.

"It is unusual not to press charges, miss." Sergeant Ridgeway seemed disappointed.

Sister broke in almost too quickly. "Yes, well, er, Sergeant. That's what Miss Roberts wants – and so be it."

"Very well. But it stays on file. One step out of line and we'll have you. Right?"

Charlie Griffin knew when he'd been beaten – and 'had'. How, he had no idea but he was sensible enough to know when to admit defeat.

A short statement exonerating Lisa from any suggestion of theft was signed by the gardener, and then he was unceremoniously seen off the premises by an apparently indignant Phyllis.

Sister briefed Lesley up in her room with a very grateful Lisa looking on. The Brigadier, who had planned every detail of the operation, had deliberately stood well back from its implementation. This was a staff matter and she was very clear that she wanted it to be seen as such. What was of paramount importance to her was that none of the other residents should ever learn anything about it. Lisa was very precious to them all and having been monstrously threatened by her rejected and undesirable suitor, should be allowed to resume her life amongst them as if the whole sorry episode had never happened.

Phyllis went off home to congratulate her 'two boys' and prepare a special meal for them before they went off to their night shift. So public spirited, so selfless. They'd pop one of the bottles of vintage champagne from the four cases George had found on a waste tip the other evening…

Ainsley lowered The Times. "What happened about Lisa?"

Life had returned to normal and the usual post-breakfast newspaper read was getting underway in the lounge. Lesley put her finger to her lips. Only the Cavaliers who had been in the summerhouse at the beginning of the week were meant to know about the unwanted suitor and the less said to the others the better.

"All sorted out, Ainsley." She added with extra emphasis, "think no more about it."

"What's this?" A Roundhead was intrigued.

A tricky moment was saved by a crunching of gravel as the minibus arrived at the front door.

"Ah, the wanderers return. Jolly good." Basil and, if they were honest, all the others, had missed Freddy and Clarence, for all their infuriating habits. They gathered in the hall to welcome the two of them back and Basil immediately noted that although Clarence was obviously tired, his back seemed straighter and he looked almost younger and fitter. His opening statement was pure Clarence Cuthbert.

"Hello all. Had a grand time. Excuse me," and with that he disappeared into the cloakroom.

The Cartiledge Rolls Royce purred along the country lane towards Thorpe Haven. Beside the large bulk of Simmonds, the chauffeur, sat the tiny figure of Gloria Cartiledge.

"I hear you did splendidly, Roy. Well done. Cooked that chap's goose all right."

"Thank you, madam. It was a pleasure. A bit of a demotion though. I was an Inspector in my last play. 'An Inspector Calls'. An excellent production."

"I've often thought that Mr Cartiledge should join your Amateur Dramatic group. He's very good at histrionics."

"I rather fear, madam, that he might be a little too, er, powerful in performance."

The little hat on top of the hair bun shook with laughter. "Quite right, Roy. Ah, here we are. Time Sergeant Ridgeway shared a cuppa with his fellow conspirators."

After a jolly tea – teas were always jolly when Gloria was around – and with Clarence tucked up in bed for a rest after an especially long embrocation session administered by Lisa, it was time to pepper Freddy for information about the pilgrimage trip to Ypres.

It had obviously been a great success. They had been taken on tours around the battlefields and war cemeteries and each evening had attended the ceremony at the Menin Gate followed so poignantly by the 'Last Post'. Clarence had found the names of his old comrades, Charlie Parfitt, Reg Spittalfield and Bob Symes, carved in stone on the walls of the gate amongst the fifty-five thousand others who had no known grave. It would have been very emotional and exhausting for anyone, particularly an eighty-four year old, and yet Clarence, buoyed up by actually being there at last and fulfilling his duty to his dead colleagues, had borne up well. Now he could sleep in peace.

Freddy was enjoying telling them all about it. It was good to be in the 'command' position at the fireplace, all eyes on him. Rather like conducting his choir. He executed a steep climb with his hand – they'd rather missed the Spitfire sorties – and launched into what he had kept for his crowning anecdote: the best of the lot.

"The last day – good Lord it was only yesterday – we'd kept the most important tour to the end. It was a First World War exhibition in the Cloth Hall in the main square in Ypres. They have different language guided tours and I made sure we got there in time for the last English one of the day. Clarence, of course, decided he had to go to the lav just as the tour started so, rather than try to catch up, we joined the next one."

"Makes sense to me." Ainsley was sure something similar had happened once to Corporal Tremlett and prepared to tell them about it but Freddy intercepted.

"It was a German tour."

"Ah!" Basil feared that Clarence might have done his terrible German impersonation complete with half-closed left eye.

"It didn't seem to matter. Everything was written in English as well as other languages, but I impressed on Clarence that he mustn't speak because a sign at the entrance had said that you had to use your own language tour."

"Why?"

"The guides probably said things that might offend other countries. The German tour would hardly labour too much on defeat."

"Did it?"

"I've no idea. Neither of us could speak a word of German."

"I remember Corporal Tremlett…"

Tubes was quickly in, "So what happened, Freddy?"

"All was well at first but I noticed as we moved from room to room that the group was staring more and more at us. Odd, because I'd kept us at the back out of harm's way."

Lesley felt she might have the answer. "Was Clarence making his little noises?"

"No more than usual and they were very discreet. Eventually, just after we'd arrived in another room, everyone turned and stared at us. They seemed quite angry. The guide shouted and seemed most upset. Clarence had had enough. 'What's up with you lot?' he shouted. 'Ah, you are English' said the guide and they all started to roar with laughter."

"That's their trouble, do you see?" Basil felt cross. "After all that happened they still find us a joke. I'd give 'em joke." He disappeared behind a particularly noxious smoke-screen.

"No, it wasn't that. A chap near us explained in excellent English. Each time we entered a new room the guide had asked the last person – that was us – to close the door please and stop the cold draughts. Of course we didn't understand so it appeared that we didn't care."

Freddy hooted with laughter and his right hand performed a series of acrobatic turns, obviously delighted to be flying over England again.

The laughter was generous and slowly, one by one, newspapers were raised back into reading position.

As if on cue, Clarence, preceded by a heavy smell of embrocation, came in.

"Couldn't sleep. What's so funny?"

A voice from behind a newspaper piped up in a terrible German accent,

"Clozen zie door bitte, mein capitaine."

But Clarence still didn't.

17

"Is the singing going well with your Oldthorpe Choir, Squadron Leader?" Lucy Banbury shifted a chrysanthemum by a centimetre or so in her altar vase and looked through its accompanying foliage at Freddy Foster who was on the organ stool playing through a few bars of various pieces of Christmas music.

"They really are becoming jolly good, you know. Of course it's mainly carols but they're having to learn the harmonies."

The two of them were alone in the big empty church up the hill above Flaxton's main street. There were still two weeks to go to Christmas Day and although most of the town and many front windows were already awash with decorations, the church itself was yet to be dressed for the festival.

Lucy was glad of Freddy's company and pleased that, at her request, the Organist had offered him the use of the organ and the music library whenever he wished. Usually there would be a gaggle – or more appropriately, a giggle – of flower ladies bustling around, outwardly complimenting each other on their arrangements as they inwardly compared and criticised, but Lucy had missed the appointed gathering and was here a day later doing her altar vase.

"I need your advice, Freddy. Father Christmas. For the Bazaar next Saturday. I've been charged with finding one. Poor old Bernard Butterfield is being, I think the modern word is, side-lined this year. The children say that he vibrates too much and his hands are cold."

Freddy chuckled. "He should meet Clarence. They'd make a perfect pair." He played a few bars of 'The Shepherds Carol'.

"I thought it would be good for the church and Oldthorpe if you provided his successor. You're all very much a part of us now, even if the vicar does wince when he sees you all marching in. He finds the critique of his sermon by dear Brigadier Ainsley rather hard to take."

"We've tried to stop him but you know Ainsley. Typical

Tank Officer. Rushes full ahead in a straight line never thinking of whose toes he's driving over." A snatch on the organ of 'A Virgin most pure' seemed totally inappropriate.

Lucy laughed, "Who would you have in mind to take on the job?" More chrysanthemums were minutely adjusted.

Freddy swivelled round. "That looks marvellous, Lucy. I don't know how you do it. All different colours and shapes and, er, lengths."

Lucy smiled. Freddy, brought up in the thick of war and subsequently in male environments had never been aware of the beauty of nature around him. Vases of flowers weren't standard parts of Spitfire cockpits. He frowned in concentration and his left hand performed a perfect landing on a manual within the length of one octave.

"Who would I have in mind? Well, not Ainsley for a start; far too gruff. He'd have the youngsters standing to attention and expect perfect creases in their trousers. He'd probably tell them all about Corporal Tremlett." A rather marshal rendering of 'In the bleak midwinter' made his point. He paused at the end of the line, 'frosty winds made moan', his mind being led directly to Basil.

"Poor old Basil would be frightened to death." This brought forth a line or two of 'A maiden most gentle'.

He then swung round. "Of course! Tubes. Ideal. No false whiskers needed, shortish and fat." He crashed out a bit of 'The Gloucestershire Wassail'. It was as well that his submariner colleague was not present to hear this scurrilous – and yet fairly accurate – assessment of his finer points.

Lucy laughed. She'd enjoyed the musical accompaniment. "Will he do it?"

"He well might. He's a good sort and was tickled pink when some visitors to Oldthorpe brought their sprogs with them. They loved his whiskers and he even let them dangle on his knee."

Lucy stood back to view her masterpiece. "We mustn't have any dangling."

"I'll talk to him and report back. Tell me, Lucy, I've often wondered. What make are those?" he pointed at the vase of flowers.

"Chrysanthemums."

"Right-oh. What makes those chaps grow into chrysanthemums?"

Lucy slipped effortlessly back into school mode. The most junior class. A little boy with his hand up. She smiled and said softly and patiently, "It's nature, Freddy."

"Ah. I remember nature. Walks and all that. Ruth Duggan tried to kiss me."

"How sweet."

"I knocked her down before she could, though. Her tooth fell out." Freddy shuddered.

"Not so sweet."

"We must have been six or seven at the time." He launched into a spirited rendering of 'Joseph and the Angel'.

Some ten miles away from this seasonal activity in Flaxton's church, life at Cartiledge Towers was following its usual unsmooth path. It was infuriating to Gloria that however much she and her faithful, if sorely tried, retainers worked at creating a harmonious environment, just one fly in the ointment could ruin all their efforts. The fly was of course, her husband, Gregory who, being the owner of CARTILEDGE WORLD ARMAMENTS, Cartiledge Towers and Oldthorpe House was a very big, noisy fly indeed. In fact there were many who would suggest that he was more a mosquito than a fly in that everyone he landed on seemed to be infected with something or other that damaged their health.

The latest to suffer was poor Gloria who had actually brought his pestilence upon herself by delivering to him a double whammy. First she told him that she planned to entertain everyone from Oldthorpe House to dinner on Christmas Day – the first Christmas in Cartiledge ownership – and, secondly, she was sending most of the Cartiledge Towers staff home over Christmas to be with their respective nearest and dearest. Only a skeleton detachment would remain.

"You'll love it, dear. You can be the life and soul of the party."

As she said it she knew it was a mistake; her husband's brand of life and whatever snippet of soul he might have was the

319

very last ingredient any self-respecting party would want to be lumbered with.

Gregory's wrath at her jolly news was mighty for even her to behold, but amidst the bellowing bluster he knew that his little wife had a weapon more powerful than anything he could call upon; it was that blasted Nuptial Agreement regarding the distribution of the Cartiledge spoils in the event of a break-up, held in a solicitor's safe, available only on her instructions. For him it lurked in the shadows ever ready to pounce.

The Cartiledges were sitting at opposite ends of the exceedingly long dining table that he insisted they use for their meals. Both were happy with the seating arrangement, he because it suggested elevation to a class to which he would never aspire and she because it saved her hearing him eat with his mouth open causing her to hear his dentures colliding with each other.

Gregory's gaze down the unoccupied yards of mahogany took in the same small, attractive secretary he had known and for whom he had jettisoned the first Mrs Cartiledge, but now, with a rare insight, he knew that his Gloria had become a very different kettle of fish. And it all seemed to stem from the time he bought, for prospective knighthood purposes, that blasted home for retired military nobs.

Gregory decided to try a little whine, "There'll be well over a dozen, my love." Would sweet words win the day?

"Oh, well over. What with the residents and their friends..."

"Their friends?" a Cartiledge minor explosion.

"Of course. You can't celebrate Christmas without your friends. Now let me see. This table will easily seat thirty or so..."

"Th-thirty!" Gregory could only manage a whispered echo,

"That's right, dear. You can have that nice Brigadier Lesley and Sister each side of you and I'll have, um, yes, sweet Major Basil, such a gentle soul and, oh yes, Squadron Leader Freddy each side of me. That reminds me, we must have the piano tuned. We can all retire to the salon after dinner and the choir will entertain us."

Gloria was quite flushed with excitement and now raced

through her sherry trifle ladling it in as if the party was due to start in the next few minutes.

"But who's going to arrange all this? You've just said that nearly all the staff will be away." Gregory rather wished that a thunderbolt might pop through the ceiling and put his dear wife out of his agony, but then he remembered that her evil solicitor had arranged for half of everything to go to her beneficiaries in the event of her demise.

"Don't worry, Gregory dear. I'm hiring a splendid firm of caterers to do all the hard work – cost a penny or two it being Christmas Day – and the officers will help you with the drinks."

"I bet they will."

Gloria smiled sweetly. "Oh, by the way, it's formal dress. Won't that be pretty?"

Gregory found his larynx was rather constricted. The sounds that he emitted could only loosely be described as words. "I will not dress as a penguin."

Gloria couldn't help herself and spluttered over her trifle but there was no stopping her now. There was one more thrust of the knife to come.

"I've said they should wear their medals. I'm longing to see them. Such bravery."

The larynx changed back into whining mode, "But I haven't got any medals."

"Never mind, dear. Perhaps if word of your great gesture to our gallant old soldiers this Christmas gets out, you might have that knighthood gong for next year's party."

Gregory finished his wine in one large gulp. Of course. He was already mentally briefing his publicity team. How wonderful that the darkest clouds nearly always had a silver – he'd prefer gold – lining.

"I think this party might work, Gloria. My idea of course."

"Of course, my love," then she added sweetly, "coffee in the drawing room?"

"I was Father Christmas once. Dashed awkward."

Basil was in one of his more mournful moods, hunched in amongst the Cavaliers who were in their usual places in the Flaxton promenade shelter shielding themselves from the sharp

December easterly wind.

No one made any comment, partly because Basil's statement hardly warranted one, but also it would mean shifting scarves from their protective duty over the lower part of their faces. It took another effort from him to get them stirring.

"They sit on your knee, you know. Frightening. I had a…"

"Cousin?" Ainsley felt that his friend's cousins had a lot to answer for.

"Well done old chap, yes. Good guess. She sat on my knee once. I remember…"

It was Lucy Banbury who saved the day this time. She popped around the corner of the shelter and, as a man; they shuffled upright and then, making space for her in the middle of them, plonked down again.

"The coldest day so far, I think." Lucy didn't seem to have much of her that wasn't covered in layers of clothing. Now they were five multi-coloured bundles in a row.

"I'm sorry, I interrupted. You were saying something, Major?"

"I think she only had a thin…"

"Yes, thank you, Basil." It was a day for Basil interruptions and Ainsley saw his duty to be chief interrupter. "We were talking about Father Christmas, Lucy."

"There's something I must tell you, Brigadier – in fact all of you. You may not like what I have to say and it could well come as a terrible shock."

They were all attention now. Four brave men who had given their all and been prepared to pay the final sacrifice. They'd had their shocks, monumental, heart-stopping shocks, the memories seared into their brains. Now, at this late stage in their lives, there was to be another one.

Ainsley's voice was quiet, "Go on, Lucy."

A pause.

"Father Christmas isn't real. He doesn't exist."

There was silence. Then she started rocking, her laughter at first silent, then gentle, then refined, and then a little cough and it died away. Now the others took over more in relief than hilarity and in no time were bouncing around and into each other. The moment of tension was gone, replaced by relief, and this was a perfect recipe for hysteria. Any passer-by would have summoned the emergency services on seeing five tightly wrapped bundles of elderly clothing swaying and howling in the icy wind-swept promenade shelter.

When a degree of order had been restored, Lucy seized the moment and drove straight in.

"I wonder, Commander, whether you would consider being Father Christmas for us at the Church Bazaar next Saturday?"

Another silence, their thoughts divided. Ainsley and Basil, although they would never admit it, were momentarily miffed at not being asked, and Tubes was thinking, "Why me, for God's sake?"

Freddy, as the unrevealed Tubes nominator, sang quietly his own version of 'Christmas is coming, the geese are getting fat'.

"Father Christmas is coming,
Tubes is very fat…"

It didn't help at all and led to one well-filled bundle of clothing thumping a smaller one beside it.

Tubes mumbled through his scarf, "Jolly decent of you, Lucy old thing. Not sure I'd be up to it. Don't know the ropes, d'you see? A bit rusty where youngsters are concerned."

With Ainsley and Basil both having recovered from their miffs, aware that they would have categorically refused had they been asked, they felt free to offer their opinions. Ainsley fired first.

"You'd do it splendidly, Tubes. A few little human torpedoes around you would make you feel really at home. Then once they're on your knee…"

Concerned for his friend, Basil interrupted, "My cousin…"

"Girls wriggle." Freddy's hand zoomed low and went into a tight turn. "At least, they did whenever I tried to kiss them. Then they'd break away. Of course they were much older. I remember one…"

Lucy felt that they were entering dangerous territory again. "Yes, well. Can I count on you to help out, Commander?"

With a confused mix of enormous pride and immense

foreboding Tubes decided to engage the enemy. "Provided the little blighters sit still…"

"No wriggling," added Basil.

"No dangling," popped in Freddy.

"Quite." The Lucy bundle fixed her eyes on the Tubes bundle. "Well, Commander?"

"In that case I will, Lucy. What time should I look in?"

"Ah," Lucy unfroze her joints and forced herself upright. "There's a teeny bit more to it than that and, if you'll allow me, I shall offer you all tea and tea-cakes in the café away from this howling gale and provide you with the details."

With that she set off and in no time five heavy bundles of warm winter woollies were bowling along the High Street towards warmth and revictualling in the Cosy Cot. With every step Tubes became less sure of the wisdom of his decision and more certain that he wouldn't be allowed to go back on it.

Once tea and tea-cakes were in place and a slow thaw had set into their bones, Lucy embarked on a detailed briefing session for the hapless Commander. As in her teaching days she took no notice of his various exclamations as the enormity of the operation was revealed to him.

"We'll get the outfit to you."

"Outfit?"

"The usual Father Christmas outfit. Red jacket and trousers, bobble hat…"

"Bobble?"

"I expect you'll have your own wellies but they must be clean. There are white furry bands to put round the top of them…"

"Furry bands?" Father Christmas sounded a bit weak.

"You'll need to stuff a pillow inside your shirt – but not as big a one as poor Mr Butterfield. He was, er, a more normal, um, rather emaciated."

"Pillow?"

Tubes was getting more mournful by the minute. Freddy felt his friend needed a little encouragement.

"Are you sure he needs a pillow at all Lucy, the size he is?"

Tubes started to stand but was gently restrained by Ainsley and Basil each side of him. Lucy was too busy mentally ticking off the list of instructions to notice that her unwilling recruit had already nearly mutinied.

"It's lovely," she clapped her hands gleefully, "You won't need the whiskers or beard. You're just right."

Tubes seemed to have lost the ability to concentrate.

"Am I?"

"Absolutely. Oh, and don't worry, it's all been dry cleaned." She leant forward, drawing them to her. "A bit smelly, you see."

Ainsley nodded. "Little children."

Lucy shook her head. "Mr Butterfield."

"I do think, Lucy, that maybe…" Tubes was certain that the time had come for a strategic withdrawal, but to no avail; the opposing force closed in.

"You'll arrive by sleigh, having had such fun clip-clopping around the town."

"Clip-clopping?" It was a very faint enquiry.

"Mr Marchant. He's a churchwarden. His pony and trap. She giggled, "They strap a pair of antlers on him."

"Mr Marchant?" Basil knew he was being wicked and would probably be made to stand in the corner but all this wonderful disaster that was enveloping his dear old friend was just too good to be true.

"And you are whisked round the town…"

"Whisked?"

"Clanging your bell…"

"Clanging?"

"Shouting out Ho! Ho! Ho!"

"Ho, bloody Ho?" At last he exploded and the café customers, as one, swung round to him.

"Tubes, please." Basil was not amused.

Neither was Lucy. "Commander, really."

They were quiet for a moment. The café customers returned to their chewing and chatting assuming these elderly citizens were now silently embarrassed but, being totally unaware of their audience, they were no such thing. In fact they were experiencing a complete range of unseen emotions from hysteria, through delight to utter despair.

At last the forthcoming star of the show stirred.

"I think, dear Lucy," Tubes whispered, "that on reflection, maybe Mr Butterfield has another year in him. I'm sure he is much loved…"

"So sad. At last the internal bits start to give way…"

Tubes wondered if she was referring to him.

"Like dear old Clarence." Freddy did a bump landing on the table, rattling the teacups, "Sister wouldn't let him out today. She feared the cold weather might accelerate his need to…"

"Shut up, Freddy," Ainsley said it nicely but firmly. "Don't you worry, Lucy, we'll have Tubes here on parade, smartly turned out, well rehearsed with his Ho-Ho and belled up ready to mount his sleigh and take Flaxton by storm. We'll bring him in the minibus…"

"You lot aren't coming?" Father Christmas added fear to his existing emotions.

"Of course we are, old fruit. To cheer you on. Wouldn't miss it for the world, would we chaps?" Ainsley rubbed his hands together, the sandpaper effect causing heads to turn again in their direction.

Basil nodded enthusiastically. "I see it as the pinnacle – or should that be barnacle – of your career, old boy? I think I can say on behalf of all your friends at Oldthorpe that you thoroughly deserve everything you'll get."

The meaning wasn't lost on Tubes but one look at Lucy confirmed that, indeed, he was beaten. He had foundered and hit the ocean floor.

One point hadn't been covered: presents for the little brats. "What will I give them?" he asked plaintively.

Freddy clapped his friend on the back. "If you breathe too close to them old mate, alcoholic poisoning, probably."

It is extraordinary how Christmas, the season of comfort and joy and to so many the jolliest time of the year, can bring misery to a few less fortunate souls. Joining Tubes in the latter category was Gregory Cartiledge who, coincidentally, was undergoing a similar briefing for the forthcoming festivities as Commander Tubes Potter, but his was at the hands of his newly confident wife.

Yet again he silently raged at the solicitor who had so

effectively sewn him up over the Nuptial Agreement. What if he had him struck off? Would it make the whole nonsense null and void? Would a hefty wad of fivers in the right pockets achieve this? Even he, to whom a bribe was a completely natural bargaining tool, somehow doubted it. Having only ever had the country's legal system against him he feared that the idea was really a non-starter.

He'd returned from a long, hard day, during which he'd alternately bullied his workforce and wheeler-dealed his way into new lucrative contracts, only to be ordered to sit down and, even before his statutory large whisky, be told how a fair whack of that day's profits was to be used on the giant Christmas party.

"We'll have their mini-bus and the Rolls to ferry them here." Gloria sat before the blazing fire holding a notepad and biting the end of her pencil. "Or perhaps we should hire a motor coach for the evening."

"A motor coach?" a Gregory explosion wasn't far off.

"Much the best idea. Then Simmonds can enjoy the party."

"Simmonds? I'm not having my chauffeur…"

"…having to work on Christmas Day. Of course not, love. So a motor coach it is."

"Now look here…"

"At the last count there were forty-one…"

"F-f-forty…"

"One, yes. So that will comfortably fill the coach."

Merryweather, the butler entered the room just in time and handed his master a very large glass filled almost to the brim with whisky and soda.

Gloria was in avalanche mood: totally unstoppable. "Everyone's said they can come – except the residents who are going to relations, but none of the Cavaliers are, bless 'em."

"Coming?" he could but hope.

"Going to relations. No one seems able to take them."

"So we are?" Gregory demolished half the whisky in one mighty gulp.

"Isn't that fun? And all the staff. It'll do that Mrs Crumb and her family so much good to be waited on for a change."

"We can't have…"

"We'll all muck in so that Merryweather and Simmonds

can have a bit of fun as well."

When Gloria was in this mood Gregory knew better than to waste his energy trying to get her to see sense. He'd bide his time and then, when the moment was right, he'd cancel the lot. No problem. Wasn't he master, a rough, tough, feared master in his own house? He still found it difficult to realise that he wasn't! He hadn't yet got used to the fact that the boot, a trim little black lace-up job, was now very firmly on the other foot.

"We'll need presents, of course. I'm off to Ipswich tomorrow so I'll need Simmonds and the Rolls. I'll get fifty while I'm about it in case a few more turn up."

"F-f-fifty?"

"Best to be on the safe side."

Gregory staggered to the bell and gave it a vicious press. He needed to bully something or somebody pretty quickly.

"Sir?"

"More whisky. Now."

"Very good, sir. And madam?"

"How very kind of you to ask, Merryweather. A large gin and tonic, please."

"A large gin and…" Gregory stared at his wife.

"Certainly, madam."

The butler bowed and withdrew.

"I suppose I should be thankful that you don't call him Charlie or whatever his Christian name is," Gregory was moving into sulk mode. Never a good sign.

"I wanted to. It's Bing, actually. He told me his mother was a great Bing Crosby fan. But he says I shouldn't. It'd be derigger, he said."

"You what?"

Total incomprehension is often helped by a period of silence which both now observed. The unnatural quiet was broken by Merryweather reappearing with the tray of drinks. As he was leaving he turned at the door.

"It seems, sir, madam, that we already have some visitors. A gypsy and his good lady and their splendid caravan. And their horse. I have taken the liberty of providing them with a cup of tea in the kitchen."

"Does the horse like tea?" Gloria enjoyed a joke.

"Not the horse, madam. I fear I expressed myself badly. It is enjoying the grass on the rear lawn."

Gregory spluttered on his whisky, "I can't believe I'm hearing this. Get 'em out, Merryweather. NOW. Tell 'em to clear off and don't let 'em into the house again. Understood?" He was feeling much better now he had someone to shout at who couldn't answer back.

"As you wish, sir. I felt with Christmas coming…"

"Off my land. Right?"

"Very good, sir." The butler looked at his mistress and received a large wink in return. He withdrew tactfully.

Gloria, not wishing to contradict her husband in front of the staff, would deal with the matter later.

The days leading up to the Flaxton Christmas Bazaar were not ones Tubes would care to remember in time to come. He likened his first waking moments each day to those of Sir Walter Raleigh and Mary Queen of Scots as they counted down the hours towards their execution. He had seen television programmes on them both recently so they were foremost in his mind.

Neither was he allowed to forget his forthcoming trial during each day. Rarely would a fellow resident pass him without singing a snatch of 'Rudolph the Red-Nosed Reindeer' which might have been humorous the one time but became positively infuriating when constantly repeated. The fact that Tubes sported a rather red and shiny proboscis poking out through his white bristles didn't improve his humour.

Sister Newbiggin, who didn't approve of the Cavaliers showing their independence amongst the Flaxton community in any shape or form – the Roundheads, in their slavishly obedient way, rarely ventured out other than under escort – was less than charitable regarding his forthcoming awesome responsibility.

"It would be far wiser to use someone acquainted with children," she sniffed as she engaged in her regular activity of pummelling the cushions.

"Ah, Sister, how wise you are." Tubes was willing to grab at any straw. "I wish you'd have a word with the authorities."

"Nonsense," Ainsley would have none of it. "It's people

who are acquainted with children who understandably refuse to take on the job. I've always felt that the Commander has just the right sort of knees on which to perch a young sprog."

Sister huffed, puffed and left the room.

Phyllis cheered him up a bit chattering away whilst cleaning the lounge windows which by Friday were always coated with a thick layer of tobacco, mostly from Basil's pipe, causing the world outside to appear permanently foggy.

"Albert's my own personal Father Christmas, Commandeer." Tubes enjoyed the novel adjustment to his rank rather more than Brigadier Lesley who wasn't sure about being labelled a Brigand. "Always bringing me presents, bless his heart. There he was – only yesterday – at the front door with a Christmas tree."

Ainsley and Tubes hardly felt this warranted them lowering their newspapers. They read on to the accompaniment of her cloth squeaking on the glass.

"Fully decorated. Baubles and coloured lights, fairy on the top. The lot. He looked so pleased. I was gob-smacked."

Ainsley slowly lowered his Times. So, he thought, must have been the previous owner, coming downstairs in the morning having spent the evening decorating the ruddy thing to find it gone!

Tubes, so preoccupied with his imminent execution, hardly heard her, which was just as well; her next sally might have upset him at any other time.

"You're perfect for it, Commandeer. Red nose, nice and jolly – and really fat."

One of the kindest things you could say about Phyllis was that she always meant well.

Things were no happier for Gregory at Cartiledge Towers. Although the date of his execution was slightly further away, he also awoke in the mornings aware that something terrible was lined up on the horizon. Had a régime in some far-off country to whom he had recently supplied a consignment of weapons been toppled? And, far worse, would this mean no payment? The mere thought of it made him shiver. It was almost a relief to remember that the cause of his distress was only the forthcoming

Christmas party.

There was still over a week to go, but in the days since Gloria had dropped the bombshell he hadn't yet found a suitable moment to order her to forget all about it and cancel the invitations. To his horror he had discovered that a new and totally alien sensation had taken possession of him: he was frightened of her! Having made discreet enquiries of his vast, overstretched legal team at Cartiledge World Armaments he now knew that merely wiping out the solicitor who had witnessed their signatures on the infamous Nuptial Agreement would not render it null and void. In fact, he was told with evident satisfaction, nothing would.

All of this occupied his mind as he was driven to work by Simmonds in the purring luxury of the Rolls Royce. As the hopelessness of it all engulfed him, his small body seemed to shrink to such an extent that passers-by would believe the car to be empty other than for the large imposing figure of the uniformed chauffeur.

Gregory wasn't used to having conflicting emotions and he found it all incomprehensible. At the root of the problem, although it would be hard for him to so define it, was his love for Gloria. Such an emotion had never happened to him before and it was probably for this reason that he didn't even contemplate the obvious solution to the nuptial problem, which was to eliminate 'the other party'.

Love being the weird, unexplainable thing that it is, Gloria herself would not have been surprised that no such dastardly thought had entered her husband's head. She, too, was in love with him, why she couldn't fathom, but there it was. It being so, she wanted to let him down gently regarding the party so, knowing him only too well, she made a few telephone calls; she hadn't worked as his secretary at CWA for all those years for nothing...

At the usual whisky hour she made sure his glass was well filled, smiled sweetly at him and set to.

"About the party, love."

"I don't want to know."

"Yes you do, dearest."

"I don't. It won't happen."

"I'm sure Her Majesty the Queen will be disappointed at your lack of interest."

The whisky bubbled in the glass as Gregory spluttered.

"Vernon Rogers at the Flaxton Chronicle is so keen to do a piece on it in his 'Social Events' column and I'm sure the dear Queen reads all her Empire's newspapers. 'Ah', she'll say, 'Give that wonderful Gregory Cartiledge a gong, Philip. Orf you go'."

Gregory just stared.

"Of course if he has to add a bit saying that you have cancelled it…"

"What if I refuse to attend?"

"…or weren't present…"

There was a pause, a viciously pushed bell, a refill of the whisky, a gin-and-tonic for the baiter and then a further pause.

"No medals, though." The rout had set in.

"What a shame. You'd have looked grand in yours."

"Eh?"

She took a hefty gulp of her G & T. "You know those four dodgy régimes you've put into power with your guns and things in the past year? Well, I've had a few phone calls made by your Personal Office." She opened her notebook and flicked through to a page, "Ah yes. By Christmas Day there will arrive in the post –

The Amanthian Silver Star with Emerald Cluster.

- this evidently includes a vermilion and puce sash.

The Buancirion Order of the Giant Goat with Guava Leaves.

- this also has a garter.

The Manderavitch Golden Guano with Wand, and

The Organdan Cross of Saint Luciano, First Class.

-this has sash, garter and sword."

Gregory just stared, the whisky forgotten. What an amazing woman this was. That he was worthy of such love – and these awards – he was in no doubt but, to his unutterable surprise, he felt tears irritating his eyes.

"I think it best…" he found his voice was inexplicably breaking, "if I stay at home for the next few days to help with the preparations. No stone must be left unturned."

Damn, thought Gloria. I hadn't intended that at all.

Gregory went to the window and stared into the blackness. He stood, feet apart, right hand wedged between his waistcoat buttons. Nelson, Wellington, Napoleon, he saw them all standing around him, Gregory Cartiledge, Knight of the Garter, bedecked with stars and sashes and crosses and other garters and, maybe, even a plumed helmet.

He smiled. Yes, he could see it all.

What he couldn't see, due to the dark evening and a convenient copse of trees, was a gypsy caravan with a horse tethered nearby.

18

Tubes Potter opened his curtains on the Saturday morning of the Christmas Bazaar and saw, to his satisfaction, that it was drizzling with snowy-white winter rain. In his innocent ignorance he assumed that at least one part of the purgatory that lay ahead, the journey in the tumbrel around town, would be cancelled.

Behind his door hung the dreaded outfit, delivered in two carrier bags by Lucy and so shamelessly displayed to the Cosy Cot customers over further tea and tea-cakes. Now, carefully arranged by Nurse Lisa on one of her hangers, it gazed mockingly down on him, an absurd buffoon's fancy-dress in which he was to be shortly encased and mortally embarrassed.

Being the determined man that he was – although determination had hardly been a feature of this whole disaster so far – he refused to dress up in the outfit at the house and so, to the great disappointment of those not attending the bazaar, they saw off in the mini-bus a morose, grumpy Tubes rather than a jolly Father Christmas.

The journey to his place of execution started with happy banter from his fellow Cavaliers and a few childishly reworded snatches of Christmas carols, but it slowly dwindled to a silence alongside that of the victim. As they approached Flaxton the rain turned to snow and the surrounding barren coastal strip started to look very pretty – a scene that totally eluded Tubes who, as if facing the scaffold, stared unseeing out of the window.

Things became worse for him, if that was in any way possible, on arrival at Mr Marchant's where he saw, tethered patiently outside, a pony fretting under a pair of ridiculous plastic antlers, attached to a trap disguised very effectively as a sleigh. Lucy and the Churchwarden welcomed them all with an enthusiasm well befitting the occasion but not Tubes's mood. They piled into the house and were plied with hot punch and mince pies whilst Ainsley and Basil dressed the protesting Father Christmas in his outfit.

"I can't possibly canter around town in the snow."

"Mr Marchant has kindly provided you with an umbrella." Father Christmas's attendants were becoming unseasonably tetchy.

"That won't help." So was Father Christmas.

"He and the pony have no such protection. Think yourself lucky. Here's your bell."

"Bugger the bell!"

"Tubes, really. Hardly what one would expect from old Santa Claus."

"Bugger Santa…"

"Now stop it, Tubes. The honour of Oldthorpe House is at stake."

"Bugger Old…"

A knock on the door saved further unnatural evocations from the mouth of what had once been a proud, highly decorated Commander in Her Majesty's Royal Navy.

"Time for the off, I think, Commander Christmas – I mean – oh you look splendid." Lucy was finding the moment very traumatic. As a new member of the Bazaar Organising Committee she was only too aware that her worthiness for such a responsible office now rested firmly in the hands of what she perceived to be a dangerously volatile contributor. The augers were not good.

Off they set at a gentle trot, Mr Marchant, proudly togged out in a hired coachman's outfit, steering the pony which obviously detested its stuck-on antlers, and Tubes in full Santa regalia behind them. The snowflakes blew into his face and he felt a strange and unwelcome wetness where wetness really shouldn't be. He was cold and the pony-cart evidently had square wheels – and yet, strangely, Tubes suddenly found that he was enjoying himself!

The transformation from sulk to serenity was particularly noticeable in his wielding of the hand-bell. What began as a tiny tinkle blossomed into a mighty peel of clanging as the pony and trap hit the High Street and people started waving and cheering. In no time children were rushing along each side of the makeshift sleigh, and provided Tubes kept the bell at full clang thereby drowning the language, he could assume that they were shouting encouragement to him.

After a short while he felt so in command of the situation that he tried a tentative "Ho," and by the time the ersatz reindeer reached the turn to the promenade he was bellowing "Ho! Ho! Ho!" fit to bust.

As the amazed crowds grew on the pavement and at doors and windows the latent blatant showman in him suddenly blew. He banged his feet, waved his arms, away went the umbrella and, with a fine emulation of Adolf Hitler merged with Benito Mussolini he rose from the seat and wildly acknowledge the adulation of the good people of Flaxton-on-Sea.

The pony, improbably called Pandora, and her owner had never experienced such a cacophony in or around them, certainly not in the twilight years of Bernard Butterfield's reign as Father Christmas, but their reaction was not so much excitement as panic. With ears back and teeth bared, Pandora leapt to the chase, breaking into a trot, then a canter and, in no time, an all-out gallop. Mr Marchant hung on for dear life and Tubes found himself on his back with his wellies waving in the air as Father Christmas hurled northwards along the promenade, scattering everything and everybody in his path.

They were halfway to Thorpe Haven by the time Pandora, realizing that the only sound remaining was her own hooves, wondered why she was exerting so much unaccustomed energy. So she stopped.

Neither Mr Marchant nor Tubes said anything; not a word. With a slow clip-clop they retraced their steps into town and up the hill to the church hall. What was it, wondered Tubes, that had made him so thoroughly enjoy himself? It had been almost as good as firing one of his beloved torpedoes, maybe even in its intended direction.

So it was a heavily breathing Pandora and coachman but a serenely smiling, if wet, Father Christmas who arrived at the hall to be met by a group of mothers clasping fearful babies. The youngsters cheered and jumped about trying to pretend, as instructed, that this strange apparition in a damp red balloon of an outfit was indeed the one-and-only, the original Father Christmas.

"Ho! Ho! Ho!" Clang, clang, clang. The whiskers and beard parted to reveal what the children might describe as a cheerful grin. Their parents saw it as proof that major dental treatment was required.

Anxious, damp, happy little hands clasped his and led him up to the hall. With another clang of the bell and a Ho, Ho, Ho that even startled the assembled Cavaliers, Tubes entered the festive interior and was ushered between the laden stalls to a corner decorated with a Christmas tree, fairy lights, jolly children's paintings – and his throne.

With military precision poppets were popped onto his knee. Some gurgled, others screamed in fear at the furry face a few inches from theirs, most were too shy to say anything and had to rely on their mothers' running commentary providing names and their particular present requirements, and a few added to his damp costume with their own supply of warm wetness.

Through it all Tubes beamed and ho-ho-ho'd and against all orders dangled and cuddled, thoroughly enjoying himself. He was a triumph. His colleagues couldn't believe it. Had their grumpy, intransigent, sulking old friend been substituted en route for this paragon of virtue, this lover of tiny sticky mites?

The bazaar was proving to be a roaring success. Buying was hectic. Many unwanted knick-knacks, kindly donated, were bought by friends and would be unwittingly given back to the original owners as presents, and the vicar arrived ready for the Grand Raffle that would follow the triumphant exit of Father Christmas.

And then, at the height of the fun, disaster struck.

"Ho! Ho! Ho!" Clang, clang, clang. Everyone turned to the door as, fully decked-out in an identical uniform, Father Christmas trotted into the hall!

True, it was a far thinner, some would say emaciated version but to all present, particularly the thoroughly bewildered children, Father Christmas Number Two, complete with bell, it undoubtedly was.

It didn't take long for the regulars to recognise this second version as none other than the unlamented, discarded Bernard Butterfield. Being short-sighted, he was well into the hall before he saw Tubes on his throne surrounded by a group of wide, troubled and incredulous young eyes.

"Who the devil are you?" bellowed Butterfield in a very un-Santa-like voice. Not jolly or friendly at all.

Tubes hadn't hounded Her Majesty's enemies through the murky waters of the world's oceans to be fazed by a little local difficulty such as this.

"Ho! Ho! Ho! Jolly good. Someone's off to a fancy-dress party, children. You've taken the wrong turn, dear boy. Ho! Ho! Ho!" With that he violently clanged the bell, causing most of the tiny tots to burst into tears and wet themselves again. A number of the elderly present were minded to do the same.

Bernard Butterfield had been a Father Christmas far too long to be put off by booming voices, children screaming and puddles on the floor. He advanced on Tubes who rose to meet him. The two stood within inches of each other.

"You are an impostor, sir." Bernard was quivering with rage.

"And you, sir, are a bounder." Tubes knew as he said it that it sounded ridiculous. What was he doing standing nose to nose with another grown human being before an audience approaching hysteria, trading such banal insults?

"We'll see about that. Take off that outfit. And those whiskers." With that the old man grabbed Tubes's beard and gave a mighty tug.

The bellow, a heady mixture of fury and pain, transfixed everyone, young and old alike. Even the bellower jumped at the ferocity of it. For such young children to witness a stand-up fight between two grown Father Christmases would have undoubtedly scarred them for the rest of their lives but, just as Tubes was about to lay out his aggressor amidst the puddles with one naval upper-cut to the jaw, a large, powerful woman who was obviously used to taking command took the bewildered Mr Butterfield by the arm – it appeared to the onlookers to be a vice-like grip liable to amputate the poor man at the elbow – and steered him towards the rear door. She barked over her shoulder, "One of Santa's helpers, children. Must have raided his wardrobe."

When the protesting Mr Butterfield had been led away, the organisers wisely decided to bring the bazaar to a close as quickly as possible. It was obvious to them that the six to ten year-olds were growing increasingly sceptical of the deceit being played on them by their parents. Was this the *real* Father Christmas? *Was* there a Father Christmas?

Their doubts were briefly assuaged by the bravery of one tiny tot who decided to test the plausibility of his mother's assurances and, grabbing a handful of Tubes's white whiskers, tugged for all its jolly little might.

If Father Christmas could bellow once he could bellow twice – and so he did just that. Those present swore that it even out-bellowed the first effort. The terrible noise that he let out, coupled with the fact that the beard didn't come away in its sticky little hand, sent the child howling to the far side of the room now confident that there was a Father Christmas and, more to the point, that he wasn't a very nice man.

Withdrawal from the combat zone was now a priority if all the good work was not to be undone so, with an assurance that the ordeal was over, Tubes agreed to a final bout of ho-ho-ing and bell ringing before he and his aching whiskers, escorted by the other Cavaliers, retired to the back reaches of the Church Hall. And there, sitting forlornly with a cup of tea shaking in his hand, sat Bernard Butterfield, still in his Father Christmas outfit.

With a whispered word to Ainsley, Tubes disappeared into the gents to change whilst Basil and Freddy dropped into chairs each side of the old man.

"Told me I wasn't wanted. Bloody cheek." Bernard was confused by a hand executing a stall turn in front of his face. His eyes lit up, "Well I'll be jiggered. What d'you know about stall turns?"

Freddy was so surprised by the question that his hand stopped in mid-air and then nose-dived onto his knee, "Spitfires – and Hurricanes." He was deeply embarrassed and added quietly, almost apologetically, "The last show."

"Mine was a Sopwith Camel," Bernard said mournfully, "First lot. Then a Bristol Fighter. So slow, we almost hovered over the enemy." Taking his cue from Freddy he lifted his hand and moved it hesitatingly from left to right.

Basil, feeling out of place amongst the two air aces weaving in close formation, took Bernard's cup and saucer seconds before it would have crash-landed onto the carpet and moved away. When Ainsley and Tubes joined him they looked back and saw Freddy gently helping Bernard out of his costume.

"The Anchor in ten minutes," they shouted. "See you there, Freddy – and, um, your friend if he'd like to come."

It had been quite a morning and a liquid de-briefing session was urgently required.

Christmas Day. A pouring with cold rain Christmas Day. For the first time in its present existence Oldthorpe House stood empty, its residents and staff either back amongst their reluctant relations for a few days or, thanks to the hired passenger coach, with their friends in the Grand Salon (Gregory pronounced it 'saloon') at Cartiledge Towers.

They had arrived to an ecstatic welcome from Gloria, the Master of the House having decided to put off his appearance until they were all suitably paraded to receive him.

"Come in, come in, dearies. Happy Christmas. Put your things in there. Merryweather's out the back helping. Ooh, pressies. Lovely. Gregory's somewhere. In we go. Cocktails first – and nibbles."

Clarence scythed his way through the field of runners and charged ahead, zimmer clattering, into the salon. If there were bare-breasted girls on hand he wanted a ring-side seat.

"Nibbles, Clarence," the resigned voice of Freddy shouted from close beside him, "and turn your hearing-aid up there's a good chap. You can turn it off later when everyone starts shouting."

Within ten minutes the level of happy conversation had already reached 'loud to very loud' on the hearing-aid scale. Gloria nipped up into the gallery just to look at them all. She'd always dreamed of a party like this from the first moment she'd inspected the then run-down property and, having reminded her disinterested husband of the Nuptial Agreement, made him buy it.

She sighed contentedly. The ladies all looked delightful in long dresses ranging from the conservative on Lesley to an amazing crimson tulle ball-gown complete with puffed sleeves, multiple jewels and tiara on Phyllis. George had evidently 'found' the whole ensemble in a clothes bin outside the Co-op, together with two immaculate sets of evening dress – white tie and tails – which exactly fitted him and Albert. What a treasure he was, she had whispered to Lisa, and so lucky with his 'finds'.

It was the men who really caught Gloria's eye. Most were in dinner jackets and looked very smart but one or two had really pushed the boat out finding, in the deep recesses of their wardrobes, the full-dress uniforms that they couldn't bring themselves to throw away. And such was the food at Oldthorpe House that most of them still fitted – more or less.

Ex-resident Colonel Alastair Hunter, DSO, Queen's Scottish Regiment, was resplendent in his kilt together with all accoutrements, the ceremonial skëne-dhu dagger thrust elegantly into his sock. Ainsley, not to be outdone by his old friend and sparring partner, had squeezed into the less flamboyant mess-kit of the Royal Tank Regiment, his upright stance made even more so by the stretched tautness of the material.

A giant Christmas tree covered in fairy lights and baubles stood in the window recess and the sound of carols blended with the human babble.

Gloria was overwhelmed by it all. There was only one thing missing. Deep down she knew it was churlish of her but she rather wished it might remain so: her dear husband, Gregory, master of all that he was about to survey – unless he tripped over his sword as he descended the stairs and broke his neck.

Gregory Cecil Cartiledge, Order of the Amanthian Silver Star, Order of the Buancirion Goat, Order of the Manderavitch Golden Guano and Order of the Organdan Cross of Saint Luciano (First Class), waddled, clanking, to the top of the grand staircase set magnificently in the vast hall of Cartiledge Towers.

He stopped to get his breath back and hitch up the brightly coloured – most would say garish – garters which, on his small legs, kept on falling down. He wondered whether they looked a little strange outside his trousers, drooping just below his knees, but the only alternative was to wear them inside, only then no one would be aware of the immensity of his awards. The medals, stars, sashes and, above all, the sword seemed to weigh a ton but, he reasoned, with recognition must come some hardship. He would, his dear wife with great satisfaction assured him, have to grin and bear it. Having little experience of the required facial contortion, the grin would be very hard to achieve.

The damned sword. Why did they make it so long that it tangled with his legs and tripped him in mid-manly stride? It never struck Gregory as he stood on the landing poised for descent that maybe it was his legs that were too short. He picked the damned thing up and started a slow descent. How he wished that Gloria had not vetoed his brilliant idea of having all the guests assembled in the hall, looking upwards and applauding as he came down to their level. But no, it must be a private triumph for the lone warrior.

Twice he nearly tumbled forward but bravely regained his balance and continued, heart pounding, quite overcome by his own brilliance. He heard the loud chattering from the 'Grand Saloon' and trusted that there would be respectful silence as he entered. Hadn't he seen somewhere great staves ceremoniously knocked on doors, demanding entry? If that useless Merryweather were attending his master, as he damned well would be if Gloria hadn't insisted he joined in the fun, he could assume the servile role of stave knocking.

But there *was* knocking. Not on the salon door but the great front door. Gregory paused. Where was that blasted butler? No one came. He stood alone, unsure what to do. Would Nelson, or Wellington, or even Napoleon be stumped by this unforeseen development? Certainly not. Of course not. The Master of the House squared his shoulders and made for the front door. The strutting gait that he employed for this simple – even for him – manoeuvre was rather spoilt by his initial inability to find the locks or the handle. The knocking became more urgent.

"Shut up. SHUT UP," was his un-seasonal message to the knocker but it had no effect. Eventually he mastered the intricacies and hauled it open.

"Yes. What?" Christmas cheer seemed no closer.

"Lord bless you, sir, and your family. God save us, we're in trouble and in need of help. Would you be after letting us in from this terrible night?"

Gregory just stared at the man, trying to come to terms with this sudden change of events. Standing there, dripping wet, was a handsome young fellow with sharp, strong features, his distress giving him almost a manic expression. Even Gregory could see that the poor chap was deeply troubled and the wild stare made him pull back. He remembered now; it was that damned Irish gypsy. He looked him up and down in considerable distaste – but still words failed him.

"I can see I'm interruptin' your fancy dress party and…"

"FANCY DRESS?" Gregory had his usual red-veins-standing-out problem. "I told my butler to order you to shove off? Well, shove off – or I'll call the police."

"Ah now, there'll be no need for that, sir. I'm sorry for any offence but, the Lord bless her, my wife is unwell, the caravan leaks so it does and we're in need of shelter so we are. Anything'll do, sir. Out the back maybe? I tried the kitchen door but no one's there just now, no they're not. If you could see your way…"

Behind the man Gregory saw a slight movement in the gloom of the porch. He could just make out a small fat woman leaning wearily on a pillar. Whether it was a tiny shaft of compassion that, to its own surprise, had penetrated his soul or, more likely, the need to get amongst his adoring guests, Gregory relented, just very slightly.

"There are old sheds round the back," he said gruffly. "They're dry. Use one of those. Then tomorrow first thing you're off or I'll have you run off. Right?"

"You're very kind, sir, so you are. May the Gods…"

"Yes, well." He could think of nothing more to say. Being told he was kind happened too rarely to him to have available an immediate response and so he took the easiest way and shut and bolted the door in the man's face. Then he readjusted his regalia and marched like the true Nelson – or Wellington – or Napoleon that he was towards the vast doors leading into the vast Grand Salon.

The entrance of the Master of the House was in no way as he would have wished. His plan had been to fling the doors wide and stand in the opening, resplendently framed, with right hand stuck into coat buttons in Napoleonic pose. In fact the doors were so heavy that he only got them slightly open and had to squeeze through, dislodging Manderavitch's Golden Guano star which dropped with a clatter onto the parquet floor.

The music played on, the chatter continued undisturbed and no one looked at him – well, not at first. Then, one by one, as they became aware of this other sparkling, decorated – but human – Christmas tree in the doorway, they turned and stared, struck dumb. In deep respect even the gramophone needle was lifted from the record of carols. The room fell silent.

Lesley Bristowe started it. She clapped quietly and, on cue, everyone else joined in until the room was shaking to wild applause, stamping of feet and from around the Coombe occupied territory, rather vulgar wolf-whistles. It was, of course, wildly over the top but Gregory, to whom gradation meant nothing, bathed – indeed positively wallowed – in it.

The Master of the House now realised that he had overlooked an important point of etiquette: how should he respond to this adulation? A bow, a wave or, perhaps, a salute? Bearing in mind that he was now an Officer of so many orders and awards, he chose a salute: not a very good one but still recognisable as a salute.

Alastair Hunter, always the one most likely to blot his copy-book, let out a guffaw and it almost certainly would have developed into a cacophony of derision if George Coombe hadn't inadvertently saved the day.

"Finished your chores then, squire?"

Gregory fell straight into it, "What chores?"

"I'll have a mild and bitter, ta."

The Coombe family, as one, dissolved into hysterics but Basil quickly dropped the needle somewhere onto the record and, helped somewhat by the Westminster Abbey Choir, everyone sang 'We three Kings of Orient are'.

The revellers were all pretty full of comfort and joy even before they moved to the dining room for the Christmas dinner. As with the Grand Salon the room was festooned with decorations, the two enormous chandeliers providing an air of opulence well suited to the financial status, if not the eminence, of the Master of the House.

Gloria had organised a meal of gargantuan proportions

hiring at enormous expense, it being Christmas Day, a team of caterers to provide turkey, goose and all the trimmings, blazing Christmas puddings and gallons of fine wines and liqueurs.

They sat down, Gregory at one end of the long table flanked by Lesley and Sister Amelia, and Gloria at the other end with Basil and Freddy each side of her. The Coombe family, Simmonds and Merryweather occupied the middle ground and the others were spaced between them.

Then the chatter started up again.

"Would it perhaps be easier for you, Mr Cartiledge, to remove your sword and scabbard whilst you eat?" Lesley in her long service career had dined with any number of colleagues permitted to wear swords – but never in the dining room.

"Best keep it on, Brigadier. The belt's holding up me trousers," Gregory, already well lubricated, attempted a crude wink; the result was repulsive.

"Best if you did then." Sister had her firm voice on. "Trouser dropping is not a pleasant business. We see far too much of it in our work. I'm afraid one of your scarves – the vermilion and puce one – has met the gravy."

"SCARVES?" Gregory rubbed angrily at the stains on the vermilion and puce sash of Amanthia's premier Order of Merit.

At the other end of the table Basil's eyes were watering as much from laughter as alcohol. "Midnight Mass, Gloria. Christmas Eve. Candlelit. Very pretty. Hong Kong. Garrison Church."

Freddy opposite him popped a large portion of turkey into his mouth. "Lovely service, Midnight Mass. I was always in the choir somewhere or another. Carols, anthems. Grand." He landed his fork with precision into the stuffing.

"I shall start going again," Gloria patted his hand. "Leave Gregory snoring."

"Anyway…" the story seemed to be slipping away from Basil, "the padre chap leant forward, do you see? Homage to God and all that, when…" Basil collapsed in hysterics, "his cassock touched a candle and – woof," his hands shot up, inadvertently sending a bread roll soaring over a chandelier and into the darkness beyond.

"Terrible thing, fire," Freddy seemed to be dowsing the story.

"Yes, well, he leapt around burning merrily do you see? No panic. We poured the communion wine over him. Soon put him out."

Gloria took a swig of hers. "He must have smelt really festive, Basil, covered in red wine!"

Basil nodded. "Certainly a change. He usually smelt of whisky."

He felt the story might have been sharper if he'd been allowed to get on with it without interruptions.

Back near the other end of the table Alastair Hunter had brought Ainsley and Tubes up to date regarding his exploits with the mischievous maidens of Flaxton. Sister, eavesdropping, did not approve.

"I can't imagine what Matron Montague saw in you, Colonel."

"I can't imagine what I saw in dear old Matron Montague, Sister. Sex is like that."

"Is it indeed?" There was no better lip purser than Sister when she put her mind to it.

Halfway down the table ex-Sergeant Simmonds, now reduced to the role of Cartiledge chauffeur, gazed across the table at Albert Coombe and his son George.

"Best Christmas ever, this. Hard times now so I've hardly noticed the festival passing these past few years." He gnawed at a turkey leg, a morsel fit for such a big man.

"'ard times, mate? 'ard times?" Albert didn't like to even think about such things, "I learnt a long time ago never to put up wiv 'ard times."

"That's all very well but…"

"Take last – when was it, George? The wallet job."

"Last Wednesday, Dad. I know because the day before had bin Tuesday."

Simmonds frowned. He'd had soldiers like this lad in his squad but somehow he never imagined them in civvy street.

Albert nodded. "Chap in the pub. I said to 'im I was a clair

– what was I, George?"

"Bloody smart, Dad."

"You were a clairvoyant, Albert." Phyllis was wobbling with laughter causing her crimson tulle to oscillate, in its turn causing Clarence, sitting opposite her, to do something similar.

"Well, whatever. I bet 'im an 'undred smackers I could tell 'im exactly how much money 'e 'ad in 'is wallet. Exact, mind. 'E took me on, the stupid..."

"Albert!" The tulle shook disapprovingly. Mainly because of his powerful voice, her husband had the attention of most of the table.

"Go on then, 'e said. Right then, I said."

They could all have done with rather less detail but Albert ploughed on, delighted to be the centre of attention.

"I thought 'ard – then I 'ad 'im. Two fivers and four onesers. That's fourteen quid, I said. And to cap it, a photo of a rather fat naked lady on a bed. He went white, 'is missus went red."

"I remember in the foothills..."

"All right Clarence, old bean. Another time." Freddy, the master of tactlessness showed that it takes one to know one.

"Were you right?" Having known many rascals like Albert in his service life Simmonds felt it was probably a superfluous question – and it was.

"Right?" Albert grinned at him. "Course I was right. Couldn't be wrong, could I?" He set back to serious drinking and eating.

No one said anything. Festivities had been suddenly suspended.

"Better tell 'em, Dad."

"Tell 'em what? Oh, right." Albert popped a roast potato into his mouth. "No, you tell 'em, son. You did all the work."

"Picked it, didn' I?" George punched an adjacent Roundhead gleefully. "Quarter hour earlier. Checked the contents. Sixteen Quid."

"Fourteen." Simmonds liked accuracy.

George shook his head. Didn't they know nothing? "Detail mate. Check the detail. I slipped the wallet back into 'is pocket and then I watched 'im spend a couple of quid at the bar, did me

347

sums. Easy 'undred smackers, weren't it, Dad?"

It was said more as a statement than a question but Albert nodded. He was so proud of his son that he would like to have given him a big hug there and then.

And George was equally proud of his father. "Others wanted Dad to do the same wiv 'em but me 'ands was gettin' sticky what wiv all the beer an' that."

Albert burped loudly. "Pardon. Manners. Anyway, a ton's enough for one night's work, innit."

Clarence looked around the table laden with the messy remains of the main course.

"Any more nipples?"

Those around him smiled indulgently at the old man. Bless his heart, so confused at the twilight of his life.

Freddy shook his head. The old rogue. He'd known exactly what he'd said.

Clarence looked around at them all. "I could have done with a couple of…"

"Pass the red-currant jelly, there's a good chap."

Lucy Banbury, sitting next to Tubes, felt a little explanation regarding the Father Christmas fiasco might be in order.

"Poor Bernard." She slipped a tiny portion of sausage into her mouth. "No one had the heart to tell him. They thought that if they didn't book him he'd put two and two together and realise he wasn't wanted this year."

"He did. And made five."

"He borrowed the outfit from the Methodists thinking ours must be lost. I'm afraid changing the Santa this year was my idea, Commander. I had no idea it would be such a disaster."

"It wasn't, Lucy, not at all. The greatest fun. I felt like Ben Hur."

"I'm really sorry for him."

"I don't think you need be. He wins in the end – well, according to Hollywood he does."

Lucy sighed. She'd taught many boys like Tubes Potter. "Not Ben Hur, Commander, Bernard Butterfield."

"Ah. Don't be too sorry. Bernard will be all right."

Somehow they all managed great helpings of Christmas pudding, borne into the darkened dining room with brandy flames spreading intoxicating fumes to a splendidly intoxicated gathering, and then even found space for a helping of cheese with port and liqueurs.

At long last, hardly able to stand, the guests, accompanied by Gloria but led, in true Wellingtonian style by the clanking Gregory, made their way back into the Grand Salon. The Oldthorpe residents who, during their service careers had attended many grand and glorious functions in far-flung reaches of the British Empire, would be hard-pressed to remember one that had matched this evening for sheer enjoyment. In truth they were ready for bed but Gloria had very different plans – after all, they could sleep through the day tomorrow but this was Christmas night and as far as she was concerned it could last forever.

"Come on, Freddy, get the choir organised. Let's have a sing-song."

The last thing any of them wanted to do, weighed down as they were with excessive quantities of food and drink, was sing. In all honesty they doubted whether they even could! They were spared having to make the attempt by a loud diversion: someone was hammering on the French windows. Gloria smiled and calmly went towards them but a sudden shouted command stopped her.

"No one move. Stay where you are – and that includes you, Gloria." Gregory Cecil Cartiledge, Order of this, that and the other with accoutrements, was in Nelsonic, Wellingtonic and Napoleonic command. As he yelled at them he rushed into the hall and then, a second later, reappeared carrying at the half-port a two-barrelled shotgun. He'd teach that Irish tinker a thing or two. He'd show the little squirt who was master in this house. Anger gave him strength and alcohol, courage. Flinging wide the heavy drapes he barged open the glass door.

"I've told you. Push off. Go back to the Irish bogs. GET OFF MY LAND." With that he discharged both barrels upwards into the black night.

No one moved except Basil who, being an artillery officer, flinched as the gun went off. He hated the sound of guns firing.

"Gregory!"

They saw Gloria rushing towards the window obviously intent on matching her husband, murder for murder. The mighty warrior started to turn back to face those he had protected from a Celtic invasion but as he did so he saw what he took to be a vast pool of blood on the flagstones. His heart stopped. Visions of a royal dubbing at Buckingham Palace gave way to a lifetime in a prison cell.

Then the red pool moved, groaned – and spoke.

"You great, stupid, prize imbecile. Happy bleeding Christmas."

They helped Bernard Butterfield to a chair and gave him a very stiff brandy. His Father Christmas outfit was covered in mud, his beard had finished up around his ears and his bobble hat had lost its bobble – probably decimated by a direct hit.

Gloria was in tears now. She stamped her foot and advanced on her husband. "You've ruined it. My surprise." She was only saved from hitting him by the gently restraining hand of Lesley. "How could you? You, you, you tin-pot tyrant!" She let out another wail.

Ainsley wondered whether a round of applause might be in order. After all, it was a splendid performance and her sentiments were certainly shared by everyone else present.

It was the amount of food and drink that saved the day. No one could stay angry for long, anaesthetised as they were with alcohol and weighed down with turkey, goose and all the trimmings. Bernard Butterfield, on receiving a whispered assurance from Gloria that his fee would be trebled, soon recovered and distributed presents to everyone. It was noticeable that in no time at all he was more inebriated than any of them.

"How did Gloria get to hear of him?" Basil was slurring pleasantly. Tubes found that he was seeing two of his old friend. "I got Ainsley to give her a ring after the fiasco in the Church Hall. Thought it only fair. She's paying him well."

Quiet music, quiet chatter, time for a little lull.

Just after midnight they'd tried a little sing but it really hadn't worked; the festivities had taken their toll. Now the coach was due and all of them felt ready for their beds knowing that it would be a headache day ahead and gallons of water to rehydrate them.

They were jerked back into consciousness by another knock but this time it was on the hall door. Merryweather, thankful to be back in his butler role, entered giving the statutory little cough to draw attention.

"Sir, madam. I fear we have a small crisis in the kitchen or, rather in the cottage."

The master's slurred voice was just discernable, "Deal with it, Merryweather. Your job."

"I fear I cannot, sir. It involves a – ahem – a baby."

Gloria, Lesley, all the women now came alive. The men each opened one eye and then closed it again. Women's work.

"A baby, Merryweather?" Gloria went to the door.

"New-born I believe, madam. Just before midnight. The – er – Irish lady."

Sister Amelia and Nurse Lisa led the group following Merryweather into the dark reaches of the house and into the kitchen, long vacated by the caterers and now cold and empty. They could hear it now: soft, gentle, contented crying. The butler led them out into the yard and through the pouring rain towards a lit window in the stable block.

The stable had obviously been converted into staff quarters, but one look at the interior showed that no one had lived there for a long while. The only furniture was a rough wooden table on which stood a hurricane lamp, there were a couple of wooden chairs, and in the corner a metal bed. Above the empty fireplace a faded picture of the Virgin Mary hung at a crazy angle. Everything was covered in dust and grime but the two nurses saw none of this; their attention went straight to the white-faced woman – more a girl – lying on the bed, a baby in her arms, and an anxious young man mopping her brow with a wet cloth.

"Bless you, ladies. I've done the necessary. The cord an' all. Not the first time nor most likely the last, please God in His mercy."

Amelia and Lisa moved gently into their nursing role. It had been some time since either of them had worked in maternity but theirs was a skill never forgotten.

351

"It's a boy," Sister gently kissed its forehead.

All the others were now gathered outside, oblivious to the rain. They made space for Basil, Tubes and Ainsley to go into the room.

Basil brought in the brandy bottle and Lisa put a minute drop of it to the girl's lips. The dark red of the liquid touched her cheeks.

Tubes brought the cloth from the kitchen table and spread it over the thin, coarse blanket on the bed.

Ainsley brought his thick overcoat and rested it around the shivering man's shoulders.

Precious gifts gratefully received.

And then, from the yard came Freddy's clear tenor voice, all traces of the evening's excesses gone, and the others, in harmony took up the familiar words,

> "Away in a manger,
> No crib for a bed,
> The little Lord Jesus,
> Laid down his sweet head…"

And Gregory joined in…